I0710217

NINE LEVELS

Elana Gomel

mirror world
publishing

This book is dedicated to my mother Maya Kaganskaya, a writer, an intellectual, and storyteller, who first introduced me to Demeter and Persephone when I was six years old. Gone too soon, never forgotten.

PART 1 ELYSIUM

LEVEL ONE And Syros

leo licked her lips, enjoying the pungent taste of sea salt. The spume flicked her parched skin, peppering it with tiny droplets. Her eyes were filled with a red glow as the sun shone through the closed lids. The warmth was just the right side of heat, thawing out her stiff muscles. Her soaked clothes were slowly drying into a crusty armor.

The bench creaked as somebody heavy sat on the other end. Cleo reluctantly unglued her mascara-caked lashes.

The man was indeed big and heavy, so much so that the promenade bench seemed to tilt toward him, lifting Cleo into the air like a child on a seesaw. He sat with his eyes closed, his broad face turned toward the sun. And there was a large spider on his left arm.

She gulped and scooted away, almost falling off the bench. The man did not move. The spider, as big as Cleo's fist, did not move either, but its angled legs, haloed with shiny hairs, twitched slightly, showing it was no bizarre decoration or a toy. Its golden head, sunken into its globular body, was peppered with multiple dot-eyes, each swiveling independently of the rest as they focused on Cleo.

She slid off the bench and stood up, her joints creaking and her damp jeans chafing her inner thighs. She rubbed her eyes, disregarding the fact that she was embedding the smears of yesterday's makeup deeper into her tired skin. She blinked, then looked back. The spider lazily spread out its legs across the man's tattooed arm. Each leg ended in a small, hooked claw, and its swollen abdomen pulsed with amber highlights.

Okay, so she had been drunk. Okay, so she might have hooked up with a Dutch tourist, which was a mistake – if it had happened. But one thing she was absolutely sure of was that she had not taken any drugs. Her sister's fate was the best guarantee of clean living. So, she had a pint or two occasionally. So, on this Greek vacation she had overdone the combination of retsina, Moscofilero white wine, and the shockingly sweet liqueur called mastika. But it was a vacation, for Christ's sake! Wasn't she entitled to let her hair down a bit? She ran her hand over the stubble on her head which had dried into a collection of scratchy spikes.

She edged away from the bench, refusing to look back at the big man with his eight-legged pet and walked to the parapet separating the promenade from the beach below. The sugary-white sand glistened in the blinding sunlight that stabbed into Cleo's bruised brain. The indigo wavelets licked at the beach margin scattered with shells. The beach was surprisingly empty: no tourists on tatty towels; no coolers, umbrellas, or kids. And no signs of their impromptu party that started last night when Cleo, Mick, Iris, and a couple of Dutch boys whose names she could not remember had spread their blankets in the balmy Mediterranean night on the shore of Syros.

Had they simply abandoned her and walked back to the hotel? But why? Try as she might, Cleo could not remember anything out of the ordinary except the retsina whose piney taste seemed to take up permanent residence in her parched mouth. And why was she soaked? It felt like sometime in the night she had walked into the Aegean fully clothed. Skinny-dipping was one thing, but swimming in your jeans in the midnight sea? And yet, a vague memory, like a disintegrating dream, nibbled at the edges of her mind with images of inky waves, bathwater-warm, embracing her as she swam toward…what?

Cleo squinted into the glare, expecting to see the tawny silhouettes of the smaller Cycladic islands surrounding Syros, but the blue immensity appeared to be empty. Not quite true – there was some vague vertical protrusion on the horizon, shimmering in the sunlight, but the hangover headache suddenly bore into Cleo's temples with such brutal intensity that she gasped and folded down onto the pavement. She kept her eyes shut for a moment and then swiveled away from the sea, subconsciously noting that her dark glasses were apparently gone together with her backpack. At least her credit cards were back at the hotel – if she could make it. Without dark glasses, the flaming July sun in Greece would burn out her blue British eyes and shrivel her damp British brain. Was it what was happening to her? Was she hallucinating giant spiders as a result of a sunstroke?

She climbed to her feet, holding onto the parapet, and looked away from the sea and up, toward the top of the island. Syros was a hilly cone, with the town of Ermoupoli sprawling up the rocky slope. Or at least, that was what it used to be, because what she was seeing now kicked the golden spider clean out of Cleo's mind.

Instead of the shallow slope dotted with white buildings, an enormous peak rose into the brightness, so tall and so massive that Cleo's brain refused to accept its dimensions. Surely no mountain outside of Everest could be so large! And the pictures of Everest Cleo had seen showed a mountain range, craggy summits piled up on top of each other. Here there was a single symmetrical mount, impossibly large, sticking out of the azure immensity of the sea and dissolving into the azure immensity of the cloudless sky. It was as if the modest cone of Syros was somehow stretched up and blown out, creating this geological monstrosity. She could not even see its top; it dissolved in the glittering sky.

Cleo realized she was hyperventilating, so she closed her eyes, counted to twenty, and tried to control her breathing. With her Apple watch, she could turn on the Breathe app to help her calm down, except her left wrist was bare and her mobile must be in the same place as her backpack, which was nowhere she knew of.

"Are you okay?" a woman's voice asked.

Cleo gratefully turned toward the source of the voice, trying to hang onto reality, but the impossible peak was still there on the margin of her vision, the sunlight piercingly bright on the bands of sage-green vegetation and bare limestone rock.

The woman was middle-aged, with untidy black hair and wearing a bright pink sundress. She reminded Cleo of a magpie or a crow, the way she tilted her head to the left, staring at her with curious round eyes. To Cleo's relief, there were no arachnid pets on, or around, the woman.

"Not really," Cleo confessed, letting go of her stiff upper lip. "I don't know where my phone is, and…"

She realized that her voice was trembling and coughed to save herself the embarrassment of going to pieces in front of a stranger.

"You are dehydrated," the woman declared. "Drink!"

She pulled out a battered metal thermos from her enormous handbag, unscrewed the top, filled it with murky liquid, and gave it to Cleo who stared at it dubiously. She had expected a plastic bottle, so ubiquitous in Greece that they seemed to generate spontaneously from thin air. But the copper taste in her mouth told her she needed to drink if she was not to pass out. Water was life in the Mediterranean.

She took a long draught. It was water, lukewarm and with a strange aftertaste like ammonia, but at least it was no retsina. Cleo promised herself never to touch anything stronger than lager again.

"Where are you staying?" the woman asked.

"In a tourist hotel. It's called Villa Pharos."

Cleo vaguely pointed toward the end of the promenade where a narrow winding alley led into the huddle of whitewashed buildings. It did not look very familiar, but then nothing did anymore.

"Come on!" The woman set off at a brisk pace and Cleo, too shocked to assert her independence, followed. She cast a fearful glance toward the bench where she had woken up, but the man with a spider was gone. Had he really been there?

Cleo trudged on, keeping her head down and refusing to look to her right where the impossible monolith of the mountain rose above the promenade. If she did not acknowledge it, would it go away? It was a weird thought but no weirder than everything else that was happening to her. The dazzle of the sun seemed to be dissolving reality into a fluid nightmare. All she wanted right now was to take a hot shower, discard her salt-encrusted clothes, and hide her head under the blanket, hoping to fall asleep – or to wake up.

"Are you alone here?" the crow woman asked.

"With friends."

"Where are they?"

That was a good question, which unleashed Cleo's pent-up indignation at Iris and Mick for abandoning her on the beach. She opened her mouth to say she did not know, and they could go to hell for all she cared – mates don't do things like this, leaving you alone and unconscious on the beach after a party, to be robbed or worse…

The words stuck in her mouth. She suddenly realized something she should have realized immediately when the crow woman had first addressed her.

Cleo understood the woman perfectly, but she could not tell what language she was speaking.

Cleo spoke fluent Greek. Her mother Daphne was a Greek who married an Englishman named Jerrod Brown and moved to Brighton with him. When Mr. Brown abandoned his wife and twin daughters to disappear into the limbo of deadbeat husbands and fathers, the girls were shipped to their maternal grandmother Eleni on Karystos. When they reluctantly came back to England several years later, Cleo and Cora spoke only Greek to each other. Other identical twins develop their own private languages; the Brown twins picked up the language of Homer for that purpose. Daphne, who always tried to be more British than the Queen, was not happy, but she had enough trouble surviving on the council estate to worry about the twins' national identity.

Growing up bilingual had its advantages and disadvantages. Cora seemed to have accumulated more mental bruises from being suspended between two worlds; Cleo fit in better by learning to shapeshift linguistically, picking up accents like trophies, to the point that her friends in London did not know she spoke Greek and her Greek acquaintances did not realize she was British.

But even if Cleo had automatically answered the crow woman in Greek, how could she not know what language they were speaking? It made no sense.

"I am Cleo," she said tentatively. "What's your name?"

She heard the sounds leaving her mouth, but for the life of her, she could not say whether it was English or Greek. It was…language, that was all; a means of communication. She understood herself. She knew the crow woman understood her. But it was as if the richness of many different tongues had been compressed into something uniform and bland. Cleo, like all bilingual people, felt she had different personas in Greek and in English, and now these personas were blended into an average Cleo.

As her language became invisible to her, she felt she was becoming invisible to herself.

"I'm Alexandra," the crow woman responded, and Cleo tried to roll the sound of the name on her tongue, tasting each syllable. Was it the broad A of English or the more subdued À of Greek? She could not tell.

They dove into the mouth of an alley, and she shivered in the sudden deep shade. As much as Cleo did not want to acknowledge the existence of the mountain, it was hard to do so in this unnatural coolness. In Greece in July, the tiniest patch of shadow was a blessed relief, and most of those were provided by shop awnings and an occasional arcade. Olive trees with their scant foliage begrudged shade to their tenders, but the flank of the mountain, towering above the alley, plunged it into gloom.

She glanced up reluctantly. The mountain was terraced as hillsides in Greece had been for thousands of years, but these terraces were enormous. She started counting. One, two…

The crow woman stopped in front of a chipped blue door set into the white wall.

"Villa Pharos," she declared.

Cleo wanted to say that it did not look right, but the words stuck in her mouth.

Above the wall was a painted sign with the name of the establishment, but instead of Greek letters the sign was covered with twitching spiders.

CHAPTER 2

leo ran through the twisting alleyways, tripping on cats and garbage. Her panic was so overwhelming that she began hyperventilating and finally collapsed onto the cobblestones.

Was this how Cora had felt in those last days when the drugs circulating through her wasted body had painted the world in colors of terror? For once, the memory of her twin was not the sharp spike of pain and longing she used to feel. It was almost comforting. At least if she was belatedly following in Cora's footsteps by losing her mind, the world still made some sort of sense.

A hand fell upon her shoulder and hauled her to her feet. Alexandra's round eyes blinked close to hers.

"Come on," she said and marched Cleo back to the hotel. She followed meekly. There was a certain relief in letting go of responsibility and just obeying somebody older who presumably knew what should be done.

They went back through the blue door and found themselves in a reception area. Cleo was so befuddled by what was happening that she no longer trusted her memories or perceptions. Was it indeed the same Villa Pharos where she, Iris, and Mick were staying? The whitewashed walls with bland lighthouse paintings and photographs of classic Greek statues looked familiar, but then any three-stars Greek hotel had those. The desk also looked generic and so did the clerk who stared at her incuriously. Alexandra bent over the desk and whispered something to the clerk while Cleo looked around, trying to gather her scattered thoughts. She felt as if she were falling apart into a heap of fear and paranoia, and needed to hold herself together with an almost physical effort.

Alexandra thrust an old-fashioned key at her, and this woke Cleo from her stupor. One thing she remembered clearly from their three-day stay was that the hotel used magnetic key cards, not this heavy monstrosity with an attached wooden label like something out of an old movie!

"Your room," Alexandra commanded. "Go and rest. I'll come over later, and we can have lunch."

And before Cleo could thank her, ask any questions, or object to this suddenly imposed lunch date with a stranger, the crow woman walked out, leaving Cleo in the middle of the foyer clutching the key. She cast a fearful glance at the wooden label, expecting to see a splayed spider. Instead, there was a number: 216. As far as she remembered, it was indeed her room number. Iris was staying in 215 and Mick in 134 on the lower floor. Iris had wanted them to share a room to save money, but Cleo had wriggled out of it by saying she had nightmares and was likely to cry out in her sleep. And of course, Mick didn't have to say anything, he just looked at her with those hangdog eyes of his to make sure she knew he would be happy to hop back into her bed. That was not going to happen. They were done. Cleo should have known better than to start a relationship just because she needed someone to talk to after her sister's disappearance, and even for the brief time they had dated she had not let him stay overnight. The truth was that the first years of her life had been spent sharing her bedroom with her own living reflection, and she could not imagine a different body occupying the empty space where Cora used to be.

She shambled toward the elevator and stood still, staring at the blank wall. There was no elevator.

Reality felt viscous and wobbly. All Cleo wanted now was to crawl away into a corner like a wounded animal. She turned toward the narrow winding stairs when the clerk called to her.

"Miss!"

"What?" Again, she tried to pin down the sounds leaving her lips: was it the liquidity of English or the short peppery explosion of Greek? But she could not; the words dissolved, leaving behind the bland residue of delivered meaning.

"Your friends left a letter for you."

The clerk handed her a sealed blank envelope. Clutching it in her hand, Cleo climbed the staircase, her knees hurting as if she were twice her age.

She turned the key in the old-fashioned lock and almost fell into the hushed room, shadowed with heavy beige curtains. Despite the dimness, the room was very hot. Cleo automatically looked for the climate control on the wall. It was not there. Neither was the flat-screen TV.

But her clothes were piled up on the bed as she had left them. Cleo picked up a white top with a golden embroidery around the neck. She had bought it in a small shop down by the harbor. And here were her flip-flops and her blue bikini.

But a couple of things were conspicuously missing. Her backpack. Her mobile. Her wallet. Her passport.

Cleo flopped onto the bed, hiding her head in her arms. Something fluttered onto the floor. The envelope! Your friends left you a letter, the clerk had said. What friend? Iris? A text message was more her style. Mick, who was a graphic designer, would be more likely to put an actual pen on actual paper.

Cleo tore open the envelope. She must have expected it deep inside because she did not even cry out. She just sat there, numbly, staring at the webby pattern created by the golden spiders on the piece of paper inside.

Suddenly Cleo realized she had a choice. She could lose control. She could scream. She could hide in the closet. She could beat her head on the wall. She could become Cora.

Or she could remain herself. Cleo, the methodical rational one. Cleo, the runner, the athlete, the future CFO. Cleo the survivor.

She studied the spiders. At first, she thought it was something glued or stamped on the paper, a raised design of some kind. Then she realized the spiders were alive because they twitched their long hairy legs occasionally. But they did not skitter around or crawl away as real insects would. They stayed in place, creating an intersecting net of their legs, with the nodes of their shiny bodies distributed evenly across the sheet. Cleo gingerly touched one of them with a tip of her finger. Fortunately, she was not arachnophobic or afraid of insects. It had been Cora who ran away from creepy-crawlies in Eleni's garden while Cleo poked at anthills with a stick and caught butterflies with her bare hands.

The spider, as big as her pinkie fingernail, remained in place. She traced the rounded bump of its carapace. Then Cleo closed her eyes and ran her fingers along the piece of paper. It was smooth. When she looked at the spiders and touched the paper, she could feel the three-dimensionality of their bodies, but when she did not look at them the paper felt flat.

Cleo put the letter aside and went into the bathroom. It looked more or less as she remembered it – but again, there was that niggling sense of something not quite right, something subtly different, like seeing your reflection in a warped mirror. The towels had been changed, and the small bottles of shampoo, conditioner, and body lotion replaced. They were by a well-known Greek company. With her eyes closed, she could visualize its name spelled out in fancy cursive lettering on the labels. With her eyes opened, she saw a golden spider embracing each bottle with its spindly legs.

She shed her salt-encrusted clothes and stood for a long time under hot water. She lathered her hair and body without opening her eyes. The slick bottles felt normal to her touch.

Wrapped up in a towel, Cleo went back to the room and picked up the letter again. One of the spiders seemed to stare at her with the tiny dots of its glittering eyes.

To be sure, she hunted in the room for something printed or written. There was a takeaway menu which she had picked up from one of the waterfront eateries. Now, instead of a list of salads and snacks, it was an arachnid colony.

So, that was that. Some unknown and possibly fatal glitch in her brain made her see spiders instead of letters.

But what about the man she had seen on the promenade? The man with a golden spider on his meaty forearm?

The guy definitely looked like somebody who would have the name of his girlfriend tattooed on his biceps.

Hallucinations. Cora had suffered from those, or at least, that was what her few friends claimed after her disappearance. Cora had never used this word, cryptically referring to visions and revelations when she had deigned to talk to her twin during that last disastrous year. Cleo had attributed this talk to her sister's histrionic imagination or drugs, or possibly both, but had she been unfair? Had she been a bad sister? A familiar stab of guilt went through her like a swift caress of a developing cancer. She had not saved Cora. She had let the estrangement between them grow, too convinced of her own rectitude to come to her sister's rescue. She had defined her own success by the baseline of her twin's failure. So, was it just a comeuppance she deserved? If Cora had really been sick, it was perhaps inevitable that she herself would develop the same brain disease.

Cleo tried to remember statistics for identical twins with schizophrenia. The very futility of this attempt brought her to her senses.

Even if she was sick like Cora had been, Cora's fate should be a warning. No sinking into depression. No self-medication with booze or illegal drugs. She would go to a doctor. She would go to a doctor, explain her symptoms, and well…get better. Somehow.

Not much of a plan but better than nothing.

Cleo put on a fresh pair of jeans, some underwear, and the white top. She was absentmindedly patting down her spiky hair when the old-fashioned phone on the nightstand trilled.

CHAPTER 3

The clerk's nasal voice declared she had a visitor. Cleo half-hoped that technology could neutralize the block that prevented her from recognizing languages, but it did not happen. She still could not tell whether the clerk spoke to her in Greek, English, or Dutch, for that matter. There had been a number of Dutch tourists staying in the hotel. In fact, the Dutch boys who had partied with them on the beach had also come from the Villa Pharos. As Cleo walked down, she suddenly remembered their names: Jorgen and Liam.

The hotel looked deserted. She knocked on the doors of 215 and 134 but both rooms were locked and nobody answered. She still could not tell whether it was the same Villa Pharos they had randomly chosen from a stay-in-Greece website or a different one. She could not trust her own memory. It felt like she was looking at the past through a layer of turbulent water. Certain images were stable in this vortex of uncertainty: Eleni's soft voice and comfortable embrace, the sunny olive grove where the sisters played on Karystos, her own tears as they landed at Heathrow and were greeted by the drizzly sky and gloomy chill of England. And of course, Cora's face, which Cleo saw every time she looked in the mirror at her own. But other things suddenly became open to doubts. Iris had been her friend since their days in Brixton Comprehensive – or had she? Was it possible Cleo had met her later, at the uni? Oh no, Iris had not graduated because…because why? She had dropped out…but here Cleo's memory thread stopped abruptly, as if cut by a knife.

And Mick? How had they met? Had he initially been Cora's friend? Had she introduced him to Cleo when the sisters still went out to pubs and clubs together? They had started dating after Cora's disappearance – of that Cleo was sure – and their relationship, such as it was, had fizzled out painlessly. Right? They were still friends. She could not find any residue of bitterness attached to his vague image in her mind, and decided it meant they were on good terms.

But why in the world had she thought that letting him tag along on a Greek vacation was a good idea? Perhaps it was Iris' idea. But again, why?

The spotty blankness in her head, these unexpected holes of memory, were driving her nuts. Cleo was almost glad to see her visitor; at least she did not have to focus on her own mental state.

Alexandra paced back and forth in the lobby, and Cleo was struck again by how like a crow the woman looked: hunched up, jittery, her thick black oily hair shiny like a corvid's feathers. Her ridiculously girlish sundress did nothing to minimize this resemblance. Her fingers, tipped with black-lacquered talons, shifted restlessly, scrunching up the shiny fabric.

Cleo paused on top of the stairs, seized by sudden doubt as to the wisdom of trusting this stranger. She still had options, she reminded herself. Should she just…what? Run away? Call the British Embassy? Check herself into the nearest mental hospital?

She did neither. She could feel the heaviness of the impossible mountain behind the hotel bearing down upon her. She suddenly saw herself like Atlas, the titan bent under the full weight of the world upon his shoulders. And whatever world this was, it had no place for embassies, or hospitals, or cellphones. Unless she was in a grip of an incredibly detailed delusion, she needed to understand this strange new place. And even if she was crazy, so what? Even if Alexandra was her hallucination, she needed to find out what phantoms of her occluded mind wanted from her.

Alexandra grabbed her arm, her talons digging into Cleo's flesh. She smelled like olive oil mixed with benzine. Cleo had tried too many weird Greek perfumes to make any assumptions about the source of the smell.

"We are going to have lunch at Dimitra's," Alexandra declared.

Dimitra's turned out to be one of the innumerable small eateries lining the waterfront, with a blue-and-white awning, a printed menu in a frame, and an ancient fan valiantly churning the afternoon heat. Cleo risked one glance at the menu, blinked away the golden glare from the spiders, and told Alexandra to order for both of them.

The food was a standard Greek fare: a tomato-and-cucumber salad with feta cheese, flatbread, and rice-stuffed eggplant. Cleo picked at her plate; Alexandra attacked hers, swallowing large chunks of vegetables seemingly without chewing. It was unnerving to look at, and despite her determination to wait for her to speak, Cleo was the first to break the silence.

"My wallet is missing," she said. "And I don't know where my friends are."

Alexandra threw back her head to let a piece of eggplant go down her gullet. Cleo had to look twice to assure herself the woman's beaky nose was not actually a beak.

"Not good friends if they abandoned you, are they?" she said. "As for the wallet, you have to work to make money. I can arrange something."

Cleo opened her mouth to say that she had a good job waiting for her in London – and closed it. It did not seem relevant anymore. She asked another question instead.

"What do you do?"

"I run a cleaning service."

Well that made sense, at least. She was looking for the poor and the desperate: illegal immigrants or stranded tourists who could be counted upon to be paid under the table and not ask many questions. But Cleo was not going to follow in her mother's footsteps by mopping dirty office floors and scrubbing dry vomit in public toilets, while looking for a man to rescue her from drudgery. It was not for that she had gotten her MBA!

"I don't think it's a job for me," she said.

"Needs must," Alexandra insisted. "It's a good job. Well paid."

"But I need to find my friends first!"

"You can try. But I wouldn't count on it."

"Wouldn't the police look into it?"

Alexandra cackled as if she had said something incredibly funny.

Frustrated, Cleo looked beyond the crow woman's shoulder into the azure glitter of the sea. She still could not see any other islands in the expanse of the shining water. Nor could she see any boats or ships. Another strange thing to add to the roster of impossibilities. Syros was a major port with a cruise ship terminal and a large marina. Even if all the cruise ships had suddenly evaporated, where were fishing boats and ferries?

Suddenly, something large poked out of the waves. It almost looked like a dolphin arching its back, except dolphins are black, and this…thing was rosy beige. Cleo remembered the video she had seen of pink dolphins in the Pearl River Delta, but pink dolphins were even smaller than ordinary ones; they leaped out of the water and disappeared back into the depth. This creature – if creature it was – kept rising, waving tentacles in the humid air, sticking above the sea like a fleshy sail…no, not a sail.

The thing went back into the waves with a splash, but its image remained imprinted on Cleo's retinas. No matter how her mind refused to accept it, she knew what she had seen.

An enormous hand rising out of the sea.

She squeezed her eyes shut to banish the image, and when she opened them Alexandra was pouring more tepid water into her glass.

"You won't get much work done in this heat if you don't drink," she remarked.

"I don't want to work here," Cleo retorted. "I want to go back home."

"You can't leave Ano Syros," Alexandra said.

"Is it the name of the town? I thought it was Ermoupoli."

"Ano Syros is the name of this Level."

"Level of what?"

"Orcus."

CHAPTER 4

leo straightened up with a groan and wrung excess water out of her cloth. The cloth was old and coarse, and the dirty soapy water splashed onto the floor in drops of liquid filth. She momentarily envied her mum who at least had had access to rubber gloves and modern cleaning materials. Now, of course, Daphne, safely ensconced in her new suburban home in Fulham, probably hired another single mother to do her cleaning.

Still, it was not too bad. Cleo's hands had grown dry and red, but Alexandra had given her some olive-oil-based concoction, which seemed to do the trick. And in the oppressive heat, the water evaporating off the stone floor provided a sort of primitive air-conditioning. The real thing was unknown here – in Orcus.

The name sounded faintly familiar, but Cleo was not sure whether it was from a video game, a fantasy movie, or one of Eleni's stories about gods and titans. Cleo was not a big gamer, so she decided it was something Eleni must have mentioned, but she could not recall the context.

For several hours after her conversation with Alexandra, Cleo had suspected she was dead, even though the enormous mountain blazing in the incessant sunshine from the cloudless sky was not her idea of hell —which she did not believe in anyway. She was quickly disabused of this notion. Dead people did not suffer from back pain and swollen feet. Dead people did not have to count their coins to pay for a tatty room and wilted salad for lunch. Dead people did not have to sneak to the bathroom in between dusting and sweeping. All of these were Cleo's daily reality now.

She was still staying at the Villa Pharos, which was now revealed as a cheap fleapit for hired laborers rather than a genuine tourist hotel. Not that there were many tourists here. Cleo had not seen anybody in the hotel who seemed to be there for pleasure rather than out of some kind of necessity: scuttling figures in the hallway, their backs bowed, their faces averted, refusing to answer her when she hailed them, and quickly diving into their rooms when she tried to catch up with them. And the whereabouts of Iris and Mick remained a mystery.

She dunked the cloth into the bucket filled with soapy water, draped it on the mop, and went back to polishing the splintered flagstones. This house was different from the ones she had done before. It was a family home. Until now, Alexandra had sent her to what appeared to be offices. They were located in impressive buildings with Doric columns and chessboard floors, but inside the buildings were subdivided into darkish cramped rooms filled with untidy paperwork in old-fashioned filing cabinets. Cleo hated them because abandoned piles of papers teased her with a solution to the mystery of her whereabouts, but every time she picked up an official-looking document, golden spiders crawled on the white surface, sending splinters of harsh light into her tired eyes.

She still hoped to wake up one day and to find that the glitch in her brain had dissipated. But it never happened; she could not read anymore. Every piece of writing Cleo saw was transformed into a congregation of spiders.

She had tried an experiment. She stole a blank sheet of paper and a pencil from one of the offices and tried to write her name in English and in Greek. But as she started on the curve of a C, a large spider reared up from the white paper, threatening her with its clacking mandibles, the hairy front legs waving in the air. Normally the spiders were passive but this one, her creation, seemed unusually aggressive, and Cleo quickly dropped the paper.

She finished the stone floor and picking up her cleaning tools, then went through the door into what appeared to be the family's sitting room. She did not know how many people lived here, but judging by toys scattered around, there were children.

The sitting room was bursting with a profusion of ill-matched knickknacks, from black-and-red embroidered table runners to miniature copies of classic Greek statues. Cleo recognized Aphrodite of Milos who appeared to be somewhat less toned than her original and Heracles with the bulging muscles of a bodybuilder. The furniture was heavy, carved out of dark wood, and there was no TV or even a radio set. In fact, Cleo had not seen any sign of modern media technology. Wherever Orcus was, it seemed to be stuck in some vague early twentieth century. On the other hand, people wore shorts, sundresses, and t-shirts, and she saw a couple of antique-looking cars on the ring road that went along the shoreline, though they did not venture into the maze of narrow alleyways that constituted the city proper.

The pitiless sun was streaming through the un-curtained window; there was no respite from the heat until it rose to the zenith and started descending behind the massive peak. Squeezing her eyes against the glare, Cleo started dusting a sideboard and paused. Among decorative plates and embroidered samplers, she saw a couple of framed photographs.

She picked one of them and studied it. Her spider affliction did not extend to images, even though any inscription on a picture would be transformed into a plump arachnid. This photograph did not have any writing on it. Nevertheless, it was creepy. A family of four: father, mother, and two kids, posed on the waterfront with the expanse of turquoise waves in the background. The father and one of the kids had empty black holes for eyes.

At first, Cleo thought that somebody had scratched out the eyes, but this was not the case. Something must have been done to the picture before it was printed. The father, a heavyset man in a polo shirt, and his daughter with thin dark braids, had black splotches where their eyes should have been. The mother, a pleasantly smiling plump woman in a white sundress, and a little boy by her side, had not been disfigured, and the contrast between them and the others was shocking.

Cleo picked up another framed photograph, depicting the same family at the entrance to what looked like a wedding hall, with an arched doorway and some unreadable – to Cleo – sign above. All four looked entirely normal.

A front door banged, and Cleo heard footsteps in the hallway. She quickly put the photograph back and started vigorously polishing the sideboard.

A boy came into the room. Cleo recognized him as the one in the pictures, even though he looked a little older. She smiled at him. The boy peered at her shyly and ran away.

His mother entered. She had changed for the worse since the pictures were taken. She had put on weight, and her body had a shapeless, defeated quality, as if she no longer cared how she looked. Cleo expected her to grunt a greeting and walk out. The inhabitants of Ano Syros did not seem to have the easy expansive hospitality of Greek islanders Cleo remembered from her childhood with Eleni. There was a furtive guardedness about them that she found off-putting. In the almost-week since she had woken up on the beach, she hardly spoke to anybody besides Alexandra.

On the other hand, how could you carry on a proper conversation if you did not know what language you were speaking?

She was pleasantly surprised, therefore, when the woman introduced herself.

"I am Katerina," she said. "You must be our new cleaner? Nyx told me about you."

Cleo figured "Nyx" must be Alexandra.

"I'm Cleo."

"Would you like coffee and some loukoumi?" Katerina asked. "I just bought a batch."

Cleo instantly agreed; coffee sounded great, and so did a break from cleaning. She followed Katerina into the kitchen. The coffee was made the old-fashioned way, by boiling it on the stove in a copper pot.

Could she have been thrown back into the past? It sounded mad, but no madder than any other theory she could come up with.

Not that time travel explained spiders in her eyes or the impossible peak whose weight she seemed to feel on her shoulders even when she could not see it.

They sat at the table covered with an old-fashioned embroidered tablecloth, displaying a map of past meals in a collection of faded stains. Cleo took a piece of loukoumi. In England, it would be called Turkish delight; in Greece, with its painful history of the Ottoman occupation, this name was never used. To her surprise, it was bright red instead of the traditional green of mastik. She bit into it; an acid sweetness flooded her mouth, the tastes clashing instead of neutralizing each other. She barely restrained herself from spitting it out.

"So," Katerina asked, "how long have you been working for Nyx?"

"A couple of days," Cleo said. "I'm new here."

She expected Katerina to ask her where she was from, but the woman did not.

"Cleo," she repeated instead. "Nice. A good name."

"Cleo is the muse of history, I know."

"The spinner of stories. With a name like this, you will have a lot of attention. Do you have any family?"

Cleo sipped the sweet thick coffee that tasted like tar mixed with sugar. Katerina's bluntness did not surprise her; it was common in the Mediterranean, if not in England. Living between two cultures, Cleo was a natural chameleon, easily adapting to either.

Though adapting to Orcus would take some doing for sure.

"Mother and…and sister."

She had not spoken to her mother for a year, ever since Daphne passively accepted the police's verdict that Cora had killed herself by swimming off into the sea. Her clothes were found neatly folded on the beach at Weston-Super-Mare. No note. No body. But a history of depression and drug abuse. An easy case to write off. But not for Cleo.

Katerina looked at her expectantly over the gilded rim of her coffee cup and suddenly Cleo felt words pouring out of her like blood from an unhealed wound.

"My sister and I are twins," she said.

Not "were" twins. Are.

"Her name is Cora," she added, as if her sister's name was an additional claim on her continuing survival.

"Really?" Katerina leaned forward and Cleo was flattered that this stranger was actually taking interest in her story.

"It's a powerful name," Katerina said, staring at Cleo with what appeared to be a mixture of respect and apprehension. "Cora is Persephone, daughter of Demeter."

Eleni had insisted on the girls learning ancient Greek mythology. Instead of cartoons and comics, they were brought up on tales of gods, monsters, and heroes. Cleo liked them as a child, and later, at school, her acquaintance with Homer and Hesiod eased her way into better grades and successful scholarship applications. Cora had been even more engaged with their heritage, enrolling to study classics at the university before dropping out.

Katerina was still looking at her expectantly, and Cleo snapped back into the present. Starved for human attention – not to mention information – she wanted to keep the conversation going.

"I know the story," she said. "Cora was the daughter of Demeter, the goddess of harvest and fertility. Cora was abducted by the god of the underworld. Demeter went looking for her but when she was found, it turned out that Cora had eaten food of the dead and had to stay in the underworld half of the year. When she is there, the world is enveloped in winter because Demeter misses her daughter."

It was a Cliff Notes version but accurate enough.

"Yes," Katerina nodded. "A powerful name, as I said. We honor names in Ano Syros. Is she here too?"

Cleo opened her mouth, but suddenly, she did not know what to say.

Could Cora be in Orcus?

"I…don't know."

"Maybe she was Called," Katerina said. "Like my husband and daughter."

"I saw the pictures," Cleo ventured.

Katerina nodded.

"My husband Tobias and my daughter Alena. Called. I don't know to what Level and why."

There was grief in her voice but also resignation like a callus protecting the tender spot in her memories. Cleo recognized it; she had grown calluses of her own.

"How many Levels are there?" she asked.

"Nine, of course. But I don't know what one of the Nine would want from a bookmaker and a little girl. Oh, well. Sorry for keeping you away from your work. Could you do my son's bedroom now?"

Cleo knew when she was being dismissed. She climbed to her feet, casting about for a way to end this conversation on an equal note.

"What is this loukoumi? I never had anything like this."

"It's pomegranate flavored."

CHAPTER 5

hen Katerina's house was done, Cleo picked her tools and supplies, put them in a large canvas bag, and marched out. She was paid by Alexandra – Nyx – weekly and did not have to have any financial interactions with the people she worked for. It had suited her just fine – until now.

She was trying to fit the things Katerina told her into the picture of the world she knew – and could not. But was it because they did not fit, or because the picture was flawed? She could almost see the holes in her memory, eating up her sense of self like hungry worms. And this image engendered a powerful sense of revulsion. It was not her! How had she just accepted her situation so meekly, dragged by the outrageous – even impossible – events like a piece of flotsam? It was not Cleo – the responsible one, the smart one, the ambitious one! Cora had been passive…but Cleo forbade herself from thinking about her twin. Perhaps the police and Daphne were right, and Cora was dead. But Cleo was still alive, and whatever world she had been thrust into, she needed to figure out its rules and find a way of getting back to her real life.

The tart and sweet taste of the loukoumi lingered in her mouth, intense despite the quantities of tepid water she had drunk. Cleo decided to look for a cheap place to have a bite.

Instead of going back to the Villa Pharos – Cleo could not believe that she had been thinking of that rathole almost as "home" – she walked slowly up the narrow alley winding on the shallow slope where Katerina's house stood between its whitewashed, red-roofed neighbors. The evening sky blazed in rose and gold, and the heavy heat of the day had not yet dissipated. But towering above her like a giant about to crush an insect was the silhouette of the mountain, rising precipitously above the town and the sea, black against the garish colors of the sunset.

Both Alexandra and Katerina had called the town Ano Syros, but this could not be the island of Syros where she and her friends had been partying. This peak must be twenty times as high as the highest elevation of the island. When her mother had married the rich creep Cleo refused to call stepfather, they took a trip to Switzerland and Daphne flooded her social media with carefully edited selfies in front of Mont Blanc. But Mont Blank was an irregular massif, a pile of rocky bulges and protuberances, as if the earth was flexing its muscles. The peak in front of Cleo was eerily symmetrical, so much so that for the first time she asked herself whether it was artificial.

No, it could not be! No skyscraper in the world rose to such dizzying heights. And yet this mountain was a perfect cone, its pointed top lost in the dazzle of the flaming sky.

Actually, it was not exactly cone shaped. It was staggered in levels. Nine Levels, Katerina had said. It was significant somehow, but Cleo could not catch the slippery recollection that was wriggling on the margin of her mind.

Somebody barreled into her, almost pushing her off her feet, and making her drop her bag of cleaning supplies. Cleo yelled at the man, who ran up the alleyway without pausing to apologize and disappeared into the maze of tiny lanes. Indignant, Cleo picked up her bag.

"Don't step between a man and his Call," a voice said.

A portly guy was setting the dining tables miraculously squeezed onto the narrow sidewalk. Taverns here were no different from the ones in Ermoupoli, with red-checkered tablecloths and bottles of olive oil and vinegar. In Greece, each tavern would have a sign with its name in Greek or English, or both. Here, the signs – at least, to Cleo's eyes – bore only a harvest of spiders.

"A little ouzo?" the man suggested, lighting tea-candles on the tables.

Cleo shrugged and sat down, her calves aching from cleaning and climbing. The man put a small glass of fiery liqueur in front of her. She downed it, hoping it would expunge the taste of the loukoumi that was still coating the roof of her mouth. It did not.

"Where was he going?" she asked.

"To the way up, I guess. The stairs. Did you see his eyes? Pitch-black."

Cleo was about to respond with something catty about the guy's belly being more prominent than his peepers, but she suddenly remembered the black splotches in the pictures of Katerina's husband and daughter. She gestured for more ouzo.

"So," she asked, "do your eyes go dark when you hear the Call?"

The tavern owner nodded.

"But you never know which of the Nine Calls you and why," he whispered, lowering his voice, and spitting on the ground. Cleo knew it was done to ward off mati, or the evil eye, so she was not insulted. Spitting, wearing an amulet, or crossing oneself were common measures of protection. But it occurred to her that despite the piety of Greek Orthodox believers, she had not seen any Christian symbolism in Ano Syros: no icons, crosses, or onion-shaped church domes.

Oh well, another puzzle to add to her rapidly growing list!

"I want to go to another island," she said. "What ferry do I take?"

The tavern owner gaped at her, and then tittered.

"Ferry? You have to pay the ferryman, of course. Are you sure you want to do that? A pretty girl like you! Why would you want to go?"

"Because I don't want to be stuck here, no offense to this town!"

The owner shrugged his meaty shoulders.

"There are only two ways out of Ano Syros," he said. "One is up, but you cannot take it unless you are Called. And the other one is across the water. And for that, you need to give a coin to the Sharp-Seeing One. But seriously, you don't want to do that. Stay here. Look, you are a beautiful lady. I'm a married man but my friend Alexis…"

"I'm not interested!" Cleo interrupted, all too familiar with the blurred line between flirting and harassment.

She fished some coins out of her pocket to pay for the ouzo.

Wherever Orcus was, it was not in the Eurozone. The coins, and the occasional bill that passed through her hands, looked unfamiliar. And each had a spider sitting on it, obscuring the inscription. It unnerved Cleo, so she learned to tell the value of each coin and bill by their size. As long as she did not look, they felt normal to her touch.

She threw a coin onto the table and got up to go.

The owner's oily smile grew wider.

"On the house!"

Cleo did not want any freebies, so she pushed the coin toward him. He squinted at it. A shadow passed over his ruddy face.

"I don't want it! But if you really decide to get off Orcus, you may want to keep it!"

And before Cleo could ask any questions, he turned his back on her, attending to a bunch of rowdy guys who emerged into the alley, their arms slung around each other's shoulders. She studied the coin, doing her best to overlook the plump arachnid twitching its brassy mandibles at her.

The coin twinkled like gold in the candlelight. It was not gold, though, but bronze, and insofar as Cleo could see beyond the spider, it bore the relief of a woman in a classic Greek peplos with a veil over her braided hair and holding flowers. She could be any Greek goddess or just some allegorical figure.

Suddenly, Cleo felt exhausted.

She trudged back to the Villa Pharos, thoughts churning in her head. Pharos meant "lighthouse" but anything less like a lighthouse than the gloomy fleapit was hard to imagine. She would have to look for something better – except she was not planning on staying in Orcus for much longer. There had to be a way out!

A whirr of wings above her head made her look up. A flock of large black birds wheeled in the indigo sky. A murder of ravens! One of them plummeted down, almost brushing Cleo's face with the fringe of its oily feathers, and landed on the pavement, cocking its round eye at her.

Cleo snickered; the raven reminded her of Alexandra.

Offended, the bird hobbled away, tossing a contemptuous caw in Cleo's direction.

"Birds of the night," she muttered. Something stirred in her mind, some vague association, but it was gone quickly. Not knowing what language she spoke – what language she thought – left her feeling flattened and insubstantial, like a piece of blank paper.

Before taking the alley that led to Villa Pharos, Cleo craned her head, for one last look at the mountain. In the dark, she could not see the staggered levels. The thing loomed into the night, vague and inconceivably large. There were no lights on its mighty flanks. It was black on black.

CHAPTER 6

leo sneaked to the marina just before dawn. The streets were cool and shadowy. Another murder of ravens wheeled in the pearly sky.

There were boats here. She had seen fishermen in the market with baskets filled with thrashing silvery sea bass and slowly unwinding octopuses. She could bribe or talk one of them into taking her to another island. And from there, she would find her way back. Cleo did not fool herself. She knew she was not in her familiar world of Euro-crises, urgent deadlines, and boozy office parties. But this world, the world of the impossible mountain, must impinge on her familiar reality somehow. After all, she was here. And even though she could not remember the transition, it stood to reason that if she had passed through some door, it could open both ways.

The marina was small and tucked away from the waterfront promenade. There were just a couple of fishing boats. She walked along until she stopped, her eyes snagged by something both familiar and unfamiliar at the same time.

A rather dilapidated boat rocked placidly on the silvery surf. A man in shorts and a floppy hat was hauling a heavy net onto the bow. Cleo could not read the name of the vessel, but she could see that it was decorated with a somewhat discolored picture of an open eye: a blue iris on the white background, surrounded by stylized curls of lashes and staring at the world with the uncompromising hauteur of an age-old symbol.

Cleo knew this symbol as did anybody who spent any time in Greece. An amulet against the evil eye, a mati or nazar, it overflowed every tourist shop in the Mediterranean, twinkling on necklaces and bracelets, stamped on coasters and mugs, printed on towels and t-shirts. No tourist could possibly escape Greece without buying at least one of them.

Except that Cleo had not seen it anywhere else in Orcus.

The fisherman finally turned around, as if feeling her gaze. He was elderly, with wrinkled, sun-damaged skin and weathered but still heavily muscled arms. He had a tattoo of some sort on his left forearm, and he wore a large pendant of mati on his chest, similar to the one painted on his boat.

"What do you want?" he asked gruffly.

"I want to get off this island," Cleo said. "Take me to Mykonos. I will pay."

The man burst out laughing.

Cleo bit her lip. She now realized she was mistaken about the man's age. He was not as old as she had thought but rather middle-aged, with large dark eyes shadowed by heavy eyebrows and a prominent nose.

"Nobody leaves Orcus," he said.

"That's not what I was told."

"Then whoever told you this was lying."

Cleo took out the bronze coin. Without looking at it – she did not need any more spiders in her life – she thrust it at the man.

"I'll pay the ferryman," she said.

The fisherman's bushy eyebrows met as he studied the coin. Then he looked at Cleo, and she had to revise his age down again. He looked to her to be in his forties.

"You don't know what you are asking," he said. "You think you can go back to your old life but it's impossible."

"I want to try."

She could see his tattoo better. It was of a large three-headed dog, scowling lugubriously from under the tattered sleeve of his faded shirt.

He looked at her and smiled, showing large sugary-white teeth.

"This coin is legal tender on Orcus and beyond, in the entire Archipelago," he said. "It is issued by the Ruler of the Final Level, and no matter what I think of her, and those who serve her, I am bound to obey. I will take you away if this is your wish. But remember that there is no turning back."

"I don't want to turn back!" Cleo responded heatedly. A tiny, almost inaudible voice in her head objected…but she resolutely shut it down. She had not asked to be brought to this crazy island that was like, and yet so creepily unlike, her own world! She did not want to wake up every morning in the shadow of this crushing mountain. She did not want to stare at the letter written by her friends and see crawling spiders. She wanted her life back. Even impoverished by the loss of Cora, it was preferable to blundering around surrounded by mysteries like some grown-up Alice in the Greek version of a demented Wonderland.

The sun climbed higher in the sky and lit up the fisherman's face. His eyes sparkled, and his black curls escaped from under his floppy hat.

"Hop in, then," he said.

She scrambled into the old and creaky boat. There was a smelly puddle of bilge water at the bottom that soaked her trainers. At the bow lay a large net festooned with white floats. The boatman powered up the external motor, which reeked of gasoline and produced an alarmingly rattling sound, but Cleo did not mind. Her heart sang as the oppressive mount of Orcus receded behind her, and they emerged out of the marina into the open water. Small wavelets gently licked the peeling wood of the boat. The sea glittered as if a handful of diamond dust was thrown into the water. Pinks and oranges of the sunrise gave way to the crystalline blue of the Aegean morning.

"I'm Cleo," she said. "What's your name?"

"What do you think my name is?"

His voice was as fresh and melodious as a mountain spring. The smooth skin of his arm stretched the three-headed dog tattoo into a cartoon pooch.

"Charon," Cleo said. "I think your name is Charon."

He looked back at her, still smiling. He looked younger than her, barely clearing twenty.

"And you still want to take a ride in my boat?"

"Wherever you are taking me cannot be worse than Ano Syros."

"You are wrong about that. And I have changed my name. Many of us did after the Upheaval. Call me Koresh."

Cleo knew it meant something in Greek, but she could not pinpoint what. Her language blindness was driving her mad. She dipped her hand in the seawater, enjoying its salty kiss, and told herself that she was alive, and no old stories would frighten her into scuttling back into the Villa Pharos.

Old stories about the three-headed dog guarding the entrance to the underworld, and about the ferryman of the dead.

"It means 'far-sighted'," the fisherman said, and his teenaged voice broke. "And this," he touched his pendant, "helps me see the dangers ahead and ward them off."

Cleo involuntarily glanced back. She did not want to, but she needed to confirm that the peak of Orcus was actually receding, dwindling into an ordinary mountain in the shiny sea instead of the oppressive weight that had been hanging above her like an incubus in a nightmare, draining her resolve and her memory. The glare stabbed into her eyes, and she promised herself that when they reached Mykonos, the first thing she did would be to buy a new pair of sunglasses.

She still could not see anything apart from the dance and glitter of the sea. If this world obeyed the familiar rules of geography, they would be gliding into the Mykonos harbor already. The Cycladic islands were close to each other. But by now she knew that space was as pliant as time here. And to see how pliant that was all she needed to do was to glance at her boatman. He looked to be about fifteen now.

Cleo bit her lips. If she believed she was escaping Orcus, then she was. No matter how young Koresh was getting, surely he would not dwindle into a helpless infant!

A girl could hope.

Finally, she spied something among the waves, a dark splotch of some kind. It looked too small to be an island, but distances were hard to judge in the open sea.

Koresh suddenly killed the engine, and they bobbed on the rising swell.

"What...?" Cleo asked.

He pressed his fingers to his lips. A curly-headed child, ten or eleven, cute as only Mediterranean kids could be.

"We need to go back," he whispered.

"No!"

A big wave rocked the boat, drenching her with its spume.
Another wave was coming – but it was not a rising storm. The wind
died down. The waves were caused by a giant body surging up from
the water and looming like a dirty smudge on the shining surface of
the sea and the sky.

Cleo stared up, unable to reconcile any notion of size with what
she was seeing. Was there really a naked man striding toward them,
the sea foaming around his shins as if he were fording a shallow
creek instead of the deepest part of the Aegean? His skin glistened
red, snakes of naked muscles crawling along the powerful arms and
skinny legs, as if he were flayed. His shovel-like hand reached
toward the boat, thick swollen fingers, each the size of her forearm,
straining. Cleo remembered the hand thrusting out of the harbor on
that first day Alexandra had taken her to lunch. She later convinced
herself that had been some strange marine organism – an enormous
starfish, perhaps – but there was no question that the creature
advancing toward the boat was humanlike, for all that its height
must have been at least fifty feet.

Humanlike in everything but his face. As Cleo blinked away the
dazzle, she could see clearly that the creature's cauldron-like head,
sitting on his broad shoulders without the benefit of a neck, had a
single giant eye located in the middle of its forefront. There was
nothing else, no mouth or nose. But the eye, as large as an entire
human head, swiveled and strained out of its orbit, almost plopping
out and swaying in the cradle of rubbery muscles. Its watery pupil
dilated, showing the black hole of a mouth studded with tiny sharp
teeth inside.

Koresh crouched down, weeping. A child, no older than six.

"Go!" Cleo screamed, reaching from behind him and trying to
turn on the engine. Koresh seemed to wake up. His small fingers
were no match for the tough cord of the ignition, but together they
managed to power up the boat and turn it around. The mount of
Orcus was a gauzy cone on the horizon – too far, Cleo thought
despairingly, forgetting that five minutes ago she could not wait to
leave it behind.

The boat sped on, but the cyclops only rebounded his efforts to
catch up. Angrily plowing through the sea and causing the boat to
rock madly, he bent forward, trying to grab the rudder. A whiff of
acrid metallic stench like raw meat and sulfur mixed together

washed over Cleo. The creature was indeed flayed. It had no skin. Its wet flesh bled meaty juices into the sea. Its eye bounced excitedly, and the maw inside it gaped wider as the cyclops worked hard to catch up with the boat.

Cleo pulled at the lever that regulated speed, and the boat shuddered and leaped forward. It sped toward Orcus, which grew more substantial as they were coming closer. Risking a glance back, Cleo dared to hope that they would be back in the harbor before the monster caught up with them. The cyclops' bony birdlike legs were not quite a match for the mechanical speed of technology.

And then the engine cut out.

The boat bobbed on the swell, as fragile as a walnut shell. In the sudden silence, Cleo could hear the wet splash of the cyclops' pursuit and the sucking sounds made by the eye as it strained against the raw weeping restraints of its orbit.

Another sound. Cleo looked down, into the bottom of the boat, where a toddler whimpered, the oversized tattoo all but covering his sticklike arm and crawling up his neck. Cerberus' three heads poked into his hairline. The mati pendant dragged down his thin neck.

Cleo reached down and yanked the pendant off the boy. Standing up in the rocking boat, she lifted it up and thrust it into the voracious face bending toward her. The blue enamel iris set into the white and gold background flashed in the sunlight.

"Go away!" she yelled. "Your evil eye has no place here! I banish you with this sign!"

The cyclops hesitated. His sausage-like fingers lowered as he loomed over the boat like a grotesque lighthouse, the raw flesh infested with sandfleas and shrimps. From so close up, his stink was suffocating.

Cleo stood her ground, trying to still the trembling in her hands.

The cyclops dropped into the sea, causing a surge that drenched the boat. Rubbing away the salt, Cleo saw him swim away. There was another eye, identical to the front one, set into the back of his head. It was watching her malevolently as the creature dived and disappeared underwater.

The horror of what had almost happened washed over her. Cleo collapsed to the bottom of the boat, sobbing and shaking. The pendant slipped out of her nerveless fingers.

The steady tuk-tuk of the engine made her look up. The boat was gliding into the harbor of Orcus. Koresh, now a young man, tinkered with the net. He moored the boat by attaching a line to the dock and turned toward her. Wrinkles like cracks in a dry riverbed fanned out around his eyes.

"You cannot leave," he said. "One of the Nine wants you here. I do not know why, and I do not want to know. After the Upheaval, I, who was once the servant of the Fates only, have become a plaything of broken time. I wish I could help you, but I cannot. All I can do is to give you my Eye. The Eye of Charon. It may not protect you anymore but at least it will remind you of your courage. There are worse things to be reminded of."

Mumbling thanks, Cleo slipped the mati pendant over her head and climbed out of the boat. Her legs trembled so much that she almost fell onto the overheated pavement of the waterfront. Steadying herself by holding onto the dock, she rested and then started up the cobbled alley toward the Villa Pharos.

She passed a small tavern under a striped awning. And stopped. And stared.

The tavern was called Aris. Cleo's eyes greedily drank in the clean outlines of Greek letters – and not a spider in sight.

CHAPTER 7

Cleo unfolded the letter her friends had left for her.

She had gone back to talk to the clerk at the desk several times, trying to find out where Iris and Mick had gone, but it was useless. The man blatantly denied they had ever been here, even though he had given Cleo their letter. The rooms they had occupied had different tenants now.

But now she could read again! On her way back to the Villa Pharos, she had paused to read every shop sign, every street name, every poster and announcement. And there were a lot of those. Cleo studied a poster stapled to the old-fashioned announcement board on the street corner. In bold letters it called upon the citizens of Ano Syros to resist the Crow's attempts to profit from illegal immigration from the Archipelago, and to report every case of human trafficking to the authorities. Somebody with a sharpie drew a crude bird silhouette on top of the poster and added a couple of very rude epithets, which strained Cleo's knowledge of street Greek. But she did understand another addition; the person with a sharpie had crossed out the word Crow and wrote Nyx instead.

Nyx. Alexandra.

It would not surprise Cleo to find out that her boss was involved in human trafficking, but why denounce her on posters instead of arresting her? Were the local authorities so impotent? And now when she saw it written down, the name Nyx – Νύξ in Greek – seemed vaguely familiar. Wasn't this the name of a goddess? The goddess of night, to be precise. But from what Cleo remembered, she had been a minor and obscure figure, not like the powerful Olympians. Nyx, daughter of Chaos.

On her way back to the hotel, Cleo was on a lookout for any sign of the return of her affliction, but there were no spiders. Fat flies lazily buzzed in the syrupy sunshine, unafraid of being eaten by animated letters. Not that Cleo had ever believed the spiders were real. Something had been wrong with her eyes or her brain. Some…spell? It seemed ridiculous even to think that but what else would you call it? Cleo squeezed the mati pendant, which Koresh had called the Eye of Charon and which she had hidden under her shirt. It made her feel better.

Along with the capacity for reading, she regained her ability to distinguish languages. Most signs were in Greek; a couple were in English, not always grammatically correct. In this sense, she could have been back in the Cyclades. But after her abortive attempt to escape and her interaction with Koresh, she knew for certain she was not.

Koresh…Charon. The ferryman of the dead. Had he been taking her to the underworld or…out of it?

She returned to her room, locked the door, and took out the shabby envelope. Cleo closed her eyes, took a deep breath, and unfolded the note. Now she would get the answers she needed!

She stared in shock at the sheet of paper, scribbled over to the point that it was more black than white. Used to Iris' text messages, she had expected something short, punchy, and with no capitals or punctuation marks. But this looked like some Victorian missive, written by an asylum inmate who tried to squeeze their entire life story onto a single leaf torn out from the Bible. In fact, the writer had turned the sheet over and written in the blank spaces between the lines. Cleo could read now, but only what was legible. And this thing was not.

Looking closely, she realized there had been two writers. Iris' cursive had always been atrocious, and the lines she could identify as written by her friend looked like spiky hedges with bird nests tangled in the thorns. The second hand belonged to somebody with better calligraphy. It must have been Mick. During their brief affair they had communicated exclusively by text, so she had never seen his handwriting, but being a graphic designer, it was reasonable to assume he would know how to write legible cursive. Still, the words were so economically spaced that she could only read some of them before they ran together into an indecipherable mess.

They punched at her like blows.

"Attacked".

"Called."

"Arachne".

And four complete sentences, triple underlined, the pen tearing through the paper in jagged scars:

Cora is here.

You must go up.

You must climb Orcus.

Find your sister.

CHAPTER 8

ater. Check.

Spare clothes. Check.

Money…

Cleo paused, studying the coins in her palm. Now that the spider enchantment was gone, she could read the inscriptions, but they did not leave her any wiser. The coins were called drachmas – unsurprisingly since drachma had been the coinage of both ancient and modern Greece. They bore different denominations and blurred profiles of men and women who could have been anybody from Alexander the Great to the current Prime Minister. They offered no clues to the nature or government of Orcus.

The brass coin she had given to Koresh was gone, but there was another one which looked similar, though it was made of silver. The relief on it depicted a woman crowned with a triple crescent.

She put it all into her new backpack, which she was quite proud of. She had bought it with her cleaning wages in one of the innumerable small shops dotting the promenade. They stocked everything from flip flops and cheap embroidered dresses, to sweets and greeting cards. Cleo studied the merchandise, but while she did not see the label "Made in China", neither did she see anything that would be wildly out of place in any discounted shop in Athens or London.

With her old backpack gone, she finally settled on a large sturdy affair made of waxed canvas with brass-studded shoulder straps. She filled it with underwear, her remaining jeans and tops, and water bottles. The letter from her friends went into a separate pocket, carefully zipped.

At first she wanted to wait for the dark, but then realized there was no need. Nobody was keeping tabs on her. Alexandra would show up every three days with the address of the next job and the payment for the last one, a significant portion of which was immediately transferred to one of the faceless interchangeable clerks who manned the reception desk and stared through Cleo as if she was not there. She was free to go when and where she pleased.

She had to find the way up. Climb the mountain, reach the next Level. The tavern owner had mentioned "stairs", so Cleo decided to start there.

As she put her hand on the door handle, she heard a rustle in the hallway outside.

She paused. The hotel was normally as silent as a grave. This noise was unexpected and therefore disturbing. And it was hard to identify. It sounded as if a large bag filled with sloshing liquid was being dragged through the hallway.

Cleo peered out through a crack and then slammed the door, leaning against the fragile wood, her heartbeat thunderous in her ears.

Did her hallucination come back in a worse shape than before? No, that was real. A sharp musty stink trickled into the room, making her eyes water.

The rustle ceased. Something heavy pushed against her on the other side.

The door had no latch; the only way it could be locked was with the key, either from the inside or the outside, and the heavy key was on the bedside table.

She leaned into the door, putting every ounce of her weight into keeping it close, but her slender frame was no match for whatever was pressing from the outside. The door flew open, shoving Cleo with such a force that she stumbled and fell on her backside. The thing squeezed into the room.

All the golden spiders of Cleo's hallucinations were but a poor approximation of the huge creature that advanced upon her, its abdomen as swollen as an IV bag and filled with bright yellow goo that seemed to swirl in hypnotic patterns. Eight legs, whose metallic chitinous gleam and sharp claws were even more threatening by contrast with the gelatinous body. The narrow thorax covered with hairy plates, viscous liquid oozing from the cracks between them. But worse than all of this was the head.

It was not the head of a spider with moving mouthparts and multiple eyes. Perched upon the thorax without the benefit of a neck was the head of a woman.

The fact that she was beautiful made it even more horrifying. Or rather, she had been beautiful. The face was marble-pale and spotted with livid patches of decomposition. The head was dead.

But its bloodshot eyes tracked Cleo's movements as she scrambled to her feet, trying to put as much distance between herself and the creature as possible. Lips the color of spoiled meat moved, and the thing said something, but in her panic, Cleo did not get it. All she wanted was to get away.

With her back against the wall, she fumbled with the window and managed to swing it open, never taking her eyes off the thing creeping closer to her. It did not skitter like a true spider but rather walked with a slow ponderous inevitability of a nightmare. It opened its mouth and spoke again. The black tongue wriggled like a grave worm.

"You must not leave."

Cleo remembered that her room was on the third floor.

The cobblestones of the pavement below scowled at her like hungry teeth. She was risking much worse than a cast on her arm or leg.

So it was either broken bones or being eaten by a giant spider with a dead woman's head. No contest. Cleo climbed onto the windowsill.

She straddled the sill, hanging on to the frame for dear life. A loud flapping sound behind her startled her so much that she almost let go.

The spider crept closer, its spoiled-meat stench clogging Cleo's nostrils.

Something flapped by her, and then another black shape, and another. Three large crows erupted into the room. They converged on the spider, strafing her from above, their curving beaks and wicked-looking claws reaching for her eyes. The spider hissed and opened her maw wide. A jet of foaming liquid shot out, its acrid stink filling the room like smoke. Cleo's eyes watered and her hand slipped off the window frame. She swayed, precariously poised above the sheer drop to the unforgiving pavement below.

Somehow, she managed to hang on. Splinters of wood burrowed under her nails as she gripped the frame and hauled herself back into the room. Crouching below the windowsill, she watched the three crows attack the spider. They dove and swooped, their beaks gaping and their taloned feet extended. They were hampered by the smallness of the room, but they seemed to hold their own, despite the liquid missiles of poison the spider spat at them. One landed on a crow's wing, and its feathers smoked as if splashed by acid. The bird cried out hoarsely and fell onto the floor, limping away into the corner, but its companions continued their fight undeterred and the spider apparently decided to let it go. Casting one last baleful glance at Cleo with her dead eyes, she turned around and slunk out of the room. Cleo sank onto the floor.

The two unharmed crows flew out and disappeared into the chaos of rooftops, but the one singed by the spider's venom remained. It hobbled toward Cleo with its beak opened wide and sideways eyes glistening malevolently. She felt around for some sort of weapon to chase the predatory bird away.

There was no need. As the crow advanced, it grew in size, towering above Cleo. It wavered, clad in a sort of bluish haze, and its feathers melted into a black mass that flowed smoothly down its elongating legs and straightening body. Its beak was absorbed into its face and stretched into a mouth, its eyes migrated from the sides of its flat head toward the front, and the very pissed-off Alexandra glared at Cleo.

"How often do I have to get you out of trouble?" she demanded.

Cleo climbed to her feet, feeling foolish, but embarrassment was quickly supplanted by indignation. She did not ask to be thrust into a world of giant spiders and were-crows!

"If you gave me some info at the beginning, you wouldn't need to!" she yelled back. "What was this thing? Why does it want me to stay here? And who are you? Alexandra or Nyx?"

Alexandra sighed and sat down on Cleo's bed. Cleo noticed a large discoloration on her pink dress, as if she had been splattered with acid.

"Well," she said, "it is strictly on the need-to-know basis here, but I guess you do need to know a couple of things."

"Thanks!" Cleo muttered sarcastically, sitting on the single rickety chair rather than sharing her bed with the crow woman.

"First," Alexandra said, "you cannot leave Orcus. I heard of your…escapade with Charon. He was a fool to take you, and more of a fool to give you the Eye, but the old man always had a weakness for pretty ladies."

"Am I dead?" Cleo asked. "Is this why I cannot leave?"

Alexandra cackled.

"No," she said, "but at the end, it may amount to the same thing."

"What does it mean?"

"This place is the prototype of which your world is a shadow. We call it the paradeigma or original, while your reality is an antigrafo or copy. Have you heard of Plato's Cave?"

Cleo had. According to Plato, the world was a shadow of some other realm, and people were like bound prisoners in a cave, watching unsteady reflections on the walls and mistaking them for the real thing. The original reality was the world of essences, while the human world was a reflection or imitation of it.

She had never thought of this description as anything but a metaphor. Apparently, she had been wrong.

"So the human world is Plato's Cave, and Orcus is the reality?"

"Yes."

"How did I end up here?" Cleo demanded.

Alexandra shook her head.

"This I don't know," she said slowly. "It's not that easy. Some people just…fall into cracks, I guess you'd call it. Quite a lot, actually. All the missing, unhoused, unhomed, lost. But they don't as a rule end up on this Level. And the fact that Arachne shows such an interest in you indicates that there is more to it than a simple slip out of the world where you have nothing to hold onto."

"Arachne is the Spider?" Cleo asked.

"Yes."

"Did she put…a spell on me? Making me unable to read? But why?"

But this was the question Cleo could answer herself.

The Spider did not want her to read the letter her friends left for her.

She reached to the backpack, pulled out the letter, and unfolded it, hoping against hope it would be more legible now. It was not.

Two different hands. The scratchy, spiky writing was Iris'. The more rounded flowing script was, apparently, Mick's. But it was not that half the letter was written by one of them and the second half by the other. Rather, the second writer had filled in empty spaces between the sloppy lines of the first one, so the entire thing was a mess of intersecting, upside-down words and sentences. Had they run out of paper?

Cleo focused on Mick's writing.

It was a bad decision…but here we are. I'm sorry about all of this. I should not have…and then the sentences tangled with Iris' inexpert cursive into something unreadable. We didn't want to leave you, but we can't stay…come back…and then, the key phrase, underlined multiple times.

You must go up.

Cleo looked at Alexandra.

"Why must I go up?" she asked.

"People stay on their own Level until they are Called. If you are Called, you must go up. You can't stay on this Level anymore."

"How many Levels are there?"

"Nine."

"What's on the top?"

"I don't know."

"You don't know?" Cleo repeated incredulously. "How come? Aren't you Nyx?"

Alexandra smirked.

"Some people believe so," she said. "It's good for business. But no, I am not. I have never left this Level. I am Nyx' antigrafo."

Cleo knew the word – in Greek, it meant "copy" – but she had never heard it applied to people.

"People in your world call us avatars."

Now it made some sort of sense. Avatars of deities were a common motif in many mythologies.

"A copy," Cleo murmured. "A copy of a goddess. So, do you have her power?"

"Some of it, because I am the first impression, a primary. The further away from the original, the less resemblance. But if people want to think I am Night herself, let them. I don't mess with the Nine. I have my cleaning company, I pay taxes, and I support this town."

"In other words," Cleo retorted, "you exploit strays like me, and then pretend to be a goddess to silence your critics. A great business model indeed!"

"It works. Anyway, trust me, Elysium is a much better place than anything above it."

"Elysium is this Level?"

"It's this Level and the two above it. There are nine Levels, and three Zones, each comprising three Levels. The Zones are Elysium, Asphodel Fields, and Tartarus."

"So, where am I supposed to go?"

"Wherever your Call leads you."

Cleo rolled her eyes, about to say that she heard no Call, and while she would be happy to get out of this hole (not to mention it being infested with giant spiders), she was going to do it on her own…and then the words dried out in her mouth.

Because she suddenly felt it, as strongly as she had ever felt anything in her life: a tug in her brain, as if a fishhook somehow embedded itself in her innermost being and was slowly but inexorably pulling her, reeling her in…

"Yes," Alexandra said with her customary smirk. "You are being Called."

CHAPTER 9

aving the Call in her head was like having a migraine that never quite struck but never went away.

Before her disappearance, Cora had often complained of migraines. Cleo had attributed it to her sister's gluttonous consumption of prescription drugs. When they were teens, she had tried to keep up with Cora's ever-changing, ever-growing list of medications until she gave it up as hopeless. Cora never saw a pill she did not like. She collected diagnoses as other people collected souvenirs. Anxiety, depression, bipolar disorder, an unspecified personality disorder…Cleo had never believed any of it. Her identical twin was as healthy as herself, which meant healthy. Cleo had never taken anything stronger than an antihistamine or more mind-altering than a glass of wine or a pint of lager.

But now, the throbbing in her skull was driving her nuts. It was not pain exactly but more like the inner equivalent of a mosquito buzz that could make you flail around in anticipation of a sting. The throbbing was not in her temples, as migraine often is, but rather on the very top of her head. It eased a bit as Cleo left the hotel and started climbing the steep narrow alley, sipping from a bottle of tepid water. The afternoon heat lay as heavy and viscous as honey on the siesta-deserted streets.

Alexandra did not accompany her, for which Cleo was profoundly grateful. She had had enough of the crow woman's company. An antigrafo of Nyx? Whatever. Despite the way she had defended her against the spider, Cleo did not trust Alexandra one bit.

Speaking of the spider – she looked around fearfully, but the alley was empty, the windows shuttered, and the marquees of businesses folded. Arachne. Eleni had told the twins her story, and Cleo remembered it, but she could not connect it with her current predicament.

Plato's Cave…well, according to Alexandra, it was Cleo's world that was the Cave, and this world – Orcus – was the real thing. But was Orcus the entirety of this world, or just the mountain? Alexandra had been rather ambiguous on that point.

Anyway, it did not matter. All that mattered now was finding the way to the next Level. Alexandra did not know where it was or did not want to tell. But she did imply that it would be hidden; no big arrow with a sign for stairs.

Cleo passed by the tavern she recognized as belonging to the creep who had tried to chat her up. Now she could read its name: "Cosmo's Nook."

Cosmo himself poked his head from the door. His eyes lit up when he saw her.

"Hello, beautiful!" he cried.

Cleo hurried by, wishing, not for the first time, she had the Medusa-like capacity to turn people to stone with her gaze. To her consternation, Cosmo ran after her.

This was beyond the usual Mediterranean macho posturing. This was harassment! Cleo turned to face him, baring her teeth in an angry scowl. The pounding in her head did not improve her mood.

"Get away from me," she enunciated in street Greek, glad to have regained her capacity to distinguish languages.

"No, no!" Cosmo waved his muscle-bound arms, bursting from the cut-off sleeves of his t-shirt. "You don't understand! I know you are following the Call! I respect the Nine. I mean, I'd like to have another glass of ouzo with you but…"

"What do you want?" Cleo barked.

Cosmo glanced over his shoulder and leaned closer to Cleo, blasting her with the smell of a pine-scented aftershave.

"There was a man here," he whispered. "Hair like a dog's fur and mouth like an arsehole."

"So?"

"He told me you would be passing by. He asked me to show you the way up."

Mick?

That was an unkind description, and Cleo could not quite connect it with her ex-boyfriend. Mick was…quite handsome. Wasn't he?

Why can't I remember his face?

"When was it?"

"A week ago, give or take."

"Was he alone?' Cleo asked. "Did he have a blond woman with him?"

"No."

So, where was Iris?

"You know where the stairs are to the next Level?" she asked.

Cosmo nodded.

"I do. I hope never to use them myself, but I can show you."

Cosmo exited his tavern and went up the alley, which had now narrowed into a cobbled passage, snaking through a sprawl of whitewashed houses with small, curtained windows. Cleo followed, fighting off the sense of unreality. It looked too much like the Greece she had loved as a child living in her grandmother Eleni's house. It should have been homecoming. Instead, she was lost in what felt like a bad dream. Was she really going to climb some impossible mountain, following the Call of a daimon or a deity?

The alley made a sharp turn, squeezing between a blank wall and a house on the hillslope, its courtyard littered with junk. A heavyset woman came out of the house carrying a zinc tub and stared curiously at Cleo.

Cosmo stopped in front of another blank wall running perpendicular to the other one. Set into the wall was a plank door painted blue, with the rickety handle hanging loose. The planks were splintered and peeling.

"That's it?" Cleo asked dubiously.

Cosmo nodded. And then his eyes strayed behind Cleo's back, and his fleshy mouth gaped like a fish's. He turned around and bolted down the alley. The woman in the courtyard dove back into the house, the tub clattering down the porch.

Cleo looked back.

Standing behind her, close enough to touch, was a Woven Woman.

At first Cleo thought she was a dolly or mannikin of some kind. The body was woven together of multicolored yarns hung in untidy hunks of brown, blue and beige. Its arms were knitted sleeves, one much longer than the other. The ragged hem of its rough skirt swept the cobblestones. There was nothing inside the skirt; sunlight glittered through the holes in the weave. Its head was a blank oval of twisted strands of fiber. An unsuccessful attempt to give it some sort of facial features ended with splotches of darker weave, randomly peppering the front of its head.

And then the head moved.

The intertwined strands twitched, forming a hole, and a segmented golden leg popped out. Then another. A fat spider was squeezing through.

Cleo grabbed the door handle, and it came off. The golden spider was almost out of the Woven Woman's gaping mouth, and another one was coming through the weave of her gullet.

Cleo beat on the door, splintered wood piercing her skin, and drops of blood renewing the faded paint. One of the spiders dropped onto the ground by her feet. It reared on its hind legs, mandibles clacking. An exhalation like a whiff of stagnant air touched Cleo's cheek, and a hoarse voice, choked with some clickety obstruction, tried to form words.

The door gave way, and Cleo fell through into the dimness and cool.

CHAPTER 10

leo's heart hammered so hard she began hyperventilating. She slid onto the floor at the foot of the door, leaning against it with her entire weight. What if the Woven Woman and her spider babies tried to follow her?

But nothing was happening. No sound was coming from beyond the door. In fact, the dim space where she found herself was as quiet as a grave. As if to underscore the similarity, the air was moist and smelled of raw earth. It was cool, and Cleo, used to the balmy Mediterranean heat, shivered involuntarily.

At least it was not dark, otherwise she would have had a panic attack. But the light, though thin and soulless, gave her the courage to get to her feet and look around.

She was at the bottom of a narrow stairwell. In front of her, a spiral staircase wound around a rusty metal pillar. The walls were of raw concrete and stained with damp. The light was provided by old-fashioned bulbs fixed above the narrow landings. All in all, it looked like the back entrance to an abandoned industrial building. But when she looked up, the stairs went on and on, disappearing into the murk.

Hoisting her backpack on her shoulders, she started climbing.

Pausing on the first landing, she looked down, still fearful that the Woven Woman might follow her. But the door through which she had come was still closed, and the stairwell was still silent. Or was it?

As she resumed her climbing, she heard an echo of her footsteps. She stopped. The echo stopped too – but with a microsecond delay. The dying susurrus of the clanking sound made Cleo shudder, and suddenly, the dull headache of the Call flared up into a piercing burst of pain. She swayed. The stairs had no banister. Cleo saw herself plummeting down onto the raw concrete below, her blood seeping from her broken body and slowly creeping toward the door like a scarlet amoeba. She grasped the central pillar, but she was sweating despite the chill and her hand slipped off the rusty metal.

Cleo forced herself to sit on the stairs and put her head down between her knees, taking deep breaths.

I'm not Cora, an inner voice like the buzzing of a mosquito whispered to her. I'm not Cora. Cora was weak. Cleo is strong.

And then another voice, deeper and more sonorous, speaking in Greek.

You are like the Dioscuri, the star twins, one mortal, one divine. But they always stood by each other, and now they are in the sky together. You have to stand by each other, girls. Always.

And a retort in English, a high-pitched whine.

Stop filling their heads with nonsense, Mum!

Eleni and Daphne, their grandmother and their mother. Eleni had passed before she had to mourn Cora. And Daphne just did not care. She had reluctantly gone through the bare minimum of filing a police report after Cora's roommate informed her that her daughter had disappeared from their grotty bedsit. Neither Daphne nor her creep of a husband had followed it up. As for Cleo…

I called the police again. I did.

Three times only.

The Dioscuri, the star twins.

Castor and Pollux. Helena and Clytemnestra.

The sisters were pretty unlucky, weren't they?

Find your sister.

Cleo forced herself to get up, still clinging to the central pillar. She wrenched the water bottle from her backpack and took a sip. She listened. The stairway was silent.

She looked down. Nothing.

I don't like heights.

Cora used to say it.

Cleo started climbing.

And the echo came back.

Her footsteps on the corrugated metal of the treads sounded obscenely loud in the narrow tube. When she looked up, she could not see the end of the staircase. How tall was it?

Nine Levels, Alexandra had said. The mountain was high, but not infinitely so. From the sea promenade, Cleo had seen its summit.

She forced herself to climb faster. Her heart hammered in her chest; lactic acid flooded her thigh muscles. She had not run in a couple of weeks, but surely she could not have lost her fitness so quickly!

When she stopped to catch her breath, the echo stopped too – with a delay that seemed a bit longer.

Cleo inched toward the edge of the tread, hanging over the yawning void that seemed to beckon her to take just one more step. She looked down. She could no longer see the foot of the stairs and the door she had come through, but there was no sign of anybody following her. She strained her eyes, trying to pierce the murk. The light was bad.

And then it got worse, as a naked electric bulb below flickered and went out. Darkness rose in the well like stagnant water.

Abandoning all caution, she ran up the stairs. The metal rang hollow, and the echoes, magnified by the concrete walls, boomed like malicious voices. Her foot slipped, and she lurched toward the edge. She grabbed the pillar, hanging on with one hand, breaking a nail as she tried to dig into the unforgiving steel.

Another bulb went out. From the corner of her eye, she caught an indistinct smear of movement. She strained her eyes, trying to convince herself it was only a play of shadows. Something stirred within the pool of darkness, surfacing.

A hunched-up gray figure was hobbling up from the landing below. She only caught the general impression of a long, cowled head, a humped back, something flapping like enormous sleeves or a cloak…but she did not pause to study it. She sprinted up the slick stairs, the spiral sucking her up like a twister. The creature below was no longer trying to hide. It hopped frantically after her, its sleeves – or were they wings? – churning up the stagnant air.

Another bulb went out, but this one exploded, showering her with slivers of glass. The light curdled into a barely diluted darkness, but its dregs were enough to illuminate a severe rectangle in the curving wall on the next landing, and the word Exit painted in red dripping letters. She threw herself at the door which remained immobile. A whiff of stench like rotten meat wafted from below.

"It's the fucking exit!" she yelled in frustration, hammering on the door.

The door did not budge until she suddenly realized what was staring her in the face this entire time. There was a handle, positioned exactly where it should be. She turned it, pulled, and the door swung inwards. Fresh air flooded the stairwell.

She stepped out and gaped at the unexpected view.

LEVEL TWO Happy Meadows

leo stared at the street of sprawling single-family homes and manicured lawns. The homes were ranch-styles houses and stucco McMansions. The lawns were so immaculate they did not seem real. It looked like the set of some American suburban drama.

She glanced behind her and saw the closed door set into the blank wall of a shed. She had no desire to open it.

She stepped out onto the sidewalk. The entire place was empty and eerily silent.

Something else was missing in addition to people. Cars! The road was empty, and there were no cars parked at the curb. But the houses had garages, so perhaps there was no street parking around here?

Around where? Whatever she had expected, it was not this suburban utopia.

Alexandra had said that Orcus was the parádeigma, the prototype, of her own world, but it made no sense. If it was populated by gods and daimons, shouldn't it be more like the classic depictions of Olympus, with chiton-clothed Zeus, Apollo,

Aphrodite, and the rest of the divine crew? Alexandra had not claimed to be a goddess herself, but she had said she was an avatar of one. And Charon, or Koresh, as he now called himself, was certainly a mythological figure, the ferryman of the dead. But where were the rest of the Olympians? Cleo tried to remember the Homer and Hesiod she had read for her A-levels, but even though the details were fuzzy, she was pretty certain that neither of them had anything to say about suburban living!

Koresh had mentioned the "Upheaval". Could it be that there had been some catastrophe in the Orcus that had decimated its inhabitants? It would not be the first time. Zeus dethroned his father Cronos, who had previously overthrown his own father Uranus. The murderous squabbles of deities were the main subject of Greek mythology. And why not, considering that the murderous squabbles of humans were the main subject of history? If the two worlds mirrored each other, this was to be expected.

The street seemed to lead nowhere, running straight between two rows of manicured front yards. The peak of Orcus brooded above it, giving a spooky unreal feel to the postapocalyptic silence. The sun dipped behind it, and Cleo started when a streetlight blinked into a feeble glow. But it seemed to be an automatic action as there was still no sign of people around. The air was purple with the dusk, but while a couple more streetlights turned on, all the windows in the houses she passed remained dark.

The silence and deepening twilight were spooky. In Ano Syros, narrow alleyways were always thronged with people late into the night, but this looked like a ghost town.

She had walked aimlessly for a while, turning onto another identical street. The dark houses were disorienting, but even more disorienting was the fact that the terrain was as flat as a pancake. She had gotten so used to the slope of Ano Syros that she forgot how to navigate a suburban maze. It had been easy to find her way on the First Level: the sea below, the sprawl of whitewashed houses climbing toward the town's boundary above. But where was the sea? And how come the street was so horizontal when she was now higher on the mountain? The peak was still here, hanging over this incongruous suburban enclave like a massive ghost, but she could not figure out the layout of this Level. It did not help that there was no moon tonight and that the people living here apparently considered street lighting a luxury rather than a necessity.

There was a sudden sound, shocking in the hush; a loud flapping and whirring as if a large ungainly bird flew over her head. She saw something dark and indistinct – as big as a buzzard – pass by, but the thing landed in the backyard of one of the houses, and she did not feel like venturing into the tangle of shadows to investigate.

She was unnerved by this strange place. Cleo loved cities; Cora had been more of a nature person. As children, both had been happy living in the Greek village with their grandmother, but suburbia always seemed to Cleo to hide dark secrets beneath its manicured exteriors, chaos bubbling just under the bland surface. How much of this impression was due to Netflix she was not sure, but she would rather be in the alleys of Ano Syros – not to mention the streets of London – than wandering these faceless subdivisions.

Cleo passed a particularly large house with a wraparound porch. Something made her look back.

A feverish orange glow bled from the French windows.

She ran back, but the lights went out as she climbed onto the porch and knocked on the door. She knocked again. No answer. She pressed her ear to the door but heard nothing. If there were people inside, they kept quiet. She had a nightmarish vision of an entire family crouching on the floor, their still heads like mushrooms in the dark. She shuddered and went on.

But now it became a new rule in this obscure game. As she passed a house, its windows would light up. But if she went back and knocked on the door, the lights would instantly go out. Whoever lived here knew of her presence but did not want to reveal themselves.

She had had enough. She was tired and hungry, her feet hurt, and she did not plan on sleeping outside. The blank street unspooled in front of her like a ribbon, leading nowhere.

Instead of hammering on the door of the next house, she cupped her hands around her face and peered into the window. She could see nothing but shadows. However, on the grass next to the porch lay a gardening trowel. She picked it up; however, the idea of breaking into somebody's house was, of course, shocking and unacceptable. But, as Eleni had often said, What cannot be cured must be endured. If you have no choice, you do whatever it takes.

"Hello!" a voice said, and the porch light came on.

Cleo whirled around, still clutching the trowel. The figure on the porch stepped forward.

It was a teenaged boy, around thirteen or fourteen, dressed in baggy shorts and a t-shirt with a print of a peacock.

"Do you want my mom and dad?" the boy asked. "They are out. I'm home alone."

Cleo could just gape at him, so taken aback she was. The boy was speaking English with an American accent. The sense of being in some TV sitcom was overwhelming.

The porch light fell on his face as he stepped forward, and Cleo knew it was no sitcom.

The boy was extraordinarily good-looking. Not in the blandly handsome way of a TV actor but rather like a classic statue made flesh. His face, despite being unquestionably that of a teenager, had the kind of perfection that seemed ageless, and somehow inhuman. No hint of adolescent acne marred his preternaturally clear skin, which gleamed with a sort of marble sheen. His blond curls lay close on his head like flower petals.

"What is this place?" she demanded. "Why are you playing this stupid game with me?"

"What game?" the boy asked. The subtle mockery in his voice, as if he knew what she was talking about but pretended not to, just to throw her off, made her doubt his age. She remembered how Koresh had shifted from an old man to a child and back again during their aborted boat ride. But this was different; the boy's physique remained unchanged, it was only his expression and his easy self-confidence that belied his apparent age.

"Are there other people here?" Cleo asked irritably. "Where are your parents?"

"My foster parents. I am adopted."

"Thanks for sharing," Cleo muttered. "So, can I talk to them?"

"They are away but coming back soon. Why don't you step in? You can wait for my parents inside."

Cleo suspected it was a bad idea, but wandering through this creepy suburbia in the dark did not appeal to her either. And if worst came to worst, she could probably tackle a teenager.

She followed him into the house, through a small hallway leading into the open-plan living space. There was something odd about it, and it took Cleo a couple of seconds to figure out what it was.

The room was modern-looking; it felt like she had stepped back into her own time from the old-fashioned ambience of Ano Syros.

But while every living room she had ever been to had a TV or an entertainment system, this one did not.

Still, it was creepily reminiscent of her mother's suburban paradise, with a leather sofa set and a breakfast bar, separating the living space from the kitchen. It was dimly illuminated by several artfully scattered mood lamps, which did little to dispel the gloom.

The boy perched on the edge of the table, while Cleo, tired and drained, gratefully sunk into the well-padded sofa. He was still studying her with what appeared to be a wry amusement.

"I'm Cleo," she said to break the uncomfortable silence. "What's your name?"

"Cleo," he repeated, stretching it out into a droop of vowels. "Cleo?"

"It's my name. And you are?"

"I'm Or."

That was not a Greek name, though why should it be? They spoke English, after all.

"It means 'light', or 'bright'," he added. "A beautiful name, don't you think?"

Cleo stared at him. Was this barely pubescent boy flirting with her? Or was there some private joke she was too dumb to understand?

"So where are your parents?" she repeated brusquely.

"At a block party. I hope they'll come home soon. Because if they don't, they may not come home at all."

"What? What kind of party is it?"

"A hunting party." Or smirked. "Would you like some tea? You look like you could use it."

"Sure," Cleo agreed. She could use a hot drink. And a sandwich or two, or whatever they had for tea here. And since the kitchen was open-plan, she could keep an eye on Or.

He busied himself with putting the kettle on and getting teabags out of the cupboard, while she leaned back, enjoying the familiar give of modern furniture. That was better than the Villa Pharos! Except for the fact that she had no clue where she was, or what she was supposed to do here.

So, what the hell was going on?

The feeling that she was in some bad movie was overwhelming. She was on the Second Level of Orcus, the Platonic world of essences according to Alexandra, and this faux-American suburban paradise was as incongruous here as a sore thumb.

You must go up.

Find your sister.

Mick and Iris had written this. Iris, her BFF, and Mick, her…whatever. But how would they know that Cora was in Orcus? And should she trust them?

Cleo tried to recall their faces but ended up with a blur. She knew that her transition to Orcus had played havoc with her memory. Certain things were crystal-clear – her childhood with Eleni, her sister's gradual deterioration and estrangement from her – but others were…not exactly forgotten but hazy, shrouded in a mental equivalent of London fog. She knew where she worked, but the details of what her employment consisted of were as elusive as a dream. She knew the vacation in Greece had been Iris' idea but could not remember why she went along on a short notice. Didn't Iris have some sort of…sudden vacation? No! She sent her son to stay with her mother! Yes, that was it! Iris had a child, and her mother volunteered to take him off her hands for a week, so they decided to hop to Greece, just the two of them. Cleo was relieved that she could remember these details; it seemed to indicate that her memory was returning. But now another mystery presented itself. Why the hell had they let Mick tag along if it was supposed to be a girls' vacation?

Her brief fling with Mick had been one of those unfortunate hookups that are not so much unpleasant as embarrassing. She had been gutted by Cora's disappearance and had nobody to share her conviction that her sister was still alive. Nobody but Mick. He had always been around, ready for a pub crawl or a movie marathon on a rainy afternoon. And wasn't he the only one of their friends to agree with her that Cora could not have drowned?

What about Iris? Had she been supportive? Yes, but… Another piece of memory suddenly dropped into her awareness, but like a piece of a lost jigsaw puzzle, Cleo did not know where to fit it. Iris disliked Cora.

Why? Cleo felt increasingly frustrated by her inability to connect random chunks of her past. But even more so, she was plagued by the nagging feeling that somewhere in those unremembered events lay the key to her ending up in Orcus.

Nobody – neither Iris nor their mother – believed that Cleo would know if her twin was dead. Nobody but Mick. He had accepted what Cleo told him. Yes, they had drifted apart, but they were still Cora and Cleo, Cleo and Cora, two halves of a single fertilized egg, two peas in the pod of their mother's womb.

Dioscuri, the divine twins.

Eleni, their grandmother, had taught the twins the stories of their Greek heritage. Had she perhaps known they would be thrown into this strange world? Was it possible that she herself was here somewhere?

Cleo felt a burst of hope, but it was extinguished almost immediately. Eleni was dead, taken away by a freak storm. Cleo had seen her laid out in the church, the Orthodox service a barely heard accompaniment to the sobbing of her friends and cousins. Cora stood by, dry-eyed and stone-faced, while Daphne was carefully navigating a crumpled tissue around her mascara. It was the last time she had seen her mother and sister together.

No, Eleni was dead, and the dead did not come back to life. Not even in Orcus.

Are you sure?

Koresh was Charon, the ferryman of the dead. Instinctively, Cleo touched the blue Eye of Charon, tucked in under her plain black t-shirt.

But Charon was willing to take her out of Orcus, at least until the flayed cyclops showed up. This was not in any story she could remember.

So perhaps myths got it wrong, as myths often did.

Or perhaps something had happened in this Platonic world of essences to distort it out of recognition.

Or came out of the kitchen bearing a tray with two mugs and a plate of cookies. Cleo's mouth flooded with saliva, but she was disappointed when she tasted the food.

The tea was actually some herbal concoction, bright-red and with a nauseatingly sweet smell, but the cookies tasted like sugared cardboard. Still, Cleo was too hungry to be picky. She ate several cookies and took a long draught of the tea, grimacing at its color that stained the sides of the mug in blood-red.

"What is this?" she asked Or, who was sipping his own tea with the delicacy of a duchess.

"Pomegranate infusion. Good, isn't it?"

Pomegranate? Cleo remembered the loukoumi she had eaten in Katerina's house. People sure liked this fruit in Orcus! Something niggled at the back of her brain – something she might have heard from Eleni or read somewhere – but no matter how she tried to pin down the elusive memory, it dissolved into the shadows of her occluded past.

"What is this place called?" she asked Or.

"Happy Meadows."

"Suburban paradise?"

"There are worse places to be, as you probably know," Or responded cattily.

Surely a teenager would not talk like this! Cleo studied his face, expecting to see the fluidity of Koresh, but Or remained the same, though his insufferable smirk grew wider.

"So, who are your folks?" she asked.

"I have foster parents. And a sister, but she is not here."

"Where is she?"

"In the place where you are going," Or responded casually. "And like you, she is not coming back."

"What? Where do you think I'm going?"

"The summit. The top. The Final Level."

"How do you know that?"

Or shrugged.

"Who are you?" Cleo demanded, putting down her mug. The cloying sweetness of the pomegranate made her nauseous.

"I told you who I am," Or replied. "If you are too stupid to understand, it's not my fault."

Cleo felt like slapping his beautiful face, even though getting mad at teenagers was a losing proposition. Boys like Or had been a bane of her adolescence: privileged, spoiled brats who believed themselves entitled to any girl from a working-class family. But those boys had been pimply, gangly bullies, while Or was…something else.

Or. He had said his name meant "bright" or "light". And he had a sister.

Something clicked.

"Is your sister your twin?" she asked.

"Yes. But she had gone over to the losing side. Stupid of her. Arty was always an idealist."

"Artemis," Cleo said. "Your sister's name is Artemis. And you are Apollo, Phoebus. The Bright One."

Or smiled.

"You are not as dense as you look," he remarked placidly.

Avatars. Copies.

"Watch your mouth! Because you are not a god, are you? You are an antigrafo. A…" – what did Alexandra call it – "a copy."

"It's better than nothing. After the Upheaval, this is all that's left."

"What's the Upheaval?"

A raucous noise came from outside; a discordant cawing, the beating of many wings and the screech of many misshapen throats.

CHAPTER 12

leo rushed to the window and stared, open-mouthed, at the procession coming down the sleepy suburban street.

At first, she thought Alexandra had come back with her murder of ravens. But no, these were not birds.

The creatures filling the night with their grim celebration teetered on bony chicken legs and flapped tiny, plucked wings, but they walked upright, their fuzz-covered obese bodies curving in a parody of the female shape, with meaty hips above skeletal thighs and slack breasts. Their shoulders sloped down to incongruously small wings, but their faces were the worst: folded and pleated, with large staring eyes, gaping nostrils, and the mouth distended into a fleshy beak studded with tiny teeth. They gabbled and honked and whistled, but Cleo could hear chewed-up remnants of articulate speech, ugly broken words spat at the world like poison.

"Moms are coming home," Or remarked with a mocking grin. "Dads will be here soon."

Cleo realized she needed to get away, and she also realized she had no strength left. The ascent through that horrible stairwell had taken too much out of her. She could not keep running.

She sunk to the floor. Or regarded her like something nasty stuck to his shoe, and that teenaged arrogance rose her to action.

"You have to hide me!" she snarled at him.

"Why would I?"

"Because of this!" She pulled the Eye of Charon out of her shirt.

She did not know whether it would have any effect on Or, but it was the only thing she had.

Or whistled through his teeth.

"Wow! Where did you get this?"

"Never mind! Just help me hide away from these…harpies."

That was not a metaphor, she realized. These creatures were harpies.

He hesitated, distaste plainly written on his chiseled features.

"All right. Come with me."

He led Cleo to the bedroom on the upper floor. It looked like a typical teenager's bedroom – or what a typical teenager's bedroom might have looked like before Cleo was born. There was no TV. No PlayStation. No computer or cellphone charger. But there were colorful posters on the walls, which Cleo did not have time to study because Or opened a large walk-in closet and pushed her in.

"Just be quiet," he whispered. "She will go to sleep soon."

And he slammed the door, leaving Cleo in the dark, surrounded by hanging clothes that brushed her face with invisible fingers every time she changed her position. She scooted into the corner of the closet and curled up, trying to make herself as small as possible. The musty smell of dust and sweat tickled her sinuses, and she pinched her nostrils to prevent herself from sneezing.

Harpies: half-women, half-birds. Cannibals. The brief glimpse of them filled her with dread and revulsion but at least she knew what they were. There was power in knowledge.

Despite everything, fatigue won over, and Cleo dozed off.

The smell of salt and sage, the turquoise glint of the sea, Cleo running on the white sand…

How can she see herself from the back?

Cleo-not-Cleo picks up a bright red fruit that has been deposited by the waves. The pomegranate is shining like a star in her hand. She bites into its leathery skin.

She woke up suddenly, jolted by silence. The faint noise penetrating the closet from the outside had ceased. She groped in the dark, but her outstretched fingers encountered only layers of heavy clothes. She was disoriented, blundering into sharp corners and clanking hangers. How big was the closet? Where was the door? She was beginning to hyperventilate, claustrophobia kicking in. What if Or had locked her in?

Her eyes adjusted to the dark and finally spotted a thin line of light. She lunged toward it and pushed the door. It gave, and she peered through the crack into the empty bedroom, dimly illuminated by a nightlight in the shape of a winged horse.

The door onto the landing was ajar, and she heard voices from downstairs. She crept onto the landing and crouched behind a post that supported the railing, then looked down into the kitchen.

Or was sitting at the table. And in front of him, perched upon the barstool, was a harpy.

From up above, Cleo was able to see the creature better, and she wished she could not.

The thing was the color of lard, her skin under the scant covering of fuzz oily and pale. Her feet were like a giant chicken's feet, yellow and bony, with black talons. They scrabbled nervously as she was speaking.

"I'll try to talk to him, but you know what he is like…"

It was strange that her beak-like mouth could produce comprehensible words, but it did, despite the phlegmy undertone as if her throat was permanently clogged. In front of her was a plate heaped up with barbequed meat, and as she was talking, she lifted a piece with her foot and bit into it, spilling meat juices onto herself. Her wings were useless atrophied appendages, but they flapped as she was talking, underscoring her points.

Or was sitting upright and staring at the wall. He was not eating. His face was expressionless and his voice was toneless and low when he spoke.

"It cannot go on like this. If we don't get some order here, this Level will be destroyed. And Nyx is already eying upper Levels. As his strength wanes, hers will grow."

"That bitch!" the harpy clucked contemptuously. "And his strength is not waning! Briareus is stronger than any of the Nine, and you know that. It was bad luck that we ended here, in Elysium. Just you wait. We will rise, as the rest of them fall."

Briareus?

"He may be strong, but he is also brainless," Or said. The harpy spat a chewed-up piece of meat at him. The disgusting projectile hit

Or in the face and slid down onto the floor. He did not even bother to wipe off its oily track.

"Watch your mouth! Speak respectfully of your Dad!"

"Yes, Mom," Or mouthed, and as grotesque as the scene was, it reminded Cleo of kitchen-table conversations with her own mother. Well, as bad as Daphne had been sometimes, she had never spat at her daughters. Not to mention the fact that she was human.

"But you know that our population is dangerously low," Or went on in what Cleo mentally characterized as an "adult" voice – trying to sound rational while your parent was being obstreperous and cranky. "People are getting restive. You can't keep them locked up in garages forever."

"We can always Call more people from the First Level."

"Nyx won't allow it. She may be weaker than…Dad, but she is smart. And remember, she has access to the Archipelago."

The harpy sighed; it was a very human sound coming from a monster.

"All right, I will talk to Dad. He will be home late. You must eat something, Or. You are getting too thin. You are not anorexic, are you?"

Or shrugged, but as he was about to respond, he lifted his head and his eyes locked with Cleo's who, fascinated by the conversation, had leaned out too much and exposed herself.

For a moment that seemed as long as eternity, they stared at each other.

"No, I'm not hungry," Or finally said. "I'm going to turn in. Night-night, Mom."

"A kiss for Mommy," the harpy said, stretching her sagging neck and offering her wattles to her son, who planted a perfunctory peck on her lardy cheek and started climbing the stairs. Cleo scuttled back into the bedroom.

Or came in and closed the door behind him. He sat on the bed and hid his face in his hands.

"I can't congratulate you on your family life," Cleo finally said.

"They are not my family. I told you, I am adopted. These are my family."

He pointed to the posters on the wall.

They were very beautiful and totally appalling – rather like Or himself. On the left side, a large poster, exquisitely rendered in brown and sepia, showed a woman in childbirth. She was positioned in such a way that her distended vagina faced the viewer, with a baby's crown pushing out. Her face was obscured by her domed belly and her hands clutched the ground she was lying on, which, in fact, was another woman's body, much larger than her own and covered in rocky protrusions. This woman's face was a rough-hewn slab of marble, with the black opening of a screaming mouth. In the middle, another poster, this one in full color, depicted a heap of dead children, splattered with blood, their twiggy limbs thrown in disarray. At some distance but larger than life, two figures stood hand in hand: a boy and a girl, their prepubescent bodies naked and their faces covered with black veils. The boy held a bow and the girl an empty quiver. And the final poster was in black and white. A grotesque figure writhed on the bone-covered ground, its long arms rooted in the ground and sprouting a thicket of disheveled pines. Its stomach was split, and an enormous wing was poking out of it. To indicate sizes, a couple of diminutive human figures ran away from the tortured giant.

Cleo studied the posters.

"Where I come from, teens have K-pop bands on the walls, not obstetrics aids," she scoffed, trying to sound superior. She felt out of her depth. She pitied Or but was also increasingly afraid of him.

"These are family pictures," he said. "That," he nodded toward the woman giving birth on a slab of rock shaped as another woman's body, "is my sister and me being born. This is our mother Leto and our aunt Asteria. Our stepmother would not let us be born on any land, so our aunt had to help out by becoming land, if you know what I mean. And that," pointing to the middle picture, "is Arty and me taking care of some loudmouth who insulted our Mum. The last guy is Tityus, and you don't want to know what happened to him, but let's just say that you don't want to mess with our family."

"I know the stories," Cleo said. "The birth of Apollo and Artemis, the killing of the children of Niobe for insulting Leto, the punishment of Tityus who tried to rape her…but you are an antigrafo, not the god himself. Where is the real Apollo?"

There was such bleakness in Or's face that she had to look away.

"Dead," he said.

"Apollo is dead?"

"All the Olympians are."

"So who are the Nine?"

"You will find out soon enough. If you manage to live that long."

"Are you going to feed me to your harpy Mum?" Cleo demanded.

Or chuckled mirthlessly.

"Mom is okay," he said, "it's my Dad you need to be afraid of."

"Briareus."

The giant with fifty heads and a hundred arms, so strong that he and his brothers were appointed the guards of the defeated Titans in Tartarus.

"He is the Ruler of this Level," Or said.

The upside-down cosmos, the mountain of dead gods...Cleo knew she had to figure it out somehow. But right now she needed to escape.

"Show me the way up," she said.

Or hesitated, then sat down on the edge of his bed, covered with a luxurious spread embroidered with peacocks that seemed to move and shift, fanning their tails. The bedroom was very nice, Cleo noted subconsciously, and it did not smell of teenaged sweat or clutter. Instead, the sweet aroma of hyacinth wafted in the air, fresh like a flower rather than with the chemical edge of an air-spray.

"You are Called," he said. It was not a question.

Cleo nodded.

"I thought he Called you at first."

"Your foster father?"

"Yes. He does it more and more recently. The people who live on this Level...they are just not enough."

"Not enough for what?"

But she could figure it out.

A hunting party. Harpies are cannibals.

No cars.

The garages are where they keep their prey. Locked up.

The roast meat on her plate.

She felt vomit rising up in her throat.

"Is this why you invited me to wait for them?" Cleo hissed. "You motherfucker!"

"I didn't ask for that!" Or hissed back. "Yes, I am an antigrafo of the god of light, and it gives me zilch. Nothing. He couldn't stand up to the monsters, what do you expect me to do? When I grow up, my loving parents may decide to have me for lunch. And no, lady, before you ask, I'm really thirteen, not three thousand years old. Antigrafos are mortal. Just like you."

"Why don't you run away, then?"

"Where? He is the Ruler of this Level. I can't go up unless I'm Called, and who would Call me? And nobody can go down."

"This makes no sense," Cleo moaned. "It's not in any myths I know."

"Things have changed," Or said. "I know you have all kinds of stories in your world, but did it ever occur to you that these stories are shadows of shadows?"

Plato's Cave…

"Whatever," Cleo said. "I need to go up. You have to show me the way. Please."

Or hesitated, but then shrugged.

"All right," he said. "I have no idea who Called you or why, but it's somebody higher up. I don't want to mess with the rest of the Nine. Figure it out for yourself."

Cleo should be relieved at his decision but another, even more urgent, need interfered with her composure.

"Sorry," she said, somewhat embarrassed to appeal to a teenage boy, "but first I need the loo."

CHAPTER 13

he en-suite bathroom was all green marble and wall mirrors, with a sunken tub and a plush cover on the toilet seat. Posh enough, but not what Cleo imagined deities used.

Did it ever occur to you that these stories are shadows of shadows?

Maybe she should not try to rack her brain for bits of knowledge gleaned from Eleni's mythological tales. Orcus confounded her expectations at every step, and the correspondences she looked for either did not materialize or were the opposite of their supposed originals. Better if she approached it with an open mind.

Cleo washed her hands at the marble sink and studied her face in the mirror.

After Cora's disappearance, she went through a period of avoiding mirrors altogether. It was too painful to see her missing twin staring back at her. Not all identical twins look exactly alike, but she and Cora did. Eleni was the only one who was able to tell them apart without a helpful mark on their clothes; Daphne could not. Their mother had been both jealous and proud of their doubled beauty. Curls as rich and dark as the midnight sky, eyes the color of the sea at dawn, skin as white as sea foam; the Mediterranean seemed to have marked Cora and Cleo as its own. Daphne had tried to make money out of them by submitting their kid pictures to some stupid breakfast-cereal beauty pageant, and that had been the only time Cleo remembered her grandmother enraged, screaming at her daughter at the top of her voice and threatening to sue for custody of her grandkids. After they entered adolescence, Cora and Cleo diverged in the relationship with mirrors, as they diverged in everything else. Cleo's attitude to her appearance was pragmatic: she knew beauty was an advantage, and she was determined to make full use of every advantage she had in achieving her professional goals. Cora tried everything in her power to destroy her beauty. And yet, even her reckless plunges into anorexia and drugs left no mark on her appearance. Cora and Cleo had remained spitting images of each other until Cora's disappearance.

When it became clear that Cora was not coming back, Cleo had done something she would have never considered doing before. She had shaved her head as a sign of mourning. Now she winced as she saw the uneven dark fuzz on her skull, sticking out in wild curls. Well, if Orcus had hairdressers, she might want to visit one! At least her best feature, her aquamarine eyes the color of the Mediterranean, required no enhancement.

Except they were no longer blue.

Cleo stared into the dead-black orbs with which her reflection regarded her. The mark of the Call. Unlike the pictures in Katerina's house, the darkness did not stain the whites. For a casual acquaintance, she might appear to be wearing tinted lenses, but she knew better. Her irises were now the color of pitch, swallowing her pupils. She no longer looked like herself.

She no longer looked like Cora.

She finished washing up and went back to the bedroom where Or was lounging among his peacocks.

"So where is the way up?" she asked.

A thunderous noise answered her as the entire house shook. Or rushed out, and Cleo followed.

Looking down the staircase leading to the ground floor of the house, she saw that the landing below was piled up with...tubes? Pipes? She leaned over the banister.

Her eyes adjusted to the dim night light. Now she could see, though she still could not believe what she was seeing.

The landing below was covered by a gigantic, splayed hand.

Fingers, each as long as Cleo's leg, twitched slightly, as if their owner moved in their sleep. They were tipped by crooked rugose nails and attached to a spade-shaped palm that could squash her like a mosquito. The wrist disappeared into the darkness of the bedroom door standing ajar. No way could the downstairs bedroom contain a body commensurate with the size of the hand.

"He is waking up," Or whispered.

Another hand, equally large, snaked out of the bedroom. Or pulled Cleo back. Above his shoulder, Cleo glimpsed a giant hand finger-walking up the stairs, and a shrunken body, tiny by comparison but probably as big as hers, being dragged in the wake of the monstrous appendage.

Or slammed his bedroom door. The floor juddered. A crash echoed in the stairwell, and something thumped against the window. The night was alive with heavy flapping, as if a flock of geese were throwing themselves against the house. A face pressed itself against the glass: an ugly lard-colored face, its mouth-beak squashed, the scanty hair on its head blown away, disclosing bald patches.

Somebody was screaming. In the property next door, the garage door opened, spilling light onto the lawn, and several people rushed out. Or drew the curtains, cutting off her view.

"You need to go!" he said.

"Where?"

Or took off his shirt.

Cleo backed off, looking for a weapon. He was a teenager, barely out of childhood, but she did not trust him one bit.

"The way is through my closet," he breathed out hurriedly.

"What?"

"Don't argue. Just...go. And put this on."

He threw his shirt at her. The peacock at the front fanned its tail, the shiny eyespots winking at her.

"If the clothes attack you, he'll protect you."

Cleo numbly took the shirt, put it over her own, and hoisted her backpack onto her shoulders. Outside, the sharp staccato of enormous nails clicking upon the stairs grew louder.

"Go!" Or yelled.

She cast one last glance at him as she opened the closet door and squeezed inside. He was naked from the waist up, and the marble pallor of his skin gleamed in the faint night light. Even in her confusion and fear, Cleo could not help but notice how beautiful his body was. Not hot, or sexy, or ripped. Or's body had a kind of impersonal, absolute perfection. Each muscle, each fold of skin, each bone was exactly what it should be, and it was impossible to imagine him grow, or mature, or age.

Antigrafos are mortal…

"Will you be okay?" she asked, despite herself.

He grinned crookedly.

"As long as I am young enough to be the child of the house. Family life. They are big on it. Now, please go. And if you find out who the Ruler of the Final Level is, just…kill them. It can't be worse than it is now."

Cleo slammed the closet door shut.

She was instantly plunged into a cottony silence, which was a relief after the cacophony outside. Otherwise, it was hardly an improvement of her situation. She was in total darkness, surrounded by musty, densely packed clothes, and she had no idea how to proceed.

"How hard could this be?" she muttered and groped forward, fingers brushing against heavy scratchy fabrics that seemed impregnated with dirt and dust.

She had gone for about five minutes when she stopped. This made no sense. Even if the closet was as deep as the entire length of the house, she should have reached the back wall by now. Not for the first time, Cleo bitterly regretted the loss of her smartphone – if nothing else, she could have used the flashlight app – but there were no smartphones in Orcus.

She drew in the dusty, mothball-smelling air and sneezed. The sound was instantly swallowed up by the curtains of clothes that hemmed her in. But now the silence seemed to be underpinned by a stealthy susurrus, a low whisper. Cleo strove to hear, but it was so faint that it might have been an illusion, her brain filling the unnatural silence with sound. She started walking again and was instantly tangled in a large coat that seemed to embrace her with its dusty sleeves. She wriggled free and ran into a large, frilled dress, her face pressed into the crinkled fabric that somehow insinuated itself into Cleo's mouth. She spat out the folds that tasted of mice and old age, and pushed away two dresses that had materialized on both sides of her, slapping her across the face with torn lace and shredded velvet. A cloth belt, stiff with ingrained dirt, wound itself around Cleo's neck, choking her.

She managed to pull it off and crouched down on the floor. Hems whiplashed above her like branches in a stormy forest. The darkness was so deep that phantom bursts of blue blossomed in her eyes. Cleo groped in the dark and a zipper fastened on her fingers like a hungry mouth.

"Think!" she whispered to herself.

Had Or tricked her? Apollo could be cruel, but he was no trickster. Did antigrafos share the characters of their originals? Apollo was the god of prophecy, but the pronouncements of his Sybil were often so coded that they entrapped the unwary who trusted their literal meaning. Or may not have lied when he told her that the way to the next Level was through his closet. The question was how to find the exit.

Cleo started crawling but instantly ran into a soft barricade of musty blankets that slipped over her like an avalanche, and she had to scramble back in order not to be suffocated. The problem was that in this darkness she did not know what direction was forward. She could have been walking in circles for all she knew.

Wait! The clothes were hung on hangers, weren't they? And hangers had to be attached to rails. If rails ran parallel to each other across the closet, she could follow one and so get to the wall. And then it would be the question of following the wall until she found an exit.

When they were kids, it was Cora who whimpered about the monster in the closet and the witch under the bed, to the profound displeasure of their mother. And it was Cleo who shushed her sister and threw open the doors of the manky cupboard in their bedroom to show that there was nothing frightening there. Now she needed to be her own voice of reason.

She cautiously raised herself up to her full height, squeezing between two rows of unquiet clothes, and lifted her hand, groping in the dark. Her fingers snagged on snapping fasteners and writhing collars, but finally they touched something smooth. A rail! She grasped the cold metal, blessedly inert, and tiptoed through the passage created by two parallel rows of hangers.

The clothes must have realized what she was up to and redoubled their assault. Something shaggy swiped her across the face like a bear paw, and she was almost swept off her feet when other fur coats joined in the attack.

Battered and pummeled, she kept her head down and pressed on. Her backpack was almost torn off her shoulders by a man's shirt whose buttons gripped it like hungry teeth. She yanked it back and kept going. A long ribbon suddenly looped around her neck. She sputtered. She grabbed the ribbon with both hands, pulling it away. It writhed like a snake, trying to tie itself around her wrists. She tried to shake it off and discovered that she could see.

The light was not coming from any external source; it was coming from herself. She looked down. The peacock print on Or's shirt fanned its tail and its sequined eyespots glowed with pink radiance. Ahead, she saw a free passage among the hangers like a narrow path in the forest.

A large bushy hat leaped down, fastening itself to her face. The moth-eaten fur got into her eyes and mouth. The peacock honked and reared off, coming loose from the fabric. It pecked at the hat until it fell off.

The clothes rustled indignantly and spat clouds of dust, but kept their distance. The peacock subsided back into the print, and when she brushed the front of her shirt she encountered only sequins.

Finally, after what felt like hours of walking, she saw light ahead. She emerged into a sort of hallway, dimly illuminated by the sunlight dribbling from around the crooked door at the end.

The enraged clothes at her back thrashed like trees in the storm-tossed woods. She pushed the door that swung out and deposited her in the real woods

LEVEL THREE Forest of Masks

The contrast was so great that Cleo was momentarily blinded by the sudden onslaught of brightness. The green smells of mulch and new leaves tickled her dust-clogged sinuses, and she sneezed several times in rapid succession. She took a deep breath, unglued her eyelids, and took a look at the Third Level of Elysium.

She was standing in a sunny glade surrounded by trees with light trunks and bright-green leaves that looked like poplars. She glanced back and saw the splintered wall of an old barn and a door standing ajar, but when she peered inside she saw an earthen floor and cobwebs draping empty corners instead of the zombie closet.

The position of the sun indicated it was late morning, which was confusing to say the least. She tried to calculate how long she had spent fighting musty clothes, and while it felt like an eternity, she could not believe it had been more than two hours or so.

She was still clutching the ribbon that had tried to garrot her but was now as passive and obedient as any other swatch of fabric. It was a long piece of linen with the elaborate hand embroidery of cross-stitched red and black patterns surrounding a stylized image of a man with a bow pointing it at a serpentine creature. Cleo thought it represented Apollo slaying the monstrous snake Python. She had seen this kind of embroidery, traditionally done by Greek peasant women, in the Benaki Museum in Athens. It was a beautiful piece of work.

She rolled it up and stuck it in her backpack, together with the peacock t-shirt, which she pulled off. It was humid and warm in the woods.

The trees were widely spaced but the ground was uneven, tufted with grass and strewn with deadfall. Yellow, white, and purple wildflowers clumped up in sunny patches. The massive peak of the mountain loomed, green and grey, above the treetops. She tried to gauge if she was any closer to the summit, but it looked as high as ever. In any case, technically speaking, she had not gone up. The zombie closet was horizontal, not vertical, but she knew that this was a different Level from the harpy- and giant-infested suburbia of Happy Meadows. Even the air smelled different here: green and sappy. But something was missing. It took her a moment to realize what it was. In Ano Syros, washed by the restless waters of the Mediterranean, the air was always scented by the sea, in all of its myriad incarnations, from the bracing sting of a summer breeze to the angry bitterness of a storm. Here, the sea smell was gone, and Cleo suddenly felt bereft.

But she had more immediate worries. She was starving. The pomegranate-flavored cookies Or had given her were a distant memory. She pulled out her water bottle and took several sips, but it was a poor substitute for a meal. Hoisting her backpack, she determinedly set forward in the direction of the peak.

A quick flash of movement in the stand of laurels to her right stopped her in her tracks. She stood still, straining her eyes to see through the dappled screen of leaves and branches. A bird wheeled in the azure sky, but it was too high up to see what kind – or even if it was a bird.

A branch broke with a crack like a gunshot. Something was hiding among the trunks. And then a quick streak of movement as it ran away, too quickly for her to get a good look. She only caught a glimpse of a shaggy coat like a sheep.

Food. Rest. Way up. In that order. The Call was tugging at her, a fishhook embedded in her brain.

She walked on but she had no idea where she was going. There were some faint tracks in the woods, but they petered out when she tried to follow. She did not like it; she was a city girl, always more at home in bustling streets and shopping malls than in nature. And despite the sunshine lying on the ground in emerald splinters, these woods felt dark, confusing, and hostile.

The mountain seemed to lean toward her like a giant observing a mouse at its feet. It appeared somehow more solid here than it had been in Happy Meadows – and closer. She could see upslope to long slicks of scree and hanging valleys, outcrops of eroded rock like ruined castles. She did not see any sign of human habitation or anything clearly demarcating other Levels, but Cleo had already realized that the topography of Orcus was not set in stone, so to speak, but changed depending on the Level, the point of view, and probably other things she did not understand.

A rustle behind made her whirl around.

"Stop following me!" she yelled at the tangle of leathery-leaf bushes. "Show yourself!"

Again, nothing. And then, a sly titter.

A huge head poked out from the curtain of green.

The moon-shaped face was set in a threatening scowl, its slack-lipped mouth agape. Its giant nose overhung the mouth like an icicle on the edge of a well. Flat yellow eyes stared fixedly from under the sloping forehead. And worst of all, a huge spider was crawling out of the mouth.

Cleo gulped and backed off, grasping a tree branch as a pathetic substitute for a weapon.

The monster wriggled out of the bushes. Its head was easily one-third of its entire length. The spider's chelicerae were raised threateningly but it did not move.

Cleo exhaled in shock.

The spider did not move because it could not. It was flat, painted on the canvas of the false face: a trompe l'oeil golden arachnid.

The monster removed its head.

It was an elongated helmet-like mask, sitting on the creature's shoulders. What was revealed when the mask was off was not as threatening, though equally strange.

Welcome to Narnia, Cleo thought sourly. The creature was no Mr.Tumnus. He was a satyr, though different from their sanitized kid-friendly representations. He was slender, with bronze-colored skin and a mass of curly hair. Above the waist, his flat shallow chest and long thin arms seemed to belong to a child; below the waist, the thick wooly pelt covered backward-jointed legs terminating in very large, splayed hooves. But the greatest difference from the Narnia movies was the satyr's face. It was not as grotesque as the mask he had removed but neither was it cute. In fact, it was not even human. The face was chinless and jutted out in a muzzle, created by the fusion of the long nose with the slit-like mouth. The close-set eyes had no whites, and the pupils were oblong like the pupils of a cat. The ears were tiny, buried in the spill of the curls.

The satyr walked toward her with a curious mincing gait. Cleo did not let go of her branch, even though the creature was smaller and lighter than her. It – or rather he, for it was definitely a "he", even though the pelt partially covered his genitalia – sniffed at her, his wet gaping nostrils dilating. From close up, she could smell him as well. The satyr reeked of sweat and something rancid like old vinegar.

"I don't want any trouble," Cleo said. "I have to go up. Can you show me where the ascent to the next Level is? Umm, maybe you could also show me where to get some food? I'm starving."

The satyr mewled.

"Can you talk?"

The satyr mewled again. A long, wet tongue shot out of his muzzle and licked Cleo's cheek. She jumped back, wiping her face.

"Oh no you don't!"

He pranced on his sinewy legs before her, as if showing off. She really didn't like it. Many chaps believed dropping their pants was enough to make a woman swoon, but this…thing didn't even have pants!

"Silen!" somebody shouted from behind the trees.

The satyr visibly wilted, and drooping his head like a guilty dog, trotted over to the owner of the voice who emerged into the clearing.

It was a woman holding a bow. And then another joined her. And another.

Cleo was surrounded by a group of identical women, armed with bows and arrows. They were bare-legged, wearing abbreviated woolen garments cinched at the waist by a leather belt. They glared at her through the eyeholes in their masks. Brightly painted and oversized like the mask of the satyr, it was these masks that created the impression of the women being identical. They all depicted the same face with bright blue eyes, pouting lips, and golden rows of braided hair.

Each mask's mouth was distended by a hairy spider crawling out of it.

Cleo told herself the spiders were not real, but they seemed uncannily realistic, as if frozen in the process of emerging out of these women's mouths. And what kind of people would wear revolting masks like these?

She lifted her hands.

"I don't want any trouble," she repeated in English and Greek. "I'm just going up."

"Take off your mask!" one of the women commanded in Greek, her voice booming from the aperture between the spider's chelicerae.

Confused, Cleo brushed her naked face.

"I have no mask!" she retorted.

"Take off your mask!" the woman commanded again, and the others lifted their bows, arrows quivering and ready.

"I have no mask!" Cleo yelled, losing patience. "What the fuck do you want from me?"

Her voice broke, and to her consternation she felt tears brimming in her eyes. This was too much! She had come to Greece for a vacation, for fuck's sake! She had not signed up for climbing an impossible mountain, being pursued by giant spiders, or harassed by harpies!

Cleo sobbed, tears and snot running down her face. She knew she was undignified and pathetic. She knew she looked like Cora in her worst moments, and she did not care anymore. She was done!

One of the women lifted her hand and loosened something at the base of her neck. She removed her mask, and Cleo wished she had not.

Under the mask, the woman had no face; she had no eyes, nose, or mouth. There was only an expanse of moist white flesh, dribbling with raw moisture. Perched on the athletic shoulders of a huntress, this no-face was the most horrifying thing Cleo had ever seen. She gagged involuntarily, taking a step back.

The woman put her mask back on, and Cleo breathed a sigh of relief. In the space of several heartbeats, the grotesque spider mask had become almost homely, now that she knew what was under it.

"Are you a woman?" one of the huntresses asked. She was the same one who had addressed Cleo first, demanding she take off her mask. Now, as her shock had been discharged in bawling, Cleo began to notice that apart from the masks, and possibly what was hiding under them, the women were different. Some were light, some dark, some slender, some plump, some looked barely out of childhood, some had the crepe skin of age, but the masks imposed a mocking uniformity on them, as if they were participants in some demented carnival.

Forcing herself to disregard the mask, Cleo saw that the woman talking to her was taller and heavier than the rest, and her costume was more elaborate. Her tunic was decorated with bits of fur and feathers, and the belt was studded with brass.

"I am a woman," she confirmed. Cleo was wearing jeans, trainers, and a hoodie, part of her vacation wardrobe that had made it with her to Ano Syros. Perhaps if this Level was modeled on Ancient Greece, the huntresses were unsure of her gender because of her clothes. Pants were regarded as barbaric in antiquity, and only non-Hellenic males would wear them.

"Then you need a mask," the woman said, "or the Triple Moon will steal your face. What is your name?"

"Cleo."

"I am Ursula," the woman said. "Follow me."

Cleo did, trying to fit the name to her understanding of this Level. The archer girls looked like nymphs, companions of the huntress goddess Artemis, though she could not understand the deal with the masks as it was not part of Artemis' lore. But Ursula was not a Greek name.

Neither was Or, though, and he turned out to be an antigrafo of Apollo. "Or" meant "bright" or "light", according to him – though Cleo did not know in what language – so it made sense he was an avatar of the god of light. Cleo happened to remember the origin of the name "Ursula" because one of her friends in college was obsessed with onomatology, study of names. Ursula meant "bear".

In Greek, árktos. Artemis.

The sunny, cheerful woods soon changed into something darker. The trees crowded together like whispering hags, their splayed branches drinking daylight and letting through only scant rays that broke into slivers of light, littering the forest floor like gold coins. The trees were mostly broadleaf – horse chestnut, beech, ash, and oak – and they all seemed to Cleo to be deformed in some way, craggy and squat, draped with beards of moss and colonized by slicks of brightly colored lichen. The wildflowers had disappeared, unable to compete with dripping mushrooms and curly ferns. The archer girls followed her like a flock of ghosts, while Ursula strode through the forest with the lumbering grace of her namesake. Pale shadows flitted among the shadowed trees.

Stumbling through the deadwood, Cleo tried to console herself with the thought that at least they were not harpies. There were plenty of female baddies in Greek mythology, from sirens to maenads, frenzied followers of Dionysus, but these nymphs were companions of Artemis, virgin huntresses, and they were supposed to be nicer to women than to men. Artemis herself was the patron of female independence and, confusingly, childbirth, so she should have been easier to deal with than Briareus.

But Or had said that all Olympians were dead. So, who was this woman? Artemis' antigrafo? If yes, then who was the Ruler of this Level if it was not her?

There was a gleam of black water like obsidian through the trees, and they came out at a small lake. Its boggy banks were overgrown with ferns and cattails, and its surface was littered with dead leaves. Ursula went around the lake and Cleo saw what the trees had hidden so far: the flank of the mountain, rising precipitously into the sky. There were no foothills; the massive peak thrust out of the flat plateau, seeming to lean threateningly over the woods. The vertical rock scowled threateningly with the broken teeth of crags. There was no path leading upward, and Cleo could not imagine climbing up this sheer rock face; she was no mountaineer.

Ursula made her way toward a curtain of creepers draped over a large hole, but she did not enter the cave. Instead, she sat on a boulder that served as a rude bench and stared at Cleo. Or rather, her mask stared at Cleo who shuddered, thinking of the moist membrane under the painted canvas.

Ursula reached up. Her fingers, laden with stacked bronze rings, fumbled at the edge of the mask and she pulled it off.

She was not faceless like the nymph. In fact, she was rather striking, with heavy cheeks, a sharp jutting nose, a slash-like mouth, and narrow lidded black eyes. Her hair was oiled and braided, arranged in a tight wreath around her head.

"Why are you wearing these things?" Cleo asked belligerently. She dropped onto another boulder, her feet throbbing with fatigue.

Ursula made a soughing sound and opened her mouth. In the black cavity, the stub of a cut-off tongue writhed like a slug.

She put the mask back on.

"The Triple Moon takes away the girls' faces at daytime, and their minds at nighttime," she said, matter of factly, in her deep, throaty voice. "But she could not take either from me, so she took my tongue."

Cleo swallowed, fighting nausea.

"Who is this Triple Moon you are talking about?" she asked.

"The Ruler of this Level."

"Does each Level have a single Ruler?"

"Yes. You met the Ruler of the Second Level, didn't you? When you enjoyed the hospitality of my brother – the coward who hides in the house of his worst enemy, in order to prolong his worthless existence!"

"Briareus, the Fifty-Headed One. He was one of the Giants, wasn't he? What the fuck is he doing in a suburban home?"

The painted mask could not smile, but Cleo had a distinct impression that behind that horrible spider-enhanced artificial face, the real face of the woman who called herself Ursula was contorted in a grin.

"Why do you think we who live in the world of essences are any less prone to change than you who live in the world of shadows? You think that essences are timeless, but what is more of essence than time itself?"

"That's philosophy, such as it is. I want to know what actually happened."

"The Upheaval happened."

"The Olympians were killed. All right, it wouldn't be the first revolution among deities. Cronos killed Uranus, and then Zeus castrated Cronos and locked him up. So, did Cronos come back? Or the Titans rebelled?"

Ursula shook her head.

"Worse. The Upheaval happened in the Archipelago, of which Orcus is only a part. And now we are ruled by the dregs of darkness, the worst of the weakest, and the weakest of the worst. Unfortunately, the last have become the first, and they are wreaking havoc on the creation out of petty malice and hunger for revenge."

Cleo frowned. It felt like Ursula was avoiding a straight answer, but she did not want to press too much. The sharp arrows of the huntresses were a good reason to tread carefully, and she was still unnerved by the spider masks that reminded her of Arachne. She licked her chapped lips, feeling another stab of hunger in her empty stomach. As if reading her mind, Ursula clapped her hands.

"Food for our guest!" Ursula commanded, which was the best thing Cleo had heard in a long time.

An archer girl appeared bearing a wooden platter with pieces of grilled meat and flatbread, and a ceramic pitcher with some murky liquid inside. Cleo hesitated. She was a half-hearted vegetarian, but she was also ravenously hungry. Her mouth flooded with saliva at the enticing scent of charred meat, which probably came from a recent hunt by these very women. She was not going to insult her hosts by rejecting it!

She muttered thanks and bit off a small piece. The richness of it took her breath away. It was as if an infusion of life-force spread from her mouth through her entire tired and battered body. She took another bite and another, and promised herself that if – when – she got back home, she would have a steak every week. The meat was so delicious that she had to force herself to eat the flatbread also, figuring she needed the carbs. The flatbread had the consistency of an old shoe-sole, but she determinedly chewed through it, sipping from the pitcher. The liquid was sour wine diluted with water.

Ursula did not eat or drink, apparently unwilling to remove her mask. The archer girls melted back into the woods.

"So," Ursula said, "you met my brother."

Cleo looked around for a napkin, and not finding any, wiped her greasy palms on the grass.

"Or? He did not seem very fond of you, truth be told. But are you really siblings? Or is it only your parádeigmas, your originals, who are?"

The mask could not show expression, but Cleo felt that Ursula was surprised.

"You know about parádeigmas and antigrafos?"

"I do. Copies of gods, imprints of archetypes."

"Indeed. To answer your question: yes, Or and I are really siblings, just as our parádeigmas, Apollo and Artemis, were. And if your next question is why we live on different Levels, it is because I arranged to be Called. I just could not abide staying with those monsters who pretended to be our parents. I am older than Or, as you may have noticed, and I remember our human parents."

"Are you born of humans, then?"

"Of course. These monsters killed our real parents when Briareus took over the Second Level with the help of the harpies. Or was just a baby."

"So, you arranged to be Called by the Ruler of the Third Level," Cleo said slowly, remembering what Or had said about his sister. "And is it better here?"

Ursula was silent for a long time, and her voice sounded hoarse when she spoke.

"It's better to be a hunter than a hunted."

CHAPTER IS

Cleo tossed and turned on the deer skin, an outcropping of rock digging into her back. She pulled another smelly skin over her head and sneezed again. She had complained about the hard bed and thin mattress in the Villa Pharos; now she thought of that crappy motel room with nostalgia. Not to mention the fact that it had a bathroom with a shower, while all the Third Level of Orcus had to offer in the way of amenities was an algae-infested pond and a latrine.

But what really kept her awake was uncertainty. She had reached the Third Level. What next?

Ursula had told her she could remain with the troop. But apart from the fact that the last thing in the world she wanted was to run around the woods with a bunch of masked savages, she could not stay here. The Call was still pulsing in her brain like a nascent migraine. Somebody on an upper Level wanted her. And she wanted her sister.

But Ursula had been rather insistent she stay, at least for a couple of days. She had also claimed she did not know where the ascent to the Fourth Level was, which Cleo did not believe for a second.

A wail came from the darkness outside. Cleo did not know enough about wilderness to tell whether it was animal or human.

There was something else Ursula had said that buzzed in Cleo's head like a poisonous fly.

One of the Nine wants you. And the Nine are merciless.

Who were the new Rulers of Orcus?

There had been several revolts against the Olympian gods in mythology: Titanomachy, when Zeus and his siblings fought Titans, and Gigantomachy, when the triumphant Olympians fought monstrous giants born of Gaia. The Upheaval must have been the last and most successful revolt, in which, if Or and Ursula were to be believed, all Olympians were slain, leaving behind faulty copies or avatars of themselves. But who took over? Nyx, the goddess of Night, a minor and obscure deity; Briareus, a Giant, child of Chaos; and on this Level…Ursula had mentioned the Triple Moon. Cleo had thought it was a figure of speech, but now she suddenly remembered the triple-faced goddess of witchcraft named Hekate.

Chthonic deities. Gods and goddesses of darkness, chaos, destruction, and violence.

Cleo had also asked Ursula about the Archipelago, remembering that the name cropped up in the conversation between Or and the harpy.

"Orcus is not the only mountain in the sea of stories."

"So, the world of essences is not just…well, Greek?"

"Your world is a reflection of this one, an unstable picture painted on the wall of the cave by the fires of creation. But reflections and originals can exchange places. You have become stronger, and your dreams and nightmares have been seeping into our world, contaminating it. And you have had a lot of nightmares recently."

Cora is here.

Find your sister.

That was the only thing that mattered, right? Cora had disappeared from the world. So had Cleo. Cleo had found herself in Orcus. Cora must be here too.

The letter said so.

The letter? How would her friends know that? And where were they? Iris, with her mane of blond curls, the only vivid detail of her appearance Cleo retained. Iris, with her laughter and her love for her son. Funny that Cleo could not remember the boy at all, but she remembered that Iris was a single mother, fiercely protective of her child, and working her ass off to support both of them. As for Mick… The mild Mick. The inoffensive Mick. The loyal Mick. Loyal to Cleo and to Cora, or Cora's memory, which he shared with Cleo. A good friend, if not boyfriend material.

But how would he, or Iris for that matter, know anything about Orcus and Cora?

For the first time, it dawned on Cleo that the letter may not have been written by her friends at all.

Distant laughter and shrieking came from the outside, and then a swift patter of hooves. Cleo turned again and tried to block her ears. Were the nymphs cavorting with the satyrs? The memory of that blank featureless membrane under the mask gave her the creeps.

The Triple Moon takes away the girls' faces at daytime, and their minds at nighttime.

A dark figure appeared at the entrance to the cave, blocking the firelight. Cleo sat up.

The figure edged into the cave, and she recognized him. The satyr named Silen. He was still wearing his oversized spider mask, but now Cleo understood its purpose. Somehow the inhabitants of this Level could not speak without them.

"What do you want?" she hissed.

The satyr came closer.

"Come with me," a distorted, almost electronic-sounding voice enunciated.

Cleo shook her head.

"Not on your life!"

"They are going to kill you."

"Who are they?"

As if in response, a shrill inhuman scream ran through the forest. Silen grabbed her hand and dragged her to the exit from the cave.

"I lead," the creature insisted, his voice devoid of inflection, words running into each other. "I lead you to ladder. Up."

"Why?"

"The Witch-goddess is hunting."

A ponderous movement beyond the cave. Cleo could not see what it was, but she heard tree trunks snap under its passage. Silen dropped down to the ground, and she followed suit. The movement receded, and he pulled her out.

The forest was filled with a mélange of night noises. Something hooted in the dark canopy, and a heavy body flapped above her head. A sharp staccato of dry clicks broke through the darkness like automatic fire, followed by a long wail. A snatch of laughter followed, metallic and inhuman.

Cleo stumbled through the bristling shadows, colliding with tree-trunks and running into curtains of vines. Her eyes had trouble adjusting to this unrelieved night. Silen was a smear of barely discernible movement ahead. She opened her mouth to call out to him when he turned and pressed his finger to his mask's painted lips. Suddenly, Cleo realized she could see him quite well.

Silvery light threw a handful of coin-like reflections onto the ground. The moon floated above the treetops, full and bloated, her pregnant belly dragging her down. And then another smaller moon popped up, separating itself from the parental body like a spawning jellyfish, and immediately budding off yet another, even smaller, orb. Three moons of diminishing size rose up above the massive peak, flooding the forest with ghostly light and turning the mountain flank into a chiaroscuro of black gaps and silvery spires.

Silen made a moaning sound and turned to Cleo, his hands flapping urgently.

"Hurry!" he hissed from behind a painted mouth. "The nymphs are hunting!"

She heard a shrill ululating cry from the depth of the forest, and Silen grabbed her hand, dragging her through the underbrush. Ahead, on the towering side of Orcus, she saw something like a scratch – a straight line that was visible only because it was straight, standing out against the chaotic background.

"Ladder!" Silen whispered.

Cleo balked. The stairs leading up from Ano Syros were bad enough, but she would be damned if she crawled up some rope on this vertical rise! She was not a bloody mountaineer!

"Not going there!" she responded. "We will be sitting ducks!"

She remembered the sharp-tipped arrows in the nymphs' quivers. The three moons' illumination was almost as strong as daylight.

Hoarse baying tore the sudden hush.

Silen was frantic, pulling at Cleo. His stringy muscles could not move her; these childlike arms were no stronger than they looked. But the baying of hunting dogs did the trick. She started running. Fortunately, while the moonlight exposed them to their pursuer, it also made it possible for Cleo not to break a leg by stumbling through bushes and deadfall.

The trees thinned, and they found themselves in the open space between the edge of the woods and the flank of the mountain. Littered with scree mixed with old bones, the space provided no concealment. Silen dropped to his belly and started crawling toward the sheer stone wall bisected by a hanging ladder. It looked impossibly fragile, woven of slender ropes, and Cleo could not see its upper edge.

An arrow whistled above her head. Cleo followed Silen's lead by dropping down and crawling toward the rockface. The ululating cries of the hunting nymphs and the braying of their hounds were deafening. Crouching behind a boulder, Cleo grabbed Silen by his shoulder.

"I can't climb this!" she whispered. "We need to find another path!"

Silen turned to her. The mask was devoid of expression, but she could smell his fear.

Something whistled past her, and an arrow embedded itself in the mask, knocking it off his head. His exposed muzzle was that of a frightened animal, his eyes revolving madly, foam dripping from his flapping tongue. He rose on his hairy legs, about to bolt. Another arrow pierced his throat, and Silen toppled over. Warm droplets sprayed Cleo's face. She frantically crawled toward the wall, simultaneously debating with herself whether she should just surrender. Ursula had treated her reasonably well, after all.

Cleo reached the wall and grasped the sides of the hanging ladder. It felt sturdier than she expected. Rough fibers scratched her hands. She lifted her head cautiously and looked back.

The edge of the forest boiled with furious movement. A furry shadow separated itself from the melee and rushed forward, then another. Large unkempt dogs, their hides filthy with mud and excrement, their yellow fangs glistening in the light of the triple moon. But it was the sight of their prey that made Cleo squeeze the ladder with numbed fingers and lift herself up, putting her trembling feet on the lowest rung.

The prey was not a deer. It was a man.

Naked and caked in dirt, he stumbled toward the wall. His lacerated feet bled heavily, leaving smeared tracks on the scree. His face and chest were scratched, and there was a puncture wound on his arm. But even in the brief glimpse she had of him, Cleo knew he was no inhabitant of the forest. Something in his pathetic nudity spoke of comfortable clothes, soft mattresses, and long lunches. His face, distorted by panic, was clean-shaven; his hair was freshly cut.

Now the huntresses emerged into the light. Their maskless faces, restored to having human features, were crudely dabbed with ochre and blood. They were also naked, but their nudity looked completely natural. They were pack animals hunting lone prey.

At night, she takes away their minds.

The dark-haired girl running at the head of the pack had blood dripping down her thighs from her vagina. She paused to dip her fingers in it and licked them.

They carried bows and crude spears. Some of them had bronze knives tied to strips of rawhide around their waists. One of them threw her spear at the running man. It embedded itself in his back. He spun around and another spear lodged in his gut. He toppled onto the stony ground, trying to pull it out and failing, his soft hands sliding off the blood-slick shaft. The huntresses yelled and cheered, but there were no human words in the sounds they made.

And beyond them…Cleo caught only one glimpse of what it was, but it was enough. A crude giant shape, bulging with protuberances like cancerous tumors. Some of them were breasts. Some were faces, mad and laughing.

In her misshapen paw, the Ruler of the Third Level held a slack human body, waving it around like a kid with a new toy. The body was badly mutilated, but from the remnants of clothing clinging to the oozing wounds, she recognized Ursula.

Cleo pulled herself up.

She clung to the ladder, vertigo making her head swim. The idea of climbing it seemed incomprehensible. She risked one glance upwards and almost let go of the ropes as she saw the flimsy construction snake up the smooth wall and disappear behind a sharp outcrop. But then she looked back and saw what the huntresses were doing.

They converged upon the prone figure of their kill. The man was not quite dead; Cleo could see his legs twitching. But they did not wait for him to die. The huntresses started butchering him with their bronze knives and he screamed like a wounded hare. She could not look. She started climbing, her wheezing breaths cutting her chest like sharp blades.

"Cleo!" A hoarse shout reached her, and she risked looking down over her shoulder, her fingers digging into the ropes of the ladder as if her life depended on them – which, of course, it did.

The giantess strode forward, kicking the cannibal nymphs aside with her splayed feet. She indeed had three faces, as Hekate the Triple Goddess was supposed to, but they were randomly distributed across her body: one on her chest, one on her left shoulder, one on the intersection of her meaty thighs. The front of her head was blank, the same mushroom-pale wet membrane Cleo had seen under a nymph's mask earlier in the day.

All three faces were those of Ursula. One was laughing, one was shedding tears, and the last one was mumbling something, its expression sly and unhinged. The giantess had dropped Ursula's body and it lay splayed and partially skinned under her feet.

"Come back! Danger is up!"

A tripartite chorus of tortured voices emerging from three slack mouths.

Cleo would have laughed if she could. From the corner of her eye, she saw the murdered man reduced to a pile of raw muscles and bloodstained bones, and naked women carrying away hunks of steaming flesh.

"No!"

She turned away and climbed on. Any moment, she expected to feel the dull thud of an arrow piercing her back. Something swished by but it was not an arrow. A bronze blade embedded itself in a crack in the rock, millimeters from her head. Cleo glanced down and saw one of the naked women, her bare face slack and smeared with blood, at the foot of the wall, her arm still raised. Cleo grasped the knife and wrenched it out of the crack. She was about to toss it back but hesitated. She put the blade into her pocket and kept climbing, refusing to look back at the huntress.

Cleo surrendered herself to the mindless rhythm of her ascent. One hand grasping the rough rope above her head, one foot lifted and planted on the next rung, the second one following, repeat again and again. Her fear of heights burned everything out of her mind, even fear of death. She was not a woman anymore with memories of the past and premonitions of the future. She became a puppet, a mindless marionette, automatically repeating the same pattern of movements. Grasp the rope, lift the right foot, lift the left foot, grasp the rope… There was no passage of time. Just the endless, viscous moment, which kept her in its grasp like a spider in its web.

Until Cleo's torn fingers encountered emptiness.

The shock of it woke her from her trance. She risked squinting back, down the rock wall.

The moonlight was still bright, but there was only one moon in the sky. Above Cleo, the smooth granite edge of the wall loomed into the starry sky. The ladder was draped across it and disappeared from view. Below…

She knew she should not look down, but the seduction of the void was too great. She risked one glance into the ocean of the empty air, and felt her muscles turn into water, her fingers slipping, gravity embracing her and pulling her into a final plunge.

Cleo groped above her head and grasped the ladder as it curved around the ledge. She pulled herself up, and the same force that almost killed her suddenly turned her friend, as the upper part of her body flopped onto a flat surface and she inched forward. Her center of gravity shifted, and she felt the hardness of stone under her hips and thighs.

Cleo lay prone for a long time, until the cold woke her from her stupor. She turned her head.

The ladder was fixed to two sturdy iron spikes embedded in the rock. She saw that one of them seemed a little loose. The next climber might find themselves taking a one-way shortcut back to the forest.

She wondered dully why the nymphs had not shot her. Could it be that the moon madness Hekate had imposed upon them made it hard for them to aim well? Or could it be that Hekate had actually wanted her to escape? Could it be that she did not want to mess with whoever Called Cleo?

Ursula was dead. Hekate had killed her. Why? Because she was an antigrafo of Artemis, a rival moon goddess?

Ursula had treated her well. Without the nourishing meal Ursula had given her, Cleo would have never had the physical strength for her ascent.

The meal. Roast meat. Hunt.

Cleo remembered the butchered man.

She turned her head and vomited until nothing was left in her stomach but bile.

PART 2 ASPHODEL FIELDS

LEVEL FOUR/Dream City

Cleo dragged the sodden bedclothes out of the large zinc tub and put them into a manual wringer. The bloody crank was stuck again, and she pushed it with her entire body weight. The contraption reluctantly turned, making obscene intestinal noises.

She regarded it with loathing. Couldn't the deities of Orcus import some modern washer-dryers from the shadow world? She decided to ask Zach about it.

She glanced ruefully at her chapped fingers. The olive-oil concoction Alexandra had given her in Ano Syros would have come in quite handy, but Alexandra was not here.

She sat down heavily on the small wooden stool, resting her aching thighs. She thought about her mother, and her early struggles in menial jobs. Trying to survive in England after her divorce, Daphne palmed her daughters off on Eleni, and the girls thrived in Greece. When Daphne married her well-off husband, she claimed the twins back. Cleo adapted easily, but Cora took the transition hard and responded with slipping grades and outbursts of temper, which made Daphne send her into therapy. Cora claimed that her stepfather was abusive, but Cleo knew it was not true. He was just a jerk.

How was Cora faring on the mountain of dead gods? Had she also been Called? Of course, she must have been. There was no other way to ascend Orcus.

Cleo rubbed her temples. She had gotten used to the Call, its persistent throb receding to the barely noticed accompaniment of her daily struggles. But it did not mean she had forgotten about it.

From under the leaking canopy of the laundry shed, she watched the gray drizzle that painted the cobblestones with the colors of depression: charcoal, steel, and tarnished silver. The imposing houses across the road ran like smudged watercolor paintings. She shivered, missing the sunny skies and dry heat of Ano Syros. The weather on the Fourth Level vacillated between dismal downpour and foggy spray, making her laundry job all the more difficult.

When the bedclothes were wrung out, she put them into a large, lidded basket and carried it into the street. The drizzle had petered out, and the pewter-colored disk of the sun peeked through the rift in the clouds, briefly illuminating the outlines of rooftops against the churning gray. The tallest silhouette was that of a large building with a triangular roof: the Sleep Clinic. Otherwise, the sky was empty. There was no mountain.

That had been the greatest shock to her as she had shakily stood up after her climb from the Forest of Masks. In the predawn chill, shivering and miserable, she stared at the single moon veiled by thin clouds and the black mass of buildings dotted with sparse lights ahead. But above the buildings, there was only the sky.

On all the previous Levels, the peak of Orcus had loomed above her as persistent and enigmatic as the Call in her brain. Its presence would not let her forget where she was. Even in the flat suburban maze of Happy Meadows, the mountain was a reminder of the monsters and deities that inhabited it. But here, on the Fourth Level, the mountain was gone. The town ahead seemed to spread out into the murky distance of a flat plain.

She looked back. The two iron spikes that anchored the rope ladder were still there, one of them tilting drunkenly. The ladder hung over the edge. She cautiously approached it and stared down into what appeared to be a disused quarry, the uneven chalky wall falling into a pit in a series of ledges. There were some broken remnants of tools and machinery at the bottom. No Forest of Masks.

From the quarry, a paved road led toward the town, hedges separating it from the muddy black fields on both sides. She started walking. When she came closer to the scatter of industrial sheds marking the beginning of the urban space, she saw a large sign. Painted in psychedelic swirls of purple and yellow, it said: "Welcome to Dream City, where your dreams come true". At the time, she had not realized it was a threat, not a promise.

And here she was, dragging the basket of laundry on the uneven pavement. She stopped and consulted her list of clients. At least the Arachne curse had been lifted and she could read! Fancy trying to decipher the address of Mr. and Mrs. Nikolaidou from a jumble of spiders!

Her shoulders and arms burned with fatigue, but she took a deep breath and bent to pick up the basket when it was lifted for her.

"Hello, beautiful!" a cheerful voice said.

Zach fell in step with her and deftly hooked the basket's strap, placing it on his own shoulders.

He grinned at her. Small and nimble, with deep black eyes and curly brown hair, he was almost a head shorter than Cleo. But he was strong. His long arms, bare despite the damp and chilly air, were sinewy and bulging with muscles.

"That's the one," Cleo said, pointing to the imposing row of brick houses with white columns and stained-glass inserts in front doors. But the house in the middle was barely more than a ruin, its windows blind with cardboard, its front yard filled with debris.

She walked to the door of the first, undamaged, house and used a bronze knocker shaped like a poppy. The owners took all the possible precautions against dreaming, which is why they were Cleo's best and most reliable clients, having their bedclothes washed every two days without fail.

Mrs. Nikolaidou opened the door. She was a large, comfortable-looking woman wearing a traditional short jacket and embroidered skirt. The costume reminded Cleo of Eleni, who occasionally donned clothes inherited from her own grandmother. She hated the reminder, because in all other respects Mrs. Nikolaidou was Eleni's opposite. Even in her sixties, Eleni had been beautiful, but it was hard to imagine Mrs. Nikolaidou had been attractive even at sixteen.

Her suspicious eyes seemed to withdraw from the world into their deep lairs, while Eleni's had always been opened wide to take in as many sights and colors and people's faces as possible. Eleni had been a born storyteller. Mrs. Nikolaidou regarded stories as a dangerous contagion, which, in a sense, they were. Stories inspired dreams, and on the Fourth Level dreaming was not safe.

She snatched the basket from Zach and thrust a handful of coins into Cleo's hand.

"Day after tomorrow?" Cleo asked.

Mrs. Nikolaidou hesitated.

"You may come tomorrow," she growled and slammed the door. Cleo and Zach exchanged glances.

"You will have to look for another client," he remarked.

Cleo had to agree with him. Increasing the frequency of laundry, clearing out your house, putting new shutters on your windows – all of these were signs that Oneiroi may soon pay you a visit. And the ruined house in the middle of the terrace was a visible reminder of what was left afterwards.

They went down the street, the laundry basket getting lighter with every house they stopped by, and Cleo's purse getting heavier with coins. By the time the basket was empty, she had enough money for her weekly rent, with something left over for food and even a couple of drinks.

"Let's go to the Winged Horse," Zach suggested. "My treat".

"All right."

They walked toward a side street where a hanging pub sign glistened in the rain. The houses here were taller and narrower, and squeezed together in terraces broken only by an occasional black maw of an alleyway. Dream City was more urban than Ano Syros, with wide pedestrian malls, multi-story apartment blocks, and streetcars. At night, the streets were flooded with the feverish orange glow of sodium lamps, which, in Cleo's opinion, did not improve the inhabitants' chances of restful sleep. Instead of multiple small shops scattered everywhere in Ano Syros, the people of Dream City got their necessities and their luxuries alike from the long avenue of department stores, specialty establishments, and large groceries. It looked like Oxford Street in London. Cleo used to love shopping there.

Didn't she?

Cleo struggled with large holes in her memory, which seemed to grow bigger every morning as she woke from heavy slumber, her recollections unraveling like a poorly knitted sweater. She knew she had come up to Dream City from Ano Syros, climbing the mountain of dead gods, but everything that had happened to her before that had become fluid and uncertain, as if seen through a layer of running water. She had read somewhere that dreaming was necessary for memory retention. She did not dream, luckily for her. Was that the reason for her partial amnesia? But then, she wouldn't be alive for long if she got into the habit of dreaming. Life or memory? Not a hard choice.

Even so, she missed certain amenities with the fierceness that proved to her that her other life in London was no delusion. Washer-dryers, for example. Or private cars. Dream City only had large rambling trucks delivering veggies and milk, and spewing clouds of black exhaust. Or phones. She had given up the hope of seeing a mobile, but since the Fourth Level seemed to be stuck in some vague mid-century era, she had been looking for the red flash of an iconic British phone booth. But there were no phones in Dream City, public or otherwise.

They approached the narrow oak door of the pub as the rain intensified, making them sprint for shelter. From the corner of her eye, Cleo noticed that the owners must have renovated the sign. Instead of the faded dabble of a sorry-looking nag with chicken wings, a brightly colored painting of a prancing stallion spreading meticulously drawn swan pinions graced the entryway. But Cleo felt the water squelching in her worn trainers too keenly to stop and admire the craftsmanship. She rushed in after Zach into the warm, fusty interior. They were lucky to find a place by the fire. She shivered as her damp clothes steamed.

Zach went to the bar to order for both of them. It was the third time in a row that he paid for her meals, even though he was hardly rolling in money himself. Was she taking advantage of him? Zach had befriended her, found her a place to stay, helped her with the laundry, and would often buy her lunch and dinner. Was he hoping for something more than friendship? If so, he sent no obvious signals, and Cleo was relieved. She liked Zach well enough, but there was something slippery and eel-like about him. And he refused to tell her where he was from or how he ended up in Orcus.

He came back to their table with mugs of warm spiced mead. Cleo took a sip and made a face. It tasted like something you would get at a charity Christmas party, but at least it chased away the chills.

She idly watched the rest of the patrons. It was still early, and the pub was only half-full. Her eyes fell upon a thin middle-aged man. He sat alone, tapping his long skeletal fingers on the table. An empty glass indicated he had been drinking something stronger than mead.

Zach noticed the direction of Cleo's gaze.

"He is getting ready for a visit tonight," he whispered.

Cleo had already found out that talking about the Oneiroi, or anything to do with dreams, was considered bad form in the city. But Zach delighted in breaking rules, or at least edging as close to breaking them as he could without actually endangering himself.

"How do you think he knows?" she asked.

"Like they all do. Remembering his dreams."

When you remembered your dreams they became real, seeping into reality and leaving their residue, whether as images or actual objects, on your bedclothes. And then the Dream Police paid you a visit.

Worn out by her laundry job, Cleo slept deeply, hours of darkness flowing by without leaving any imprint either on her memory or on her rickety bed. She washed her bedclothes for hygiene, not to disguise the blood of a killer-under-the-bed nightmare or the rainbow of a flying-like-a-bird pleasant dream.

Cora used to suffer from night fears, screaming and waking up Cleo when the twins shared a room after their return to England. Cora would not have survived here a single night, Cleo thought. Cora must be on a Level above.

A pouty waiter brought their order of fried cheese sandwiches. After her experience in the Forest of Masks, Cleo went back to avoiding meat.

"Did you ever remember yours?" she asked Zach.

"I'm still here, am I not?"

"I mean before Dream City. Come on, Zach, we are friends. You are not from the Fourth Level, are you?"

"Few people are."

"But some are born here, right? I mean there are kids…"

There were children in Dream City, though fewer than in Ano Syros and never on their own. On the First Level, kids ran around everywhere as they did in Greece, but in Dream City, they were always accompanied by parents or guardians. Cleo did not know if this had any significance.

Zach shrugged.

"Look. Cleo," he said, "if you want to survive here, you better not ask too many questions. You know that."

"No, I don't!" Cleo fired back. "I hear all kinds of bullshit, but nobody gives a straight answer. I am being Called by one of the Nine, but I don't even know who the Nine are!"

A couple of heads turned in her direction. Zach shushed her.

"People think it's bad luck to name them," he whispered.

"But I want to know!"

"Later."

"Are you from another part of the Archipelago?"

Zach frowned but then his gaze shifted to something behind Cleo's back. She turned.

Two new visitors just entered the tavern.

CHAPTER 17

The two young men made a beeline for the bar, where they ordered gin sours and started laughing and chatting with the bartender. Their high spirits made them stand out; few people were so jolly in Dream City. But there was something else about them that caught Cleo's eye. She was not sure what it was. One was tall and rangy, a runner. Cleo's eyes automatically searched for a Fitbit on his wrist, but these had not made their way into Orcus. Clad in jeans, a graphic hoodie, and fresh sneakers, his blond hair sun-bleached, or simply bleached, he projected a kind of easy self-confidence that Cleo used to find attractive until a bad breakup some years ago.

His companion was not so showy but, in a way, more interesting. He was shorter and stockier, with long brown hair and a trim beard, clad in a button-down shirt and khaki pants. The runner's face was so deeply tanned that it looked darker than his blonde hair; the bearded guy was the opposite: pale, almost pasty-looking, but with eyes the color of plums. There was a tattoo peeking from under his collar. He nodded a couple of times, while his friend talked incessantly, but the pub was filling up, and Cleo could not hear him in the drone of voices.

"Fancy the runner?" Zach grinned. "Or the crawler?"

Cleo kicked him on the shin.

"What are you, Tinder? No, they just look…normal. Do you know them?"

"Not really," Zach said evasively.

The blond guy seemed to feel Cleo's gaze and turned around, dazzling her with a dentist-perfect smile. He really was good-looking, and not in a creepy way like Or. He said something to his companion and the two of them rambled over to Cleo's and Zach's table.

"May we join you?" he asked. He spoke in English but with an unplaceable accent. Since regaining her ability to read and distinguish languages, Cleo had been listening attentively to all the multiple tongues spoken around her. There was a lot of Greek, some English, and a couple of times she heard languages she could not identify, but the linguistic babel gave her little clue to how these people ended up in Dream City or why.

"I am Hendrik," he said, offering his hand. "And this is Tomas."

Cleo and Zach introduced themselves. Hendrik immediately ordered drinks for the four of them and launched into a tirade about the weather. Tomas hung back, listening but saying little.

It turned out that the two young men worked for the Sleep Clinic, which was the biggest, most imposing structure in Dream City; a grey monstrosity with a frowning pediment, rows of tiny windows, and two blank-walled wings. People who were beginning to remember their dreams, were troubled by insomnia, or found strange objects in their bedclothes could go to the Clinic and seek help. Cleo had heard rumors that besides draining their life's savings, the Clinic did little for the patients, but they kept coming out of sheer desperation. When your dreams became too tangible to ignore, you were ripe for a visit from the Oneiroi. And when it happened, no help could be asked for or given.

"So," she asked Hendrik, "are you a doctor?"

He laughed.

"Me? No, I'm just a security guard. "He," he pointed at silent Tomas, "is the smart one."

"I am a nurse," Tomas said.

His accent was more pronounced than Hendrik's, and suddenly Cleo knew what it reminded her of: Jurgen and Liam, the two Dutch boys at that ill-fated beach party that ended with her waking up in

Orcus. She eyed the young men suspiciously, but try as she might, she could not recall Jurgen's and Liam's faces, or any particulars of their interaction.

"So, is it true what they say about medics at SC?" Zach suddenly barged in. He had been largely silent since the young men joined them. Cleo sensed his discomfort, but she did not know him well enough to tell whether it was some macho bullshit or there was something more to it.

Hendrik lifted an eyebrow.

"What do they say?"

"That you act like bloodhounds for the Oneiroi."

There was a sudden lull in the hum of conversations filling the pub, and the word reverberated like a pistol shot. Heads turned, lips were pursed, foreheads creased. Mentioning Sleep Demons was something between a social faux pas and a religious taboo, but apparently the other patrons decided it was not worth getting involved in. The hum resumed, and the four of them were left alone.

Hendrik looked angry, but it was the quiet Tomas who responded.

"The Oneiroi don't need our services," he said. "We are trying to help people to keep them away."

"If so, you are not doing very well." Zach sounded more belligerent than Cleo had ever heard him before. "Look at the city! How many houses have been destroyed in the last week alone? How many people killed?"

"Listen, mate," Hendrik drawled, "we don't make rules here."

"Who does?" Cleo asked.

The three men stared back at her: Zach with a frown, Hendrik with a smirk, and Tomas…Cleo could not decipher his expression, but it gave her the chills.

"You know, Cleo," Zach said uneasily.

"No, I don't know!" she flared up. "Why are we pretending we are on a pub crawl when we are stuck on a mountain that does not exist? I am supposed to go up because somebody Called me, but who? This is some fucking Greek underworld – or is it overworld? I don't know what happened to my friends. I don't know how to get back to my own world. I don't know how to reach the next Level. And I can't even ask who the fuck is in charge here?"

"And do you know who is in charge where you come from?" Zach asked pointedly. "The Prime Minister? The EU? The bloody US President?"

She stabbed her finger at him.

"Okay, Zach, enough of this bullshit! You are like me, right? Stranded here? So, the truth. How long have you been here?"

Zach looked as comfortable as a man sitting on a tack. It was Tomas who spoke.

"Hypnos and Thanatos," he said. "The conjoined twins."

Cleo turned to him.

"What?"

"You asked who made the rules here," he said. "It's them. Or maybe him. They have grown into each other, so you can't tell where one ends and the other begins."

Cleo swallowed.

"This is the Ruler of this Level?"

"Yes."

It made sense. Hypnos was the god of dreams and Thanatos the god of death. A perfect fit for the city where dreams were deadly.

"What fun! So, how do I get out of here?"

Tomas shook his head.

"You can't," he said.

Cleo blinked, as the electric bulb over her head suddenly flared into urine-yellow light. She did not realize the night had fallen while they were sitting here. The incessant drizzle smudged the boundaries of darkness and light.

Hendrik's face looked unnaturally sallow in the puddle of yellow illumination, his beach-boy good looks gone. He turned to the front door, as if hearing some inaudible noise.

In a moment, it was no longer inaudible. The door came crashing down in a swirl of black wings.

The Oneiroi had arrived.

CHAPTER 18

The tavern was filled with a confused melee of bodies as patrons fought to make it out the door. Chairs crashed to the floor, tables were overturned. A woman shrieked, a man screamed.

Zach caught Cleo's wrist and pulled her down under the table.

"Keep quiet!" he breathed into her ear. That was superfluous; even if Cleo had been inclined to give a voice to her fear, the sight of dream daimons would have rendered her mute.

She had heard enough about the Oneiroi since her arrival on the Fourth Level of Orcus. They were the local bogeymen, a combination of the Night Policeman and the monster under the bed. Except, of course, they were real. But until she actually saw them, she had not realized just how real they were.

Their velvety bodies stood out from the panicky background of the crowd as if they possessed more than three dimensions. Like a doll glued upon a photograph, the Oneiroi rendered everything and everybody else flat and inconsequential. They looked like a cross between giant bats and dark angels. Their sleek torsos were covered with dense silky fur, but their arms and legs were bare and as fleshless as a skeleton's limbs, ending in bony claws. Their leathery wings had an incongruous fringe of oily black feathers along their rims. Their faces were smooth and flat, a combination of a doll and a monkey, with sloping foreheads, gaping wet nostrils, and pouting lips. Their eyes were the worst. They were empty holes, as if somebody drilled into their skulls. But inside these holes, an occasional ruby spark flared up like the headlights of a distant train in a deep tunnel.

There were many of them, but Cleo could not tell how many – they seemed to flow together and separate like drops of mercury. They converged upon the thin man sitting alone, who Cleo had noticed when she and Zach had walked in. He was on his feet, backing off toward the exit. One of the Oneiroi casually swiped its taloned finger across the man's throat. It erupted in a geyser of red, and the man crumpled.

But it was not over. A new commotion started at the front door. People were thrown around like bowling pins as another feathered hurricane burst into the tavern. It was white, not black, and much larger than the Oneiroi, but it possessed the same more-real-than-real hallucinatory vividness. It took Cleo a couple of seconds to process what she was seeing.

The creature was the winged horse from the pub sign, now three-dimensional, active, and obviously pissed.

Cleo gaped, her own danger forgotten, as she watched dreams fight dreams. The Oneiroi flowed together into a monstrous clump of taloned limbs and slashing wings as they attacked the horse. But he was not about to give in. His head expanded into an enormous fleshless skull, easily as big as his entire body, and his wings were sucked back into the flanks to emerge as an additional pair of legs. The six-legged horse kicked with its iron hooves at the flailing octopus of the merged Oneiroi, while the swollen skull, miraculously supported on the maned neck, opened its maw and breathed fire upon its enemy. The clump of Oneiroi screeched like a whole fleet of police sirens, piercing Cleo's eardrums. Bottles and glasses from the shelves above the bar rained down in a shower of glass shards. The screams of the patrons almost rivaled the volume of the Oneiroi.

Why were they not trying to flee? Cleo and Zach had the misfortune to sit too far away from the entrance, hemmed in by the fighting monsters, their cozy fireplace table now a trap. But the rest of the people in the pub: why had they not rushed out the door?

And then Cleo saw why. The door was not there anymore.

A blank wall bulged and shuddered like a distended stomach where the entryway had been, rivulets of plaster flowing down and solidifying in misshapen stalactites. Tables and chairs near this distortion were being drawn into its vortex, lengthening into uncouth forms as they were being swallowed up by the expanding maw of fluid space.

But then it was not just inanimate objects. A pudgy man was sucked into the distortion, kicking and screaming. The wall gulped him down but then solidified again, so his legs were left protruding out of it like a bizarre decoration.

Meanwhile, the Oneiroi underwent another metamorphosis. With the fluid illogic of a nightmare, the melted clump of their bodies reconstituted itself as another winged horse, bigger than its rival and just as misshapen. It only had four legs, but its skull-head was almost split in two by a gaping mouth with a lolling blue tongue. It spat a stream of foaming water at the white horse, quenching his fire. The white horse hissed and reared, melting down and reshaping itself into an ugly-looking goblet that gulped down the water. The black horse flowed into a single one of its legs with the hoof the size of a table and stomped on the goblet. The shards scattered but then became a swarm of rats running toward each other.

The distortion was growing, spilling over onto the floor that became as soft as molasses, sucking down furniture and guests as the duel of nightmares continued. Its edge was creeping closer to the table under which Cleo and Zach huddled together.

"We need to get out!" Zach whispered.

"A great idea! Why haven't I thought about it?"

Zach stood up, overturning the table.

"What...?" The white and black horses had now become two enormous columns of flesh, plaited together like two anacondas trying to strangle each other, but the crash of the table made them pause. Open eyes popped out along the lengths of the columns like clusters of grapes, focusing on Zach and Cleo. A tentacle sprouted from the black column and reached toward them.

Zach grabbed Cleo's hand and pulled her toward the fireplace, where the fire still sputtered feebly, consuming the last of the wood. He wrenched away the grate and lifted a poker.

The iron rod lengthened and split, becoming two intertwined snakes that reared and hissed. And while this transformation was going on, another one started, this one involving Zach. Of all the bizarre things happening around Cleo, this one struck her like a physical blow because it involved the man she had thought of as her friend.

Zach turned toward the black and white fleshy columns and thrust the snake-topped rod toward them. They retreated, falling apart, each reconstituting itself into a horse, and each horse shrinking until they were no bigger than ponies.

Zach – or the creature Zach had become – pulled Cleo toward the fireplace that grew as they approached, becoming a rectangular gateway framed in brick. The fire spread itself out under their feet like a carpet.

Cleo did not want to step on the writhing flames, but she hardly had any choice. She followed him into the fire that retreated deferentially as they rushed through the brick tunnel. The gateway behind their backs blinked into nonexistence as they passed.

CHAPTER 19

"Hermes?" Cleo growled.

She and Zach huddled in her tiny, rented room, sitting on the floor because the ancient blind on the window had finally dropped like a withered petal and the night peered through. Oneiroi visits were not necessarily deterred by curtains and shutters, but it felt better not to see the riot of nightmares outside. And the clash in the Winged Horse had apparently roused the spectral population of Dream City into frenetic action. The gibbous moon outside was periodically obscured by a swish of batlike wings or a sinuous movement of a flying serpent.

"Sort of," Zach mumbled.

He had reverted back to his usual appearance – a tatty jumper, unruly hair, round black eyes – but Cleo vividly remembered the man – or god – who had rescued her from the pub. The marble-white nude body, glistening like a beetle's carapace and topped with a winged silvery helmet covering the entire head, so that the face was just a blank shiny expanse of liquid metal like mercury. The only article of clothing on that inhuman body had been a pair of winged sandals.

But now there was no sign of divinity in Zach's woebegone expression, just as the snake-entwined rod that had opened the way out of the pub was again a simple poker.

"The caduceus," Cleo said, pointing to the poker. "Hermes' staff. The god of roads, doorways, shepherds, merchants, and thieves."

"And dreams," Zach added ruefully.

"So, you are…what? The Ruler of Dream City?"

"I wish. No, that Dutch creep told you the truth. The Ruler is – or are – Hypnos and Thanatos."

"So, what are you? Who are you? What the fuck is going on? How are you still alive if the Olympians are supposed to be dead?"

Zach sighed.

"All right," he said, "let me explain."

"Long time overdue," Cleo muttered.

"First, I am not Hermes. I am his antigrafo. But you know how lithographic copies are made? If you take multiple prints off the same plate, only the first ones are close to the original. The more you make, the more distorted they become."

"So, second- and third-degree antigrafos are like…what? Bad prints?"

"Some of us are pretty accurate imitations of our parádeigma. Some are much further removed. Some don't even know they are copies, or don't remember their originals."

"And where are you on this spectrum?"

"Close enough to Hermes to have some of his powers, but certainly not the first impression. I don't know if the first impression is even alive. Hermes, my parádeigma, is not."

"Who killed him?"

"The Nine."

"And they are…?"

"Nyx, Briareus the Fifty-Headed One, Hekate the Triple Moon, Hypnos and Thanatos, the Furies who are One-in-Many, the Mother of Monsters, the Mistress of Stone and Glass, the Child Eater, and the Barren One."

Cleo shivered. Some names sounded familiar from mythology. Others just evoked the sense of vague and unfocused dread.

"The chthonic deities? Evil ones?"

Zach shrugged.

"Whatever you want to call them. But remember that good and evil are human constructs. And not even shared by all humans."

Cleo knew. Greek mythology was not like Christianity with its clear-cut division of angels and demons. The Olympians often behaved in terrible and destructive ways, while the creatures of the underworld could be helpful and kind. But what she had seen on Orcus so far did not quite fit this paradigm either.

"So, why did it happen?"

"Remember what I said about smudged prints? It works with worlds too. Our world is imprinted by conflicting Platonic realities, but it also influences its originals back. And I don't need to tell you how fucked up our world is."

"There is a two-way street between Plato's Cave and whatever is outside?"

"You asked about the Archipelago," Zach said. "This is what it is. Every culture has its pantheon, right? Its underworld, its gods and demons. And each pantheon has an island to itself. The Archipelago is a cluster of realities."

"Each of them has a mountain?"

Zach shook his head.

"Orcus was a pit," he said grimly. "Now it has become a mountain. It has grown. And the Ruler of the Final Level won't rest until our world is remade in its image."

Cleo felt as if her head would explode, stuffed with too much information all at once. She pleaded fatigue. But even in the bedroom, with the door closed, she could not fall asleep..

Cleo tossed and turned, while Zach snored peacefully on the couch. They decided it was too dangerous for him to go back to his own flat while the Oneiroi rampaged in the streets.

He had agreed that she should go up to the next Level next as soon as possible. He also said he would go with her. Once the Oneiroi had seen what he was, he was a marked man. The Ruler of the Fourth Level would not tolerate an antigrafo of the rival dream-god among their cowed subjects.

"How can you?" she had asked. "I thought you needed to be Called to go up."

"Not necessarily."

He had sounded evasive, and she decided not to press the issue for now. Whatever answer he gave, she could not be sure it was the truth. Now that she knew who he was, she trusted him even less.

A more immediate problem was that neither of them knew where the ascent to the next Level was located. They talked about it, and he suggested they try the Sleep Clinic. It was the tallest building in Dream City. Since the mountain itself was hidden in the Asphodel Fields, as opposed to its oppressive presence in Elysium, this seemed rational and she agreed.

But now she could not sleep, ruminating over what he had told her – and also, what he had not told.

So, he was an antigrafo of Hermes. Why not? She had already met antigrafos of other dead Olympians: Apollo and Artemis. But if what she had witnessed in the Forest of Masks was real, Ursula, Artemis' antigrafo, was dead. So avatars of gods were mortal, and could be killed by gods or by other mortals. This chimed with her knowledge of Greek mythology. Gods, on the other hand, could only be killed by other gods. In the Upheaval, the Olympians had been slain by the chthonic deities, the Nine.

So far so good, but the rest of it made little sense. Zach all but confessed he was from the same world as Cleo. So what was he doing in Orcus? How did he get here?

For that matter, how did she get here?

She squeezed her eyes shut and tried to remember the beach party, but it felt like pouring water into a cracked cup, the stream of memories slipping by and leaving behind only the muddy residue of a trauma.

She needed to get some rest before tomorrow, but trying to force sleep to come to her only made her wide awake. Considering that in Dream City your nightmares could literally kill you, sleep was not the most restful activity imaginable, but humans could not go long without sleep. She had read somewhere that sleep deprivation could cause hallucinations and delusions – in other words, dreaming while awake, which was the surest way to remember your dreams, thus making them real and having the Oneiroi come for you. The malevolence of the Ruler of the Fourth Level – or should it be Rulers? – was on full display in this Catch-22.

Tired of it all, Cleo kicked off the blanket and went to the tiny bathroom. On her way back, she glanced into the equally small living room where Zach was ensconced in a pile of blankets, snoring softly. Hermes, huh? She tried to remember what she else knew of Zach's parádeigma. Hermes was not to be trifled with, despite being one of the "younger" gods, the progeny of Zeus and the nymph Maia. With his caduceus he could open any door, and his role as a divine messenger meant you should listen to whatever he said. He was a restless god, the deity of travelers and wanderers.

And he was also a trickster, the patron of liars, prone to games and deception. If Zach was anything like his parádeigma, she should be careful of his forked tongue.

But who was she to complain? A woman with two nationalities, two languages, the broken part of a lost duo.

Lost? No. Cora was here. She had to believe it. And she had a proof of her conviction.

Cleo picked up her backpack, unzipped a side pocket, and took out Iris' and Mick's letter.

The densely scribbled lines in two different handwritings, meandering across the page and crossing each other, were not easier to decipher with frequent viewing. If anything, they seemed even more impenetrable. The underlined sentences, though, were still legible.

Cora is here.

You must go up.

You must climb Orcus.

Find your sister.

If the letter was not written by her friends, then by who? The same deity who had Called her? One of the remaining Rulers? And if so, did it mean that this deity had Cora?

And where were Iris and Mick? Back in Greece, looking for her? Cleo imagined her friends in a police station, trying to explain to the bored Greek cops that the third person in their party had miraculously disappeared from the beach. Not likely they would be listened to or believed!

But while she could visualize the Ellinikí Astynomía or Hellenic Police station easily enough, her friends were nothing but vague blobs. She suddenly remembered that Iris had worn a silly t-shirt with a rainbow and a unicorn. Yes, she bought it after Cleo told her that the name Iris belonged to the goddess of the rainbow. She could remember the t-shirt but not Iris' face. How was it possible that her amnesia was so randomly and maliciously selective?

She put the letter back into her stuffed backpack and lay back in bed, determined to wrestle her racing brain into submission. She knew that forcing oneself to sleep did not work, but with a perversity of defiance she wanted to try.

Since she could not remember Iris or Mick, she decided to focus on something she could remember. How about…yes, meeting Zach?

When she finally made her way to the city from the precipice leading down to the Forest of Masks – or the disused quarry, depending on point of view – it was early morning and the streets were deserted. She was bone-tired and cold in the chill, misty air. Casting a weary glance at the long lines of single-family homes interspersed with blocks of flats, she sat on the curb, trying to get her strength back after that horrifying climb.

"Are you okay?" a male voice asked.

She lifted her head and looked at the small wiry man standing by her. He was wearing modern clothing, which disposed her in his favor after the wild savagery of the Forest of Masks. He also looked non-aggressive, keeping his distance, and there was a genuine concern in his voice.

"Not really," she said. "What is this place?"

"Dream City," the man replied. "You are new here, aren't you? Come, there is a coffee shop here, they open early."

Indeed, she could smell the aroma of coffee wafting from around the corner, and it instantly made her rise to her feet. As she followed the man, she saw a banner above the street. In bright purple letters on the yellow background, it said: "Dream City. Where your dreams come true."

The letters ran together, forming a violet arch. The yellow curled around it. A two-tone bow. Then the purple sprouted a dark blue band, which lightened into light blue, which became green, the cheerful color of spring leaves. And the yellow birthed orange, which birthed red, which became scarlet, dark and clotted, and oozed down in viscous slicks, obscuring and tainting the colors of the rainbow, while behind it somebody was screaming, and rough hands squeezed her arms, and something smelly was pressing against her mouth…

She shot up in bed, drenched in sweat.

She had slept. That was something. And she had had a nightmare, which was something else.

She stared at her pillow.

Her dream had not dissipated completely as dreams normally do. It was still present in the shape of a multicolored smudge where her head had lain.

CHAPTER 20

leo went through the stuff in her backpack. Climbing Orcus had taught her the skills that mountaineers, survivalists, and long-distance hikers knew from their training. Always pack basic necessities, make sure you have water and calorie-dense snacks, adjust the weight to your strength. Her backpack, more tattered and scuffed now than when she had bought it in Ano Syros, was still holding together. Some underwear, a couple of t-shirts and jumpers, a water bottle, dry fruit. At the bottom, her fingers encountered something made of metal. She pulled the bronze knife one of Ursula's nymphs had tossed at her when she was climbing the wall separating the Third Level from the Fourth.

She regarded it with revulsion. The thing was archaic and crudely made, and it looked like it belonged in some Bronze Age museum. Orcus' propensity for combining relatively advanced everyday technology with ancient prehistory unnerved and irritated her. She felt like tossing the knife into a trash bin, but she hesitated, running her finger along the blade. It was pretty sharp and came to a wicked point, still serviceable after the encounter with the wall. She put it back into a separate compartment, along with other mementoes of the Levels she had climbed, which included the peacock shirt Or had given her and the embroidered ribbon she had picked up as she struggled with zombie clothes in his closet.

She poked Zach, who was still snuggled up in the living room.

"We need to go," she said.

The Sleep Clinic was the tallest building in Dream City, towering above its neighborhood of apartment blocks. It thrust into the drizzly sky like a miniature copy of Orcus itself.

They climbed the broad stairs toward the grand entrance, which was flanked by two generic statues of women in flowing draperies, each holding a pitcher. Who were they supposed to represent? She had no idea. When the twins had lived in Greece, Eleni had taken them to the National Museum in Athens and showed them statues of gods and heroes. When they relocated back to London, Cleo and Cora had gone to the Greek Rooms of the British Museum and studied the Parthenon sculptures and Elgin friezes, depicting gods, goddesses, centaurs, athletes, and warriors. Cora would go back again and again, while Cleo had stopped after a while, trying to focus on the here and now, rather than wallowing in Greek nostalgia. Now she regretted not spending her every free moment there. Knowledge was power, and clearly her knowledge of Ancient Greek mythology was insufficient, since it offered no useful guide to the topography of Orcus. The four Levels she had traversed so far seemed to be haphazard, strung on the mountain like a handful of mismatched beads. What was the connection between the quasi-Mediterranean streets of Ano Syros, the manicured lawns of Happy Meadows, the wild woods of the Forest of Masks, and the depressing urbanity of Dream City?

Wait, there it was. Cleo stopped, struck with a sudden realization. There was a sort of order in this chaos. Ano Syros was a city, Happy Meadows – a suburb, the Forest of Masks – a wilderness, and Dream City…well, as its name indicated, it was a city again. Alexandra had told her that Orcus was divided into three Zones, each with three Levels, so perhaps each Zone had the same spatial order, from urban to wild.

"Let's go!" Zach hissed in her ear.

Cleo nodded, following him through the heavy doors that were propped open to allow the trickle of early visitors to pass. But she was proud of her insight. If she was right, she now had some inkling of what the next Levels were going to be like.

Inside the gloomy foyer with a sweeping staircase leading to the upper floors, a drowsy concierge in a gold-buttoned uniform asked their business.

"Dream disturbance consultation," Zach responded briskly.

"Eighth floor." The concierge sounded bored. "Take the stairs."

"What about the elevator?" Zach asked. "This lady hurt her ankle."

"Out of order," the concierge barked. "Stairs!"

And he even waddled from behind his desk to make sure they climbed the staircase.

"I can walk," Cleo muttered to Zach as they joined a straggle of visitors, some of whom seemed in greater need of an elevator than her.

"We need to go to the top as quickly as possible," he whispered back. "Oneiroi can sniff us out."

Remembering what had happened last night, she had to agree.

"And what happens at the top?"

"I am an antigrafo of the god of doorways, remember?"

He was carrying the poker-caduceus stuffed into a golf bag.

The inside of the Sleep Clinic looked like any boring office building. Long corridors with brown linoleum floors and rows of identical doors, an occasional island of uncomfortable-looking chairs, dead fluorescent lights. Cleo looked for vending machines but did not see any.

They had climbed seven floors but did not seem to be anywhere near the top. Winded, she perched on a chair and pulled out a water bottle from her backpack.

"Here you are!" a voice shouted.

Cleo looked up.

Hendrik! One of the two Dutch guys who had been with them in the Flying Horse. Instead of the casual clothes of the evening in the pub, he was decked out in the same purple uniform with gold buttons as the concierge below.

She felt Zach tense beside her.

Hendrik's smile was broad enough to display an impressive array of sugary-white teeth, but his eyes were cold. He came over and stood towering above them. Cleo knew it was deliberate.

"We have an appointment," Zach said, getting up. Even so, he barely reached Hendrik's shoulder. "Fancy running into you, but we are in a bit of a hurry."

"Appointment? Where? I can take you to where you need to go. Skip the queue."

"No need, thanks!" Zach moved to walk away, but Hendrik did not budge, blocking his way.

"Come on, mate!" he drawled. "Why rush? The lady looks like she could use a breather."

"I'm fine!" Cleo got to her feet and stood beside Zach. "Thank you for your concern, but we should get a move on."

"Cleo!" another voice called from the cavernous corridor leading away from the landing, and another familiar figure made its way toward them. Tomas! The second Dutchman!

The two of them stood shoulder to shoulder, blocking their way. Despite their dissimilarity, there was something spookily alike about them. It was not in facial features or stature, but in the identical expression of barely contained glee.

Cleo assessed the situation. They could make a run for it, but Hendrik was right about one thing: she was unaccountably tired and was not sure she could outrun the two men. Shout for help? They were not alone; other patients and visitors trickled up and down the stairway and walked through the corridors, but one glance at their ashen hopeless faces told Cleo they would not intervene on their behalf. Uniformed guards dressed like Hendrik were sprinkled among the visitors, keeping an eye on the proceedings.

Zach must have made the same assessment because his posture relaxed somewhat.

"All right," he said, "can you take us up? Appreciate your help."

If Hendrik sensed the irony, he showed no sign of it.

"What's your problem?" he asked.

"Residue," Cleo replied.

Hendrick raised an eyebrow.

"Really? Well, that's…serious."

"So can you take me to a doctor?" Cleo insisted.

"Sure. Come with me."

Dream residue was how Cleo had made money in her brief career as a laundress. The stains she had to wash off bedclothes were not ordinary sweat or dirt. There were colorful orchids on bedsheets, cooing doves on duvets, dragons on pillowcases, and worse things: screaming, distorted faces; dead bodies surrounded by blood splatters; naked blindfolded women. These were not weird designs by the manufacturers, as they could be washed off, but the next day the owner would reappear, shamefaced, carrying their bedclothes decorated with an entirely new menagerie of nightmarish imagery. Cleo had been puzzled by the whole thing until Zach enlightened her.

These images were literally nightmares: the residue of dreams that percolated out of the sleepers' heads and sedimented into reality. This process, which Zach told her was entirely involuntary, was the greatest – perhaps the only – crime in Dream City. Remembering your dreams and externalizing them eventually resulted in a visit from the Oneiroi, which was the last thing the sufferers saw in reality or in dreams, provided they were even able to distinguish between the two at this stage. Dream residue on bedclothes was only the first stage; if not caught by the Oneiroi, the dreamers would eventually begin to project their nightly visions in tangible objects and living beings, like the sign of the Flying Horse. Such objects and beings would acquire independent existence, harassing the citizenry even after their unwilling creator was executed by the Oneiroi.

Naturally, people regarded the advent of remembering their dreams with horror, much like in Cleo's world people would react to the news of an incurable cancer. This was why the Sleep Clinic existed: to offer a smidgeon of hope to the desperate who thronged its massive edifice, hoping for a cure. Whether any such cures were ever effective remained unclear.

"I'll take you where you need to go," Hendrik said, but instead of leading them up, he turned around and started walking down the stairs. Cleo protested.

"I'll take you where you need to go," Hendrik repeated. Cleo looked back; Tomas was close on her heels, cutting off their route to escape. She met his opaque gaze and shivered. There was something implacable about his soft face. Despite Hendrik's impressive physique, she was more wary of his silent companion.

Zach fell in step, and Cleo, remembering his caduceus, thought they would be able to escape if needed, so they trudged back down the same seven flights they had just trudged up.

The stairs continued beyond the foyer, leading into the dim maw of the basement. Cleo stopped.

"I'm not going there," she said.

CHAPTER 21

endrik caught Cleo's arm and twisted it brutally. She felt her joints crack, but the pain only infuriated her. She aimed a kick at Hendrick's crotch. Hendrik must have had at least thirty pounds and six inches on Cleo, so the fight was unequal, but adrenaline surging through her veins made her reckless. She writhed, scratched, and kicked, all the while expecting Zach to come to her rescue, but it did not happen. When Hendrik finally brought her down to her knees, her arms behind her back, she saw why.

Tomas was holding Zach's caduceus, aiming it at Zach himself. The two snakes, black and white, twined around the rod, hissing, venom dropping off their bared fangs. Zach's face was expressionless.

"I should have killed you both when I had the chance," Hendrik hissed. "Now, They want to see you. I don't know why."

"Enough!" Tomas said softly. "She is important, not him. Let's take them down and let Them sort out what to do with her."

Hendrik nodded sourly and pulled Cleo to her feet, then forced her down the stairs. Zach followed, with Tomas holding the caduceus in the rear.

Even as they descended deeper into the gloom of the weak buzzing light illuminating the concrete steps, Cleo's mind was working feverishly.

I should have killed you both when I had the chance.

Surely, he did not mean in the pub! Then where? Had they met before that? Where? When?

The two Dutchmen had looked familiar…

The Dutch boys on the beach…Jurgen and Liam.

She twisted around, looking at Hendrik's face.

"Did you bring me here?" she asked. "Did you bring me to Orcus? What did you do with my friends?"

"Your friends were unfinished business. We finished it."

All fight went out of Cleo, as she was dragged into the unnaturally deep basement.

Iris and Mick were dead? But then, who wrote the letter?

And what did they want from her?

"Why am I important?" she asked Hendrik, but got no response. The light fixture above the staircase sputtered and went out, and they were plunged into near-darkness. Cleo tried to look back to see if Zach and Tomas were following, but Hendrik cuffed her on the side of the face with casual brutality.

They were descending for a long time. The stairs narrowed precipitously, only leaving room for them to walk single file. Hendrik's meaty fingers were clamped around Cleo's wrists like handcuffs as he prodded her forward. The stairs got increasingly steep as they wound around the vertical stairwell, plunging down into the gloom toward the unseen bottom. The light dwindled to a murky, reddish, uncertain glow. The electric fixtures of the upper floors were supplanted with guttering torches set into iron brackets. The walls were no longer plaster but damp rock, drops of moisture clinging to ledges and protrusions and glittering with torchlight reflections. They were deep into the innards of Orcus.

The pit that became the mountain…

"Are you going to kill me too?" she asked Hendrik.

He snorted.

"You would have been dead already if we wanted to kill you. No, somebody up above wants you, and we have to obey. But first, our Ruler wants to find out what you are."

"So, the higher up they are, the more power they have?"

"Enough of that talk," the soft voice of Tomas sounded from above. If voices had texture, Cleo thought his would be like black velvet splattered with dry blood. "You'll find out soon enough."

Hendrik pushed her so forcefully she almost lost her balance and tumbled down the stairs. Regaining her footing, Cleo continued her descent. She sneaked a glance back, but Hendrik's bulk blocked her vision of Zach. She could not hear him either, but she could sense Tomas' presence like a heavy weight suspended above her on a frayed rope.

The stairs ended abruptly in front of a large door made of blackened wood and bound with rusty iron bars. It had no handle and no keyhole.

Hendrik produced a huge, angled key from one of his pockets and pushed it into the wood, which it entered as smoothly as a knife entering butter. The door groaned and swung open. Beyond it was darkness.

CHAPTER 22

The rank mushroom smell wafting from the maw of the door reminded Cleo of Eleni's cellar, which she had explored once as a little girl. She and Cora had lifted the heavy hatch, and she peered into the large, cavernous space breathing out pungent odors. Cora balked at descending the steep ladder, but Cleo did it and slipped on the last rung, falling down and hitting her head on the cement floor. She did not remember what happened next, except waking up in Eleni's arms and hearing her twin's sobbing. Eleni put a lock on the cellar, which only fueled the girls' imagination as they whispered about the green-skinned monster imprisoned there. Much later, when Cleo and Cora came to their grandmother's house after her death, the cellar was open, but when exposed to the light of day it held nothing more frightening than a couple of jars of spoiled pickles and some bottles of cheap wine turned into vinegar. Now, as the smell of acid rot assailed her nostrils, Cleo was reminded of that childhood trauma.

Tomas grabbed her hand and pulled her over the threshold. She shivered at his touch. His hand was neither cold nor warm, and somehow its dry silkiness drained her strength. He was not dragging her with force, but she could not imagine resisting.

She looked back but saw no sign of Zach.

Hendrik slammed the door behind her.

She was plunged into absolute darkness that settled over her like the lid of a coffin and she started hyperventilating. She was back in the cellar.

She cried out, but the dark seemed to flow into her throat like pitch, blocking her airways. She could not force her vocal cords to vibrate, her lungs to draw air, her eyes to see even the phantom sparks that the brain conjures up in the absence of light. She tried to touch the wall, but there was nothing in front of her trembling fingers. She could not even smell the mushroom-like stench anymore.

Was this what death was like?

She forced her feet to move but there was no traction; she seemed to be walking on ice. She collapsed on the floor and could not feel its hardness.

She lifted her invisible hand to her face and bit deeply into her thumb. The pain was real and tangible, and she held onto it like a drowning man on a plank. The pain spread through her nerves and muscles, and brought her body back, cell by aching cell. She now felt the throbbing in her tired legs, the bruise on her shoulder from the encounter with the flying horse, the dryness in her parched mouth. And then her senses kicked into high gear. The rank damp smell flowed back into her nostrils, making her cough.

She remembered that the heavy lump beneath her was her backpack.

With trembling hands, she rummaged inside until her fingers closed over the sequin-embroidered fabric. She traced the outlines of eyespots.

She pulled out Or's peacock t-shirt and put it on.

At first she thought it would not work, but as she stared disconsolately at her trembling hands, she realized that she could see them.

The light coming off the peacocks was so dim that it illuminated very little of her surroundings, but it was as welcome as a tiny spring in the waterless desert.

She was in some sort of cave, but the light was too weak to make out any details except a glistening curtain of flowstone on the wall near her. Drips of moisture crawled down the curtain, and the air was cold and damp. Jagged silhouettes loomed ahead like a garden of rock cacti.

As her eyes adjusted, she saw something else in the depth of the cave: a weak reddish glow. It might have been an illusion, but at least it was a goal.

She cautiously crept forward, toward the glow. Stalactites dripped cold water onto her head, and slick stalagmites reached toward them with the pleading fingers of stone. The floor of the cave was wet and slippery, and a couple of times she took a fall. The light glowed ahead but did not grow brighter, and she still could not make out what it was.

The ceiling of the cave rose up and the stalactites disappeared. She sensed she was in a much bigger cave. Something flapped above. Bats?

The glow suddenly blinked into nearness. It happened so abruptly that she was left with the vertiginous sensation of time moving in discrete jumps, like a faulty recording, instead of a smooth flow.

The glow was emanating from a large circular firepit like the ones wealthy suburbanites installed in their yards for garden parties. Like most such firepits, it was made of ornamental rocks and bricks with an open bowl in the middle. But unlike any firepit Cleo had ever seen, it was hanging vertically in the air. The flames in the middle danced merrily across the burning pieces of wood, which defied gravity by staying in place. The tongues of fire did not strain up but stretched toward her like welcoming hands.

She stared at the impossible firepit, feeling chills crawl down her spine despite the pleasant warmth emanating from its center. Its disregard of the familiar rules of reality made it an outrage. She remembered a quote, though she could not remember the source: a definition of evil is a rose suddenly bursting into song. This floating firepit, as irrational as a singing rose, frightened her more than any slavering monster would.

Until, alerted by another flapping sound above, she glanced up.

The rocky ceiling of the cave was thickly covered with hanging bodies. Leathery wings fluttered and sleek furry bodies twitched, but these were not bats. The ceiling was festooned with Oneiroi.

She must have gasped because one of the creatures, hanging upside down with its taloned feet wedged into a crack in the ceiling, opened its empty eyeholes and flashes of fire inside illuminated its mushroom-pale face. She stood still, paralyzed with fear and revulsion. The Oneiroi lapsed back into its slumber.

The firepit suddenly flipped over, hanging upside down. The flames continued to burn, with their tips pointing toward the floor of the cave, which was covered with furry lichen like gray hair. In the dancing firelight, she saw that there were three sets of footprints leading into the darkness beyond the hanging firepit, where the cave abruptly narrowed down into a tunnel with smooth obsidian walls like a lava tube.

She hesitated, Oneiroi hanging above her like the harvest of nightmares, but she could not stay here forever.

She walked around the hanging firepit, trying to make as little noise as possible, but her feet sunk into the squelching lichen on the floor with a gulping noise. Oneiroi stirred, flapping their hybrid bat-crow wings, large black feathers raining upon her. The mushroom smell intensified, almost choking her.

Abandoning all caution, she ran, but as she passed by the upside-down firepit, the flames reached out to her, purposeful and hungry like the tentacles of an octopus, and caressed the sleeve of her shirt, catching it on fire.

She screamed and threw herself onto the ground, where the wetness of the lichen put the fire out, but not before it raised angry blisters on her arms. She scooted back. The upside-down fire spread to the sides, barring the entrance to the tunnel. And above her, the Oneiroi were waking up. One of them disengaged from the ceiling and floated down toward her, its wings swishing in the stale air. The fiery sparks in its eyeholes flared up, mirroring the dance of flames in the fire barrier before her.

She pressed her back to the sidewall. The Oneiroi advanced toward her, its pouty mouth stretching in an ugly smile disclosing broken, blackened teeth. More of its brethren floated down from the ceiling. The fiery barrier expanded, generating a curtain of flames at the entrance to the tunnel.

Her hand instinctively crept to the Eye of Charon hanging around her neck, but somehow she knew it would be of no help. The Eye belonged to the open skies and the azure waves of the Mediterranean. It guarded against the dangers of the sea. It removed the letter-blindness of the Spider. But it would be of no use here, in this claustrophobic nightmare-infested underground.

With trembling hands, her arm burning from the lick of the flame, she pulled off the peacock t-shirt and threw it into the firepit.

Peacocks were symbols of clear vision. If anything could counteract the illogical nightmare of Oneiroi, it would be them.

The peacocks screamed and brayed, their fanning tails catching fire. The heat whooshed at her, singeing her face. Her short hair shriveled and smoked. She threw herself onto the damp floor and rolled in the lichen, blinking away the smoke. When she could see again, the air was filled with firebirds.

Their plumage was composed of glittering tongues of flame, their eyes bright coals, their beaks burning wicks. The birds rose in a shiny flock and attacked the bats of nightmares. The descending Oneiroi collided with the firebirds. Some caught fire immediately and plummeted down like smoky comets; others managed to strike back with their sharp talons, separating the birds' heads from their bodies. The beheaded birds fell apart into a shower of coals. The cave was not cold anymore. A maelstrom of fire raged above her, threatening to consume her. Her face and lungs burned from the smoke, and her clothes were peppered with holes where sparks landed on the fabric.

She did not wait for the conclusion of the battle being conducted in eerie silence, the hiss of fire and the swish of Oneiroi wings the only sounds in the deep hush of the cave. Slapping away the sparks, she rushed toward the entrance to the tunnel and pushed through the narrow opening. The smooth black walls closed around her as the firestorm was left behind.

CHAPTER 23

leo squeezed through the lava tube. At first, the fire raging behind her back generated enough residual light for her to be able to see ahead – not that there was much to see, just the mirror-smooth lava-polished walls. Then the tunnel curved to the right, and she was in total darkness again. But it was different from her entrance into the cave because the air was not dead. A tangible draft caressed her face, bringing a whole bouquet of strange smells – not the rank mushroom stench of the Oneiroi but a combination of a heavy orchid-like perfume with something that reminded her of a roadkill festering in the sun.

I'm not claustrophobic, she reminded herself. Cora was. I am not Cora. I am Cleo, and I can do it!

Talking herself down helped. When they were kids, Cora and Cleo had encouraged, and occasionally dared, each other to stand up to bullies or to their mother. Without Cora, Cleo had to rely on her own inner voice to act as her twin.

She pushed forward, her fingers stretched out in front of her face like the tentacles of an anemone tasting the inky water. The darkness was so absolute that once again she began to experience a strange sense of dissolving in it, her body and her senses going numb. She deliberately hit the tip of her scuffed trainer on the wall. The pain was muted and remote.

I could always go back, she told herself, but she knew she could not. There was no room to turn around in the tube, and she had walked too far to backpedal. Forward was the only way.

Time became stretchy and immeasurable. She had been walking for minutes, or hours, or years. Pieces of her were rubbed away by the smooth invisible walls, leaving the shivering core of her stripped-down identity naked.

Until there was a light ahead.

She stopped and blinked. To her starved eyes, it felt like a rude imposition. An exit? A hallucination? She could not tell. She crept forward.

She stopped when the illumination was strong enough that she could see her own fingers against the rock wall. They looked bloodless, drained of color and vitality. Paradoxically, these pitiful gray digits brought her back to herself. She squeezed her face, rejoicing in the reality of her own body, and peered around the bend in the tunnel.

The light was coming from the larger space ahead. It was not the dancing firelight she had encountered in the big cave, nor was it the mean electric illumination that grudgingly dripped through the endless corridors of the Sleep Clinic. This light was rather dingy, but it did not look artificial. It reminded her of a rainy day in February.

Her eyes took some time adjusting – not just to the dimness of the light but to the sight in front of her. She could see it, but she could not see – or understand – what it was.

This was a smaller round cave, bubble-sleek, with gray marble walls. The domed ceiling was, thankfully, free of Oneiroi. There was no light source; the rainy glow seemed to be dispersed in the air like a luminescent fog.

And in the middle of the cave was…a man? A very big man, perhaps? Or two men, sitting very close together, their arms thrown around each other and buried in the rags of their clothing. Or…

Neither of the above.

The thing in the middle of the cave was two bodies partially melted and blended with each other. One body was that of an old man, its exposed parts wrinkled and covered by crepe-like skin. The other was robust and stocky, its chest hairy and bronzed. The bodies were connected at the heads, and the joined trunk, exposed by discolored rags the creature wore as clothing, was swollen and lopsided, with two mismatched arms and three legs, the middle one created by the fusion of two. Their heads were glued together into a lumpy parcel with a saddle in the middle, where the thin white hair of one intertwined with the raven locks of the other. Their faces were not on the same level, so the four eyes of the composite were askew, blinking at her from the piebald mass with two noses and a long, jagged maw created by the wrinkled old mouth joined to the thick-lipped scowl.

It stood up, tottering, and Cleo gulped when she saw how big and tall it was. Its double pate brushed the ceiling of the cave. The three legs jittered, as if it did not know in what order to move them. The maw opened and two tongues flopped out, dripping saliva. It tried to speak, but nothing came out except inarticulate mewling.

She backed off, trying to squeeze her numb body back into the tube. Anything was better than this – even the Oneiroi! But then she was pushed from behind with such force that she was propelled back into the marble cave like a champagne cork flying out of the bottle. She slipped and fell close enough to the double monstrosity to be flooded with its mingled stench: rot and orchids.

Tomas followed her out of the tunnel and regarded her like something he had found sticking to the bottom of his shoe.

"The god wants you," he said. "Make obeisance to the Ruler of Dream City!"

"The god?" Cleo scrambled to her feet, sliding along the wall as far from the double monstrosity as she could. "This is a god? You shitting me? This lump?"

Tomas' dark face grew darker, as if flooded with blood. His shoulders twitched, and another head popped up beside his own. At first, Cleo thought somebody was peeping over his shoulder, but then she realized what she was seeing. A smaller head bubbled up from his shoulder, joining his own. It was the size of a baby's head, but its features were familiar. Hendrik!

"Watch your tongue!" Tomas/Hendrik hissed simultaneously. "You are in the presence of one of the Rulers of Orcus. Bow down to Hypnos and Thanatos, our parádeigma!"

Hypnos was the god of sleep, the ruler of the Oneiroi. Thanatos was the god of death. They had been brothers in the original Greek pantheon, but nowhere in this pantheon was there a place for the misshapen idiotic hybrid of sleep and death that ruled Dream City.

What had happened in the Platonic world of essences to generate something like this?

But right now, Cleo was not concerned with the past but only with the present. The stench of the double deity was suffocating, and the two-headed antigrafo jeering at her blocked the only exit from its cave.

"You have to let me go!" she insisted. "One of the Nine wants me! They are Calling me, you can see it!" She pointed to her pitch-black eyes. "You can't keep me here!"

"Really?" Tomas/Hendrik jeered. "We know who wants you, and she is not the prime mover she thinks she is! We didn't get rid of Zeus to bow to her!"

Cleo, with her back to the cave wall, looked around in desperation. The bulk of the double-headed monster pressed closer to her in odious intimacy, and its wasted arm reached to her with claw-like fingers, while the heavily muscled arm rose above the creature's head, hanging over her like a club. She whipped out the Eye of Charon and pointed it at the Hypnos/Thanatos. The double mouth tittered, drooling.

A loud click sounded behind Cleo's back, and someone grabbed her t-shirt. Not even seeing who it was, she grabbed the hand in return, and was whisked into a tunnel that suddenly gaped in the smoothness of the marble. The wall closed behind her as she lost her footing and sprawled on the hard floor, banging her head. When the stars in her field of vision subsided, she was lifted to her feet.

"Took you long enough," she muttered to Zach.

CHAPTER 24

This was not a rocky cave or a lava tube, but rather a dismal basement of some office building with fluorescent lights and a scuffed linoleum floor. Cleo had never been as happy to find herself back to civilization, as uncertain and skin-deep as it was.

Zach looked no different than he had when they had entered the Sleep Clinic (was it only this morning?). She had only caught a brief glimpse of him streaming with liquid gold before he reverted to his human persona, but he did carry his caduceus, and it was in its true shape.

"I can't do miracles!" Zach responded sulkily.

"Really? A god like you?"

"I'm not a god, I told you! I'm…"

"An avatar, I know. An antigrafo. Just like these two guys. How did you get away?"

"I pinched a pen from Tomas' pocket. Who is carrying pens nowadays, I ask you? Anyway, he did not even notice."

Hermes was also the god of thieves.

"And I used it to open another door and to sneak out. They did not want me anyway. They were only interested in you."

They had been walking through the empty corridor when they came across a deserted café with dusty tables and ancient-looking pastries under glass domes. Cleo's mouth flooded with saliva.

"Coffee break? Zach suggested.

"Great minds think alike."

The glass door was locked, but it swung open with one touch of the caduceus. The pastries were as stale as they looked but still edible. In the fridge there were water bottles, which bore familiar Greek labels. An ancient coffeemaker reluctantly hissed into action, producing two cups of burnt brew.

"So," Cleo asked, sipping the bitter beverage, "why are you helping me?"

"We are mates, remember?"

"I don't remember, actually. But yes, I think we are mates, or were. When your name was Mick."

Cleo did not know when the realization had come to her. Possibly during that nightmare-haunted night she had spent in Zach's flat. Or maybe later, as they were trying to escape Hendrik and Tomas, who she recognized as the Dutch boys on the beach, Jorgen and Liam. But by now it had established itself in her brain with the unquestionable certainty of truth.

Zach was actually Mick, her once-boyfriend and a vacation partner.

She could not understand why she had not recognized him immediately. Something in her memory was seriously awry; more seriously than she had realized. And she suspected Mick had somehow modified his appearance just as he had changed his name. Had he really been that small and wiry in London? Had his hair been that luxuriantly curly like clusters of grapes, as Ancient Greeks liked to describe it? Had he really resembled statues of Hermes so much?

She doubted it. But in any case, there was no longer any question about his identity. At least one of her friends was here. How much of a friend he really was remained to be seen, though.

"Why did you lie to me?" she asked.

"I didn't! I just…I did not know how much you remembered and I did not want to upset you. I was not in the greatest shape myself, trying to put the pieces together. They say that when a person from the shadow world enters a Platonic reality, their memory is impacted, sometimes severely, sometimes less so. Lots of people here are from our world. Most of them only have bits and pieces of their identity left."

This sounded plausible, but Cleo was more concerned with another issue.

"What happened to Iris?" she asked.

"These bastards…they…they went after her. Just as they said. I couldn't do anything."

"They killed her?" Cleo asked, feeling the weight of the words in her mouth like teeth-crushing stones.

Zach nodded miserably.

"And you escaped?"

"Yes."

"Did you know who…what you were?"

"No. I was Mick, a graphic designer, your ex, on a Greek vacation with friends. But when…when it happened…I fought. But you saw them. They looked different in our world but just as creepy. They overpowered me. And then there was this…hole in reality. I don't know how else to describe it. They were dragging you through, and you were screaming…I jumped after you. And found myself on the promenade in Ano Syros. It looked almost the same as in our world, but when I stepped through, I remembered. I was disoriented, of course. It's not every day that you realize you are an avatar of a deity. But I saw them dragging you somewhere and followed them. And then, a woman barred their way and forced them to let you go."

"A woman?"

"Not exactly. She had a crow's head. She was one of the Nine, I think."

"Nyx," Cleo whispered.

Zach nodded.

"She said something, and they ran away. By this point you were unconscious. She told me to take you back to the beach. It was horrible, the way that beak opened and closed and made humanlike sounds but not really human speech. Anyway, I did as she said. I wanted to stay with you, but Nyx told me I needed to go up and I had to obey. I waited until dawn. You were unconscious but breathing. And then I…went up."

Cleo frowned. Zach's – Mick's – story made sense, but she suspected it was not the whole truth. He was keeping something from her, but she thought there was time to pry it out of him later.

"We need to go," he said. "Hypnos and Thanatos may be idiots, but They are stubborn."

Cleo nodded, collected some water bottles, and they set off. She had one last question, though.

"Why did you write the letter?"

Zach shook his head.

"I didn't write any letter."

"There was a letter left for me at the Villa Pharos."

"Iris, perhaps?" he suggested.

Hermes, the god of thieves, merchants – and liars.

CHAPTER 25

hey found a stairway leading up. They passed several floors with empty hallways lined with closed doors. Cleo was beginning to be creeped out by the desolation and was relieved when she heard the sound of footsteps descending toward them.

The relief abruptly vanished when the person rounded the turn and faced her. The woman was gaunt and barefoot, her face sallow and bruised. She was dressed in a thin hospital smock, open at the back. Her eyes were glazed. She shuffled by Cleo and Zach, seemingly without noticing them, and continued down the stairs. On her bony exposed back rode a creature like a hairless monkey with a pink malevolent face. It looked back at Cleo and wheezed through its tiny teeth.

"Nightmare-ridden," Zach murmured. "Oneiroi lunch."

They stopped at the next landing, which had a window as it was above ground. Cleo looked into the drizzly landscape outside, the dirty sky frowning with another wave of rain, and shivered. She could not wait to get out of Dream City. Whatever waited on the Fifth Level could not be as bad!

Zach poked his head around the corner and exhaled in triumph.

"There!" he whispered, pointing at the opposite end of the hallway where an old-fashioned elevator gaped with its cage door folded to the side.

They ran through the hallway, the dirty loose carpet unpleasantly wriggling under their feet. The wooden elevator was in the openwork metal shaft, suspended from the complicated web of cables and pulleys. The cage door was open, but the door of the cabin was locked and there seemed to be no obvious way to get in. Zach pointed the caduceus and the snakes reared up.

A heavy weight landed on Cleo's shoulders, knocking her down. She screamed as the sharp talons of an Oneiroi raked her arms, and the creature's sulfurous breath singed her face. Zach struggled with the caduceus, as the snakes seemed obstreperous, hissing angrily and lashing at him. Cleo managed to push the Oneiroi off and scrambled to her feet. At the mouth of the hallway, she saw several more creatures, scuttling on the ceiling like giant insects. The Oneiroi she had kicked off spread its mangy wings, preparing for another strike.

The wooden door clicked open, and they tumbled through.

The cabin had once been upholstered in scarlet plush, but it had worn into a dirty fuzz on the walls and the bottom. There was a panel of large buttons on the wall, and Cleo promptly pushed the uppermost one.

The doors remained open.

"Close the cage!" Zach yelled, still struggling with the snakes, who had unwound loose from the rod and were crawling up his arms. Cleo, who hated snakes, felt nauseated. She turned her back on him and pulled the folding metalwork of the external cage. It remained stuck.

The Oneiroi were galloping toward the elevator. One of them pushed its taloned arm through the door. Cleo finally managed to move the cage, and it started to close with a metallic screech. But the Oneiroi was stronger than her, squeezing its wormy body inside and pushing the door back.

Cleo pulled out the bronze knife she had kept from her ascent to the Fourth Level. It was crude and unwieldy, but she had seen the huntresses use it to kill a man. It would have to do.

She brought the knife down upon the Oneiroi's skittering arm.

The creature screamed, the first loud sound she had heard it make. It was inarticulate and animalistic, like a wounded hare's screech. Black viscous blood dripped onto the floor.

She struck again, and the Oneiroi withdrew. At the same moment, the wooden door shut with a thunderous clap, and the elevator shuddered into motion, lurching up.

Cleo turned her attention to Zach and saw, with horror, that the snakes were now free of their rod and were winding around his body instead, binding his arms to his trunk. The black snake was crawling toward his throat, its neck swollen into a cobra-like hood. Zach's face was red with exertion as he tried to free himself, struggling like Laocoon and his sons being strangled by the giant snakes sent by Apollo.

Or's all-knowing smirk flashed before her eyes.

She struck the black snake with her bronze knife. The creature lunged at her, venom dripping from its curving fangs. The nausea came back, accompanied by faintness, as her legs threatened to give way.

Distantly, she heard Zach's panting as the snakes were crushing his chest, cutting off his air supply. And at the same time, her own chest felt locked, as if with an echo of his suffocation.

She lifted the knife and aimed for the creature's head, but the blade slid off the diamond-hard scales. The snake hissed. A bolus of venom splattered against her leg. She backed off, pressing against the wall of the elevator. It was only a matter of seconds until one of the snakes wound its slithery body around her, leaving its companion to finish off Zach.

She pulled out the ribbon she had gotten in the transit from the Third to the Fourth Level, a linen band embroidered with the image of Apollo slaying Python, and tossed it at the snakes.

The ribbon unfolded into a straight rigid line as it flew through the air, transforming into a golden arrow that struck one of the snakes in the head. The creature fell to the floor, then the arrow sagged into a ribbon again and wound around the second snake. Cleo heard the crunch of shattered vertebrae.

The elevator was rising jerkily. The snakes lay on the floor in a limp coil, intertwined with the blood-splattered ribbon whose embroidery was obliterated by dripping crimson. Cleo's vision was still dim, and she felt she could not get enough air.

Zach hugged her.

"Breathe," he whispered.

Cleo pushed him away.

"What the fuck?"

"I don't know what happened. Until now, the caduceus obeyed me. Maybe it's because I've reached my limits. Or maybe Hypnos and Thanatos did something to it."

It was not what Cleo was asking, but she was too exhausted to insist. All she wanted now was to complete the ascent and to be out of Dream City as quickly as possible.

The elevator came to a juddering stop, but the door remained closed. Zach tried to pull it open with no effect.

"Are we on the Fifth Level?" Cleo asked.

"Have no idea. Never been up here."

Why not? If Nyx ordered him to go up, why was he stuck in Dream City?

Suspicion and exhaustion fighting for control of her mind, Cleo added her efforts to Zach's with no avail. Suddenly something heavy thumped on the top of the car. It shuddered and dropped a couple of inches. Cleo screamed.

Another thump. Another drop. Dream City was pulling out all stops in unleashing its flood of nightmares: claustrophobia, snakes, falling…

She dug her fingers into the wall, breaking her nails, as if she could keep the fragile cabin from plummeting down.

The elevator ground to a stop, and the door reluctantly crawled open. Beyond the metalwork of the cage, green leaves glowed in the golden sunlight. Warm, pleasantly scented air wafted into the blood-stinking cabin.

She folded back the cage door and stepped into the spring. Zach made to follow but paused to deliver a spiteful kick to the dead snakes.

The white one lifted its flat head and struck at him with its venomous fangs.

Cleo heard Zach cry out, but it was overlaid with a metallic clang as the doors of the elevator slammed shut, and the cabin dropped back into the depth of its shaft.

CHAPTER FIVE The Hives

Cleo lay in a fetal position, the thick honey of sunlight filtering through her eyelashes. Yellow plumes of grass nodded above her head. Her body was slowly relaxing, sinking into the rich, peaceful earth. Dimly, she thought how wonderful it would be to lie among the flowers forever, listening to the lullaby of the buzzing bees and breathing in the sweet smell of narcissi. Even though her eyes were closed, she could visualize the flower's white crown with the golden trumpet in the middle. She felt as if she was thawing out, the damp and mold of Dream City being drawn out of her muscles by the Mediterranean heat. The smells and the sounds were those of Greece, and she felt soothed by them like a child in her mother's arms. She was drifting away into a doze, dreams crowding at the threshold of her mind, eager to draw her into their secret city…

She sat up, her heart hammering, all thoughts of sleep forgotten. After Dream City, she did not know how she would ever sleep again.

But the peace and warmth of the countryside were real. She looked around; she was lying in a field of tall nodding grass, its ochre-colored tassels whispering in the light wind. Wildflowers were scattered around in fragrant clumps – small narcissi, orange poppies, pink and white clover. Large bumblebees lurched from one flower to another, droning like miniature airplanes. Above the heads of grass, the graceful tapering silhouette of a cypress bisected the heat-bleached sky.

No towering mountain obscuring half the sky.

Was she back in her own world? Back on the real Syros or Mykonos?

But then the peak was not visible from Dream City, either. Apparently, in this Zone, finding a way to go up was more complicated than on the first three Levels where at least she could see her goal. What had Alexandra called the three Zones, each comprising three Levels? Elysium, the Asphodel Fields, and…Tartarus? There was something wrong with this nomenclature, but Cleo could not be bothered to figure it out now. More immediate concerns intervened. If she was on the Fifth Level, in the middle of the Asphodel Fields, she needed to find out what this place was all about. Previous experience had taught her that each Level was beset with dangers, and that knowledge was the key to survival.

Wincing from the pins and needles in her legs, she stood up. She would not be surprised to find out that the elevator that had brought her up from Dream City was gone, but then she saw the shaft sticking out from the middle of the field like a giant wire-mesh chicken coop. She approached and tried to push the single button on the panel, but it was unyielding. She squinted into the grated interior, but nothing moved inside the dark well threaded with cables.

Zach – Mick – was gone. She needed to accept this and move on.

She was instantly ashamed of her indifference. He was her friend. Her ex. He had saved her life in Dream City several times.

But he had lied to her.

Still, he was her only connection with the real world. Even though she was not sure what "real" meant anymore.

She looked around. Cypresses stood in a trim line beyond the border of the field demarcated by a low stone wall. But this was no wilderness; there were roofs poking out from between the trees.

It made sense. Cleo went through the topography of Elysium in her head: city, suburbia, wilderness. The Fourth Level in this Zone was Dream City. If she was right, the Fifth Level would be suburban or maybe rural.

The trauma of Happy Meadows still lingered. For some reason, even the horrors of Dream City had not affected her as much as this hellish parody of a suburban family with a harpy for the mother, a misshapen giant for the father, and a smirking wise-ass teenager, an avatar of the god of light, for the son. Had there been something about that triad she had missed?

Well, there undoubtedly had been many things she had missed. A lot of unnoticed details, discarded observations, wrong facts. And the one fact she did not want to think about. Iris, her friend, was dead.

But Cora was alive. She knew it. She had known it when everybody – the police, her mother, her stepfather – had declared her twin dead.

Cleo had refused to come to the memorial. Had refused to lay flowers on the empty grave. Had cut off the relationship with Daphne. All because she knew in her bones that her twin was alive somewhere.

And now she knew where this "somewhere" was. Here, in Orcus, on the mountain of dead gods.

The letter confirmed it, but Mick claimed he had not written it. Was he lying? And if yes, why?

Mick/Zach. An avatar of Hermes, the trickster god. He had saved her life in Dream City more than once. According to him, he had tried to defend her from the abduction by the antigrafos of Hypnos/Thanatos. But could she believe him? Could she believe anything he had said?

She had liked him well enough to hook up with him, though, again, she could not remember any details. It felt like the holes in her memory were patched up with the cement of generalized information. And yet, there was a sense of trust and friendliness when she thought of him. Since her memories were so unreliable, all she could go on were emotional labels that remained attached to blurred and elusive images. Eleni – love and grief. Cora – love and grief. Iris – love and grief, now that she was told that her friend had been murdered.

Seems like a theme, right?

Even so, how could she not have recognized Zach as Mick when he had run into her in Dream City? There was no way their meeting had been random. He must have been waiting for her. And yet, he had not told her who he was; he had not tried to jolt her memory.

She felt like the accumulated questions were an avalanche, hanging over her head, about to crash and bury her in the debris of indecision and doubt.

You must go up.

This was the only certain thing. The Call was just a reminder of what her inner voice had been telling her since she awoke on the beach in Ano Syros. She was here. Cora was here. She would climb the mountain. She would find her sister. And the answers…they would come when she finally looked into the face of her twin, the face that was her own.

Still, she lingered in the field, breathing in the smells of dry grass, flowers, pine resin, and mastic trees, and listening to the soothing drone of cicadas. She could use this time to hydrate and grab a bite, she decided. She glanced at her arm under the worn sleeve of her hoodie. Her knuckles and wrist bones were as prominent as pebbles under the dry skin. She was losing weight, a process she had not needed even in her teen years. When other girls obsessed over the impossibly thin influencers on Instagram, Cora and Cleo ate whatever they wanted and watched their bodies shape themselves into the smooth slenderness of classic statues.

She sat in the shadow of an old olive tree and opened her tattered backpack, pulling out a water-bottle and a bar of pressed dry fruit she had gotten in Dream City. It was made of apricots and plums, but colored bright scarlet with pomegranate juice. She bit into it and winced: the bar was intolerably sweet, and apricots and pomegranates did not seem to enjoy their forced pairing.

The shadow of a memory brushed her mind like a butterfly wing, but it was gone before she could catch it. She dutifully chewed through the leather-tough fruit, repacked her possessions, and strode toward the houses beyond the tree line.

CHAPTER 27

At least it did not look like Happy Meadows. No manicured lawns, McMansions, or picket fences. When Cleo walked through the narrow belt of cypresses, she found herself among mature olive trees scattered on the shallow slope. And at the bottom of the slope were several farmhouses surrounded by barns, stables, and various sheds. The houses looked old: honey-colored thick stone walls, narrow windows shadowed by wooden shutters, tiled roofs. Sturdy Mediterranean architecture to keep you warm in winter and cool in summer. Beyond the farmhouses lay small vineyards and fruit orchards. An idyllic view.

But this was Orcus, and if she had learned anything in her ascent, it was that each new Level was worse than the one below. The Cyclops and crows of Ano Syros felt almost homely compared to the wild huntresses and Oneiroi. She watched the farmhouses, but if there were people inside they hid behind the stonewalls. She took a deep breath to steady herself and touched the nearest olive tree for luck. She loved olives' stolid trunks, their deeply fissured but silky bark, and narrow silvery leaves. One of the oldest domesticated trees and the staple of the Mediterranean, the olive had always been associated with Greece for her.

The trunk squirmed and bulged up under her touch.

She was thrown off balance, as much by surprise as by the tree's sudden animation. Snatching her hand back, she scrambled away from the olive, which shuddered as if straining to pull its roots out of the powdery soil. The bulge grew and split, and a small, sleek head popped out.

The creature wriggled out as far as she could go, which was not very far, as she blended with the trunk below the waist. The bark shaded off into her skin, greenish, deeply furrowed, and crumpled. The creature's face was pug-nosed and goggle-eyed, with a small mouth lined with tiny sharp teeth.

Creature? No, Cleo knew what she was seeing. One did not need to be an expert in Greek mythology to recognize a hamadryad. Still, Cleo was somewhat disappointed as her video-game-inspired images were blown away by brute reality. The hamadryad was neither beautiful like classic Greek statues nor sexy like game characters. She possessed no pneumatic breasts or flowing locks. Her chest was almost flat, and her hair was matted and twined with twigs and dead leaves. Her eyes were black and glistening like pickled olives in a jar, and she stared at Cleo with what appeared to be a total shock.

"I am sorry," Cleo said, deciding that conciliation was the best approach. "Did I startle you? I did not know it was your tree."

The hamadryad's mouth opened and closed like a fish's, but she remained mute.

"Can you tell me more about the Fifth Level?" Cleo persisted. "As you can see, I am being Called, and I have to go up. I could use some guidance."

"Maiden," the hamadryad said in an oily voice. "Run away while you still can."

Maiden? Really?

"Run where?" Cleo asked.

"You will never reach the Final Level," the hamadryad went on. "And if you do, you will wish you haven't."

"This is what they keep telling me," Cleo muttered. "All right, so how can I go back to my own world?"

"You can't," the hamadryad said.

"Well, thanks for nothing."

She started down the slope toward the farmhouses.

"Beware the bees that collect the honey of vengeance, maiden," the hamadryad declared, something viscous bubbling in her throat.

"I don't care about stupid bees! Just tell me where the ascent to the next Level is!"

"Near is far, far is near. This is the law of Orcus"

Cleo rolled her eyes, but before she could inquire about the meaning of this nonsensical riddle, the hamadryad popped back into her tree, the bulge of her passage smoothing out.

"What the hell?" Cleo asked rhetorically. At least, until now all the Levels seemed to be more or less "modern", for lack of a better term. Even in the Forest of Masks, its cavorting satyrs and naked huntresses spoke contemporary Greek. The hamadryad's language was so archaic that Cleo was not sure she understood her correctly. And being addressed as "maiden" rubbed her the wrong way, not just because it was ridiculous, but because the word that the hamadryad used, kore, sounded like her sister's name.

CHAPTER 28

The wooden gate in the plastered wall of the nearest compound was ajar. Cleo peered into the courtyard where a small fountain decorated with the statue of a naked boy holding a bow burbled softly in the afternoon heat. The courtyard was paved with blue ceramic tiles, and two large amphoras stood at the entrance to the main house. But like everything else here, the compound appeared deserted. The only sound was the soothing buzz of bees and bumblebees in the flower beds on both sides of the house.

"Hello!" she called out, but elicited no response. It reminded her of Happy Meadows. Suburban living sure bred isolation!

She gingerly stepped into the courtyard and called out again. This level was positively paradisiacal compared to the damp nightmare of Dream City, and it made her suspicious. At this point, she expected the worst from Orcus, especially in the light of the hamadryad's histrionic warning.

"Hello!" she repeated, and this time she got a reaction.

The statue jumped off its pedestal and tottered toward her.

Cleo started when she realized it was not a statue. It was a boy, perhaps three or four years of age, and stark naked. His body glittered with drops of water, but his tight blond curls were dry. He stared at her with an inquisitive expression that seemed too old for his angelic face. His uninhibited nudity seemed to indicate that imitating garden statuary was par for a course for him. Cleo, not used to dealing with kids his age, cleared her throat.

"Erm," she said, "are your parents at home?"

The boy turned around and walked to the front door of the farmhouse. Cleo followed. Before he reached it, the door opened, and a woman stepped out.

The woman was round-cheeked, with wavy black hair and a big smile disclosing a gold tooth. She was dressed in an old-fashioned embroidered blouse and a long peasant skirt.

"Who are you?" the woman asked. She did not sound hostile or wary.

"I am a guest. I ask for this house's hospitality."

Hospitality had been a very big deal in Ancient Greece, with many myths detailing the gruesome punishments Olympians meted out to those who abused or harmed their guests. The patron of hospitality had been Hestia, and while Cleo suspected she was as dead as the rest of the former divine crew, the archaic speech of the hamadryad inspired her to appeal to old customs.

"You honor us with your presence," the woman said. "I am Sophia. And this is Yannis."

Cleo introduced herself.

"Come in, come in!" Sophia led her into the large kitchen at the end of a dim hallway. "Sit down, please. And you" – she turned to Yannis – "go and put on some clothes! You are not a baby anymore!"

The child scurried away while Sophia bustled around, putting dishes on the table and keeping up an uninterrupted stream of chatter, from which Cleo gathered that the farmhouse belonged to Sophia and her husband Vassilikos; that they lived there with their six children, of whom Yannis was the youngest; and that they grew grapes, figs, olives, and peaches, and kept goats and bees. The father and the rest of the kids were out in the fields, but they would be "blessed" when they came home and met Cleo.

Before long, the scrubbed kitchen table was groaning under the weight of cucumber and tomato salad with feta cheese, olive oil, tzatziki, and freshly baked flatbread. Cleo's mouth watered, and she realized just how hungry she was and for how long she had not eaten good Mediterranean fare. The food in Dream City had seemed to partake of its watery ambience, while the meal she had eaten in the Forest of Masks…she did not want to think about it. She demurred at first, not wanting to eat before the rest of the family, but Sophia insisted and Cleo decided she could do with a second helping later on.

As she was finishing the delicious piece of freshly baked bread dipped in fragrant olive oil and sprinkled with herbs, the noise outside announced the arrival of Vassilikos and the older children. They all filed into the kitchen, one after another: three boys, two girls; Giorgios, Dion, Andres, Thalia, and Lyra. The kids ranged in age from Giorgios, a strapping lad who appeared to be in his early twenties, to Lyra who was about eight. They all looked like their parents: dark-eyed, with curly or wavy dark hair, and open and welcoming round faces. None was particularly handsome, but they all seemed to be salt-of-the-earth, polite, and hardworking. Vassilikos, an older version of his sons, gave Cleo a hug and told her that they were honored to have her. Clearly, whatever the fate of Hestia, the old tradition of hospitality was very much present on the Fifth Level of Orcus.

And that was precisely what gave Cleo a pause. No matter how sweet the air was, fragranced with scents of flowers and warm greenery; no matter how guileless and ordinary her hosts looked; no matter the amazing food – she was still in Orcus. If each Level was worse than the preceding one, how come that the nightmare-haunted Dream City was followed by this idyll? And if indeed each Level was ruled by one of the Nine, who was the Ruler of this one? Cleo tried to remember the order in which Zach had listed the Nine but could not. And who said that Zach was a reliable source of information anyway?

Thinking about Zach spoiled her mood, so she was relieved when Sophia asked her whether she wanted to freshen up before dinner, and led her to an upstairs bedroom, which had a bed made up with clean sheets, embroidered hangings on the walls, and a ceramic vase with fresh wildflowers on the side table. Across the hallway was a bathroom with basic but adequate plumbing. she was glad that parallels with ancient Greece did not extend to the exact copy of their sanitary arrangements, which, while superior to the rest of the world at the time, were not up to the standards of the twenty-first century. But that, of course, raised the question of why Orcus contained that weird mishmash of different technologies and styles, as if sampling history at random. Perhaps that was exactly what it did. The Platonic world of essences would not be bound by chronology.

Then what was it bound by?

CHAPTER 29

The dinner was delicious: large rounds of feta cheese swimming in olive oil, lamb roast, cardamom-flavored flatbread, stuffed grape leaves, and fried eggplants. Vassilikos produced several bottles of homemade wine, which, while a bit raw and tart, was a perfect accompaniment to the food. Cleo was amused to see that at the dinner table, all the kids, including Yannis, had a splash of wine added to their water glasses, which had still been traditional in rural Greek households when Eleni was young.

In every way, the evening meal seemed like a picture of the past filtered through the rose-colored glasses of nostalgia. The children in colorful clothes sitting demurely around the scrubbed table laden with fresh food; the parents, smiling at each other as they talked to their guest; the general atmosphere of happy domesticity. The kids, including the oldest Giorgios spoke when they were spoken to, allowing their parents to steer the conversation, but Cleo sensed no harsh disciplinary vibes. They all looked happy and healthy. Cleo was surprised to see an unfamiliar little blond girl when the six of them trooped to the table, until she realized that the girl was in fact Yannis, wearing a short dress. But then she remembered that boys in nineteenth-century Europe wore dresses until the age of five. Yannis did stand out among his siblings, though: his hair was the color of honey and his blue eyes reminded Cleo of her own, or rather her own as they had been until the Call painted them the color of pitch. The rest of the family were dark-haired and brown-eyed, and none as cherubic as Yannis who kept quiet at the table, so Cleo was not sure whether he could speak.

The meal had been preceded by a moment of silence when Vassilikos bowed his head and mouthed something inaudible. The rest of the family joined in, while Cleo tried to figure out what deity they were praying to. Certainly, not the Christian God; there was nothing in the house that resembled an ikon or a crucifix. This was peculiar. Considering how deeply Orthodox Christianity was embedded in Greek culture, shouldn't the Platonic world of essences reflect it in some way?

Why do you think this is the only mountain? Or island?

The mysterious Archipelago. Orcus must not have been the only one of the many mythical worlds that influenced Plato's Cave.

Cleo was so stuffed that she barely crawled up the stairs to the guest bedroom. Washing her face, she studied it in the mirror. Her ascent of Orcus had planed off all softness, revealing the sharp angles of her cheekbones and the straight line of her nose. Her skin was tanned and roughened. Her hair had grown out and curled in untidy black ringlets. The now-black eyes, enormous in this gaunt face, went so well with her new image that she had to remind herself they used to be blue. She realized she liked this new Cleo, and this realization brought a stab of guilt because she no longer looked like Cora. It felt like losing her twin all over again.

She peeled off her travel-stained clothes and found to her pleasant surprise that Sophia had laid out a long, embroidered nightgown, which she slipped over her head with a sigh of contentment. She stretched out among the clean crisp sheets and blew out the candle. The house had no electricity, but she did not miss it. After the horrors of the Forest of Masks and Dream City, she wanted to savor the simple rural pleasures of this unhurried life. She even let herself consider lingering here, on the Fifth Level. The Call was still tugging at her, but she thought she could overcome it, reducing it to the barely noticeable buzz at the back of her mind. Surely she deserved a break!

She let herself imagine sunny days and quiet nights scented with the perfumes of figs and lemons as she drifted to sleep.

A blond frizzy-haired woman is kneeling before a small child and gently adjusting his tiny jacket. It's raining; straight rods of steely water are pummeling the pair and washing away their colors, leaving behind gray outlines. The blue of the child's jacket sloshing down the pavement in an aquamarine stream, the woman's blondness dripping into a puddle of yellow… Two colorless shadows frozen into a tender gesture of motherhood.

Not colorless. A gush of bright scarlet flows down the woman's fingers, painting the child with bold strokes of blood.

Cleo woke up, her heart beating so strongly she was gasping for breath.

Iris.

And Iris' son.

She could not remember the boy's name and it drove her to distraction because she had been his godmother. Iris had dropped out of the uni to have her baby, though she went back later to complete her degree. She was blessed with understanding and supportive parents, and perversely, Cleo remembered them well, despite having almost no recollection of the child who would be seven or eight by now. And the boy's father? Iris had never disclosed his identity, and it felt quite natural to Cleo who had always been a part of a family of women. Eleni had been eighteen when Daphne was born, her father a sailor who disappeared into the sunset, leaving no forwarding address. Cleo's own father did the same, though he had at least had the grace of bestowing his name on his twin daughters. With no child support and only a couple of random visits, Cleo and Cora had grown up fatherless. Iris had done well for her son on her own, and she was a more affectionate mother than Daphne had ever been.

But if she was really dead, the boy would be an orphan. Or…Cleo was struck with a horrible thought. Was it possible Iris' son had been with them on the beach?

No, no way. No matter how unreliable her memory had become, she distinctly recalled that the vacation was planned as a throwback to their student days, an opportunity to recapture the carefree spirit of youth. No, Cleo's son (what WAS his name?) was safely home in Fulton with his grandparents, who must have been gutted by her disappearance. Or worse, murder, if her body had been left on the beach in Ermoupoli.

And were the police looking for her and Mick? Were they suspects in Iris' murder?

Cleo realized that her racing thoughts were taking her places she did not want to go. She stirred restlessly under the blanket, kicking it off. Her heart was beating fast. The window was open, the white curtain billowing in the soft breeze, and the giant harvest moon flooding the room with silver radiance. The air was mild, but she shivered.

She got up to close the window, averting her eyes from the moon. It had been full when she ran away from the huntresses: the face of Hekate, the Triple Goddess of witchcraft, asserting her dominance over the Forest of Masks. Under the cloudy skies of Dream City, the moon had gone through its phases unnoticed, as the city's subterranean Ruler brooded in darkness. And now it was full again.

She closed the window, muting the insistent striation of cicadas, but she knew she could never go to sleep again. Not after her dream.

She lit the candle and pulled the letter, scuffed and worn, from her backpack.

Zach/Mick had claimed he had not written it. And of course, if Iris had indeed been killed by antigrafos of Hypnos/Thanatos, she could not have written it. Then who had? And why had Arachne put a spider spell on her to prevent her from reading it?

Cleo traced the convoluted lines of writing, intertwined like vines. The more she studied the letter, the less she was able to make out anything at all. The impression that it had been written in two different hands was hard to shake off, but she was now beginning to see common features in the text. Was it possible that it had been written by one person pretending to be two? But why? Even if somebody had wanted to deceive her by faking a letter from her friends, what was the point of deception if she could not understand what it said?

The door to the bedroom creaked open. A tiny figure toddled in.

Cleo started and suppressed a scream when she saw who it was. Yannis, in a white nightgown, stared at her with big luminous eyes, his expression solemn. Moonlight glimmered on his tight curls.

"What's up?" Cleo asked brusquely. "Can't sleep?"

She was instantly ashamed of herself. How could she talk like this to a toddler? Perhaps he just woke up from a nightmare and needed comforting.

Yannis climbed onto the bed and settled among the pillows, still keeping his eyes on her. Cleo winced. There was something in his gaze – a combination of innocence and knowingness – that rubbed her the wrong way.

"Listen," she said, "let's go find your Mama."

"My Mama is dead," Yannis said.

His voice was honey-sweet and honey-sticky, settling over her like a flood of intoxicating perfume. It was a man's voice, the most beautiful one she had ever heard. Having it come from the mouth of a small child was obscene. She scuttled away, almost falling off the bed in her haste to put as much distance between herself and the creature as possible.

"Who are you?" she whispered.

CHAPTER 30

Yannis smiled, his cheeks dimpling adorably. And then he spread his arms, the gauzy sleeves of his nightgown flapping like white wings…until they were really wings, sprouting from his shoulder blades, downy pinions unfolded, feathers like mingled silver and gold gleaming in the moonlight. His body shot up and grew like a silver tree. It towered above Cleo, adult now and terrifying in its perfection. She glanced at his face and staggered back, as if from a blow. Nothing she had seen in Orcus could compare with the sheer power emanating from his inhumanly flawless nudity and his inhumanly serene face. Or's cheeky attractiveness had been like a candle to a firestorm in comparison with this man's – or god's – overwhelming beauty.

She slid off the bed and knelt on the floor, careful to keep her eyes down. The feathery wings rustled like leaves in a windswept forest, and no matter how hard she tried not to look, she could see that they were changing color, turning feverish pink.

"Look at me, maiden," the honey voice dripped over her.

"I am unworthy, son of Aphrodite, the mightiest of gods," she said. "I am unworthy to gaze at your face."

The rosy wings fluttered above her, the colors of dawn dancing on the margins of her vision, and she felt an almost overwhelming need to look up, to meet his eyes, to touch and be touched…

I have never been in love.

I don't know what love is.

This is my chance to find out.

This is my chance to lose myself.

She bit the inside of her cheek until the salty taste of blood flooded her mouth. At the same time, she heard a low chuckle, and the towering presence above her shrunk and receded.

Cleo risked one glance through her lowered lashes. Yannis, a baby boy, was curled up on her blanket, smiling at her with an un-childlike complicity.

"You are stronger than you look," he remarked. His voice was the same honey adult voice, seductive and thrilling.

She remained on the floor. Her heart was still beating so fast she was afraid she would pass out.

"But you know nobody can resist me," he continued. "Not even my uncle."

It took her a moment to figure out who he meant. The family relations of the Olympians were so convoluted that any genealogy expert would give up in disgust trying to figure out who was whose sibling, spouse, uncle or parent – or all of the above.

"Isn't Zeus dead?" she asked.

He nodded.

"He is. And so is my mother. Killed by the rebels."

"So, who is in charge now? Orcus seems a bit…disorganized if I may say so."

He grinned. There was something revolting about this cynical smile on a baby's face.

"Well, that's a really good question, isn't it? And this is why they all can't wait to get their hands on you."

"Me? Why me?"

"You are important," he drawled. "Surely, you have figured out that much already. But it does not answer my own question."

"Which is what?"

"What to do with you. I can take you away, you do realize it, don't you? I can make you my slave. I can make you do anything I want, and you'll serve me out of love, not fear."

Cleo's blood ran cold.

Eros, the god of love, the son of Aphrodite, was not a cute little prankster dispensing roses and chocolates. He was not a Valentine's Day cliché. He was the god of lust and desire, of procreation and passion. He ruled over urges that people were ashamed to name and animals were powerless to resist. Sex was the lynchpin of creation, and Eros held it in his hands.

But was this creepy child Eros or one of his antigrafos? And if the latter, how far was he from the original; how much of Eros' power did he really possess?

She decided that pretending to be cowed was a good strategy, not that it required much playacting. She was genuinely terrified, and the worst thing was her fear was underpinned with hot excitement. She was grateful that Yannis had reverted to his child form, no matter how it repulsed her now. Anything better than to fall in love with the god of love!

"I realize it," she said. "I know nobody can resist your arrows. Where are they, by the way?"

He smirked again.

"I don't need arrows!" he responded. "One touch would be enough to make you mine. Let me show you…"

"No!" she interrupted hastily. "I believe you. But why would you hinder me? All I want is to be out of here. I want to go back to my own world. I didn't ask to be in Orcus!"

The whine in her voice was genuine enough, and she let the tears of frustration that filled her eyes roll down her cheeks. Let him think she was just a pathetic whimpering thing, unworthy of his attention! From her readings in mythology, she knew that Eros liked challenges.

"Too late," he responded. "Anyway, your world, as you call it, is a shadow of this one. It's not like it's any better out there. Chaos is coming back, and we will all suffer unless a new order is established."

"Have you been in my world?" she asked cautiously, remembering like with Mick/Zach, this was one way to find out if Yannis was an antigrafo or the parádeigma himself.

"Why would I go?" he responded. "You are so attached to your dead devices, you forgot how to use your living bodies. Anyway, this is not where the real action is. It's here. Unless the Nine agree on their leader, your world won't exist for very long."

"But you are not one of the Nine," she persisted. "Who do you back?"

He opened his mouth but was interrupted by a sudden loud noise, like the buzzing of a giant bee swarm. And for the first time in their interaction, the expression on his face was not mocking superiority. It was abject fear.

CHAPTER 31

leo rushed to the window, but Yannis caught her hand and pulled her back with strength beyond his tiny frame. "Don't look!" he whispered.

But she did, from the corner of her eye, and still the confusing mélange of silver light and moving shadows, filtered through the gauzy curtain, was impossible to make out. What she saw, or thought she saw, was a vast moving body composed of separate flapping entities; an enormous roiling cloud that obscured the Moon and plunged the bedroom into a noisy darkness. The buzz intensified until it sounded like a myriad of dentist drills. He curled up into a tiny ball, hiding his head under a pillow, like a helpless little child that he was not.

And then the cloud passed, and the silence returned. It was deeper than before because the cicadas had stopped their song.

"What was that?" she whispered, her head still pounding.

"It's bad luck to name them," he whispered back.

"You are a bloody god!"

"So were my parents. So was my uncle. They are all dead."

She frowned. He had a point. Whether Yannis was Eros himself or his antigrafo, the fact was that his mother, Aphrodite, the all-powerful goddess of beauty and love, and his father, Ares, the god of war, not to mention Zeus, the king of the Olympians, had been overthrown and presumably killed by the chthonic rebels. Where had they gotten their power? And were all the Olympians dead? What about Poseidon, the ruler of the sea; Demeter, the goddess of vegetation and growth; or for that matter Hades, the god of the underworld? Why had not Cleo thought of him before? Orcus was like a negative of his underground domain, a pit turned mountain. Was Hades still alive, then? She did not know why but the idea gave her the creeps.

A soft sound brought her back to her present situation. Yannis was crying; fat tears rolling down his cheeks.

"They are all dead…" he repeated forlornly.

He looked like a little boy, frightened and alone, cowering in the bed of a stranger, and her heart melted – until she remembered the gale of brute potency coming off his adult form. But still, Eros or not, he was also a toddler, and Cleo awkwardly patted his shoulder. He threw himself into her lap, his short arms around her torso. She rolled her eyes – she was not good with kids – but she folded him in a hug, hoping he was not going to transform into a naked man in her embrace.

The bedroom door was flung open, and Vassilikos and Sophia appeared on the threshold, still in their night clothes and looking very pissed.

"We have welcomed you as an honored quest," Vassilikos bellowed, "and this is how you repay us? Trying to steal our son?"

"What?!" Of all the nonsensical accusations! Cleo let go of Yannis and tried to push him away, but he clung to her as tight as a leech. "I don't want your son! What would I do with him?"

"What is he doing in your bedroom then, in the middle of the night?" Sophia demanded.

"He came in by himself. He…" Cleo hesitated. Did the parents know who their baby boy really was? She decided not to open this particular can or worms. "He had a nightmare, he told me. He just wanted comfort."

"You are lying!" Vassilikos shouted, advancing upon her, and Cleo saw, with a sinking feeling, that he held a butcher knife in his raised hand. His pastoral placidity was gone, supplanted by uncontrollable rage. "Our son is afflicted. He cannot speak. If he had a night fright, he would seek comfort from his parents, not a cunning stranger! I saw how you looked at him! You are either a barren woman seeking to steal a child you cannot have, or something even worse!"

"Even if I wanted a child, which I most certainly don't, yours would be the last one I'd choose!" Cleo yelled back. She shook off sobbing Yannis and reached under her pillow, her fingers groping but encountering only emptiness. "Yannis, tell him!"

"Liar!" Vassilikos shouted. "Witch!"

He lunged toward her, the raised knife gleaming in the moonlight, while Sophia grabbed the squirming child and held him tight. Cleo finally found what she was looking for and pulled it from under the pillow.

The window burst open, showering her with slivers of glass. A swarm of fluttering, buzzing bodies filled the room.

There were so many that Cleo, battered and overwhelmed by the swirling maelstrom of wings, could not draw a breath, as if all the oxygen in the room had been sucked out. Crouching on the floor, she got only fleeting glimpses of giant bees, their vibrating bodies striped in black and dirty yellow, their wings red as if dipped in blood, their stingers dripping foaming venom, their faceted eyes glistening with humanlike fury. The swarm whirled in the center of the room like an indoor tornado, breaking mirrors and overturning furniture. The bees melded together into a boiling mass, whipping her with its palpable rage, its buzzing tearing through her brain. And then the mass subsided onto the floor, falling apart again into individual components, only now there were fewer of them. They kept flowing toward each other like drops of mercury, bees combining and melting, reshaping themselves with scurrying insectile rapidity that she could hardly follow. At the end only three figures remained, standing in the middle of the trashed bedroom.

They looked like an unholy hybrid of a woman and a bee: slender bodies with tiny waists and swollen abdomens resting on stilted legs, four transparent wings stained and splattered with what appeared to be dry blood, fleshless arms gleaming with chitin. They wore dirty rags wound around their shallow chests. But their faces were the worst: human enough to be contorted with anger, insectoid enough to be implacably alien. Flat and nose-less, with bee stingers flickering out of their pouty mouths, they had the compound orbs of an insect but composed of human eyes, squashed together into a bulge. The eyes blinked desultorily, some weeping, some staring blankly. They were all different, as if harvested from different individuals and roughly sorted out by color. The creature on the left had all the eyes in her compound orbs brown, the creature in the middle had green, and the one on the right sported a selection of watery blue and gray.

Yannis whimpered.

"The Kindly Ones," Cleo said under her breath.

Now she knew why Yannis/Eros had refused to name the Rulers of the Fifth Level of Orcus. The Erinyes, or Furies, relentless pursuers of transgressors and criminals, were so feared that their names were supplanted by euphemisms, such as the Kindly Ones or the Just Ones. Of course, they were neither kindly nor just.

But what were they doing here? Surely, no crime had been committed.

The Furies spoke all together, their voices coming out in perfectly syncopated drone from three mouths, the stingers dripping foamy venom.

"Laws of hospitality have been broken."

CHAPTER 32

assilikos and Sophia fell to their knees, banging their heads on the floor and begging the Furies to spare their lives. A couple of their older kids, woken by the commotion, peered into the room, and spotting the Erinyes, promptly disappeared. Yannis burrowed into the bedclothes. Cleo opened her mouth to protest – this was just a misunderstanding, she wished no ill will to her hosts – when the three insectoid figures turned to her and advanced together in a sort of coordinated scuttle.

"A guest owes respect to their hosts," the brown-eyed one intoned. Cleo suddenly remembered their names: Alecto, Tisiphone, and Megaera. But what difference did this make? They were not individuals but blind communal forces of conformity and discipline. Their beelike appearance was perfect for what they were: enforcers.

"This guest broke this obligation by trying to steal a child," the green-eyed one pitched in, her voice indistinguishable from her sister's.

"A crime has been committed and requires punishment," the blue-eyed one concluded. In unison, the three of them converged upon Cleo.

"What the fuck!" The accusation was so baseless that Cleo was practically paralyzed. She frantically tugged at Yannis' hand, but he refused to stir, wailing in a pitiful voice and acting to perfection the role of a traumatized baby.

What an idiot she had been!

She stood up and let go of Yannis, who lifted his head for a split second and gave her a wry glance before redoubling his crying. The Furies' compound eyes stared at her impassively, and she shuddered when she realized some of them were rotting. Eyes of the dead.

She would not be added to this collection, punished by grotesque bee women for a transgression she had not committed! But what could she do? The Erinyes were implacable and invincible. The gods themselves trembled before them. And now, with the gods dead, there was nobody to appeal to.

She realized that she may die in the next five minutes. And strangely, her strongest feeling was outrage. To die for a transparent setup!

To die without knowing what had happened to Cora.

But she still had something – something as flimsy as a dream, but better than nothing. She grasped it in the folds of her nightgown, ready to pull it out.

But the Furies did not attack – at least, not immediately. They threw up their skeletal chitin-glistening arms, and sharp-pointed stingers emerged out of their bony palms, flickering in unison with the stingers in their mouths.

They produced a thunderous buzz, piercing Cleo's eardrums like an awl. She collapsed to her knees. Vassilikos and Sophia rushed out of the room, and Yannis curled up into a ball.

And then the Furies fell apart.

Each of them disintegrated into smaller copies of themselves, and these miniature Furies, buzzing and beating the air with bloodstained wings, rose up in a dense cloud. Swarming and roiling, each Fury kept dividing up, generating fractal copies of herself, until the room was black with a seething cloud of venomous bees, engorged with rage and righteousness. They converged on Cleo.

She whipped up the dream-residue object that she had found on her pillow when she woke up for the last time in Dream City.

It was a net woven of gold and silver, its fibers shimmering with all the colors of a rainbow.

The yellow and purple birthing blue and green birthing orange and red…Iris screaming in the background, as Cleo is being carried away by rough hands…

The residue of a nightmare, a repressed memory materialized into an object, a message from her dead friend, or a cunning trap set by the Ruler of the Fourth Level…Cleo did not know what it was – just that it was her only weapon.

She threw the net at the swarm of Furies. Her hands shook, so she aimed badly. But

the net flew straight, expanding as it did. The angry buzz of the Furies rose into a thunder, and Cleo felt like her eardrums would burst. Blood trickled from her nose.

The net unfolded like a fisherman's trawl and burst into the radiance of all the colors of the rainbow. It curved around the swarm and closed neatly, containing the bees inside. It fell onto the floor, expanding into a large ball and vibrating under the frantic attacks of the Furies. They tried to chew through the fibers, and the net shuddered, but it held.

She rushed to the door, leaving the trapped swarm behind. Hurling pell-mell down the stairs, she ran into one of the sons. To her surprise, the boy stepped aside, letting her go. A brief fumble at the front door, and she was out, in the jasmine-scented Mediterranean night.

CHAPTER 33

leo cowered among the rows of vines in the vineyard, shivering as the adrenaline burnt itself out. The moon, soft and white like a round of feta cheese, was dropping toward the horizon, and the predawn sky was lightening up into the indigo color of the sea. But there was no sea on the Fifth Level, and no obvious way to locate the Sixth Level either.

She hugged her knees, feeling the hardness of her bones under the embroidered nightgown. The bare soles of her feet bled; she had cut them on sharp stones while running away from the farmhouse. So now she had no clothes or underwear, no shoes, and worst of all, her backpack had been lost together with all the useful odds and ends she had accumulated in her ascent and with the letter. No matter how often she told herself the illegible letter was irrelevant, since she could not read it in any case, she could not let go of the feeling that it was important.

At least the Eye of Charon was still with her. She never took it off, not even in bed. She touched the blue circle pierced with a black pupil against the white porcelain background, and remembered stalls overflowing with cheap pendants, rings, and keychains with a mati —

the evil eye – design in every touristy market. She could have brought handfuls of them into Orcus had she known!

But all she could do now was wait until dawn and then…she realized she did not know what to do next. This was the most hopeless and defenseless she had felt in her entire ascent. Being without her clothes and her backpack contributed to her vulnerability. Her River Island jeans washed until they were as soft as velvet, her M&S knickers, and her trainers were her connection to her own world, her own reality, which, in her heart of hearts, she still felt to be more real than this topsy-turvy world of essences that seemed more and more to resemble a disjointed feverish nightmare.

There was a rustle – clods of soil tumbling down the hillside – and she saw a dark silhouette approaching. She instinctively crouched even lower down, but of course widely spaced vines provided no real cover, making her look as ridiculous as a child pulling the bedclothes over her head to be invisible. Defiantly, she stood up.

The pinkish glow of the dawn illuminated the intruder's face. Giorgios, the eldest brother!

He was carrying her backpack and her clothes and shoes, which he lay on the ground at her feet.

"I also have some food and water for you," he offered, adding a cloth bag bulging with flatbread and a water flask.

Cleo was so taken aback that she did not know how to react. She studied the boy's face. He was older than he had appeared at first – more or less her own age. And while, thankfully, he had nothing in common with the scorching beauty of Yannis/Eros, he was quite handsome, with melting brown eyes and thick dark hair.

"How did you know where to find me?" she asked suspiciously.

He shrugged.

"How far could you go in the dark? I just walked around the farm. The Kindly Ones are gone for now. Back to their Hives."

"What Hives?"

He pointed at something behind her back and she turned around. She did not understand how she had missed it until now, but then she realized that the farmhouse nested in a hollow, and she was now high up on the ledge.

Outlined against the tender colors of the morning sky were cylindrical structures that reminded her of kilns. Made of gray pebbles and chips of stone, they narrowed toward the upper end like rockets. Surrounding them were clouds of black dots. The Hives were too far for her to figure out what the dots were, but they must have been bigger than ordinary bees to be seen. The Hives stretched out into distance; she could not count their bullet-like spires as there were too many.

"Is it where they live? The F…The Kindly Ones?"

"Yes."

"But there are only three of them!"

He shook his head.

"Maybe there were once. But now…they are innumerable. One-in-Many, and Many-in-One."

"Do they rule this Level?"

"Yes. They punish all transgressions by stinging you to death. But only they decide what a transgression is. And people pray to them to punish their neighbors, or family members, or…"

"I get the idea," Cleo said glumly. A community torn apart by mutual suspicions and denunciation, fear and self-righteousness snowballing until nobody is left untouched, the poisonous honey of anger and revenge dripping into the sweetness of their rural existence… There had been many such communities in her own world; echoing Orcus or influenced by it, who knew? And did it even matter?

"They only come out at midday or full moon," he said. "They will come after you for what you have done. Or what they decide you have done."

She had no doubts they would.

"So, I'd better make myself scarce," she said. "Turn around!"

Giorgios did so obediently, and Cleo pulled off her nightgown and dressed in her jeans and hoodie with a sigh of relief. She hesitated, looking at the nightgown. She had accumulated some spare clothes during her ascent, never sure when the next opportunity to run a wash would come around. All her spares were clean now, as laundry was literally what she had done for a living in Dream City. Still, the nightgown was beautiful and handmade…

No! She dropped the nightgown among the vines. There was something rotten about the Fifth Level that set her teeth on edge; she wanted no mementoes of it.

"If you want to go," he said, "you'd better do it now, before my parents find you. They are very angry with you. They believe whatever Yannis tells them."

"That little bastard…" she spat. "I don't know how you put up with having a kid brother like him!"

He smiled crookedly.

"Yannis is the oldest of us," he said. "He was born before me."

"What? How?"

"Do you know what he is?"

"Yes. An antigrafo of Eros. Even though he claims to be Eros himself."

"He is not. But he is the first imprint, so he has a lot of his power."

"How do you know?" she asked suspiciously.

"Because I am also an antigrafo of the son of Aphrodite. But a second impression, a weaker one, rubbed away like a poorly made cast."

She stared at him. Warm brown eyes like hot chocolate shaded by long lashes, eyes in which you could lose yourself if you were not careful, a Cupid's bow mouth, skin like burnished bronze… She flicked her gaze away but not before a wave of warmth spread through her making her knees feel like they were made of melting wax.

"I see," she said weakly, trying to get a hold of herself. "So, how do you two get along?"

"Not well. He thinks that he is a god. I know I am only a man. He thinks our parádeigma made the right choice. I know he damned himself and all of Orcus."

"What choice?"

"To side with the Nine."

"Eros? The god of love? Why?"

He shrugged.

"Jealousy, anger, rage? Who knows? We don't have access to our originals' memories, and the Upheaval happened before I was born. But I know it had something to do with an abduction."

"An abduction?" This was the first time she heard about it.

"You better go," he repeated. "I'm sorry, I wish you could stay longer…"

There was a note in his voice that she understood all too well, but her revulsion from the Fifth Level was stronger than her desire to linger in his company. Fortunately, he did not seem to have Eros' invincible arrows either…

She peered toward the farmhouse, but nothing was stirring there. She needed to skirt it to get where she was going. She started walking down, and he fell in step with her.

"Can you leave this Level?"

He shook his head.

"No. We are bound to our own Level. You may go up only if you receive a Call from one of the Nine who rules higher than where you are."

"Not much freedom here."

"No. This is why I despise my brother. He thinks that this prison is the best of all possible worlds. He craves power."

"Power of his arrows?"

"He does not have the arrows. Our parádeigma has given them to the Erinyes. Did you see their stingers?"

"What the fuck!" Despite her hurry, she stopped, shocked. "Arrows of love in the hands of these…monsters?"

"Love and hate are close together, and so are desire and rage."

He was right, of course, but she felt sick when she thought of the distortions in her own world this combination produced. Fanatical true believers, righteous torturers, mass killers, rapists, and murderers.

"But where is Eros himself?"

"He has become part of the swarm."

Serves him right, she thought.

They stepped onto the track circling the farm, shaded by sweet-smelling fig trees, and a figure stepped from behind one of them, barring their way.

CHAPTER 34

annis grinned at them, white teeth painted pink with the light of dawn as if with blood. His blue eyes were also bloodshot, and his entire body seemed swollen, engorged like a leech's. He was in his Eros form but the beauty that had overwhelmed Cleo earlier was now subtly transformed into something bestial and grotesque. His wings, fluttering jerkily, were flushed with scarlet, and red rash marred his marble-like skin. He was naked, and Cleo thought she could do without the reminder of what Eros' power over human sexuality actually entailed.

"Where are you going, brother?" he asked. "Don't take our guest away. She has not experienced our proper hospitality yet."

Giorgios rolled his eyes.

"Come on, brother," he responded, "you have done enough damage for one night. Calling the Kindly Ones upon our home! Mother and Father will never get over it! And cover yourself up. This is a decent household!"

"That's your problem, brother!" Yannis hissed. "You don't understand our heritage. You don't understand the power we wield. You are just a poor copy, a second-hand imitation. Don't stand in my way!"

Cleo realized it was time to interrupt this sibling rivalry show.

"What do you want from me?" she asked Yannis. "I am Called, you can see it. One of the Nine wants me, and it's not your bee-swarm. I have to go up. Why are you messing up with your Rulers?"

"You don't know who Called you," Yannis responded, "but I do. Trust me, you are better off taking your chances with the Kindly Ones. They are my Rulers, and I obey Them."

He lifted his hand, making a gesture as if beckoning somebody, and Cleo heard a faint buzzing in the distance. Giorgios had said that the Furies only swarmed at the full moon and at noon, but what if he was wrong? She flexed her muscles, ready to sprint up the track, but then Giorgios tackled Yannis, bowling him over.

The two rolled in the dirt, trading blows. Giorgios' body shifted slightly, growing stronger and more supple, sketchy wings fluttering at his back for a second before disappearing. Yannis' wings remained and at first seemed more of a hindrance than help as they dragged in the dirt, one breaking with an audible crack. But then he rallied and slashed his brother's face with one wing, sharp pinions drawing blood. The buzzing was coming closer.

Cleo knew she had to run. But where?

The enigmatic words of the hamadryad popped up in her head.

Near is far, far is near. This is the law of Orcus.

What if the ascent to the next Level was precisely where she had exited into this Level?

It was not certain, but nothing was. All she wanted now was to leave this sickening parody of the Greek countryside behind as fast as she could.

But she could not abandon Giorgios. He was trying to help her. But what could she do? Coming between two brawling guys was not a good idea, even regardless of their semi-divine powers.

As she hesitated, something fell onto her hair from the tangle of vines above. She automatically swept it off and screamed when a huge spider dropped onto the ground at her feet.

The spider shone like a gold coin, its furry legs blurring as it scampered toward the men. It leaped onto Yannis' face, and the antigrafo squealed, letting go of his brother's throat and rolling in the dirt, frantically trying to dislodge the spider that squatted on him, spreading its plate-sized body across his eyes.

Giorgios jumped to his feet, bleeding from numerous lacerations but with no major wound. He grasped Cleo's hand and together they rushed up the track and around the farmhouse. Cleo risked one last glance back. Yannis had shrunk back to his child form, and what she saw was a gigantic spider clinging to a bawling toddler. Had she not known any better, she would have run back to save him.

They stopped when they exited the farm, outside the courtyard with the fountain, which now splashed into an empty basin with no statue.

"Arachne," Giorgios whispered. "She is trying to protect you."

The same Arachne who had taken away her ability to read in Ano Syros? The same Arachne who had almost made her jump out the window?

It made no sense, but then, nothing in Orcus did.

"Have you seen the Spider before?"

"No, but I heard stories. She is fighting the Nine."

Cleo knew she should go, but she lingered. The fact that she knew exactly the source of her procrastination did nothing to diminish the allure of Giorgios' chocolate eyes and dazzling smile.

"Would you go up if you could?" she asked, hoping for a yes.

The smile grew even more dazzling, and then faded.

"I am an antigrafo of Eros, but I am also Giorgios, son of Vassilikos and Sophia. I can't leave my parents and younger siblings."

"I understand," she said. "Well, thank you for..."

The buzzing grew louder.

"You must go," he said, but before she made a move, he pulled her close and his lips met hers.

As she climbed upslope, Cleo could still taste this kiss, and she knew that any time in future she kissed a man, the taste of dark honey, and sweet pomegranate, and dawn-rosy wine would interject between her and her lover. Few people are kissed by the god of love, but those who are, never forget it.

CHAPTER 35

leo made it to the olive grove before the buzzing grew thunderous. But when she glanced back, she saw the swarm blanket half the sky, churning with roiling motion like an insect tornado. Except that the bodies composing the swarm were much larger than insects.

She looked around. The contorted gray trunks squatted in the powdery soil like trolls, their narrow leaves rustling in the breeze. The sun was higher in the sky, and the first wave of heat touched her face. She felt at home among the sounds, smells, and warmth of the Mediterranean, but she knew she had to make it out of this Level as soon as possible. She did not know why Arachne had come to her rescue, but she did not trust the Spider; nor did she think a lone creature would be of any help against the Many-in-One or One-in-Many, whatever the hell the swarm of Furies called itself. Her dream net was gone and, in any case, trying to trap this tornado of rage would be like draining a lake with a teacup.

The problem was, she did not remember which olive tree contained the hamadryad, , so she frantically knocked on the swollen branches and exposed gnarly roots.

A large bee landed on her exposed arm. She swiped it off and saw with a gasp of revulsion that the creature had miniature human hands growing out of its thorax. She picked up a stone and smashed the thing, but more and more were plummeting down from the churning sky, some as big as sparrows and all having some human feature incongruously glued to their insect bodies: splayed feet at the end of skittering legs or grimacing faces instead of a bee's blank-eyed head. And even bigger creatures were beginning to descend, their transparent wings vibrating over skeletal bodies.

She whirled around, her back to a tree, one hand clutching the Eye of Charon. She did not think it would work, but it was the only weapon she had.

The tree opened up behind her back, and she almost tumbled into the dark interior. A bark-covered hand clutched her arm and drew her in, then the trunk closed smoothly.

She expected it to be dark inside the tree, but it was not. A pale greenish radiance streamed from the smooth walls. She was in a vertical hollow, a wooden tube extending up and down much farther than the tree itself. She was clinging to a shelf jutting out from the curving wall, too narrow to be comfortable. She risked one glance down where the glow was swallowed up by the seemingly bottomless drop and pushed herself into the unyielding wall behind her back. The wall did not give but the wooden arm that supported her tightened around her wrist. The hamadryad looked at her with distaste.

"I warned you, maiden," she declared in her oily voice.

From close up, the hamadryad looked like an animated doll – a sort of half-made Pinocchio carved out of the tree core. Below the waist, her body blended with the pale wood and above the waist it was only generically human – cylindrical breasts with no nipples and sticklike arms with no musculature. Her face under the crude furrows meant to represent hair was not capable of many expressions but now it clearly radiated disapproval.

"I know," Cleo said contritely. "I should have listened. I am sorry. But now would you please help me go up? I need to get to the Sixth Level."

"Why do you think it would fare better for you?"

"I don't," Cleo confessed. "But I can't stay here and my Call is as strong as ever, so it means whoever is Calling me is on a higher

Level. All I want to do is to get out of here and return to my own world. And this is the only way."

"Is it really all you want?"

Cleo averted her gaze as if caught on a lie.

She was not sure why she did not want to talk about Cora with the inhabitants of Orcus. Was it because she dreaded hearing that they knew nothing about her twin – or hearing that they knew something?

"I am looking for my sister," she finally said. "She disappeared in the shadow world, in Plato's Cave. I believe she is here."

"Do you believe that whoever is Calling you is also holding your sister hostage?"

"Yes," Cleo said. "I do."

The hamadryad's wooden face turned toward her, and the holes drilled in the wood stared at her with no expression.

"After the Upheaval," the hamadryad said finally, "Orcus has emerged into the light as the pit turned into the mountain. But sometimes light can be worse than darkness. Your world is plunged into chaos because of the Nine Levels and their Rulers' squabbles. But our world mirrors its own shadow, as it falls into greater disarray. And the rot is spreading across the Archipelago. The Weaver is trying to hold the web of stories together, but I don't think she can. Still, I will help you for her sake. I'll show you the way up. But beware of what you find on the Sixth Level. Here in the Hives, trees are your friends, but they may not be in the Plantation."

"I got it," Cleo muttered, "nobody here is friendly for long. Can you tell me more about the Sixth Level?"

The hamadryad shrugged, which produced an alarming clack like the snapping of a twig.

"I cannot leave my tree," she said, "so I have never been to the Plantation, but stories travel up and down our roots and branches. The Sixth Level is a wilderness where a maiden like you can be whisked away, never to be seen again."

This was hardly helpful. But again, there was nothing to do but to go up. She did not believe anything she would find there could be as bad as the rural pastoral infested with swarming Furies.

"How do I go up?" she asked.

The dryad broke off one of her wooden fingers and handed it to Cleo.

"Touch the wall as you are climbing and the tree will give you footholds," she said. "But hurry, for the potency of dead wood dissipates quickly."

Cleo touched the tip of the finger to the wall, and indeed, another ledge bulged out, too narrow and smooth for comfort but enough to pull herself up. The hamadryad withdrew into the wall like a snail into its shell, the break on her hand already budding with a new finger. Before she disappeared, Cleo managed to ask:

"Who is the Ruler of the Sixth Level?"

"We don't say the name of the Mother of Monsters," the hamadryad clicked and was absorbed into the trunk without a trace. Cleo grabbed the ledge and started ascending.

CHAPTER 36

The wood was slick under Cleo's sweaty fingers. She was afraid to look down but looking up only showed the hollow tube telescoping into the distance. The greenish glow waxed and waned at unpredictable intervals, making her dizzy. And what was worse was that each ledge she clung to was absorbed back into the wood the moment she pulled herself up onto the next one. At any given moment, only a treacherously smooth wooden shelf separated her from the sheer drop down that rabbit hole.

I can do it, she whispered to herself, but the truth was she was not sure. She reminded herself she had climbed up the rock ladder from the Third Level to Dream City, but bad as it had been, at least the ladder was stationary and had rope handholds. Here she had the feeling of utter precariousness. What if at some point the hamadryad's finger simply stopped functioning as she had warned it might have? The farther up Cleo went, the more brittle it felt.

She forced herself to fall into the same mindless rhythm that had saved her on the rockface. Don't think, don't feel, don't fear. Touch the wall, pull yourself up, feel the last ledge dissolve under your feet, touch the wall… But while her body, toughened by her stay in

Orcus, labored to keep her alive, her mind churned like a pond of muddy water with a stone tossed in.

The Weaver. Arachne. Why did she help me?

The nymphs and satyrs of the Third Level. They could only speak through an image of the Spider. The Weaver of Stories, the Mistress of Language…

But she took away my languages in Ano Syros.

So I could not read the letter.

The letter written by my friends – or by somebody else?

The letter urging me to climb the Nine Levels and find my sister.

The Spider did not want me to search for Cora?

Why?

Another ledge, another pull up, her muscles screaming in protest. How far did she have to go? The hamadryad either did not know or was unwilling to say.

Cleo touched the slick wood at her chest level with the hamadryad's finger.

Nothing happened.

She stabbed the finger at the wood with barely constrained fury. It snapped in two, like the desiccated twig it had become. The pieces dropped from Cleo's hand and fell down, disappearing into the well of greenish swampy light.

She sat on the ledge, her back to the unyielding wood, her legs dangling into the abyss. So, that was that. There was nothing she could do. It was not a staircase you could run up on, away from pursuit. It was not a closet filled with animated clothes you could push through. It was not a rope ladder or a falling elevator, in which at least you had something tangible to hold on to. This was a wooden tube, as slippery as ice, with no footholds. This tiny ledge was the only thing between her and death, and who knew how long it would hold? She could easily visualize herself becoming drowsy, falling asleep, her body slumping, and then sliding off the slick shelf to plummet into the abyss. She had no doubt she would die when she hit the bottom. Orcus defied many physical laws, not the least in its impossible topography, but she had learned the hard way that it gave you no leeway on dying.

What should she do in the last moments of her life? Pray? She snorted in derision. She had met too many gods and their avatars already to have any piety left – not that she had much to begin with.

She wished she believed in an afterlife – then she could imagine a reunion with Eleni and her sister. But she did not.

My sister is not dead.

It came to her with absolute conviction. And together with it, the determination to stay alive. She owed it to Cora. Twins always stayed together, in life as in death. Even the Dioscuri, with one brother immortal and the other mortal, refused to be parted. If Cora was alive, she would try her damndest to stay alive too.

She turned her head cautiously, trying not to make any unnecessary moves. As opposed to rocks, the olive wood did not have any tiny protrusions or uneven surfaces to keep her anchored. It was as smooth and slippery as ice.

She studied the wall. It took the hamadryad's lifeforce to reshape it. What did she have that could do the same trick?

The answer was obvious. Her lifeforce was in her veins. The sap of a tree, the blood of a human being, they were the same.

All flesh is grass…

The hardest part was getting the bronze knife out of the backpack. When she moved it, her buttocks slid an inch off the shelf, and for a moment her center of gravity shifted, dragging her toward the hypnotically swirling void. She threw herself back and counted heartbeats until she was stable again. Moving in tiny increments of cautiously rationed risk, she undid the clasp. Fortunately, she had placed the knife in an easily accessible side pocket when she had packed, remembering how handy it had come in the elevator.

Its bronze edge was dull with a patina. It might have been blood, animal or human. The huntresses of Hekate did not seem to make distinctions when it came to their prey.

Cleo slashed the knife across the back of her hand.

It took several tries – the knife was not very sharp – but finally a crimson line appeared, the bright pain pushing the ache of her limbs and the fear in her mind into the background. Neither Cleo nor Cora had ever self-harmed as teenagers, but now she understood the appeal: her world had narrowed down to the burst of pain, everything else momentarily forgotten.

She pressed her bleeding hand to the olive-wood wall. She did not need to say anything; the living tree knew what she wanted, what she needed.

The next couple of heartbeats marked the longest time in Cleo's life.

The ledge was extruded with a creaking, jerky unwillingness – very different from the smoothness with which it obeyed the dryad's finger – but it was extruded, lopsided and narrow, yet a lifeline.

She pulled herself up, more blood dripping from the cut, feeding the tree that swayed and shuddered. Where the blood drops fell, misshapen burls and horned twigs sprang out, marking her ascent.

But she did not look back. Press the hand to the wall, pull yourself up, press the hand, feed the tree… As long as there was blood in her veins, she would go up.

When her head emerged into daylight, she was not even aware of it, so caught was she in the rhythm of her ascent. With her dripping hand up, she sought the wall to press but encountered only air.

Her eyes blinked in the sudden brightness. It was green too, but it was the shadowy green of daylight filtered through leaves, not the source-less swampy light of the tree's interior.

She pushed up and dragged herself out of the hole in the enormous knobby trunk, flopping onto a branch so wide she could lie on it as if it were a bed.

She had made it onto the Sixth Level.

LEVEL SIX The Plantations

For a long time, Cleo just laid there, luxuriating in her prone position, in the fact that her battered body was safely supported by a sturdy surface, and in the warm open air that caressed her face. She was roused by the throbbing in her cut hand, which still bled. She needed to clean and bandage it, she realized. Orcus probably did not have antibiotics, even though Ano Syros and Dream City had small pharmacies, which, to her regret now, she had neglected to explore. She should have stocked up better before her ascent! But if the topography of Orcus really corresponded to her mental map, with each Zone divided into three Levels, one urban, one suburban or rural, and one wild, the next Level up might be more civilized. Whether this was a good thing remained to be seen.

But first she had to go through the Sixth Level, so she sat up, groaning, and took stock of her surroundings.

In one sense, she had been right: she was in the forest. But this forest was nothing like what she had expected.

In the Forest of Masks, the trees were ordinary European kinds — ash, poplar, pine, horse chestnut, and spruce. In the Hives, the landscape was Southern Mediterranean, with cypresses, figs, and olives. But this place looked like a rainforest, or maybe some CGI backdrop for a fantasy movie.

The trees were enormous, tall and rotund, with paunchy trunks. She was perched on one easily thirty feet in diameter, and its top disappeared into the canopy far above her, formed by similar giants, their splayed limbs tangled in a profusion of vines and creepers. Its ashen bark was deeply fissured and disfigured with pendulous burls and swollen protrusions. The leaves were tiny, pointed, and almost gray. It looked like a monstrous olive tree affected with elephantiasis. Other trees around her also seemed diseased or deformed in some way. They were widely spaced, but the canopy filtered the sunshine, plunging the forest into twilight. Looking down the sheer drop of the trunk, she could see very little undergrowth. The soil was barren, littered with deadfall.

Well, as interesting as the local flora was, first things first: she took out her water bottle, washed out the cut, and bandaged her hand the best she could with a strip torn off her spare clean t-shirt. Then she considered how to get down.

The horizontal branch she was sitting on was very broad at its base but quickly narrowed down to a clutch of small twigs and leathery leaves. Below it, the trunk bulged out in swellings and lumps that might offer a decent purchase for hands and feet, but she was sick of climbing. Still, what cannot be cured must be endured, as Eleni often said. Cleo sighed and got ready to start, when she saw a large vine hanging off an upper branch and almost touching the ground.

She inspected the vine, not sure whether it was some sort of parasite or an air root. The thing was fleshy but tough, the thickness of her wrist, and covered with the dull, reddish fuzz that blended with the somber palette of the forest. She gave it a couple of experimental tugs, but the vine remained firmly attached, coiling down like a sleepy python. Grasping the living rope and locking it with her feet, she swung off the branch and lowered herself, hand over hand, down to the forest floor. The vine was warm and sticky, and she was relieved to find herself on the firm ground.

Her hand was bleeding again. She grimaced, but then realized it was both her hands that were stained red. Not blood, then, but the vine's sap, the same color as blood and with the same metallic stench. Putting it out of her mind, she took stock of her surroundings.

The trees were grotesque. She had never been to the tropics – the planned trip to Thailand had been scuttled in favor of Greece, and she briefly wondered whether she would be climbing some mountain with demons and bodhisattvas had she gone there instead. But even her scant knowledge of tropical rainforests gleaned from nature documentaries told her this forest was weird. Each enormous trunk was covered with bumps and tumors. The bark was peeling off in curling strips like dead skin. The scant foliage was of strange colors and textures: yellow and beige, or bluish and teal; leathery, desiccated, or drooping. It was warm and humid, and the air smelled of burnt spices and squashed bugs.

The trees formed long shadowy aisles. Because there was almost no undergrowth, going was easy. She could walk in any direction she wanted. The problem was, she had no idea where to go. She looked up, but even if the peak of Orcus were visible from this Level, she would not be able to see it through the trees. Nor could she see the sun. She chose a direction at random and started walking.

Soon enough, the monotony of the forest became almost unbearable. No flowers, no grass, just contorted bulbous trunks squatting in the bare dirt like gigantic gray toads, their scaly limbs obscuring the distant sky. Swollen vines dangled in the dead air like hairy serpents. And worst of all was the total silence, with no birdsong, insect buzz, or rustle of branches. The air was heavy and still. she was beginning to miss the cicada sough of the Fifth Level or even the urban bustle of Dream City. Shouldn't a forest have some life in it?

Finally, she did hear something: a faint plopping sound like drops falling out of a faulty tap. The sound was coming from behind a tree whose bloated trunk was covered in overlapping triangular scales like shark teeth. She poked her head around it to get a better look.

A large vine was swaying in the air even though there was no wind. The vine was injured: there was a gash in its stem, and it was bleeding. Fat scarlet drops fell onto the dusty ground, making a circle of sodden soil beneath. The sap did not flow freely but dripped down, viscous and oily.

She suddenly felt somebody's gaze and quickly turned around. Nobody was there; the shadowy aisles were as hushed as an abandoned church. She looked back at the bleeding vine and traced it up to where it emerged from a branch. It was not a parasite as she had thought, but rather a part of the tree itself. It emerged from a tumorous burl which at first looked as shapeless as any other deformity on these diseased giants. But as she studied it, she realized the burl bore a strong resemblance to a human head, albeit a human head melted and twisted. Beneath the lump of a nose, a crevice crudely imitated a mouth, and from this crevice, the vine dangled out like a clownish tongue.

The wood-head seemed to stare at her with two empty holes.

She quickly darted behind another tree, but now her eyes were opened, and she could see that all the hairy vines were attached to the trees via burls or swellings, each with a passing resemblance to a human head. The trees had faces that stuck their snakelike tongues at her.

She remembered the hamadryad, but these wooden faces looked inanimate. In fact, they seem to phase in and out of pareidolia. Perhaps she was just seeing things, her brain, overflowing with the grotesqueries of Orcus, conjuring visions.

In any case, the trees had done nothing to her. The vines, disgusting as they were, seemed harmless. She hoisted her backpack higher and walked on.

It occurred to her that she had become accustomed to monsters. Maybe too much so.

CHAPTER 38

head of her, the forest came to an end. Daylight was streaming through the gaps between the trunks.

She emerged into a strange landscape unlike anything she had ever seen. It was a dell dominated by coral-like rock formations thrusting out of the matted white grass. Swollen trees did not disappear completely, but they were smaller now and widely scattered among the rocks. The sky was cloudy and gray, and the setting sun left watery streaks of muted color on the horizon. The rocks were fretted, holed, and spiky, and looked like they belonged underwater.

She was alone, and just like the forest, the rocky dell was silent: no bird calls, insect buzz, or sounds of human habitation.

All the previous Levels had been populated. Even the wilderness of the Forest of Masks was filled with nymph huntresses and satyrs. Her encounters with inhabitants of Orcus often made her wish for solitude, but now she felt at a loss. She needed a guide to point her to the way to the next Level, not to mention food and shelter.

The sun dipped below the horizon, and the rocky clearing swarmed with twilight, darkness rising from the ground like stagnant water. She did not fancy stumbling around the rocks and breaking a leg.

She decided to camp right there. It was warm; in fact, as the sun set, the air grew even stickier with sauna-like humidity. She would not need a fire, and her backpack had a rolled-up pallet that could serve as a makeshift sleeping bag. She had water, and the flatbread and olives Giorgios had given her. She chose a rock that leaned out a bit, creating a shallow cave, and unrolled her pallet.

It was almost totally dark now, and she studied the indigo sky, looking for the moon. Last night on the Fifth Level, the moon was full, but now it was missing completely. Was it only last night? Cleo was becoming convinced that time moved at different speeds at different Levels, lurching ahead or slowing down.

Zeus imprisoned Cronos, his father, god of time. And now Zeus is dead, and probably Cronos too.

Was this why time seemed so broken in the human world? Cleo remembered all too well the days doled out in increments of Zoom calls, clashing deadlines, accumulating emails, and calendar alerts. She had embraced the corporate lifestyle because it helped her to differentiate herself from her sister. Now she wondered how she had survived the infinitely regimented, and yet somehow shapeless, temporality of the office.

Time in Orcus was equally shapeless, but space was not. The Nine Levels, each with its character and its Ruler. Not that Cleo had figured out the complex web of power, competition, and alliance among the Nine, but at least, she knew where she had to go – up.

The sky was thickly sown with stars. She did not know many constellations – only what Eleni had shown them when the sisters were kids, walking with their grandmother in the velvety fragrant night of the Greek islands. But no matter how she searched for the Hunter and the Twins, the sky remained alien. Giving up, she stretched out on the pallet to try to get some sleep – and saw more stars on the ground.

She sat up. The dark barrier of the forest was sparkling with lights. At first, she thought these were fireflies, but they were too bright and too colorful. Blue, emerald, pink, and violet, they blazed brighter with every passing second. Each giant tree was decked out in wreathes, garlands, and clusters of shiny magic.

Cleo watched, spellbound. There was something innocent and fairy-tale-like about the lights that reminded her of corny but endearing Christmas displays. Not all of them were immobile. Swift streamlets of green and blue sparks ran up tree-trunks into the canopy where they bloomed into explosions of color. An occasional burst of red or orange illuminated an entire tree, and then fell apart into spheres of luminescence hanging off the boughs like enchanted fruit. The hairy vines glowed with dim scarlet. Even the face-like burls where the vines emerged were lit up like carnival masks. Lilac and yellow gleams danced around them.

In her ascent of Orcus, she had seen sublime beauty and soul-scorching ugliness. She had faced down monsters and communed with avatars of gods. But she had never seen anything so pretty.

She got up and walked toward the trees, and felt as if the innocent charm of the illuminated forest was washing off the accumulated levels of grime Orcus had deposited on her mind. The mountain of dead gods finally offered her something to enjoy.

She stopped some distance away from the tree line, trying to figure out what the lights were. They did not seem to be glowing insects or luminescent plants. They were incorporeal, flitting in and out of darkness, pausing in thin air or attaching themselves to the trees.

She was about to cross the boundary of the forest, just to see the lights better. And then she stopped.

She hated herself. Couldn't she just succumb to an innocent impulse? Just for once – not thinking about consequences, not weighing pros and cons, not analyzing or trying to understand? Just…doing something because she felt like doing it?

You are such a stickler, Cle! Such a dried-up, calculating, soulless corporate lackey! Take your "success" and shove it! I want something better from life. Something different!

Cora's voice.

Cleo took another step toward the sparkling forest. And stopped again.

She was who she was: a cautious, analytical, plan-ahead Cleo. She was not Cora.

The forest sparkled and beckoned her in. Lured her in.

She was in Orcus, the pit that became the mountain. She did not know who the Ruler of the Sixth Level was.

The hamadryad mentioned "the Mother of Monsters", but that could have been half of the female chthonic deities. And there were also nymphs, oceanids, demons, semi-goddesses, and a whole host of other supernatural creatures. Ancient Greeks were very prolific in inventing scary creatures and providing them with extended families.

She peered into the glittering depth and saw a quick movement. Something rustled. A swaying bush? But there was no wind. A scuttling animal? But she had seen no life in the forest.

She could not make it out. The flashing and blinking of the lights broke up her field of vision.

She turned her back on the light show and went to pick up her backpack, then find another place to bed down for the night.

Only her backpack was no longer there.

The pallet was still in the lee of the rock, but the backpack with everything she had scavenged on the lower Levels, everything that had been keeping her alive, was gone. Outraged by this latest misfortune, she sprinted toward the rock formations. Whoever stole the backpack could not have gone far.

And indeed, it had not. She saw a dark silhouette, faintly illuminated against the bleached grass, dragging her backpack away. It had to drag it because the thief was small, barely the size of a ten-year-old. But it was no child. Its body was warped and bent, its arms disproportionately long, and its large mophead with dreadlocks sticking out looked like the thief was wearing a shaggy Halloween wig.

"No, you don't!" she yelled and rushed toward the thief, who scuttled away. But fast as it was, Cleo's longer legs gave her an advantage and she careened into it, sweeping the creature off its feet and grasping the strap of the backpack. The thief did not want to give up, and so the two engaged in a game of tug, with Cleo dragging the backpack, while the thief clung to it like a limpet. She could see it better now, which still gave her no clue to what kind of entity it was. It looked like a monkey with the head of a madman. Its body was covered in black fur, and its long arms and short legs had prehensile toes. But its face was human, albeit distorted by a grimace of rage, teeth bared, and eyes rolled up. The "dreadlocks" were in fact twitching hairy tentacles. They writhed as the creature fought, growling and spitting.

Finally, she delivered a swift kick to the creature's human-like genitalia. It squealed, let go of the backpack, and skittered away into the maze of rocky formations. Flushed with adrenaline, Cleo carried her possession back to her makeshift camp. She found another rock, moved her pallet, wrapped the straps of the backpack around her arm, and drifted off to sleep. Just before she fell into dreams, she realized that the tentacles on the thief's head were indistinguishable from the vines in the forest.

CHAPTER 39

leo was dutifully chewing a stale flatbread and drinking tepid water from a bottle. She was looking forward to the next Level, which according to the topography of Orcus should be urban. No matter which of the Nine ruled it or what torments they inflicted on their subjects, she would face it gladly as long as she could have a cup of coffee and a hot shower. She was not a nature person.

Cora had been, though. She waxed lyrical about communing with nature and doing some dubious pagan rituals among standing stones with her equally dubious friends. Had it been easier for her to navigate the Nine Levels or harder?

Cleo went through the mental map of Orcus in her head. Three Zones, nine Levels. Each Zone had one urban, one rural, and one wild Level. If Cora was on the Final Level, who was its Ruler? And why did they want Cora, and now Cleo?

If Cora had ascended all Nine Levels, why hadn't she left a trail for her sister to follow? Surely she could have scattered some breadcrumbs for her twin!

But only if she knew that Cleo would go after her, and judging by their last conversation, this was hardly a foregone conclusion.

There must be something else…something better!

Sure, if you are willing to work for it!

Work? Getting stuck on the corporate treadmill?

Having a job is nothing to sneer at, Cora!

While the world is falling apart?

It's not falling apart.

Really? Just look around!

Okay, so what do you want? Blow it all up?

Yes! If this is what it takes!

Maybe if she really had ascended Orcus, Cora would have changed her opinion by now. Each Level Cleo had seen so far looked like a malignant Petri dish where the formerly downtrodden chthonic rebels invented new torments for humanity. Plato's Cave would be much better off if it could cut its ties with the worlds of essences where gods and daemons perpetually messed with human reality. Cleo shuddered, thinking of the mysterious Archipelago, each island shaped by some mythology's heaven and hell.

But if these worlds bled into reality, perhaps the influence went both ways. Maybe Plato was wrong in imagining that shadows passively reflected objects. Maybe shadows and objects were the same, shaping and feeding off each other.

Cleo got to her feet and stretched the kinks out of her muscles. The forest loomed before her, as ugly and forbidding as it had been yesterday, the pretty lights gone. The sky was white with haze, and all she could see were bulbous spiky trunks and swaying vines like hairy snakes.

Where were all the people? Each Level she had traversed so far had been populated. Without anybody to ask for directions, how would she find her way up? The vine-headed creature who had tried to steal her backpack did not seem a likely guide.

She decided to explore – not that she had any other choice.

Beyond the dell, the ground rose in a series of folds and dips. The swollen trees were still around but they had dwindled to dwarfish sizes compared to their gigantic counterparts in the forest. Most were hardly taller than Cleo herself. The ground was covered by the dry bleached grass. The sky was mantled with yellow-white clouds, as sullen as everything else on the Sixth Level. The landscape looked sickly, like a formerly robust man suffering from a chronic wasting disease. A strange stench hung in the air: an ancient, forgotten rot that had sedimented into something mineral.

She hated it. Of all the Levels she had ascended so far, the Sixth Level seemed to express a kind of queasy malevolence that set her teeth on edge. She really did not want to meet its Ruler, but she was afraid she would have to do it, as there seemed to be no other inhabitants around. Had they all been killed? Or were they hiding somewhere, so scared and downtrodden that they did not stir out of their hiding places during the daytime?

She crested a ridge and saw yet another hollow, but this one did not have rocks. Instead, at its center lay what looked like a large rosette of thick, fleshy stems radiating from a shaggy mass. The stems were the same as the vines in the forest, covered with dull scarlet fuzz and ending in rounded protrusions. The central mass…it looked like a tangle of dirty hair, a dust bunny that you find under the bed and throw into the bin with a grimace of distaste – except, it was as big as a truck wheel.

She decided to walk around this new specimen of the disgusting local vegetation. She skirted the lip of the hollow when the earth moved.

She was thrown off her feet, scrambling desperately, and trying to hold onto the crumbling slope. Dry white grass disintegrated under her fingers, desiccated roots pulling out. She was shaken and tossed around like a piece of wood in the tide, sand and soil thrown into her face. Her backpack slid off her shoulders, and she grabbed desperately for it, missed, and saw it roll away. If this was an earthquake, it was a peculiarly silent one; no screech of tortured rocks, no crash of broken trees. Instead, there was an enormous and smooth movement close by, something growing, towering into the lifeless air above her…

Cleo scrambled to all fours and craned her head up, watching the giant emerge from its earthy cradle.

It was a man, or a manlike thing, crude and unfinished. Its gnarly body was randomly peppered with tufts of black fur but most of the skin was bare and flushed with dark blood. Its limbs were broad and splayed; a long, bifurcated penis swung between the meaty thighs. But its head was the most striking thing about it: disproportionately large and cauldron-like, it was crowned by a nest of writhing hairy vines swishing around its maddened face like living dreadlocks. A tangle of coarse filthy hair rose like a coxcomb above it. The rosette Cleo had seen was actually the top of the giant's head sticking out from the soil where it had been buried.

It was huge, at least twelve feet tall, but in proportions and general look it resembled the creature that had tried to steal Cleo's backpack.

She kept still, hoping the giant would disregard her, but no matter how she squeezed into the crumbling slope, there was nowhere to hide. The hole where the giant had been buried yawned open below her, her backpack dangling on its edge.

The giant opened its huge mouth but what came out was not the King King-like roar she expected. Instead, a swarm of lights floated out: pink, blue, and yellow, like multicolored fireflies, their sugary prettiness in stark contrast to the creature from whose stinking maw they emerged. The giant breathed out more lights that swirled around it and floated in the direction of the forest. Then it leaned over Cleo, scooped her up, and, indifferent to her struggles, carried her away.

CHAPTER 40

he stink of the giant's body was overwhelming. The same metallic smell of old blood and old rot that hung over the forest was concentrated into a poisonous emanation, making Cleo struggle for every breath. Its thick fingers dug into her ribs with such force she was afraid they would snap. She stopped struggling and just hung loose in the creature's hands. She was convinced that it was non-sentient, so it would be as useless to plead or negotiate with it as it would be with a pitcher plant.

But what was it going to do with her? Was she dinner or were its plans even worse? She remembered the cyclops in Ano Syros. The Eye of Charon lay against her chest, but she could not reach it.

Finally, the giant stopped and unceremoniously dropped her. Fortunately, the ground was covered with dry vegetation, but she had the wind knocked out of her. Her eyes stung from the metallic stench hanging in the air like a cloud of tear gas. She finally blinked her eyesight back – and almost wished she had not.

She rose to her feet, eyeing the presence that towered above her into the dull lifeless air like the Colossus of Rhodes, one of the Seven Wonders of antiquity. The presence before her was one of the Nine Rulers of the tainted remnant of antiquity's dreams.

It was so huge that the giant who had brought Cleo before it looked no bigger than a toddler in the shadow of the massive swollen body. And it probably was a toddler. Because the body was female and maternal. The way it was positioned left no doubt about it.

It sat on the ground. Its – her – legs were splayed, and its vagina was displayed with no embarrassment, proudly, as the gateway of life and death. But as opposed to the human anatomy, the vagina was horizontal: an enormous mouth with slack gray lips between the hairy thighs, each twice the thickness of Cleo's entire body. The trunk was sagging and covered in so many tumors, swellings, and protrusions that the pendulous breasts were almost lost among the cancerous display. The skin was thick, fissured, and bark-like. This, then, was the model for the trees in the forest: their diseased trunks imitating this monstrous parody of motherhood, or maybe the other way around. The creature's quill-covered legs were like giant specimens of the forest vines, and so were her fuzzy arms, dangling from the gargantuan shoulders with no joints and no hands.

Cleo's gaze traveled upward, to the face, and stopped there, snagged by its beauty.

The titanic visage stared down at her with a sort of blank benevolence. It was free of the lumps of the body, smooth and glabrous. Its features had the timeless perfection of classic Greek statues: straight nose and chiseled lips, rounded cheeks, large eyes under the low wide forehead. The eyes were sky-blue, the only spot of color in the face that was otherwise uniformly grayish beige, even the lips without a hint of red. The hair – not vines or snakes – was plaited in the classic style, with a knot in the back, and it was the same dull scarlet as the fuzz on the vines that served as the creature's limbs. A monstrous maternal body flaunting its deformity and crowned with the head of a goddess.

"Mother of Monsters!" Cleo whispered. "Echidna!"

She remembered Eleni's soft voice as she had read the description of the "half-nymph, half-snake", the mother of too many mismatched monsters to count, a whole bestiary of creatures, from a many-headed Hydra to a lion to a sow…and the twins dissolving in laughter as Cora scribbled a crude cartoon of a fat woman cradling a piglet…and Eleni shaking her head disapprovingly, slamming the book shut…

I should have listened.

All she could remember was that Echidna was a mate of Typhon, another anarchic giant, and the two bred an endless procession of strange offspring with no regard for distinction of species. Unlike Nyx or Hekate, she was not a goddess; unlike Medusa, she was not a deified human being. Neither a demon nor a titan, she was…chaos.

Cleo backed off, the old-blood reek suffocating her, her feet tangling in the tough desiccated grass. Behind Echidna loomed a rocky hill with the dark opening of a large cave. Nothing grew on the old, weathered rocks. The Mother of Monsters sucked all vitality out of nature, leaving behind the hopelessness of sickness and decay.

There was no negotiating with this blank face. Cleo did not believe Echidna even understood human language. She turned around to flee, and a backhanded blow sent her sprawling. The giant who had brought her in stood guard behind her. And even if she could somehow outrun him, Cleo realized she had no hope of escape; rising out of the dry soil behind him were more like him: Echidna's children, all sizes and shapes, from a scuttling creature like the one who had tried to steal her backpack to clod-like misshapen barrels with squat heads and undefined limbs. And there were some who did not bear even a caricatured resemblance to humanity. She saw a pink naked four-legged creature with the face of a shaved bulldog, and another one with a curving scorpion's tail. But they all had some element that seemed borrowed from the vines in the forest. Hairy tentacles on the giant's head, pliant stems instead of bony legs carrying animal bodies, a reddish fuzz on the scorpion's tail. They started up the hillside toward her, a climbing, slithering flood of monsters, eerily silent, as their mother watched with the unvarying benevolence in her empty beautiful face. Cleo knew she was going to die.

She pulled out the Eye of Charon and brandished it before Echidna. It had an impact, but not the one she hoped for. The Mother of Monsters pulled back, her loveliness suddenly disfigured by a grimace of rage as her mouth opened in a silent scream. Above the gaping hole of the mouth, her blue eyes still stared on with unwavering serenity, and the contrast between the two was horrifying. The vegetable snakes of her boneless legs contracted and came together, momentarily hiding the obscene mouth between them. She fell upon her slack belly and advanced toward Cleo, crawling, the vines of her limbs slithering upon the ground. Cleo, caught between Echidna and her offspring, had no way out. Even the bronze knife, pitiful as it was against the tide of monsters, had been left behind in her lost backpack.

If Cora is still alive, one of us will live…

No! Cleo was not just one half of a pair of twins. She was a person in her own right. She did not want to die like this, torn apart by mindless archaic creatures out of the dawn of humanity!

She turned around, looking for a gap between the advancing monsters, still clutching the Eye of Charon and holding it up like a talisman. It did cause the things to pause. The scorpion-tailed creature backed off, its multiple legs skittering. It had human eyes but otherwise no face to speak of, just a bunch of quivering mouthparts. The four-legged thing scuttled sideways, its stemlike legs undulating with the liquid grace of an octopus' tentacles. But the giant who had brought Cleo to Echidna's cave seemed unaffected. It strode forth, the vines on its head rearing.

She looked up, searching for the outline of Orcus' cone against the dismal sky. It felt frustratingly sad to die without knowing who had Called her, and without seeing the goal she had been ascending toward for what seemed like a lifetime.

The cloud-laden sky was empty. No, wait…

A movement there, a swirl of beating wings, a darkness of flocking birds. A murder of ravens.

In this silent world, their cawing was as startling as orchestral music. They descended upon Echidna, tangling in her carefully coiffed hair, pecking at her plant-like flesh. Against her enormous bulk they looked as small as flies on a human being, but flies can madden an angry bully into retreat. Echidna's vegetable tentacles flailed madly as she tried to shake the ravens off, her mouth gaping wider and wider, but all in the same unnatural silence. Echidna had been born before the world knew sound.

Her offspring paused, uncertain of what to do, but Cleo was not about to wait. Sliding on the steep slope, her legs whipped by dry grass, her lungs burned by the dead air, she ran toward the forest.

She hid among the bulbous trunks. Their melted shapes disgusted her and so did the ubiquitous hairy vines dangling all around her. But in the forest they were quiescent, and that was all Cleo wanted.

She still could not figure out the relation between Echidna, her monstrous offspring, and the trees, but right now she had more urgent concerns. Number one was finding the way up. Whatever waited on the next Level – no, the next Zone, since she would be crossing into Tartarus – could not be worse than Echidna's domain.

No, Cleo realized. It was not right. Number one priority was retrieving her backpack.

Maybe she should let it be. She had her clothes. She had the Eye of Charon. The next Level should be urban. She could get a job, the way she had done in Ano Syros and Dream City, and replenish her supplies.

But she could not do it. In the nightmare of unknowing and uncertainty that her ascent had become, her backpack was the one thing she could rely on. It was her only friend. Containing the clothes that she had brought over from Plato's Cave, it was her only link with her own world. She had her knife, which she had retrieved from the huntresses, serving as the proof that she could not only survive but fight back. She had the coins, one of which could be her ticket back home. No, she would not abandon her possessions to a swarm of dumb monsters!

She tried to remember where the giant had emerged from the ground and picked her up. Cleo had an excellent sense of spatial orientation. Actually, it was not that hard to find your way around. Apart from the forest, the Sixth Level's terrain was a collection of ridges, small valleys, dells, and hills, all covered with the same dead-white grass and studded with eroded rocks and boulders. If Echidna was a daimon of fertility, she was not doing a very good job.

Or maybe she was. Echidna was the Mother of Monsters, a diseased, deformed spirit of rot and decay that was the obverse side of growth and flourishing. The chthonic deities who had taken over Orcus were not the opposite of the supposed gods of light. They were their complements.

She crept back to the fringe of the forest, listening. The silence of the Sixth Level had one advantage: any unusual sound carried far. She could not hear the cawing of ravens, so they must have left. Did it mean Echidna was now free to send more of her creatures after Cleo?

But remembering the blankness of that beautiful face and the vegetable bodies of her offspring, Cleo became convinced that they were truly mindless. The giant had picked her up because she happened to be there. Echidna had intended to eat her because she was in the creature's field of vision. By now Echidna would have forgotten all about her, while the creatures would revert back to the instinctive tropisms of their kind. If she were careful, she could go back and find her possessions.

Of course, Cleo could have been wrong. Echidna could have been sentient. But the fact that the ravens had attacked her with seeming impunity, despite infringing upon her domain, seemed to prove otherwise. There was no requirement for gods to be smart; only to be powerful.

She decided to wait till dusk. The light display of the forest would provide enough illumination for her to find the place where her backpack had been left behind, while she would not feel so exposed. She leaned against a rough bole, closed her eyes, and dozed off despite her best intentions, as her adrenaline burned out, filling her body with fatigue.

You are the stars… Twins always stand by each other… The Dioscuri, one mortal, one immortal…always together…

Find your sister.

Stand up to your mother.

Cleo woke up with a start. Nothing stirred in the forest. The dull gray sky in the gaps in the canopy was getting darker, fading into the color of granite, and the first sparks of color were lighting up among the tangled vines.

Remnants of the dream were dissolving, draining down into the inaccessible groundwaters of her mind, but wasn't there something about her mother?

Cleo missed her grandmother fiercely but seldom thought about her mother. Now she considered, for the first time, what Daphne must be going through. Her second daughter was missing, a year and a half after Cora's disappearance. She must be frightened and upset. Grieving? Yes. No matter how angry she was with her mother, Cleo had to be honest with herself. Daphne had loved her daughters as much as she was capable of loving anybody. Even shallow and self-centered people have feelings.

Stand up to your mother.

She did, a number of times, the last time when Cora had disappeared, and Daphne had done the bare minimum of searching for her. But Daphne was not in Orcus, so what was that all about?

She put it out of her mind, deciding that if Hypnos/Thanatos had any influence on the Sixth Level, it would be better to pay as little attention to her dreams as possible. Getting up, she stretched, trying to get rid of the needles and pins in her battered limbs.

She crossed the tree line and aimed for the hollow where the giant had hatched.

CHAPTER 41

ehind her, the forest glowed with cheerful colors, lights blooming in the canopy and running in blinking lines up and down the trunks. The illumination was fitful and confusing, but enough to show her the way.

Here was the hollow with the gaping hole in the middle where the giant had clambered out from. Some dry soil was still trickling into the hole, but the sliding had subsided. Cleo could not see her backpack anywhere, though.

She crawled to the edge of the hole. It was too dark to see the bottom. Lying on the edge, she reached down, groping in the murk.

Something gripped her wrist and pulled her down.

She yelped as she went headfirst over the edge, but fortunately she landed on the churned soil, cushioning her fall. Whatever had dragged her inside suddenly released her, so she was able to stand up. The hole was about fifteen feet deep, and the jagged opening was far above her head, barely visible as the sky clotted into the night. But the darkness below was not absolute. In fact, she realized she could see quite well as strings of lights blinked on around her.

The crumbling walls were festooned with creepers and vines. They were not quite the same as the ones in the forest: slenderer and bare, with no hairs or fuzz. Instead, they bore rows of gaily twinkling lights, yellow, pink, violet, and green.

She looked around and saw that in one place the vines continued into the wall, curving around the jagged edge of an opening. It was a tunnel, leading away from the hole she had fallen into like Alice following the White Rabbit. The Christmas garlands of the vines snaked into the deeper darkness.

What had pulled her down? She saw a coiled vine with parallel rows of bright pink dots on the ground. She prodded it with her foot, and the vine struck blindly like a released spring, trying to wrap itself around her ankle. She stepped away, and the vine subsided. Tropism. A mute vegetable groping; an instinctive reaction to stimuli. She kicked it away and peered into the tunnel. It was fairly well lit by the luminescent vines, but a couple of feet in it made a sharp turn, and she could not see where it led.

She considered her options. It was madness to squeeze deeper into the underworld of the Sixth Level when all she wanted was to get above it, but would she be able to get out of this hole? She could try to climb up using the vines for support, but what if they immobilized her instead? Would she just be hanging there, easy prey for Echidna's children?

And she needed her backpack. She was hungry and thirsty, and the mental image of her water bottle and the provisions from the Fifth Level hovered before her like a lodestar. She realized she was getting obsessed, but she did not care. Maybe it was a good idea to be mad in a mad world. She checked the tunnel; she was not (yet) crazy enough to risk being buried alive if the loose earth suddenly subsided, but the ceiling and the walls were actually rock. It was as if the hole of the giant's hatching had broken an access into a preexisting underground tunnel or perhaps a system of tunnels. She decided she was safer venturing deeper than staying where she was, so she squeezed through the opening.

The ceiling of the tunnel was low at first, brushing the top of her head, but it rose after the first turn. The tunnel went on beyond, with the same tangle of luminescent vines on the walls and the lights getting brighter. The lights were not glowing berries or fruit; they seemed embedded in the woody substance of the plants, flowing in long swarms or stuck in stationary constellations.

The tunnel did not branch, though it zigzagged multiple times. She consoled herself with the thought that retracing her steps would be easy if she needed to. She did not think she would, though; the tunnel had to lead somewhere.

And it did. She stopped short when she saw her destination.

In front of her, the tunnel widened and opened up into a rocky cavern, which continued on the opposite side, deeper into the gloom, but she was too shocked by what she saw in the cavern to pay much attention.

The vines grew through the cavern in luxuriant clumps and snarls, crisscrossing the space in webs of light. And caught in these webs were people.

They hung immobile, dark bodies against the starry background, like desiccated insects in a spiderweb. But occasionally one of them twitched or moaned. The bodies were alive.

She crept closer to one of them. It was a man, skeletally thin, his face fallen in like that of a famine victim. He had some rags on, but they were so tattered that she could not tell whether they were modern clothing or something archaic. Sharp ends of vine shoots poked from his eyes and mouth. And running away from him through the cat's cradle of vines keeping him suspended were streams of pale-yellow lights.

She examined other bodies, trying not to look too closely at the smaller ones. Each one generated differently colored lights, which were draining into the vegetable net growing through the cavern and undoubtedly continuing to the surface, eventually reaching the forest. These pitiful, barely alive bodies were the source of the pretty display that had cheered Cleo on her first night in this monster-infested wilderness. And considering that Echidna and her offspring seemed to be half-vegetable creatures of the vines, the drained people must have been the source of their vitality as well.

Cleo's lips thinned. She had wondered where the human inhabitants of the Sixth Level were. Well, she wondered no more. Here they were, batteries for their glowing trees, compost for their mindless Ruler.

How bad could it become? She had thought the Fifth Level was the worst, with its buzzing swarms of self-righteous Furies. And before that, she had believed nothing could be as bad as Dream City, where people were punished for dreaming. And before that…

Orcus was hell. Just because it was not a Christian hell did not make it any better. And perhaps there was another mountain where people were being tortured by Satan and his minions. Scary stories and dark fairy tales, punitive mythologies and oppressive religions, they were all real in the Platonic world of essences. The Archipelago of Fear. She had it backwards. It was not that Greek mythology suddenly came back to life; it was that it had never died. Every time a story of Zeus and the Olympians was told and retold, Orcus grew stronger, until it could reach back into the shadow world whose shadow it was and rearrange it to the satisfaction of its Rulers. A feedback loop of torment.

But she would go on. She would ascend Orcus. She would reach the Final Level. And there she would confront whoever was on top of this pyramid of pain and demand accountability. She did not know where this resolution came from. She only knew she would do it – or die trying.

She scanned the beautiful underground garden with its flowers of light and fruit of corpses. Among them, she saw something small. For a nauseating moment, she thought it was a baby.

It was her backpack.

She dropped onto the ground and crawled under the vines. The metallic stench of old blood burned her sinuses. Above her, the vines leisurely contracted in a peristaltic motion.

She grabbed her backpack, tugging it away from the springy vegetable coil, and scooted back. And then she ran.

CHAPTER 42

eyond the cavern of living corpses, the tunnel went on as before, but Cleo noticed that the vines lining its walls were getting bigger and woodier. Some of them were now as thick as her thighs, and though they still glittered with fairy lights, they seemed dimmer. She examined one and saw that the lights were as bright as before; it was just that the surface of the vine was furred with reddish down. The bigger the vines became, the coarser and longer the fuzz grew, evolving into a coat of matted hair. Now the vines were the same as the ones she had seen in the forest; the same as the ones incorporated into the bodies of Echidna and her offspring. They were too big to cling to the walls and now lay in swollen stacks on the floor like pythons digesting their prey. They twitched when she passed by but seemed too lethargic to stop her.

The tunnel widened. In front of her was a crude archway hacked in the rock. The vines snaked through into the space beyond.

She approached the archway and peered through.

It was a large cave, the walls glistening with crystals, the floor the same lifeless dry soil as covered the rest of the Sixth Level. The cave was open to the outside; a draft blew into Cleo's face from another entryway veiled with darkness. And between the two, on the flowstone wall, Echidna hung in the cradle of vines.

Her deformed body was as slack as a liquid-filled sack, the head lolling on the chest. Her beautiful face was serene in its repose, the empty eyes closed. The vines that served as her limbs were entwined with a web of others covering the walls of the cave, indistinguishable from the stems that crawled back into the tunnel. Echidna looked like an enormous spider with multiple legs – or perhaps, an amputee with no limbs at all. Her horizontal vagina was on full display, and as Cleo watched, a small creature with a vine-covered head and a semi-human face was pushed out, dropped to the floor, and scuttled away. Echidna did not even twitch. Cleo turned away, nauseated.

Now what? This must be the interior of the same cave Echidna had been sitting outside of earlier in the day. Even if Cleo could creep by her unnoticed, she would be simply retracing her steps. If Echidna's offspring still lurked outside, she would be in the same situation as she had been before. And even if she managed to escape, where would she go?

Where was the way up?

For the first time in her ascent of Orcus, Cleo felt the deep soul-freezing despair that Cora had once mentioned, trying to describe her depression. She sat on the floor, her backpack which she had risked her life to get – a heavy, useless lump, cutting into her ribs.

She needed a guide, and there were no guides here. This place was empty of malevolence and benevolence alike – the void of predatory nature, without intelligence, self-awareness, or care. Echidna or her offspring would devour her with the mindless efficiency of pitcher plants and Venus's flytraps devouring stray insects. There were no gods or demons here – just animals.

She missed Iris. She missed Giorgios. Hell, she even missed Alexandra.

And most of all, she missed her sister.

The thought of Cora made her get up. She decided she was going to backtrack and try to clamber out of the hole on the other end of the tunnel. Perhaps if she went back into the forest and tried to find the tree she had climbed out from, she could use it to ascend to the Seventh Level. It was a slender hope but better than nothing.

She hoisted her backpack higher and turned around to go back through the tunnel when she saw a shadow lying at her feet like a black rag. She looked back but there was no light source in the cave strong enough to make her cast a shadow like this.

She inched forward, her foot cautiously touching the shadow like a puddle of dark water. The shadow reared up, creeping up the twinkling, glowing wall. Where it fell against the vines, their lights were extinguished.

Cleo recoiled. The shadow loomed over her, an indistinct smudge of darkness against the play of lights And then it drew in upon itself and solidified, acquiring a three-dimensional heft.

A figure stood in the tunnel, barring Cleo's way: a tall slender figure, swathed in a voluminous cloak. Its head was that of a raven, with sideways round eyes and a bony yellow beak.

"Where are you going, Maiden?" the figure asked. The beak moved as it spoke, but the voice was melodious and as soft as black velvet, with no birdlike harshness.

"I'm going up," Cleo responded.

"You don't know the way."

"I hope you will show me the way."

"Why should I?"

"Because you want me to succeed. Without your ravens, I would have been eaten by this vegetable horror. I don't know why your antigrafo tried to keep me in town, but you want me to go up, don't you, Nyx, Goddess of Night, the Ruler of Ano Syros?"

There was a short silence and then Nyx motioned her to follow. Cleo noticed that the hand that emerged from under the folds of the cloak was bony and yellow like a bird's foot. She touched the rocky wall and it opened up, disclosing a staircase. Nyx went up, and Cleo followed.

They emerged on top of a tall rocky cliff. Below, she could see the expanse of the Sixth Level. It was mostly dark. Indistinct masses of trees were blinking with few puny fairy lights and stretches of empty valleys were filled with stagnant shadows.

"This Level is dying," Nyx said. "Echidna, daughter of Chaos, has all of her progenitor's power and none of his mind. She is sucking her subjects dry, and when they are all gone she and her equally mindless offspring will crawl down into the lower Levels, infesting and polluting them. She needs to be stopped."

"Why don't you stop her?"

Nyx was silent, but Cleo could guess.

"Because you are less powerful than her," she said. "But why? You are one of the primordial deities, right? The first on the scene. You are older than the Olympians. How come you are lower in the food chain than this overgrown pumpkin?"

Nyx did not respond for so long that Cleo was afraid she would say nothing. And Cleo was deadly tired of lies, prevarications, and half-truths. She needed to know.

Finally, Nyx's beak moved once again, releasing the rich chocolate-y torrent of her soothing voice.

"When the Upheaval happened," she said, "Orcus was turned inside out – a mountain instead of a pit – and all the hierarchies we were used to were scrambled. You know what happened when Zeus deposed his progenitor, Cronos?"

"A lot of bad stuff," Cleo muttered.

"Cronos was locked up in Tartarus. The deepest level of the underworld. The highest level of Orcus now."

"So is Cronos on top now?"

"Cronos is dead. Zeus is dead. All Olympians are dead, and most of the other gods as well."

"Killed by who?"

"Killed by you. Humans. Do you think your poison does not leach into our world? Cronos was the god of time, and time is order. Your history has gone off the rails. And instead of trying to set it right you are flailing around, generating more and more words, spinning more and more stories, all ruined, half-finished, unconnected. A spiderweb of stories instead of a ladder of history. Cronos died because you murdered time."

"'Time is out of joint'," Cleo quoted Shakespeare. "All right, but what about the rest of them?"

"Once time collapsed, everything was up for grabs. I am not saying we handled it in the best possible way. For centuries, we languished in the limbo of forgetfulness. But now, it's our game. You rebelled against nature, now nature is rebelling against you. We just seized the opportunity."

"Chthonic deities taking over. I can see that. But you are hardly happy with the new arrangement, are you? Nobody seems to be in charge, everybody is plotting against everybody else."

"It's true. We don't have an agreed-upon leader. The one who led the Upheaval is...well. We don't know what she is doing. Presumably, she has her own plans. But while she is trying to stay on top, the rest of us are bickering and no alternative leader has emerged. And humanity keeps on pumping out the venom of words, entangling itself in its own spiderweb. The only one who is happy about it is the Spider."

"Arachne. She is the one who tried to keep me in Ano Syros. But she also helped me in the Fifth Level. Why?"

"That's right. She bribed my antigrafo. I don't know what she offered that silly cow Alexandra, but she already regrets not listening to me instead."

Cleo felt a momentary flash of sympathy for her erstwhile employer.

"Why did Arachne want me not to ascend Orcus?"

"Because she is happy with the situation as it is. She is the spinner of stories. The chaos of human history is her natural habitat. But I guess now that you are ascending anyway, she wants to keep in your good graces."

"But I don't have any part in this mess!" Cleo cried. "I didn't ask to be brought here! I didn't ask to be Called! All I want is to find my sister!"

Nyx's bird-head turned away slightly, and she stared at Cleo with her round liquid eye.

"You have a part to play," she said finally, "even if you don't know what it is. But I am afraid that all you will do is to unleash more chaos. I wish it were different. To be perfectly honest, I wish I could get rid of you, Maiden. But I can't. The one who Called you has more power than me, unfair as it is. After the Upheaval, all of us found ourselves with new domains. Each of us is trying to engineer a different model for the relationship between humanity and its gods, much like Zeus had done after defeating Cronos and the Titans. You saw Ano Syros. This is what I want the world to be. Is it so bad?"

Cleo was silent. Compared to the rest of Orcus, Ano Syros was paradise.

"The Elysian Fields," Nyx went on. "Now the bottom of the mountain of gods. And on top…well, you will see for yourself. And then you will have to decide if that is the world you want humanity to live in."

"First, I need to get there!"

"I'll show you the way," Nyx said. "After that, it's up to you."

Cleo nodded. She expected Nyx to climb somewhere higher, but instead she went down the stairs back into the tunnel, and Cleo followed. She asked one more question.

"Who Called me?"

"I can't tell you," Nyx said. "She is more powerful than me. But I have something to give you that might help."

She handed something cylindrical to Cleo. It was a small flashlight, such as could be bought in any hardware store for a couple of pounds.

"Seriously?" Cleo's thumb hovered over the On button. She had not used a flashlight in ages, not since she got her smartphone.

"Don't," Nyx said. "Only turn it on when you need it."

"What will it do?"

"You will know when you use it."

CHAPTER 43

ollowing Nyx, Cleo found herself back in Echidna's cave. Nothing had changed; the distended bulk still hung from the tangle of vines.

"The way to Tartarus," Nyx said, "is through the body of the Mother of Monsters."

It took Cleo a moment to figure out what it meant.

"No bloody way!"

The bird-head could not smile, but Cleo was sure Nyx snickered.

"Well, then," she said, "how about over her body?"

"She'll wake up and have me for a snack!"

"I don't have many powers on this Level," Nyx said, "but I can wrap her in the velvet slumber of the night that will keep her insensate. But you better hurry! She'll wake up when the sun rises, and I won't be able to do anything then."

It was not that much different from climbing one of the trees in the forest. Echidna's body had the tough unyielding texture of a bark, and the many swellings and tumors provided convenient footholds. But she breathed, a slow stertorous sound that reverberated through Cleo, making her clumsy and careless. She slipped a couple of times, almost losing her grip. And the metallic stench was so bad that her head swam, and she had to breathe through her mouth.

Fortunately, it was not far. When she stood on Echidna's shoulders, she could see a circle of light above her head. It was not an opening in the cave's ceiling. The light that streamed through it was not the dull yellow gray of the Sixth Level. It was blue and white; the light of open skies and vast distances. A fresh breeze tickled her face, bringing in the bracing smell of salt.

She tried to reach toward the light, but it was too high. It seemed to float in the murk of the cave like an illuminated disk, its edges sharply outlined against the drab background. To reach it, she would have to stand on Echidna's head.

Grimacing in disgust, she pulled herself up, her hands tangled in Echidna's reddish curls. Her face was on the same level as the creature's serenely beautiful empty visage. Echidna shuddered, and one of her lids rose slightly, disclosing the glassy blue iris.

Abandoning all caution, Cleo pulled herself up again, her legs dangling in front of Echidna's face. The Mother of Monsters's teeth clacked in her rosebud mouth.

The top of her head was slippery, the neat rows of curls dancing as she shook her head, trying to dislodge the intruder.

The illuminated disk was just within Cleo's reach. It still had no thickness or volume to it. Not knowing what else to do, she stuck her hand through it, and felt fresh, cool air caress her fingers.

Echidna pulled in her vine-limbs, tearing the web that held her in place. The perch under Cleo's feet was tilting and shuddering.

A vine rose and whipped in the air. It wound around Cleo's neck, trying to strangle her.

She stuck her second hand through the disk of light. Her body was whooshed in, pulled up like a champagne cork flying out of the bottle.

Echidna flailed her vines around, but it was too late.

Cleo reached the Seventh Level of Orcus.

PART 3 TARTARUS

LEVEL SEVEN City Of Glass

The smell of the sea. Blue and green, salty and sharp, growth and decay. The sound of the sea. Rhythmic and polyphonous, monotonous and varied, whispery and booming. The touch of the sea. As familiar as her sister's touch…

Cleo sat up. The sea?

She was on the beach: white sand, a scatter of shells, long strands of iodine-scented kelp. The small waves of the Mediterranean licked her hand like playful puppies. Sunlight threw handfuls of glitter into her eyes.

How come?

She was going up. Climbing the mountain of gods. She should be on the Seventh Level now.

So why was she on the beach?

The beach looked familiar. Wasn't it the same one where she had had her ill-fated party with Iris and Mick and the Dutch boys? Not boys, actually, but antigrafos of the conjoined gods of sleep and death.

But if it was the same beach, had she even gone anywhere? Was the whole thing an elaborate dream or psychotic delusion? Were there even such things as antigrafos? Was Iris alive? Was Mick around instead of in Dream City?

Cleo shakily climbed to her feet. Something heavy weighed her down. Her backpack. Surely, she had not gone to a beach party with a large backpack! And why was she wearing tough trousers, scuffed heavy-duty trainers, and a black long-sleeved shirt? This was not beachwear.

She reluctantly turned away from the sea, which felt as welcoming to her as one's childhood home, and looked inland.

And knew she was not at home.

Above the beach was a promenade, fenced in with a guardrail. And above the sidewalk were slender high-rises, glittering in the bright sunlight. Blue and peach glass walls reflected back the Mediterranean glow, pointed rooftops sparkled in gem-like clusters, spires of high-tech insolence reached for the sky. She was reminded of Canary Wharf, but these buildings were more streamlined, more elegant, and squeezed closer together. It looked like the pictures she had seen of Hong Kong and Shanghai skylines. She could hardly think of a greater contrast with the Sixth Level's monster-infested wilderness.

She instantly felt better. She was ready to tackle the dangers of civilization, whatever they may be, rather than blundering around in primordial vegetative chaos. The rumbling in her stomach reminded her that cities always had supermarkets or grocery shops. The collection of coins she had accumulated in Ano Syros and Dream City rested at the bottom of her backpack, and hoisting it higher on her shoulder, she set off briskly to where stairs led up from the beach.

The promenade was empty of pedestrians. A couple of benches and a shuttered kiosk shimmered in the bright sunshine. All were covered in graffiti but otherwise the promenade was clean and tidy, no rubbish on the pavement. Beyond it was a narrow strip of rather sorry-looking grass, and then an asphalt road bordered by the high-rises that shone like giant mirrors.

She looked at the sky. The sun indicated it was around noon, which did not jibe with her escape from the Sixth Level at dawn, but by now she was used to the vagaries of time in Orcus.

Cronos is dead…

Well, the sun still moved in the sky, and the body still marked time with its needs: breakfast, lunch, dinner.

She crossed the road and saw a car parked badly in a place where parking should be illegal. It was a hatchback of some kind, festooned with graffiti like an underground rock bristling with marine life. Even the windows were blind with tags and decals. On the windshield, there was a large drawing of a black cat.

She cautiously approached the car. The front door was ajar. Inside, the scuffed seats were covered with empty snack packages and dented plastic bottles. The steering wheel was broken, which put an end to her vague hopes of driving. Where would she drive, anyway?

In the back of the car there was a child seat, empty except for a sippy cup with some ancient juice dried into a lurid orange smear.

She frowned. Of course, Orcus had kids. Plenty of them in Ano Syros, quite a lot in Dream City, and presumably in Happy Meadows too, if that suburban paradise with harpies lived up to its image. From what Or had said, she gathered he was an adopted or foster child, his monstrous parents taking in an antigrafo of Apollo as some sort of sick joke or perhaps a revenge on the Olympian god of light. But not all inhabitants of Happy Meadows were harpies and giants. There were humans too, and they must have driven their freshly washed cars with their chubby infants securely belted into their seats and drinking orange juice from their sippy cups – until the fifty-headed Ruler decided to have some fun with his subjects. And of course, the large family of Vassilikos and Sophia indicated that the Fifth Level did not lack for babies either. So there would be nothing unusual about the Seventh Level being family-friendly, or at least as family-friendly as Orcus was likely to be.

But why would the parents abandon their car in this state? The graffiti looked like gang tagging to her.

Was the Seventh Level an arena of gang warfare?

"Try London," she muttered to herself. She lived in a reasonably good area, but no Londoner was unaware of urban blight, rough sleepers, dilapidated estates filled with drugs, and dead-eyed kids brandishing knives. Her urban instincts kicked in as she scanned the empty street. She had had horror after horror thrown at her by the Rulers of Orcus, but she had been spared the kind of random physical attack that every city-dweller fears.

No swaggering gang materialized out of thin air. The street seemed to purr in the sunlight like a dozing cat.

She crossed the street to the sidewalk. The high-rises were separated by courtyards with bamboo in concrete planters and stone benches. Again, she was struck by how much more modern this Level looked compared with its predecessors. The contrast with Echidna's mutant wilderness could not have been greater.

So, who was its Ruler? Nyx had refused to name her, as she had refused to name the Ruler of the Final Level. Zach/Mick had listed all of them, but was it done in the order of ascendance, or randomly? At the time, she had not thought to ask – stupid of her! And she could not even remember all of them. Some seemed to be nicknames or attributes rather than anything familiar from mythology.

The courtyard's pavement was as clean as a corporate boardroom, but the benches seemed to groan under the weight of graffiti. Most were tags and random scrawls, but one bench had a remarkably well-done picture of a black cat staring at Cleo with its almond-shaped eyes. She walked to the nearest high-rise, cupped her hands around her face to cut out the glare, and peered through the glass wall. Inside was a deserted lobby with a security desk and a bank of elevators. The building had automatic doors but they did not move, no matter how much she waved her hands and pushed, so she sighed and decided to explore further.

After half an hour of walking, she was getting bored.

Yes, it was preferable to Echidna's mutant forest and dead meadows, but only just. The Seventh Level looked like some generic business park after a full-scale evacuation. It was composed of spires of glass and concrete stabbing into the bright sky, separated by empty lanes, courtyards, and professionally landscaped gardens with instantly forgettable abstract sculptures. There were no shops, restaurants, or people. Everything was tidy, deserted, and locked down. No matter how often she stood in front of glass entryways, waving her hands and staring at her own reflection, nothing moved. The automatic doors did not open, and revolving doors did not revolve. She caught glimpses of the buildings' interiors: lobbies, foyers, hallways, all as empty and pristine as the manicured outdoors.

Pristine, that is, except for street art. As if to make up for the soul-numbing boredom of this glass city, it was overrun with graffiti. It looked like a whole army of Banksy wannabees had descended on it. Every available surface was filled with tags, whorls, and splotches of paint, interspersed with striking images and broken splinters of words that made no sense to her. She almost felt nostalgic for the legible obscenities of London underground tunnels and trashy estates.

The images were quite recognizable, though; creepily so. They were human faces. Enlarged to the size of balloons and separated from bodies, they hung in the thicket of graffiti like strange fruit. Men, women, and children; all rendered with bold, exaggerated strokes and in monochrome gray, black and white. Their mouths were gaping open, and their eyes were popping out of their sockets. They all looked like they were screaming.

Cleo decided she preferred Hello Kitty, but the anonymous street artists on the Seventh Level apparently did not like cartoon characters. The only other images she spotted apart from the screaming faces were of a black cat, demurely sitting on its haunches and facing the viewer. It was not quite Hello Kitty but better than the screamers.

She was hungry and thirsty. In London, she had worked in one of the newer business parks, and so initially this ultra-urban maze looked like home. But as her hopes to stumble upon a party of office workers with sandwiches and drinks were dashed, she was getting increasingly annoyed.

She came through another faceless courtyard and stood in front of a slender high-rise faced with pink glass. It narrowed at the top into a cone-shaped sky floor, similar to places where expensive restaurants were popping up all over London. The high-rise glowed and sparkled like a giant Christmas ornament.

She looked around and spotted a remarkably ugly concrete statue of a frog. Hefting it, she walked over to the front door, ready to smash her way inside.

The door whooshed open.

She rushed through.

She found herself in a large atrium. It was as deserted as everything else she had seen on the Seventh Level so far, but other than that it looked familiar and welcoming: tinted-glass walls, low tables and armchairs in the waiting area, and best of all – a small coffee-bar tucked into a corner. She made a beeline for it, practically salivating.

She knocked on the counter. She yelled. She searched for a bell and found none.

Shedding her civilized inhibitions, she stepped behind the counter. There was a modern chrome-gleaming espresso machine, primed to go. There was a glass cabinet with cans and bottles of drinks, and there were racks of brightly colored cellophane packets.

Caffeine! She made herself a cup of Americano, wrenched open the glass cabinet, and took out a bottle of flavored soda. The sweetness flooding her mouth and the sugar rush were the best things she had experienced since awakening on the beach in Ano Syros. A healthy Mediterranean diet was great but there was nothing like junk food to make you feel better!

She half-expected the barista to show up and start berating her, but nobody did. The building was hushed. The silence was unnerving when she considered the floors and floors of offices above her. Were they all deserted?

She methodically raided the bar, squeezing her loot into her already full backpack. Another bottle of soda and a couple of bottles of mineral water. Snacks. These were pretty interesting. She studied the garish packaging that looked like a parody of the usual supermarket fare. Familiar names and logos were misspelled and distorted. What looked like Chinese or Japanese characters at first glance turned out to be some random scrawls. Instead of cute cartoon characters, scowling faces with bulging eyes stared at her, recalling the graffiti outside.

She tore one package open. It was filled with candy bars. She knew she should be more careful, but the temptation of junk food was irresistible. She bit into one and winced. The bar had a tart scarlet filling that assaulted her palate with clashing sweetness and sourness, but the clash subsided as she swallowed it and she unconsciously reached for another one.

She sat at the rickety plastic table next to the bar, sipping her Americano. She emptied one packet of candy bars and opened another one. Her head was buzzing with sugar, caffeine, and adrenaline.

So, she had reached the highest – or lowest – Zone of Orcus: Tartarus. The pit-turned-mountain. It should have been infested with the worst creatures of the Greek underworld: demons, many-headed dogs, serpents. It should have been ruled over by Hades and Persephone. It should have been plunged into eternal darkness.

Instead, it was bright and sunny, with all mod cons, and apparently devoid of people or any demonic entities. So far, it looked to be the best of all the Levels. And as for Hades and Persephone, Cleo was reasonably sure they were as dead as the rest of the Olympians. She still could not figure out the details of what Nyx had called the Upheaval, but it certainly seemed that a ragtag collection of secondary deities, giants, and titans had somehow taken over the world of essences and killed its erstwhile rulers. Gods could be killed by other gods. Or had there been another Upheaval somewhere else, reflected in Orcus? What if there was a hierarchy in the Archipelago and something that happened elsewhere had influenced the power struggle in Orcus?

Tired of metaphysical speculations, she decided to make use of this Level's modern facilities. Hot water would feel like a dream.

Her dirty coffee cup rested on the table, together with an emptied packet of candy bars. She did not feel like cleaning up. Her experiences in Ano Syros and Dream City left her with a healthy respect for domestic labor and a resolution never to do it again, but if the barista did come back, she needed to leave a payment. She fished a coin out of her backpack and put it on the table. She had no idea what prices were like here, or even if all the Levels used the same currency, but it made her feel better.

She looked around – and yes, a familiar sign with two sticklike figures beckoned from a corner.

Inside, it was all she had hoped for: stalls, gleaming taps and sinks, wraparound mirrors, and soap dispensers. The stalls' doors were decorated with swirling loops and whorls of graffiti, but otherwise the bathroom was immaculately clean, with no signs of vandalism, discarded needles, or condoms. Did people on this Level simply like street art so much that they put it everywhere?

Washing her hands, she sighed with contentment as a stream of hot water obediently gushed over her chapped and scratched skin. She studied her face in the mirror: she could certainly use a long shower and…

The water pooled and bubbled in the sink as Cleo stood very still, staring into the mirror. The large blue eyes of her reflection, the aquamarine color of the noonday sea, stared back.

CHAPTER 45

So, she had reached her goal? Here? On the Seventh Level?

Her eyes were clear of the black taint, and the shadowy tug of the Call in her head was gone. She probed it gingerly, like a missing tooth, but it was not there. Cleo had gotten so used to its oncoming-migraine presence that she had stopped noticing it, and now there was nothing to notice. The hook embedded in the soft tissue of her mind had been removed so gently she could not tell when it had happened.

She had felt the Call in Echidna's domain, hadn't she? It meant that the Seventh Level was where she was supposed to go. This bright empty downtown, a developer's wet dream, was her destination? Seriously?

So, who had Called her? Where was the Ruler? Who was the Ruler?

And more importantly, where was Cora?

Alexandra had told her that the lost and the un-homed often washed up in Orcus, falling through cracks in reality. Cora had been lost in the year or so before her disappearance. Where would she find herself if not on the mountain of dead gods?

But if Cleo had been Called by the Ruler of the Seventh Level, did it mean that Cora was somewhere here, too? And if yes, what was going on with the upper Levels? If the Final Level housed the would-be Sovereign of the new chthonic deities of Orcus, what did this entity, whoever they were, know about the sisters? Nyx had intimated that Cleo had some role to play in the power struggle on Orcus, but what was it?

She returned to the mirror, just to make sure that her eyes were back to their normal blueness. That was a well-designed bathroom, with mirrors curving around the large, tiled space. From every angle, her own face looked back at her.

Or was it her face?

The mirror images were changing.

She shrunk back as her reflections stared, winked, leered, and grimaced at her.

The mirrors were slicing at her face with the scalpels of fear and reshaping it into many different Cleos. They erased her body as if it did not exist, even though she could feel the drumbeat of her heart. Instead of the tiled bathroom, the space within the mirrors was filled with feverish swirls, tags, and spirals of dirty colors that snagged her faces in their twitching coils. Some of the faces swelled up like balloons, growing as big as the visage of Echidna, some were distorted into idiotic masks, and some shrunk into tiny pale ovals, blowing about like a handful of seeds. The bigger faces seemed to press against the glass and retreat back into the graffiti-filled space like fish in a giant aquarium.

Cameras, Cleo told herself. Some fucking video app. I bet they have those in every club in London.

But she was not in a London club. And the faces – her faces – were watching her with their blue eyes, now free of the dull blackness of the Call, and filled with a variety of alien expressions – mockery, malice, schadenfreude – that she had never seen in the selfies that used to populate her social media feed before Cora's disappearance. She had not been on social media since then.

She forced her feet to carry her over to the wall of herself and touched it; the mirrors still felt like mirrors, slick and smooth. So at least these were reflections or projections of some kind, and not actual faces mimicking her. She would not put it past Orcus to have some creatures capable of such a feat, but the more she studied the faces, the less she recognized them as belonging to herself.

One giant face smiled at her lewdly, its eyes heavy with the liner and mascara that she had not worn since coming to Orcus. Another smaller one was all heroin chic: emaciated, shadows as deep as bruises, and also actual bruises mottling its pale skin. She was momentarily glad to find what she thought was an accurate reflection, only to realize the girl staring at her had the long wavy black hair she had cut off after Cora's disappearance. And as she swerved around, fascinated and appalled by the proliferation of her mirror selves, she saw more and more reflections than looked like malicious parodies. One face was old and wasted, with sagging wrinkled skin. One had an ugly scar running across its cheek. One was slack and empty-eyed. Some looked only partially human. In one corner, a reflection fell apart into a swarm of miniature copies like a budding jellyfish, and all of them had no eyes – just a blank stretch of skin above the nose. Another one scowled at her with the needle teeth of a moray eel. And the big, heavily made-up face sprouted vampire fangs spotted with blood.

"Not me," she muttered under her breath. "Not me, not me, not me!"

But was she sure of that? If she had learned anything in Orcus, it was that identities were fluid and malleable. Antigrafos, smudged copies of ancient gods, plotting with – or against – their originals. Or, a lippy teenager, was also an avatar of the serene god of light. Alexandra and Nyx, Eros and his two avatars, brothers and rivals, fighting each other. Who was she, if not all the possible versions of herself floating in that soup of what-ifs? What was she? Cleo reached inside herself and clutched emptiness. And meanwhile, all around her, distorted images undulated in the virtual sea with the hypnotic slowness of kelp forests, sprouting more and more hybrid Cleos. She saw a face with the hairy vines growing out of its scalp, and another one with the beak of a raven. Cleo, being dissolved in Orcus, being taken over, thrown back into the cauldron of ancient metamorphoses, and being remade as something else.

"No!" she shouted. "I know who I am! I am Cleo! I came here looking for my sister!"

And in response, all the faces broke out in peals of deafening laughter.

The faces floated toward each other and blended together like oil drops in water. One face remained, reaching from the floor to the ceiling and staring at Cleo with an ambiguous smile.

It was her but not as she used to be – an ambiguous young woman, stubbornly climbing the peak of corporate hierarchy, kicking away the debris of grief. Not even as she was now – a hardened, whip-thin survivalist, climbing another peak with the same dogged determination. It was Cleo as a complete person; Cleo as she should have been had the fertilized ovum in Daphne's womb not split into two partial versions of the same woman. She was beautiful, as Cleo, haggard and tough, was no longer. She was serene, as Cleo, spurred on by the competition with her twin, had never been. And she was powerful, as Cleo knew she would never be.

Magnified to this inhuman size, Cleo studied herself: her unblemished olive skin, her straight nose, her Cupid's-bow mouth, her eyes the color of the Mediterranean, and her black curls, lush as clusters of grapes, which she no longer possessed. It was a classic beauty of the sort one sees in the statues whose perfection still takes one's breath away after thousands of years. With a strange detachment, Cleo realized that her beauty had been power, which had never learned how to use, and which Cora had thrown away. And now it was too late for both of them.

But she also realized something else. She looked like Eleni. Her Greek grandmother, only forty when the twins were born, only sixty when she died, was the most beautiful woman she had ever known. She had bequeathed her face to her granddaughters. Not to Daphne, her daughter. Daphne was pretty. Her daughters had the face that launched a thousand ships.

The Cleo-face returned her gaze, and finally it spoke. Its voice echoed around the room, coming from nowhere and everywhere. For a moment, Cleo was relieved that it did not sound like her, but then she realized it did – it sounded like Cora's, which meant it was also hers.

"Welcome to the Seventh Level, Kora, daughter of Chthonia, the Mistress of Harvest, the Bringer of Food, the Bountiful One."

The spell was broken. She had seen too many ways in which Orcus had twisted the classical myths into something ugly and dangerous. This was no different.

"My mother's name is Daphne, and she is the Bringer of Food to nobody but her lout of a husband," she responded. "And I'm Cleo, not Cora."

The Cleo-face's smile widened.

"You have forgotten your true nature in that shadow world, which has gone awry because it has lost our guidance. But we are coming back, to bring it to the true path. And you will be brought back too, as you always have been."

Cleo tuned out.

She did not believe a word the Cleo-face was saying. Not because it was all lies. She knew there was a grain of truth in it somewhere, or perhaps many grains, food mixed with poison, some infernal brew to dull her senses.

She tuned out because she saw something.

She studied the face again, making sure she was not mistaken – and she was not.

"Who are you, then," she asked, "telling me who I am?"

"Don't you recognize me?"

"It's not hard to steal another's face. I know people who do it for a living. Who are you, really?"

"You have been stolen, Maiden. They stole you and hid you in the shadow world. But they paid for it, all of them! The pitiless Bright One and his sister who plotted to come back to humanity and scorch it with their fire; the doddering, toothless Father of gods who had lost his mind; the fat love-goddess who could only inspire lust; the Ruler of the Underworld shrunken into an ice mummy; and the Horseman of the Sea eaten alive by his own horses! They have all paid for the injury they caused me! Now Orcus has risen, and we are coming back to take what's ours!"

The expression on that titanic face as she spat out this litany of hatred was something Cleo did not believe herself capable of. It made her even more sure of her conclusion.

"And you are what?" she asked again.

The Cleo-face broke into a radiant smile.

"Come to me, Daughter!"

The glass shuddered as the face flowed back to a normal size and a body materialized beneath it, sketchy at first, but then acquiring volume and depth. A woman's body clad in a traditional Greek chiton, one shoulder bared, the folds of the white fabric as precise and symmetrical as if carved by a chisel. The glass buckled and stretched, and the woman with her face leaned out, her marble-white arms breaking out of the mirror surface and reaching toward Cleo. Her hair, with its rich rippling locks, rose clear off her head.

"Keep away!" Cleo shouted. "I know who you are! Medusa the Gorgon, the snake-haired one! You are no mother of mine! Your only children are barren stone and glass!"

The Cleo-disguise slipped off, and just for a second, Cleo got a glimpse of what was beneath it – the ugliness and malice so profound that it burned her retinas like acid. Covering her eyes with a crook of her elbow, she groped behind her back for the door. But her fingers slipped on the smooth curving glass surface that had sucked the door in and closed over it like water swallowing a stone. Medusa was approaching; she could hear the hissing of the black snakes weaving in and out of her pitch-colored hair, blending with the curls but for an occasional flicker of a forked tongue, and an occasional gleam of a scale. It was that flicker and that gleam that had told Cleo who the Ruler of the Seventh Level really was.

Still covering her eyes, she hefted her heavy backpack and threw it at the mirror.

There was a deafening crash, and when she lowered her arm she was alone in the bathroom that was no longer as immaculate as it had been. Glass shards littered the floor, and a star-shaped hole yawned in the mirror.

Sighing, she picked up her backpack and went back into the atrium.

The barista at the counter turned around and smiled at her.

CHAPTER 46

She still could not believe it, even as he was hugging her.

She extricated herself and stepped back to study him, still unnerved by Medusa's theft of her face. But there were no snakes in his hair. He was exactly as she remembered him: wiry and whip-thin, his black eyes sparkling, his dark curls glued to his forehead by perspiration, grinning at her. The man she had known as Mick in her own world. Hermes' antigrafo.

Zach.

The last time she had seen it was in that rusty elevator cage, clanking down into the dismal domain of Hypnos/Thanatos, the Oneiroi-infested damp city. She had never expected to see him again. The directionality of Orcus had become too deeply engraved into her brain: always up. Going down was synonymous with death, disappearance, and dissolution.

But here he was, unquestionably himself and unquestionably real.

"It's good to see you." He almost jumped up and down with pleasure like a little kid. He did not seem to mind that she had abandoned him on the Fourth Level and had not tried to go back after him. On the other hand, had he not abandoned Iris and her on the beach in Greece?

Her memory was still occluded in random patches, but she knew that in London Mick had not only gone by a different name but had also looked somewhat different from Zach. She had no doubt they were the same person, but this apparent shapeshifting ability made her distrust him even more. He was an antigrafo of Hermes, the god of charlatans and thieves. He had sworn he had not known who he was in London, but was that possible? And if he had known about Orcus, had he played any role in Cora's disappearance?

He smiled, and she felt ashamed of her suspicions. He had been her friend in London. He had saved her ass on the Fourth Level. He was her only link to her former life. She suddenly realized how tired she was of Orcus and its endless metamorphoses in which nothing and nobody was what they seemed to be. Zach was her only anchor in the sea of uncertainty.

"You can show me how happy you are by making me a cup of coffee," she said. "And is there anything to eat besides cookies?"

"You've been eating those, haven't you?" He turned away, pressing buttons on the espresso machine.

"I know I'll end up diabetic but it's the choice between starvation now and diabetes later."

"It's not because of health hazards." Zach put a perfectly made cup of flat white in front of her and proceeded to brew one for himself. "They are made with pomegranate."

"I know but so…?"

And then it hit her.

Cleo was so used to pomegranate's popularity in Greece that she never thought of its mythical implications, but in the story of Persephone's abduction by Hades she was given pomegranate seeds to eat, and so was compelled to go back to the underworld for half a year. During this time, as her mother grieved for her, winter would set in and nature would grow somber and cold.

Pomegranate was the food of the dead.

"So, I am dead, after all," she whispered. "Kora, eating pomegranate seeds, imprisoned in the afterlife…"

"You are not dead." Zach came back to the table and sat down, nursing his own coffee. "Not entirely, at least."

"What's that supposed to mean?"

"True death is final in Orcus. But this mountain is positioned on the boundary between the world of essences and the world of shadows, partaking of both. People who are drawn into it are given pomegranate to eat, so they forget their origin. Did you have memory problems in Ano Syros?"

"A lot. Later, too. This was why I didn't recognize you in Dream City."

"People who live on the Nine Levels are kept in that twilight state, so they will obey the Rulers. Some remember and try to escape. But escape is becoming impossible as the Nine tighten their rule and bring more and more subjects to their Levels, binding them with the Call."

"So, this whole shtick about how this is the Platonic world of ideal forms is bullshit?

"It is what the Nine want us to believe. It is true that Orcus influences our world. It is also true that the influence is reciprocal, going in both directions. As to what the Platonic world is, or even if there is only one or a hierarchy of many, who knows? The Archipelago is vast."

Why do you think this is the only mountain? Or the only island?

"What really happened to Iris?" she asked abruptly.

"I told you. She was killed by the Dutch boys."

"Hendrik and Tomas, or whatever names they used in Greece. Then who wrote the letter? You said you followed them into Orcus, trying to save me. But the letter was left in the hotel. Who wrote it? And when?"

Zach was still sipping his coffee. Milk foam left a white mustache on his upper lip.

"All right, I…condensed it a little," he said. "I told you that I did not know who I was in our world. But I did. We antigrafos are sent sometimes to the shadow world to do the bidding of the Nine or…of other entities. Some of us suffer from shock. Amnesia. You hear about people gone missing and then turning up out of the blue with no memories? Antigrafos, many of them. But my memory was okay. I knew I had been sent to keep tabs on you and Cora."

"That's what you call it? 'Keeping tabs'?"

"I was…I am very fond of you. You know that."

Cleo decided not to go there.

"Anyway, I was doing my best. I met Iris at one of your parties. I knew she was also from Orcus. So, we teamed up to protect you."

"Iris? She is…was an antigrafo?"

"Yes."

"Of whom?"

"Iris, of course," he said, as if it were self-evident.

Iris, an antigrafo of Iris, the goddess of the rainbow, the messenger of the gods.

"We knew you'd be Called," he went on, "so, we wrote this letter. Left it in the Villa Pharos, just as a precaution, hoping it'd be sucked into Orcus if you were abducted and we could not reach you. It was, just like most of your belongings. It happens. This is why Orcus has bits and pieces of modern technology."

Cleo bit her lips, thinking of her friend. A shadow of the rainbow, sent to watch over her… It was as if her entire life had been a carefully constructed, paper-thin narrative, glued over the strange depths of the real story.

"You said you were sent to watch over me," she said. "Who sent you?"

Zach was looking over her shoulder.

"She did," he said.

CHAPTER 47

leo knew who it was even before she willed herself to turn around. The skitter of insectoid legs on the polished floor, the acidic, squashed-bug stench…

Arachne stood some distance away, as if acknowledging the depth of Cleo's revulsion and trying to placate her. But this gesture made it even worse, as Cleo was forced to recognize a personality like her own behind the dead-woman's rotting face perched on top of the arachnid bulk. She had been horrified by Echidna's vegetative mindlessness. Now she realized that the presence of a human mind in a monster's body was every bit as frightening as its absence.

The patches of putrefaction on Arachne's face had spread even further, marring what had once been a classic beauty, rather like Echidna's, or, Cleo realized with a spasm of disgust, her own.

She looked back at Zach, feeling the slow anger of her accumulated days and nights in Orcus overflow in a flood of bitter bile. This final betrayal was almost more than she could take.

"So, it did not work with your melted Tweedledee and Tweedledum," she spat at him, "and now you are selling me to that dead bug? Hope it's for a higher price!"

Zach lifted his hands, his face an almost-convincing study in innocence.

"What are you talking about? I helped you to escape Dream City, remember?"

"Yeah, like you helped Iris?"

"I couldn't do anything. I was overpowered."

"Your friend was killed by the antigrafos of Hypnos and Thanatos," the spider intervened. "She was weak because her parádeigma was one of the first to perish in the Upheaval. The longer the original is dead, the more…smudged the copies become."

"Like you? 'Smudged' hardly begins to describe this."

The dead face was taut as if caught in rigor mortis, but Arachne managed a grimace like the ghost of a smile.

"I am not an antigrafo. I am the parádeigma."

"Of whom?"

"Of that spider that helped you to escape in the Fifth Level, among others."

Cleo was silent, remembering the golden spider that intervened in the fight between Yannis and Giorgios, the two antigrafos of Eros.

"Please listen to her," Zach implored. "She is the only thing that stands between the Nine and the destruction of our world. Do you really want London to become Dream City, or LA to become Happy Meadows?"

"Some would call it an improvement," Cleo muttered, but she was weakening. Fragments of the world that was Orcus rotated in her memory like pieces of colored glass in a kaleidoscope falling into a new configuration. She turned to Arachne again, forcing herself to look into the dead face.

"I know your story," she said. "You are Arachne the Weaver. You challenged Athena to a contest, and when you won, she, in her anger, turned you into a spider. But what has it got to do with me? What are you now? Why do you look like an accident in the county morgue? And why did you put a spell on me, making me unable to read? Because it was you, right? You made me see spiders instead of letters. Had it not been for the Eye of Charon, I'd still be cleaning loos in Ano Syros."

"Yes," Arachne said, "I did it to you. I could say it was for your own sake, but it would be a lie. Or as I prefer to say, a story. Because this is what I am: Arachne, the Weaver of Stories, the

Spinner of Narratives. And this is why I crawl through the nooks and crannies of the Nine Levels, helping everybody who opposes the Nine. Helping you, even though I admit you may not see it this way. Because this is what makes a good story: it is never black-and-white, never one thing, but always many, woven together as tight as a spiderweb."

Cleo rolled her eyes.

"For a storyteller, you are not very good at your craft," she said acidly. "Could you please start at the beginning?"

"The beginning was the Upheaval. When the Nine Children of Chaos, emboldened by the evil and destruction spilling over from humanity's history, emerged from the underworld, massacred the enfeebled, sleeping deities of light, and turned the underworld inside out – the pit into the mountain. You have already been told that everything that happens in Orcus is reflected in the shadow world of humans but also vice versa. The Nine have been re-energized by your wars, your genocides, and most of all your destruction of Gaia. But they have plans for the shadow world as well, and these plans include turning it into a version of Orcus. What you see here on the Nine Levels are sketches of what the future of humanity may look like. Or the futures, if the Nine cannot agree on their leader and end up carving up the human domain. But I know what will happen if humanity is enslaved. The well of stories will dry up. Orcus is being fed by your nightmares, and when they cease it will come to an end, becoming a frozen mausoleum of dead gods and monsters. The Nine are too full of pride and honestly too stupid to understand that. But I do. I am Arachne, the Weaver of Stories. I am your ally."

Cleo bit her lips. Her confrontation with Medusa was too vivid in her mind to reject what Arachne was saying out of hand.

"So, you are doing it out of the goodness of your heart?" she retorted, but she was beginning to weaken.

"You asked me why I look like this. It's because I am fed by your stories, and they are being poisoned by the influence of the Nine. The gangrene you see in my face is the gangrene of your imagination."

"Who are the Nine?" Cleo asked abruptly. "If they are the only deities left, who are they?"

Zach looked like he wanted to interject something, but it was Arachne who answered:

"You have met seven of them. Nyx, the Night; Briareus, the Fifty-Headed; Hekate, the Witch-Goddess of the Triple Moon; Hypnos and Thanatos; the Kindly Ones who are now One-in-Many; Echidna, Mother of Monsters; Medusa, the Mistress of Stone and Glass; Lamia, the Child-eater; and Demeter the Barren."

"What?" Cleo staggered back as if from a physical blow. "Demeter? But she is one of the Olympians!"

"Yes," Arachne said sadly, "the only one who joined the Children of Chaos. Joined and led them. The one who occupies the Final Level, trying to exert her rule through Orcus. The one who is helped by her sidekick Lamia on the Eighth Level to abduct and torture children. Demeter, the Barren One. Demeter, your mother."

CHAPTER 48

They were huddling in one of the offices on the second floor. Zach had ransacked a couple of corporate boardrooms and brought in armchair cushions and some rugs.

"Where are all the CEOs?" Cleo asked.

"There are still some left in the City of Glass, but they don't come downtown anymore. Afraid of urban decay."

"Urban decay?"

"Street art. The Mistress of Glass and Stone uses it to entrap her victims."

So, the weird graffiti was Medusa's tool. This wasn't too surprising: in mythology, she had the ability to turn people to stone, and what is more stonelike than images painted on walls?

Cleo and Zach shared some stale sandwiches he had scavenged from an office fridge. Arachne refused to partake, which Cleo was grateful for. She did not want to see this dead face eat.

She fidgeted, trying to find a better position on the jury-rigged bed. Her entire body ached almost as badly as her mind.

Arachne had said that tomorrow morning they would recoup and consider their next steps. She did not want Cleo to go up and try to reach the Final Level. It would be extremely dangerous, she had said.

Dangerous for whom?

The world. Many worlds, in fact.

Arachne could temporarily protect her from Medusa, the Ruler of the City of Glass. But the Eighth Level was Ruled by Lamia, the Child-Eater, who was even stronger than Medusa. As for the Final Level…

If your mother gets hold of you, you will never be the same. She is mad, and she has enough power to drive you mad, reshaping you in the image of her hatred and resentment. I was trying to protect you in Ano Syros and in the Hives. I cannot protect you on the Final Level.

What is the Final Level called?

The Wasteland.

Beyond the floor-to-ceiling window, the sky was curdling into indigo and violet. The high-rises melded together into indistinct shadow masses, drinking away the last glow from the sky. There were no lights in any of them. The sparkling gaiety of illuminated human metropolises was absent from Medusa's malicious imitation.

Arachne had told them the City of Glass was unsafe at night, and Cleo had not questioned her any further. She felt bone-tired and yet unable to settle down or to sleep. Her brain was abuzz.

"You are Persephone," Arachne had told her. "The Maiden. Demeter's only daughter. You were abducted and hidden in the shadow world. And Demeter, already driven half-mad by the devastation humanity has unleashed on nature, swore vengeance on both the Olympians and humanity itself. Orcus is the outcome."

"Abducted by whom?" Cleo had asked.

"Artemis and Apollo. They had their own plans for humanity, of course, but they are dead, so I don't know what those were. And they plotted against the Father of Gods, much as the Nine did. But they lost to the Barren One."

"Why do you call her the Barren One? Isn't Demeter the goddess of harvest and fertility?"

"She was, before humans decided they did not need nature anymore to feed themselves or to make babies. Before they declared war on Gaia."

Cleo wanted to object. She was a believer in science and technology as tools to combat climate change. In the past, this had led to many heated arguments with Cora. But defending the green revolution was not her first priority. Figuring out her identity was.

Arachne's tale corresponded to Medusa's attempt to pass herself off as Cleo's mother. She had confirmed that Medusa wanted Cleo as a bargaining chip in her negotiation with the Barren One. Having taken over the urban level of Tartarus, Medusa believed herself to be the inevitable Final Ruler of Orcus, and apparently had some complicated plans on how to dislodge Demeter from the top of the mountain of gods. Cleo was less interested in Medusa's machinations than she was in answering a simple question.

Even if she accepted the mad proposition that she was a goddess herself, who was Cora? And where was Cora?

Unfortunately, neither Arachne nor Zach had any light to shed on this issue.

"I suspect that Artemis and Apollo somehow managed to split you into two," Arachne had said, though she sounded much less assured than when she explained the power dynamics on Orcus. "They were twins, remember, and Artemis was also a goddess of childbirth. What I know for sure is that your sister is not on any Level of Orcus I have access to."

"Don't you have access to all of them?"

"No," Arachne said, but did not elaborate.

"Demeter the Barren is mad, and if reunited with her daughter she will have enough power to seize full control of Orcus and then invade the human world to remake it in the image of the Nine Levels. When I discovered that the Maiden was in the shadow world, I needed to act. I knew antigrafos of Iris and Hermes, messengers of the gods, escaped into Plato's Cave, so I contacted them and persuaded them to guard you. Unfortunately, Hypnos and Thanatos somehow found out about you and teamed up with Medusa, the Mistress of Stone and Glass, to bring you to Orcus. And…well, you know the rest."

"What I don't know," Cleo retorted, "is why Zach and Iris urged me in their letter to go up, while you made it impossible for me to read it, so I'd stay in Ano Syros!"

Zach, who had been subdued and silent during this conversation, intervened.

"We had a…disagreement," he said, casting a nervous glance at the human-faced spider. "Iris and I thought you had to confront Demeter and bring her back to her senses. Arachne believed that it was too dangerous. Hence the spider-spell. But you managed to remove it yourself, so…here we are!"

Cleo suspected he was lying, or at least not telling the whole truth. She realized she could no longer trust him, which left a bitter taste in her mouth.

"So where is Cora?' she demanded. "Why did you lie about her? Why did you write she was in Orcus?"

"Because I knew it would make you determined to reach the Final Level."

"But is it possible that she is really there?"

"It's possible," Arachne said. "It's also possible that she is dead."

Cleo tossed and turned on the sliding cushions. The office was not the greatest place to bed down, but she had been in worse places during her ascent of Orcus. What kept her awake was not the physical discomfort or even the presence of a giant spider, looming like a black mass in the corner. It was what this spider had said.

Cleo was Persephone. And her sister was…who knows where.

She had climbed Orcus with a single-minded purpose of finding her twin alive. Would she now have to accept Cora's death? Or worse: would she be thrown back into the twilight of grief and confusion when everybody was telling her Cora was "missing", as if it explained anything. As if you could "miss" a person like a mislaid pen.

No! Cora could not be dead. Cleo would know if it was the case. Cora was part of her.

Maybe they somehow managed to split you into two…

One soul in two bodies.

And what about Daphne? Cleo was not particularly fond of her mother, but the thought that she was not her mother caused an unexpected surge of grief.

And what about Eleni? If she was the daughter of Demeter, she had no human grandmother at all. Demeter was a daughter of Cronos and Rhea, both dead.

The dark water of sleep finally closed over her.

A woman carrying a child, walking away from her. Her face averted, the child's arms around her neck. A riot of blond curls whipped by a sharp wind…

A scarlet stain spreading over the hair…

Cleo woke up. She saw Zach standing by the window.

"What…?"

He shushed her.
And then she heard it too.

CHAPTER 49

A stealthy susurrus, a whispering singsong, a soft footfall. Cleo could not identify any of the sounds coming from the outside, but she knew that there were sounds, shocking after the daytime hush. Somebody or something was awake, down in the dark streets.

"What's that?" she whispered to Zach.

"I've never been on this Level," he whispered back.

Arachne skittered toward them.

"These are servants of the Stone," she said. "We should be safe from them as long as we stay indoors."

In the dark that hid her swollen spider body and her rotting face, Cleo trusted Arachne a little more. Her voice was exceptionally beautiful, low and musical.

"What servants?" she asked.

"Better if you don't see them."

Cleo disagreed; her ascent of Orcus taught her the value of knowledge. She had faced too many monsters not to realize that the worst of them are hiding in the shadows of your imagination, faceless and shapeshifting to accommodate your nightmares.

But no matter how she strained her eyes, she could see nothing except some indistinct movement below. She remembered the torch Nyx had given her. She groped in her backpack and pulled it out.

"Don't!" Arachne cried.

Cleo pushed the button.

The bright beam of light cleaved the room and was thrown back by the glass, blinding her. When she blinked away the blue shadows swimming in her eyes, she saw her own face staring back at her.

A reflection.

She stepped forward, mesmerized by her own beauty. It was restored to her now, on the Seventh Level. Her Call was done. Her ascent was completed. She knew who she was and where she belonged. Here, in the City of Glass, where her images would take over the empty spaces of the city and remake it as her domain. Futuristic towers of glass and stone, stabbing into the sky, climbing ever higher, leaving the dirt and mess of humanity behind.

Her face, perfect and serene, smiled at her. The hyacinth curls swayed and grew, tendrils of darkness spreading like rime across the window, curling and tangling in a hypnotic web...

"Medusa!" Arachne hissed.

Cleo came closer, still clutching the flashlight, aiming it at the face that hung suspended in the elaborate curlicues of vines, or snakes, or locks of hair, covering the entire glass wall.

She tried to make out what the tendrils were, growing in a labyrinthine profusion and obscuring the night beyond.

"Turn off the light!" Arachne lunged forward, and one of her front legs brushed Cleo's wrist, reminding her of the time she had almost jumped out the window in Ano Syros to avoid the Spider's touch. Angry at the memory, she aimed the flashlight at the Spider's dead face. Arachne cried out and skittered back.

The glass shattered.

The flood of tendrils slithered into the office. It looked like an invasion of a speeded-up kudzu vine until Cleo saw that it was no plant.

It was graffiti; tags, and whorls, and even words distorted into illegibility, putting off multicolored shoots and covering the floor in a web of living paint.

It was strange but quite beautiful.

"Run!" Arachne cried out from the doorway, having retreated from the tide of images that expanded over the walls and was reaching the ceiling.

The flowing lines and streaks of paint did not have any thickness to them. A flood of graffiti crept over the walls and the ceiling, colors and outlines unfolding and blossoming into a tangle of tags, shapes, and words. Faces budded out of flowing lines like fruit on the vine.

It still seemed harmless to Cleo. How could a drawing hurt you, even if it was moving?

A broad scarlet stroke crept toward Arachne and touched her hairy foreleg.

The Spider screamed.

The stroke climbed up her leg, flattening it. The leg was losing volume, collapsing in upon itself, and settling on the floor in a two-dimensional hairy outline. The graffiti was sucking Arachne in.

Cleo stared, paralyzed. She wanted to help but she could no more intervene in the process than she could jump into a comic strip.

Arachne screamed again in rage, and with a painful crack she broke off her foreleg that remained painted on the floor. She lopsidedly rushed out into the hallway on only seven legs, graffiti in pursuit.

In front of Cleo, faces budded on the walls. Some looked familiar. Was that impressionistic sketch really Or? Was that tragic mask Ursula? Was that Gothic cartoon Yannis?

As in a dream, she stretched her hand toward them. Their painted eyes regarded her with the eternal serenity of art. Nothing she could say or do would change them. They were immortal.

She touched them. Plaster and paint.

"Watch out!" Zach yelled. She had almost forgotten about him.

Awakening from her hypnotic reverie, Cleo snatched her hand back and aimed the flashlight at the tide of images, but the light only seemed to encourage them. The oatmeal-colored walls were crisscrossed and speckled with colors and lines. And not just the walls. The parquet floor was almost invisible under the tide of graffiti. Short of hovering in the air, there was no escaping them.

CHAPTER 50

 e need to go up!" Zach screamed.

"Go up where?"

"The Eighth Level!"

He was right, of course. It had become so ingrained in her – the need to ascend. Always up, never down. Even if Arachne had told the truth, even if Demeter was unhinged, even if Cora was dead, she still needed to reach the top of Orcus. The Final Level.

They rushed into the hallway. It was as dark as the rest of the building but as Cleo pointed her flashlight at the walls, they could see the telltale tendrils of graffiti sprouting across the institutional green. The linoleum was darkening under her feet with a wave of images and words.

There was a bank of elevators at the end of the hallway, its illuminated display the only light in the shadows. They sprinted toward it, Zach overtaking Cleo.

She felt a strange sensation in her foot – not pain but loosening, as if her bones were rattling inside her skin. She pointed the flashlight down. A line of letters, hairy like a caterpillar with brushstrokes, crawled upon the toe of her trainer. She shook it off and ran toward Zach, who was desperately stabbing at the call button. The trainer was sucked into the graffiti, immortalized in a Banksy-like arrangement.

The display blinked as it showed the car descending. It was intolerably slow, crawling like a drunken slug and pausing for endless seconds on each floor.

The tide of graffiti reached the ceiling above the elevator alcove and now looked down at them with the tortured faces caught in its tangle, mouths agape, eyes screaming. But Cleo was more concerned about the graffiti crawling toward them on the floor, as it would be impossible to escape once they reached the alcove.

"Move it!" she yelled at the leisurely blinking display.

Five floors above them, four, three…

Out of the mesh of broken words, a painted arm was reaching toward her with gray sinews and razor nails.

The door swooshed open.

Zach rushed in, but she hesitated, just for a heartbeat. Seeing him inside brought back the horror of that ancient, rusty, chain-dragged elevator in Dream City that had taken Zach back into the sodden domain of living nightmares.

How did he make it up here?

"Come on!" he urged her.

She jumped inside, just as the painted arm was about to touch her bare foot.

Thankfully, the cabin did not look like the one in Dream City. It was modern and clean, and to her relief it had neither a mirror nor any art on its walls. The panel inside showed buttons for twenty-one floors above and two below. There was even a familiar P for Underground Parking.

The familiarity, the everyday-ness, of it all calmed Cleo. She pushed the uppermost button and the cabin rose smoothly. No longer lingering on every floor, it quickly reached the top. In an office tower, there would be corporate headquarters here, or maybe a sky-room with an observation deck, or a restaurant.

The door pinged open and they stepped outside.

There was no fancy restaurant with a city view here. In fact, there was no view at all.

They stood in a large cone-shaped space, dimly lit by a sort of underwater glow coming from the walls. The space was empty except for some papers lying on the floor. Cleo idly picked one up.

Zach reached out and tore it from her hand.

"Don't!" he hissed. "Don't you understand, images are deadly here!"

She only caught a bare glimpse of what was on the paper, but that was enough. A sketch of a flayed man, muscles exposed, eyes gouged, screaming, and a helmeted figure standing behind him, a two-toned staff in its raised hand.

She rounded up on Zach, but there was no time for questions. Bits of paper moved like leaves in a breeze around them, even though there was no wind. Rustling and whispering, they started bleeding lines and colors, and then a new crop of graffiti budded on the floor.

Remembering her encounter with Medusa in the bathroom, Cleo hefted her backpack and hurled it at the wall.

Had she been in a real high-rise, the backpack might have bounced off the reinforced glass. But here in Orcus, with its strange amalgamation of archaic magic and modern technology, with gods like magpies stealing human ingenuity and adapting it to their needs, safety regulations were unknown. The glass shattered with a noise like the ringing of church bells followed by a screech that pierced Cleo's eardrums.

Through the hole, a salt-laden wind came roaring, almost sweeping her off her feet.

She rushed to the hole and looked out into the glitter of sunrise on the water. But the sea was not down below; it was at her eye-level. Where the sky was supposed to be, the Mediterranean rolled its gentle swell with total disregard of gravity or perspective.

She lowered her eyes and had another bad-topology, vertigo-inducing moment. The high-rise went down, seemingly infinitely, narrowing into a pink tube and disappearing into a vortex of blue and white. It was as if space itself was folding, curdling, sucking in distance and perspective and spitting out impossibilities.

Behind her, she heard the snakelike hissing of graffiti.

"Come on!" she cried to Zach, but he did not respond. Glancing back, she saw an open doorway in the wall where there had been none just moments ago.

A tsunami of images was advancing upon her, words like stings, tags like tentacles, faces like poisoned fungi. The whole sky-room was distorting, the walls flowing together, the hole gaping wider and sending cracks through the structure that trembled as if in an earthquake.

"Fuck you!" Cleo yelled.

Backing off, she took a long run-off and jumped, letting the momentum carry her through the break in the glass.

Salty water rushed into her nose and flooded her eyes, but she quickly surfaced. The warmth of the sea felt welcoming, and she floated for a while before opening her eyes and risking a glance, only to squeeze them shut again, hit by sickening vertigo. She was suspended in the water ceiling above the slowly rotating funnel of a space distortion that sucked her in like a hungry vortex, but she was kept in place by the pull of gravity drawing her up instead of down. When she closed her eyes, she was swimming in the sea. When she opened them, she was a fly walking upside down on a ceiling. Her inner ear and her vision were at war.

She remembered pictures of vomit floating in a space station. Clamping down on her imagination, she risked one more glimpse and spied an inverted shoreline. She closed her eyes and started swimming in the approximate direction.

She was a strong swimmer. Even with her soaked clothes on, she found it easy and pleasurable to cut through the water that caressed her body like silk. The sea was hers. Ancient Greeks called the Mediterranean hē hēmetérā thálassa, Our Sea, and Cleo understood it on a primal, instinctual level as she had never understood it before.

Her foot touched the bottom. She unglued her eyes.

She was back on the beach. The world had flipped back to its proper configuration: the sand below her feet, the sky above. She could not see any high-rises. They were left behind in the domain of one of the oldest chthonic deities: Medusa whose face no mortal can see. Medusa the Mistress of Stone and Glass.

But she had seen it and survived.

She sat in the puddle of sunlight for a bit, letting her clothes dry. The memory of her awakening in Ano Syros layered itself over the present. But that had been a different Level and a different Cleo.

She had reached the Eighth Level.

LEVEL EIGHT The Cages

This would be a rural or suburban Level.

In the whirlwind of encounters and revelations, this was one thing Cleo clung to: the topography of Orcus. City, village, countryside. But as she wearily dragged herself away from the beach, the landscape unfolding before her did not look like anything she had expected.

A dismal flat plain led away from the sea, sandy soil barely held together by the roots of tough desiccated grass tufting up in untidy plumes and nodding in the gray air. There were boxy concrete bunkers scattered around the plain. Coils of rusty chicken wire snaked on the ground. Some spiky contraptions poked up from the dunes. It looked like a World War II invasion beach. She shivered as a gust of wind, smelling of old ammunition and dirty rain, touched her face. She looked back, seeking solace in the Mediterranean, but the sea frowned back at her with fretful surf and white foamy caps on the steely water. The wind was rising, and clouds shaped like flying snakes were eating into the sunlight. She searched for her backpack, but it had disappeared into the distorted space of the transition between the Seventh and Eighth Levels. Everything she had gathered throughout her ascent was gone, and she was back to where she had been when she had first opened her eyes in Orcus: wet, vulnerable, and alone.

No, she reminded herself. She had her knowledge. She had her understanding of Orcus and its topsy-turvy topography and disjointed rules. She was only one Level below the top where she would find the answers to all the questions weighing down her brain like stones, each Level adding yet another puzzle.

Gusts of wind threw rotten seaweed in her face. It felt like a storm was coming. It was getting colder with every passing minute. Shadows of scuttling clouds raced across the dunes like black cats.

No, not like black cats. There were actual animals slinking among the beach grass. And one was standing on top of a dune, staring at her.

The large cat, almost totally black except for a little white bib, regarded Cleo with regal insolence. When she approached, making kitty noises, the cat jumped off the dune and disappeared into the nearest bunker.

"I don't like you either," she muttered.

The wavy outlines of the dunes blocked the horizon. She could not see any sign of human habitation other than the bunkers. They looked extremely uninviting: old and gray, their walls pitted with scars and eroded by the elements, they squatted on the beach like monstrous turtles. But she had no other option than seeking shelter inside one of them. The wind was rising to an almost gale force, and she needed rest before she could figure out the layout of this forbidding Level. It felt more appropriate to Medusa the Mistress of Stone, but she had been left behind on the Seventh Level. The Ruler of the Eighth Level must be collaborating with Medusa, or just sharing her ugly personality.

Arachne had named her – Lamia. Her story was one of the most unpleasant in mythology, and Cleo was not looking forward to meeting her. According to various sources, Lamia was one of Zeus' paramours, which made her as unique as a raindrop in a downpour, but Hera, Zeus' wife, must have been in a foul mood one day because she had killed all of Lamia's children and took away her eyes. Lamia became a child-stealer and child-eater, a monstrous apparition of the night.

Cleo cautiously approached the bunker the cat had gone inside. There was a passage with raw concrete walls leading inward.

Dribbles of pale light from the depth of the bunker dimly illuminated the lichen-stippled walls and the uneven floor. The air was musty and cold, but there was something even worse overlaying the smell of abandonment: an organic, sewer-like stench.

She carefully edged her way into the passage. The floor had a thin layer of sand blown in, and she saw imprints of cats' paws. So, the animals did go in and out, but what for?

The passage dipped down, turned a corner, and opened up into a large space with embrasure-like windows and a broken floor. And she had an answer to her question.

CHAPTER 52

The walls were festooned with chains, and hanging from these chains like rotten fruit were bodies.

Most of them were skeletons: yellow bones, spider webs of hair, rags of clothes. Some were mummified by the salty air and glared at her with the mindless malevolence of death, their individuality erased by the mask of scowling teeth and empty eyeholes. But the worst thing about this garden of death was the size of the bodies. All of them were children.

Cleo fought nausea. No matter how many atrocities she had witnessed in Orcus, this was something new – and worse. The horror of it was precisely its ordinariness. There was no magic graffiti here or speaking masks. She had seen pictures like these in old documentaries and contemporary newscasts about war crimes and civil atrocities.

She counted the bodies – ten. The sizes seemed to indicate ages below puberty, but at least there were no babies. She could not even guess how long they had been here. Had they been chained to the wall dead or alive? Had they been left here to die of starvation? Cleo hoped they had been corpses when the Ruler of the Eighth Level had arranged this macabre display.

A black cat slunk out of the dark corner, making Cleo cry out in horror. Its presence was so disturbing in this garden of the dead that Cleo rushed out, almost tripping over the animal in her haste to get away. The story of Edgar Allen Poe called "The Black Cat" about a cat walled in with the corpse of its owner flashed through her mind, adding to her distress. It had given her nightmares when she was a child.

Outside, the storm was lacerating the beach. The air was filled with sharp needles of seawater spray and pieces of foam like a swirl of white butterflies. The sea itself was whipped into a frenzy of whitewater, the waves crashing against the shore like a herd of maddened stallions. When they retreated, broken fangs of rock poked out of the churning sand. Cleo needed to find shelter.

But she was not going to go back into the bunker with children's corpses hanging off the walls like macabre Christmas decorations. Leaning into the wind, her vision distorted by tears, she managed to scramble through the hissing sands to the next bunker and dive into its doorway.

Finally catching her breath, she looked around. This one was different because there was no passage leading inside, just a doorway opening into a large dim room with flurries of sand crawling on the bare floor. There were no chains, either, but in the corner of the room was a huddle of what looked like dirty blankets.

She did not want to see what was underneath, but she had to look. She lifted a corner and let it drop immediately.

The boy's dead face stared through her blankly with cloudy, milky eyes. Livid spots of decomposition disfigured his cheeks and forehead.

Cleo wanted to run away but could not. The thunderous rattle and boom of the storm outside warned her not to venture out.

She crawled into the farthest corner from the body and hid her face in her hands.

She had been strong because she had to be strong. Cleo, the responsible one. Cleo, her sister's support system. Cleo, her grandmother's favorite.

Lies.

She had to acknowledge it to herself. She had played a part, using her sister as a foil, to make herself stronger, smarter, better than the poor addicted, mentally-ill, fragile Cora. But they were twins. They were the same. She had deliberately reshaped herself into Cora's opposite but wasn't it only skin-deep? How could she be something other than herself? And had Cora seen through her sister's game, pushing herself deeper into dysfunction as a challenge – or even worse, as an act of love? Had she been debasing herself in order for Cleo to be successful – and smug about her success?

And was her journey through Orcus in search of her sister a feeble attempt at self-justification?

Cleo wiped the salt from her eyes. What difference did it make? If her search for her sister was ultimately about redemption, so what? Actions mattered, not the reasons for them. She would find her sister. She would take her back to the real world. Because there was the real world, with all its horrors and dangers, but also with the predictable rhythm of seasons and geography that did not change from moment to moment, and rulers that were fallible, sometimes evil, but human. Fuck Orcus, the Platonic world of essences that was nothing but a disjointed, illogical nightmare! She would find Cora and take her back. Mykonos or London or Paris or New York. It did not matter. All humanity was one, all stories were the same, all countries flowed into each other. She would bring Cora back.

Sniffling and cold, Cleo huddled in the corner with only a child's corpse for company, listening to the howling of the storm outside, when the soft padding of footsteps snapped her out of her misery.

She lifted her head, her hands groping futilely for the familiar heft of her backpack with its bronze knife, but she had nothing. Apart from her tattered, brine-soaked clothing, she was as bare as the day she came into the world, clutching her sister's hand – or so Eleni had told them. And even though later Cleo realized it was impossible, she never quite let go of the fantasy image of two little nude girls like tinsel angels floating out of some ill-defined pink cloud of their mother's womb and holding hands. And now she was alone, miserable, and defenseless. But her sister was close, she could feel it.

She jumped to her feet, ready to confront whatever new danger Orcus was throwing at her – only to look into the green eyes of a cat who backed off, its back bristling and tail swishing.

She exhaled in relief, but she was not quite reassured. The cat was bigger than the one she had encountered previously but also black and white, with striking tuxedo markings. It hissed, baring its small sharp teeth.

Cleo was not a cat person – or a dog person, for that matter. She liked animals but was too busy to have pets. Still, the presence of so many cats among children's corpses was more than unnerving – it was ghoulish. What were they doing here?

The cat turned around and slunk out of the bunker, and Cleo realized she just could not stand being there anymore, breathing the polluted atmosphere of the bunker. Any storm would be preferable.

Before leaving, she scanned the interior of the bunker again, and saw a small pile of clothing in another corner. She could not stand the sight of another child corpse, but she was so cold that her brain refused to work, slowly shutting down. She was in danger of dying from hypothermia.

She rifled through the pile. There was no corpse there, but all the clothes belonged to children. She paused, holding a pink t-shirt with the stenciled picture of a rainbow unicorn. It was just big enough that it could fit her, stretched to the point of bursting. But wearing a dead child's clothes?

What cannot be cured must be endured.

She put the shirt on over her own clothes.

The wind hit her in the face like a fist, carrying lashes of sand mixed with salt and shreds of foam. Beyond the dunes, the sea was a white cauldron of fury.

She dropped down to her belly and crawled on the sand among the tufts of coarse grass. Miniature tornadoes of sand blinded her, so she was not even sure where she was going. The thunder of the maddened surf provided some orientation, as she was aiming to get away from the sea.

Something jumped upon her back and she screamed, flailing and trying to dislodge the heavy body.

It was another cat, black and white as well, and the size of a terrier. It launched itself at Cleo, its claws shredding her jean leg and leaving the tracery of pain on her skin. She grabbed the loose hide on the cat's neck and tried to drag it away, but the creature hissed and swiped at her hand. The scratches burned like hell. She kicked the cat and cast around for a stone or a stick. Picking up what looked like a gnarled driftwood branch, she threatened the animal who suddenly stopped its attack and slunk into a nearby bunker. She cursed. Monsters were bad enough – but cats? Who knew what bacteria the creature carried on its claws?

She looked at the branch, still clutched in her fingers, and flung it away as far as she could. It was a human bone.

The gale was not weakening but she had gone far enough from the boiling sea to be able to withstand its fury. The landscape remained the same: an infinite expanse of dreary dunes, dotted with squatting bunkers. In the whipping beach grass, quick black shadows slunk from bunker to bunker. A cat, even bigger than the one that had attacked Cleo, was briefly silhouetted against the concrete wall, sparking off a moment of recognition. She remembered the graffiti of black cats on the Seventh Level. There had to be a connection! But what was it? From everything she had been told, each Level had its own Ruler. She had left the domain of the Mistress of Stone and Glass behind. So why did black cats infest this Level?

She did not want to enter any more bunkers, but she knew she had no choice. The way to the Final Level had to be through one of them, as the dreary flatness of this uninviting beach showed no other landmark that could possibly lead to her goal.

She walked into the bunker to her left through the wide arched doorway. At least she would not be plunged into darkness! She found herself in a short hall, with a sturdy metal door barring the way inside. The hall was empty.

Well, not quite. There was a glass jar standing by the wall. She lifted it and gasped.

CHAPTER 53

The jar was filled with eyes.

Human eyes – blue, hazel, and brown – floating in a cloudy solution, the eyeballs trailing clusters of nerves like deformed tadpoles. One of the eyes edged closer to the glass; its pupil dilated as it seemed to study Cleo.

Orcus had toughened her because she did not drop the jar. She put it on the floor and turned to walk out, when she heard knocking coming from the other side of the inner door.

She paused, uncertain what to do. Now that she looked at it, she saw that the door was latched from the outside with a simple bar. She crept closer. The knocking was irregular and not particularly strong, as if whoever was inside the bunker was losing hope. At least she knew it was not a cat!

"Who are you?" she called out.

The knocking died down for a second, and then resumed with renewed vigor. She remembered children's corpses in chains.

She slid the bar aside.

The door banged open and a small figure barreled out, almost colliding with Cleo, who managed to put out her arms to stop the boy's panicky flight. She grasped his shoulders, and for a moment they stared at each other.

The boy was about seven or eight: peaky, pale, with hazel eyes and blond hair. He was dressed only in khaki shorts and sandals, his upper torso bare and covered with gooseflesh. He shivered violently, trying to wriggle away from Cleo.

"It's okay. It's okay. I'm not going to hurt you. I'm Cleo. What's your name?"

"Brian," the boy muttered.

"All right, Brian, calm down. Who locked you in?"

"She…" The boy cast a fearful glance at Cleo, still trying to get away. Another freezing gust of wind through the doorway whipped his semi-nude body.

"Who is 'she'?"

Brian just shook his head.

"Where are your parents, Brian?"

"In the City of Glass."

"What? The Seventh Level? Is this where you are from?"

The boy nodded miserably.

"How did you get here?"

The boy's eyes opened wide as he looked at something behind Cleo. She looked back. Another one of the cats stood in the doorway, its black-and-white fur fluffed up by the wind, its spindle-shaped pupils dilating as it stared at Cleo and Brian. It was even bigger than its predecessors.

"Shoo!" Cleo advanced on the cat who regarded her disdainfully, but then scampered away.

"The cats," Brian whimpered.

"The cats brought you here?"

He nodded again.

"How?"

"Paintings appear on walls at night and capture people. Mum and Dad told me never to go out when it's dark. But once I saw a cat on our wall, and my friend Elfie told me cats are good and can take you away if you talk to them. So I sneaked out after the dark, and the cat came off the wall and promised to take me to the Final Level. But instead she just brought me here and locked me up with no food. I'm hungry!"

The boy sniveled, and Cleo felt helpless; she was just as hungry and had nothing to offer him.

"It's okay," she said, trying to keep a brave façade. "We will go and look for something to eat."

That was an overly optimistic goal, she thought, but what else could they do? The promise of food worked. Brian stopped fighting and apparently deciding to trust her, slid his small grubby hand into hers.

"Are there any more kids inside?" Cleo asked, apprehensive of having to care for an entire primary school, but to her relief Brian shook his head.

They exited the bunker, shivering in the icy wind that seemed to get even colder. The boy's naked upper body was getting blue as he hugged himself. Cleo sighed.

She should stop trying to save strays!

She took off the rainbow unicorn t-shirt she had found in the other bunker and gave it to Brian.

"Put it on!" she growled as the wind gleefully lashed at her.

If Brian objected to wearing a girl's pink shirt, she mentally swore she would leave him to fend for himself. But not only did he eagerly snatch the shirt and put it on, he also thanked her politely.

They headed inland.

"Why did you want to escape the City of Glass?' Cleo asked. "Were your parents mean to you?"

"No, Mum and Dad are okay. But everybody wants to reach the Final Level. There we will be made gods and rule over the Archipelago."

CHAPTER 54

As Cleo and Brian walked away from the sea, the landscape was finally beginning to change, though not necessarily for the better. The sand and coarse grass gave way to firm ground covered with creepers and a variety of short plants. Some gaunt shrubs stuck out here and there, whipping in the unrelenting wind. The bunkers were still around, hunkering in this bleak landscape like sullen behemoths. They blocked the view of the horizon, but Cleo had no hope of seeing her goal. Since entering the Asphodel Fields in Dream City, she had not seen the top of the mountain of dead gods.

Ahead of them, one bunker was almost covered in greenery. Moss, lichen, and ivy clung to its splintered walls and grew out of its multiple cracks. This one looked older than the rest, and Cleo decided it was as good a reason to enter as any. She was wiped out, hungry and thirsty, and Brian was lagging behind, barely able to move. And it was getting even colder, as the uninviting sky grew the color of a pigeon's breast: gray, lilac, and purple. The night was coming, and she had no idea where else to find shelter. The added responsibility of Brian compounded her distress.

"Wait here," she told him, and peeked into the green-festooned bunker. It was dark inside, and warmer because the bunker's tiny windows had actual glass. There were no chains and no bodies, but shelves at the back had a couple of glass jars she decided not to examine as her attention was drawn to what sat in the middle of the floor: a lumpish shape of some kind.

She crept closer and gasped.

It was her backpack.

The next minutes were spent in the frantic examination of its contents, and then in the blessed relief of sweet water sliding down her parched throat and watching Brian gulp half a bottle in a single draught. Her flatbread was still there, wrapped up in plastic film, and she shared it with the boy. Everything else was in its place: the bronze knife, the collection of coins, her spare clothes. The backpack was dry. Wherever it had ended when she tossed it through the window of Medusa's high-rise, it was not in the sea.

Cleo finally relaxed a bit. While the cats were still prowling outside – she could see slick feline silhouettes against the darkening background of the entryway – they did not try to enter their bunker. It was cold, but by using her spare clothes and huddling together with Brian, she thought they could survive the night. And if it got freezing – well, the backpack contained matches and they could collect enough driftwood to make a fire. She did not like this idea: a fire would stand out like a scream on this darkened plain, and who knew what it could attract? But at least they had this option.

Brian curled up by her side, covered by her jacket. Cleo was not one of the women with a hypertrophied maternal instinct – while vaguely considering a family sometime in the future, she found most babies and younger children annoying, but the memory of the small skeletons in chains was still fresh in her mind and she felt protective toward the boy. She patted his shoulder reassuringly.

"Sleep," she said. "I'll keep watch."

Brian's face poked from under the canvas of the jacket like a bird from the nest.

"She comes at night," he whispered.

"She? The cat?"

"No, the Cat Lady."

"Who is the Cat Lady?"

But Brian did not answer, and Cleo discovered that he was fast asleep, curled up by her side. She sighed and nested closer. Brian was an unforeseen complication, but his presence also gave her comfort.

She woke up to the sound of footsteps outside.

She sat up and listened. These were not a cat's soft padding. Somebody heavy was walking outside the bunker. Or maybe "walking" was the wrong word. It sounded like the person was groping around, shambling, stopping, and then resuming their purposeless meandering. At some point, she heard the sound of a fall and then a groan as the walker got up.

Was the person injured? Cleo decided she was not going to find out. It was dark in the bunker, with only a dim drip of moonlight pooling on the floor by the entrance. The storm had abated but the hiss of the wind was still overlaid upon the soothing splash of the surf. Brian slept quietly by her side.

She hoped the walker would just go away but no such luck. Their erratic wandering was coming closer to the bunker instead of retreating. A lumpy shadow eclipsed the entryway.

A smaller shadow detached itself from the silhouette and ran inside. Another one of those damned cats! This one was not as big as the one that had attacked Cleo. It was purely black, with not a white spot anywhere. Its luminescent eyes glowed like fallen stars as it crept closer.

Brian's breathing got faster as he stirred and tried to sit up. Cleo pressed her hand against his mouth.

"Shh!"

The cat meowed and arched its back. Its owner blundered into the bunker.

In the dimness, Cleo could not see her very well, for which she was profoundly grateful, but she saw enough: the ragged smelly clothes of a bag lady; the long thin strands of dirty hair, with the greasy scalp glistening through; the hands so emaciated they looked like a bird's talons. But worst of all was the face: gaunt and dusty. And two black slicks of blood dripping down the hollow cheeks from the empty eyeholes.

Brian whimpered.

The blind woman turned her head toward them, and her gaping nostrils quivered. Her nose was fretted and caved in as if she suffered from leprosy. She shuffled toward the shelves at the back of the bunker. A groping hand reached out and took one of the glass jars.

Cleo knew what was going to happen next, and she did not want to see it, butt the cat barred their way as she dragged Brian toward the exit. It hissed loudly, its fur sparking off static electricity.

The woman was moving with the horrible sluglike non-coordination, but she was quick. The bony fingers groped in the jar and pulled out a dripping eye. With a smacking sound, the woman inserted it into her left eyehole. The eye focused on Cleo, staring at her with mocking malice. The woman pulled out a second eye and inserted it too. The eyes were mismatched, blue and brown, but they were gleeful and watchful. The woman blinked her lash-less inflamed lids, fixing the borrowed eyes firmly in their places.

Meanwhile, more cats had arrived, blocking the exit. Cleo might have tried to break through – she had faced worse than cat scratches in Orcus – but she could not further traumatize Brian.

She faced the woman.

"What do you want from me, Lamia?" she asked. "I am Kora the Maiden. Bow down to me, you Child-Eater!"

CHAPTER 55

amia laughed.

It was a rusty sound like the screech of old machinery forced to perform its intended function one last time. Her teeth were sharpened and black with decay.

"The Maiden?" she said mockingly. "You are nobody! Your mother does not want you. You have blundered your way into the world you don't understand, lying and being lied to at every turn. You have no power in Orcus. You are nothing!"

She turned to the cats and motioned to the living wall of bristling fur that crept closer to Cleo and Brian, their putrid breath fouling the air. Brian whimpered.

Cleo felt the accumulated fatigue of her ascent fall upon her like the weight of Orcus itself. Her knees buckled and she lowered her head. Lamia laughed again.

And it was the petty malice in this laugh that made it all come back: the slights and taunts of her childhood; English kids teasing her for her Greek parentage, and Greek kids refusing to play with her because she was English; the humiliation of poverty and then the humiliation of prosperity bought with her stepfather's money; all the times she stood up for Cora and all the times Cora run away from fights, abandoning her; unanswered phone calls and unread texts.

She had survived all of this. She had survived seven Levels of Orcus. She was Kora the Maiden. She had the talismans she had collected in her ascent, but suddenly she realized she did not need them anymore.

Koresh's words came back to her:

It may not protect you anymore but at least it will remind you of your courage. There are worse things to be reminded of.

She stretched her hand toward the snarling, spitting cats, and they halted. Then she turned to Lamia.

"I am the Maiden," she said. "And you are a beast, child-eater, night-crawler. You could not keep your children safe, so you steal other mothers' kids and other women's eyes because your own have been gouged out by your lover's jealous wife. You are despicable. I could kill you, but I won't. I'll just do to you what Hera had done – take your sight, so you could only stew in your impotent rage and never see other people's happiness. I am sealing your empty eyes forever!"

And pulling the Eye of Charon from under her shirt, she thrust it toward Lamia. The blue-and-white pendant pulsed with a single burst of light and heat, scorching her fingers, and shattered. Its slivers flew toward Lamia like a hail of bullets, embedding themselves in her stolen eyes.

The scream that tore through the night silenced the whisper of the wind and the rhythmic beating of the surf. The cats turned around and scrambled out of the bunker, their claws clicking on the cement floor. Lamia collapsed, rotten blood and vitreous gel streaming down her ruined face. Cleo grabbed Brian's hand and rushed outside.

It was cold but the gale had died down, and the diluted moonlight made going easier. Cleo did not know where to go but suddenly she saw a feeble glimmer of light in the distance and made a beeline for it.

Brian kept up with her. They boy did not appear to be in shock, for which Cleo was profoundly grateful.

"Is the Cat-Lady dead?" he asked.

"I don't know," Cleo said, but she had no hope she was. At best, Cleo had managed to put her out of commission for the remainder of the night. The cats were still loose but she could deal with those.

Cleo could not remember anything about Lamia's association with cats, but the Rulers of Orcus were clearly not bound by mythological precedents.

"Is she the one who came to you in the City of Glass?" she Brian.

The boy nodded.

"Why did you follow her? She looks like an Evil Witch of the West."

"She was not ugly when she came to me and my friends. She was a beautiful lady. She promised to take us to the Final Level and to make us gods."

Lamia had indeed been beautiful once and retained some shapeshifting ability. Remembering the skeletons in other bunkers, Cleo did not want to inquire about the fate of Brian's friends.

"Why did you want to be a god?" she asked.

"To kill the word-plants and take my Mum and Dad away from the City of Glass. We did not like it there. My friend Tammy's parents were taken and turned into pictures on the wall."

"Word-plants" must have been what he called the predatory graffiti. It was as good a name for them as any.

The further they got away from the sea, the easier the walking became. The land was flat and sparsely covered with grass and dwarfish shrubs. The bunkers had disappeared, and instead there were some uninviting structures like industrial sheds or barns scattered around. Cleo felt pavement under her feet and realized they had somehow blundered onto a paved path. She kept on walking toward the glimmer of light ahead.

They came close enough to see its source.

CHAPTER 42

The shed ahead of them had its door ajar and light was streaming onto the pavement. It was not electricity; the glow was uneven and red-tinged like firelight. Cleo peeked through the crack.

There was an ancient-looking tin stove in the middle of the empty space. Huddling next to it were several kids. Cleo hesitated to hail them, but Brian forestalled her, running into the shed. She made a grab for him but missed.

"Tammy!" he cried.

One of the kids wearily lifted her head. She was the same age as Brian, or even younger: a little, tow-headed girl in a torn and stained dress with a dirty face. The other kids also stirred but made no move toward Brian. Neither did Tammy.

The kids were all bound together, a rope of some kind linking their wrists and going around their huddle. Brian almost barreled into Tammy but then suddenly stopped and tried to backpedal. Cleo's eyes adjusted to the firelight, and she saw what spooked him.

The dirty smudges on the little girl's face were dried blood. One of her eyes was a swollen meaty lump. The other stared blankly into the distance. The other kids were squirming on the floor like a litter of blind mice.

Cleo tried to pull Brian out of the shed, but the rope that bound the kids snaked toward him and lassoed his wrist. With a spasm of revulsion, she saw that it was a blood-filled gut that seemed to grow in and out of the children's flesh. Gritting her teeth, she tugged on the living rope trying to burrow into Brian's thin arm. She managed to pull it off him but now the disgustingly warm thing was winding around her own wrists. The bunch of kids strung upon the blood rope acted as an anchor, dragging her down.

"Get the knife from my backpack!" she yelled at Brian.

The boy obeyed. He was tougher than he looked, or perhaps the hammering of unceasing traumas had annealed him into premature adulthood. He fumbled in the backpack as Cleo struggled against the blood-swollen gut. The blind kids did not actively attack her, but their uncoordinated squirming made her fight harder. She tried to avoid hurting them as she tugged and pulled. She felt nothing but pity for them. As the source of the eyes on the jars, they would be fodder for Lamia when she regained her power. Cleo had no illusions that she could actually kill any of the Nine – at least, not until she had reached the Final Level and confronted its Ruler.

Her mother.

She could not think about it now. The rope was tightening its grip, digging, trying to grow into Cleo's arm, and her skin was feeling loose and dislocated.

Brian handed her the bronze knife, and she slashed blindly through the tough tegument. Thick hot blood spurted out, drenching her top. The kids cried out all together in a chorus of inarticulate pain. The gut slackened but did not let go. And where the blood splattered the edge of the knife it smoked and dulled, covered with a grayish patina.

Brain tried to help her, but his small hands were no match for the resiliency of the living rope that, driven into frenzy by its injury, whipped and wound tighter around Cleo's arms. Tammy shambled toward him, trailing coils of the bloodied gut, and collided with her playmate. Both fell onto the floor, dragging Cleo down. Brian wriggled free.

"Run!" Cleo yelled, and he disappeared through the open door.

She slashed again and again, but the knife was useless. Melted by the children's hot blood, it had become a lump of tarnished bronze. She tossed it away and struggled futilely to free herself.

"Maiden!" a musical voice behind her called, and the blood rope suddenly stopped its flailing. It no longer needed to: Cleo was securely bound at her wrists. She struggled to her feet and turned around.

Lamia stood by the doorway, the pale light of the dawn illuminating her beautiful face. She had regained the appearance that once upon a time had tempted Zeus and enraged Hera. Golden hair tightly arranged in a crown of small curls; a slender body, incongruously clad in a Regency high-waisted muslin dress; a plump scarlet mouth. Cleo remembered a poem by John Keats called "Lamia", but the poet who said "truth is beauty" would have changed his opinion had he seen this creature. The eyes gave the monstrosity away: one blue, one brown, they bulged out of the orbits, as if improperly fitted.

Lamia was not alone. Cleo stared at her companion, feeling the pieces of the puzzle fall into place.

CHAPTER 57

ach stepped forward, as if challenging Cleo.

"So, you made it here!" Cleo hissed. "You bastard! How many times did you double-cross me? You sold me out to the Dutch boys! You led me into Medusa's trap! Why did you do it? You are an antigrafo of Hermes, why the hell are you collaborating with this bunch of monsters?"

"I also saved you in Dream City," Zach responded. "Not to mention protecting you in London."

"Protecting me from what? And in Dream City, you only helped me because you wanted me to go up, right? You were in cahoots with Medusa. You betrayed me, and betrayed Arachne too. Why, Mick? I thought we were friends!"

"Friends? In other words, a temporary hookup, to take your mind off more important matters. I never had any illusions about our relationship, Cleo."

"Relationship? What relationship? We were friends. Or at least, I thought we were."

"Cora said the same thing."

"Really? So, you had a fling with Cora too? Fuck you."

"Jealous?"

"You flatter yourself. My sister never had a good taste in men, and apparently neither do I. Twins, right? But who gives a fuck about your love life? Don't tell me you ended up in Orcus because of your broken heart. What do you want, Mick? What's your game?"

A band of dawn light fell onto Zach's face, and as Cleo got a better look at him, she got another shock.

It was Zach but not as she remembered him from Dream City. He stood taller and he was dressed in brand-new designer athleisure wear, but the main difference was in his face, though it took her a moment to realize what it was.

Zach's eyes were no longer dark. They were washed-out blue.

"So, you had been Called too."

"I tried to tell you," Zach/Mick said with sadness in his voice. "But you would not listen. Just as she never did."

"She?"

"Cora."

"What did you want from Cora?"

"The same thing I wanted from you."

"Just don't say 'love' or I'm going to puke."

"Understanding. Yes, I knew who I was when I was in London. I knew who you were. The two of you had the power to remake the world. And what did you do instead? Cora with her clubbing and her drugs, and \ you with your neat corporate resume. Goddesses on the Tube, eyes glazed, posting on social media, while the world is going to hell!"

There was a genuine passion in Zach's voice, and Cleo realized that it was as close to the real man as she was likely to get. It did not make her like him any better.

"So, you put the idea of Greece into Iris' head…"

"Didn't take much persuasion." Zach smirked. "She was a better girlfriend than you, sorry to say!"

Cleo rolled her eyes.

"More fool her," she responded. "She is dead, isn't she?"

"I could not stop the Dutch boys."

"I bet you didn't try too hard."

"They wanted you for their parádeigma. I wanted you to come here. To the Eighth Level. Where my Caller lives."

"This?" Cleo strained against the living rope that was eating into her wrists, cutting the circulation, burrowing, dripping thick alien blood into her bloodstream. "Her? The Child-Eater? I could understand Medusa – maybe – but being the lapdog of this crazy cannibal? What's wrong with you?"

"The Mistress of Stone and Glass was your Caller," Zach retorted. "Didn't mean you got along with her, did you?"

"Why did Medusa want me? Why does Lamia want you?"

"They work together, Medusa and Lamia. Did you ever consider why the Nine were triumphant over the Olympians?"

"Because they are a bunch of freaks and monsters."

"No, because they have the power of the underdog. Medusa and Lamia are victims, remember? Victims of rape, mistreatment, male power…"

"Sure, great feminist heroines that they are! Stop giving me this bullshit! Medusa and Lamia are working together to ascend to the Final Level, right? To depose its Ruler. And then there will be more kids abducted and people killed. But how will they decide who rules? And what's in this for you?"

Zach grinned.

"What's in that for me? Oh, a small thing: just saving the world. As for how they decide who rules, it's up to them. We just need to depose the Barren One. And now we finally got our trump card. We have you."

There was nothing more to be said after that.

Cleo was locked up in a shed and bound by the rope woven out of children's blood.

This was more distressing than the fact she was exhausted and hungry. More even distressing than the fact her backpack, her faithful friend and reliable support in her ascent, was now an empty bag of artificial leather, casually thrown at her feet. They did not even bother to take it away. She had spent everything she had accumulated in her journey through the Nine Levels of Orcus. No more talismans. Her carefully packed spare clothing was reduced to rags, her water bottle empty, her food pouch torn. The leather thong used to hold the Eye of Charon flopped uselessly on her chest. But she could have accepted all of this. What she could not accept was the horrific sight of the maimed kids as helpless and blind as newborn kittens crawling on the floor, and of the rope tethered to their drained bodies. She had never hated anyone as she hated Zach now. Or should she call him Mick?

Her memory was returning. Was it because she had not eaten anything with pomegranate in it for a long time? She had not eaten anything for a long time, period.

Or maybe she had been editing and rearranging her memory for a long time before she came to Orcus. Creating a story in which she was the heroine and Cora the victim; in which her twin's ruined life was a foil to her own success.

She remembered Mick well now. They were in the same circles at the university. Then he moved out of her orbit, and she was mildly surprised when Cora brought him home on a couple of occasions during the brief period that they shared a flat before her twin's drug addiction spiraled out of control, forcing Cleo to move out. Cleo neither liked nor disliked him. He was a colorless spot on the edge of her awareness. Faithful Mick, reliable Mick, good mate Mick.

After Cora's disappearance, she was suddenly cast adrift. She had nobody to talk to about her sister. Their mother accepted Cora's supposed suicide with almost visible relief, prompting Cleo's angry outburst and the cutting-off of communication. Cleo had not seen their father in years and knew nothing of his whereabouts. It suddenly occurred to her that perhaps Jerrod Brown was not her father at all. Who was Persephone's father? Zeus?

Mick had been there to hold her hand when she went through a litany of regrets, reminiscences, and second guesses. A boyfriend? No way. They had slept together a couple of times, but Cleo had quickly put an end to it, explaining that she was not in the right frame of mind for a relationship. She thought he had accepted it with no hard feelings. What a fool she had been!

And now it turned out that he, an antigrafo of Hermes, the messenger of the gods, had been in cahoots with the worst monsters of the Nine: Medusa who turned her subjects into murals on the walls of her lifeless city, and Lamia, the Child-Eater. Why? How?

But then she remembered Or, living as a child in the house of his original's killers.

There was clearly something about the Upheaval and the role of antigrafos in it she did not understand, and now was the time to try to figure it out. Lamia and Zach were going to take her to the Final Level pretty soon, and then blackmail her supposed mother into giving up her power in exchange for her daughter's life.

The children's pitiful moaning distracted her to the point of madness. Cleo wanted to comfort them but the blood-swollen rope tethering them together was twisted around her wrists in such a way that every move she made drained them faster and increased their distress. She dropped her head into her hands, trying to block out the inarticulate cries of pain and to focus on her own survival, but it was as if the determination that had sustained her in the ascent of Orcus had dissolved in the accumulation of traumas. She was no longer the put-together, strong, goal-oriented Cleo. She was as weak, scattered, and unpredictable as her twin. She was becoming Cora.

Lamia and Zach had said nothing about her sister being on the Final Level. The whole thing had been an elaborate charade, a lure to lead her into their trap. Cora was probably dead. What everybody told her had happened must have been the truth: Cora had had an accident or killed herself, perhaps by emulating Eleni's drowning, and her body was lost in the treacherous currents of the cold sea or swallowed up by the quicksand. The Ockham razor: the simplest explanation is always true.

She was praying for Zach and Lamia to come back and take her away. Whatever happened next, she no longer cared. She embraced resignation like the tepid bath that did not warm you but allowed you to pretend it did. All she wanted now was just to be out of sight of these crawling, blinded children.

A small hand fell on her shoulder, and Cleo jerked upright. At first she thought one of the blinded kids had somehow managed to make their way to her, but then she saw the familiar hazel eyes and the grubby rainbow t-shirt. Brian!

She had hoped he would somehow find his way back to the City of Glass and his parents, even though she knew descending Orcus was impossible, but now she was glad to see that he had not abandoned her. This small gesture of loyalty perked her up, and she felt ashamed of her funk. Perhaps all was not lost.

But what could a small child do?

"What are you doing here?" she whispered.

"I want to help you, Miss!"

"You can't! You should hide…"

She felt the hopelessness of their situation fall upon her like a load of rocks. The Eighth Level belonged to the Child-Eater. Even if the rest of it was not as dismal as the beach, where would Brian go? How long could he hide from the cats?

He sat by her side, leaning into her.
"I want my Mum," he murmured.
"I know, Honey. What's your Mum's name?"
"Iris," Brian said.

CHAPTER 58

Lamia was back but neither as a sickeningly beautiful woman nor as the fumbling eyeless zombie she had first appeared to Cleo. The creature looming at the door was a grotesque hybrid of the two. The muslin Regency dress hung loose over the protruding bones, stained with the black mold of decomposition. The golden hair was matted with gore. The pretty face was livid, and teeth showed through a hole in the cheek where it was eaten through. But the worst thing was her expression of unhinged, mindless rage in those bulging mismatched eyes.

She reached for Brian, and Cleo threw herself between the two of them.

"Let him go!" she shouted. "Let all the kids go! If you want me to negotiate with Demeter on your behalf, let them go!"

Lamia paused.

"Let them go!" Cleo repeated. "You need me to bargain with my mother, right? You need me on your side. Let them go, and I'll come with you willingly and plead with my mother to step down. You can figure out the pecking order on your own. I will convince Demeter to leave the Final Level, but only if you release Brian and the other kids."

"Do you promise, Maiden?" Lamia asked, her voice thick and clogged with phlegm. "Do you swear?"

"I promise," Cleo said. "I swear."

"The Maiden's word is inviolable," Lamia insisted.

"Sure. Just let the kids go back to the City of Glass."

"I can't do it," Lamia said. "We can only send our subjects up Levels, not down."

"I can do it," Brian said. "I have the rainbow."

"Iris?" Cleo had repeated in disbelief and felt a stirring of impossible hope. "How does she look, your Mum?"

A mane of blond curls, a smile that lit up the room, a silly rainbow unicorn t-shirt...

Brian shrugged. She was just Mummy to him.

"Where were you born, Brian? Where did you live before the City of Glass?"

"Fulton Close".

Cleo's eyes filled with tears. She knew the address well. She still could not remember the face of the child who played with his Lego when she dropped by her friend's but she remembered the street and the tiny garden blazing with multicolored flowers in summer.

Brian was Iris' son.

"Is she with you in the City of Glass?"

He shook his head.

"My Mum is gone," he said solemnly. "My parents in the City of Glass are okay, but they are not my real parents."

"Foster parents?"

"Yes."

"Why did you want to be a god, Brian?"

"Because I am one already. I have Mum's rainbow. But I thought I would grow up quickly and kill all the monsters if I got to the Final Level. But the Cat Lady was strong, and she took the rainbow away, and locked me up. But you found it."

He touched the cheap rainbow print on his shirt.

The seven-color arc of pure light sprung around him like a halo, setting the pale lifeless dawn of the Eighth Level on fire. It curved over his head, glowing brighter with the boy's every labored breath. The rainbow, the attribute of Iris, the goddess of good news and the messenger of divinity.

Brian grabbed the end of the rainbow – actually grabbed it, his small fingers closing over the insubstantial nimbus of light and squeezing it as if it was a rubber toy – and he thrust it at Cleo.

"Take it!" he breathed.

She tried to move her bound hands but the blood rope bit into her viciously, cutting off the circulation. Her fingers felt numb and useless, heavy burdens weighing her hands down.

Brian dragged the rainbow closer to Cleo's wrists, and she managed to lift them up. He touched the glowing end to the blood rope and it caught fire.

The flame ran along the rope that bubbled and hissed, emitting a choking odor of burnt blood and leaving a track of blackened skin along Cleo's arms and legs. The blind kids keened. But the rope fell apart into sooty flakes and she was free.

She jumped to her feet. Brian, still wielding the rainbow as if it was a tangible thing, flung it toward the exit and it unspooled into a prismatic road.

"It will take us where we want to go!" he said.

Where we want to go. But where was that?

Lamia growled.

Cleo tried to scoop up the rest of the children, but they were all tangled in the blood rope and twitched together in a heavy pile. There were four of them, including the little girl Brian had called Tammy.

Brian tried to help her, his mouth moving as he said something, but whatever he was trying to convey was swallowed up in the roar coming from outside the shed like a military plane taking off above their heads. Even the blind kids stopped their moaning.

A figure stepped from behind Lamia's back and into the shed.

It was Zach but in his Hermes form, with the golden helmet, the shining metallic body, the blank face. The snakes on his caduceus writhed and hissed, and he pointed the caduceus at the boy.

Brian yanked up the fading rainbow and pulled out one of the seven bands of color – the red one. It burst into a ball of scarlet flame, which he lobbed at Zach who easily deflected it with his caduceus. The ball rolled on the floor and fizzled out in a shower of red sparks. Brian pulled out the orange band and repeated the attack, which was more successful this time. The orange flame, buzzing and roiling, flew at Zach/Hermes and struck him in the middle of his blank helmet, leaving behind a smear of soot and eliciting a howl of pain. Zach jabbed with his caduceus at Brian, and one of the snakes opened its mouth and spat a gob of foaming poison at the boy. He managed to avoid it, but it fell onto the rainbow and the yellow band started fading. Brian cried out, blisters rising on his cheeks as if the poison had landed on him instead of the rainbow.

The fight between a child and an avatar of the messenger god was so unreal that Cleo, despite having been exposed to any number of dangerous unrealities in Orcus, simply gaped at it. But hearing Brian's cry, she realized that she needed to intervene. Pain and injury were the bedrock of existence, in the Platonic universe of essences and the shadow world alike.

"Stop it!" she yelled.

Brian tried to pick up the yellow band, but it faded out of existence as he touched it. The snakes lunged forward.

"You killed Iris!" she shouted at Zach. "Leave her son alone!"

Zach lifted his snake-wound staff.

Cleo turned to Lamia.

"Stop him! Or I will kill myself instead of going with you to the Final Level! Death is final in Orcus!"

Lamia hesitated, her borrowed eyes shifting from Cleo to Zach and back again.

"You don't need him anymore!" Cleo continued feverishly. "You need me! He is an antigrafo of the god of thieves! How can you trust him? He killed my friend. He plotted with Arachne, and he betrayed her. He will betray you too!"

The Hermes disguise sloughed off Zach like a snakeskin. He bared his teeth at Cleo – a small, enraged, and empty man.

"I was trying to save the world!" he snarled. "The Barren One is destroying it. I thought Arachne could stop her, but she can't!"

"Lies! You have so many plans and schemes you no longer know who you are working for! Lamia, get rid of this traitor, and I will do whatever you want me to do, I swear! The Maiden's word is inviolate."

Zach lunged at Cleo, but then he stopped as if he had run into a glass wall. His eyes bulged.

Lamia opened her mouth. A thin red tongue snaked out, reaching for Zach, as it grew scales and fangs, turning into an actual snake. And then another. A whole bouquet of writhing coral snakes shot out of Lamia's mouth, distending her jaw until it dropped down to her chest. Her eyes fell out of her head and splashed onto the floor.

But Zach had snakes of his own. The black and white reptiles on his caduceus reared up, their hoods opening like poisonous calla lilies. They struck at Lamia's coral snakes.

Linked by the flailing, hissing snarl of snakes, Zach and Lamia engaged in a weirdly awkward dance, like two puppets entangled in their strings. Lamia, the Ruler of the penultimate Level, was stronger than a mere antigrafo, but Zach was fighting for his life.

"Help her," Cleo whispered to Brian, and it was no wonder that he hesitated. Lamia had abducted him and his friends, had stolen the other children's eyes, and would no doubt eventually devour them if she could. But to survive in Orcus, one needed to make unsavory alliances.

Brian pulled the blue stripe off the rainbow and whipped it at Zach, rotating it like a lasso. It struck the man across his face and he staggered back. The black and white snakes, already retreating under the onslaught of Lamia's tongues, hesitated. And that was all it took for one of the snake-tongues to strike. As swift as an arrow, it thrust at Zach's throat.

He lurched and fell back. Out of nowhere, a black cat leaped onto his face, its extended claws raking his eyes.

"Don't!" Cleo screamed but it was too late. Zach shrieked, his face disfigured by runnels of blood. The cat jumped onto her mistress' shoulder and dropped a bleeding blue orb into her hand. Lamia inserted it into one of her empty eyeholes.

Cleo knelt by Zach's side. His face was bloodied and puffed up; his breathing wheezed as his throat was locked by the poison. She knew she should feel pity for him, but she could not. She felt nothing. It was as if all the conflicting emotions that had swirled around him – friendship, reliance, distrust – canceled each other out, leaving nothing but void.

"Who wrote the letter, Mick?" she asked.

She did not know whether he could talk; his airways were shutting down. But he managed to squeeze out:

"You will never know."

Cleo got up.

"I will find out," she said. "Sorry, god of liars and thieves, but your time is up. The realm of essences has no need of you anymore."

She turned to Lamia who regarded her with one borrowed eye, the second one – a bloodstained ruin. She had absorbed back her snake-tongues and pushed back up her dislocated jaw. It had improved her appearance but only just.

"Let the children go," she said.

Lamia shrugged.

"I have no need of them," she replied, thick blood bubbling in her throat. "There will be many more once I am the Ruler of the Final Level."

"I bet the Mistress or Stone and Glass will have something to say about it," Cleo muttered. That was her only hope now, slender as it was. Medusa and Lamia were allies against the Barren One, but how long could they maintain their alliance once Demeter was deposed?

Lamia snapped her fingers and the blood ropes fell off the blinded children. Brian pulled the violet band off his t-shirt where only the green and indigo remained.

He turned to Cleo, his eyes big and uncertain, and she saw a faint outline of her friend's face in his.

"Go!" she whispered. "Grow up."

She wanted to add And kill all the monsters, but Lamia was listening.

Brian took Tammy's hand and the rest of the kids held onto each other in a chain. He led them onto the violet strip, which unfolded into a shimmering path. Once they were on it, the path blinked out of existence with all the kids.

Lamia smacked her slack lips.

"Well, Maiden," she said, "this is your last ascent. We are going to the Final Level."

ThE FINAL LEVEL The Wasteland

This time, at least, there was no need to search for hidden doorways, call up spooky elevators, or clamber over the body of a monster. With Lamia and Medusa flanking her on both sides, Cleo stood in front of an imposing double door set into a massive marble frame with two Doric columns. The pediment over the door depicted the story of Demeter and Persephone: the daughter abducted by Hades, the mother searching for her, and their reunion. Cleo stared at the graceful marble outlines of drapery-clad figures and felt nothing. It evoked no memories or feelings. It was an ancient tale, that was all.

The door was unusual in one respect – it was not connected to any building or structure. It stood in the middle of a depressing flat field, dotted with occasional sheds, like all of Lamia's domain. Cleo could not help but notice how depleted Tartarus was, even compared with the lower Levels of Elysium and the Asphodel Fields. The sky on this Level was permanently stormy, the sea angry, and the land exhausted, as if all three rebelled against the torture of children perpetrated by its Ruler.

Lamia, had donned yet another Romantic disguise, with a flower-decked bonnet and a high-waisted white dress. She had also picked up another mismatched eye, this one bright green, to pair with Zach's blue one. It was noticeably bigger too, bulging out of its distended orbit and dripping slow drops of blood onto her rouged cheek.

To Cleo's relief, Medusa was not wearing the face she had stolen from her. Instead, she showed up in her classic persona: a permanent expression of rage etched into her finely sculpted features, her mouth gaping in an inaudible scream, and a nest of lethargic worms on her head.

Cleo was bone tired. She had had it with these two female monsters. Once hailed as symbols of rebellion or alluring femmes fatales, they had become nothing but empty vortices of hunger and resentment. She did not know what awaited her on the Final Level, but she had no illusions Demeter would be any better. How could the erstwhile goddess of harvest and agriculture join forces with creatures of mindless destruction?

But ultimately the how's and why's did not matter. She had no feelings for her divine mother, one way or the other. She had climbed Orcus in search of her sister, and her sister was gone. Whether Cora had indeed drowned or was killed at some lower Level of Orcus did not matter. Cleo knew she would never see her twin again.

But she had a task to finish, a tale to complete. The one memory that still kept her going was Eleni's soft voice, the sweet Mediterranean night breathing through the window, and her own child self refusing to go to bed until yet another story of the argonauts, or Heracles, or the Olympian gods and goddesses, was finished. You did not leave your audience hanging, and although Cleo was her own audience now, she clung to the irrational belief that it would not always be the case. Others, whether in the shadow world or on Orcus or in some other part of the Archipelago, would know about her. For some reason she thought about Giorgios, and smiled faintly at the remembered taste of roses and dark honey.

They stopped in front of the door, and Medusa glanced expectantly at her. Cleo glared back. Medusa's fabled ability to turn people to stone either did not exist or had no influence over Cleo. Indeed, the City of Glass seemed to indicate that Medusa trafficked in images and simulations, which, to Cleo's corporate-trained mind, was how power operated anyway.

"What are we waiting for?" Cleo asked. "Can we just get it over with?"

The worms on Medusa's head rose from their stupor and flailed angrily.

"You need to be Called," Lamia replied in her thick voice. "In order to climb the next Level of Orcus, you need to be Called by its Ruler."

"And she did not Call you," Cleo sneered. "I can't blame her. So how do I get an invitation?"

"Just knock," Medusa responded, reshaping her gaping angry maw into a more functional mouth, her voice like cut glass. "Knock and she will answer."

Cleo saw that there was a door knocker in the shape of a braided ring surrounding a woman's face wearing a crown and a veil. She lifted the ring and knocked on the polished wood.

Once, twice. No answer.

Medusa's worms flailed again, and Lamia's blood tears flowed stronger.

"Nobody's home," Cleo muttered, but she felt a letdown. She knocked again. And a shockingly familiar voice said:

"Enter!"

CHAPTER 60

f the Eighth Level was a desert, the domain of the goddess of harvest was a wasteland. Of course, it was. It was called the Wasteland, as Arachne had told her.

When Cleo rushed through the door, followed closely by Medusa and Lamia, she found herself in stony terrain covered with pebbles and outcroppings of rock. Nothing grew there, but there were puddles of melted metal, rusty appliances, mounts of unidentifiable rubbish, and piles of garbage dotted the barren plain. The sky brooding over it was on fire: dim and scarlet, with tattered rags of clouds scudding over its inflamed dome. It looked like an eternal sunset, only the sun was nowhere to be seen.

But Cleo was not interested in the landscape. With mounting horror and disbelief, she stared at the two figures approaching her.

A young woman and a shrunken, dwarfish crone, as small as a child, hobbling unsteadily on her crippled feet, her toothless mouth working incessantly, her bald head barely covered by a torn kerchief. The young woman held her firmly by her arthritic hand.

The woman was perfectly familiar to Cleo. Had her memory been wiped clean by the ascent, she would have still recognized the woman, simply because she saw her face daily in the mirror.

Cora!

Not the Cora of the last days before her disappearance, thin and haggard, drugs circulating through her abused body. Not even the Cora as she had been when the sisters were so close and so alike that even their mother occasionally confused them. No, this Cora was blindingly beautiful. This Cora was regal. This Cora was divine.

Crowned with a wreath of pomegranate flowers and fruits and dressed in a purple peplos belted with a golden chain, she shone in her dreary surroundings like a precious ruby in a garbage bin. Confronted with her, Cleo felt as scrawny and dirty as a street urchin in the presence of the Queen. Her hair shorn, her body stringy and tough, her clothes worn; she was no longer her sister's double.

But it did not matter. Nothing mattered except that Cora was alive!

She ran toward her.

"Sister!"

Cora lifted her hand, her beautiful face contorted into a grimace of distaste, and Cleo was stopped in her tracks as if she had run into a wall.

"I have no sister," the musical voice said. "I am the one and only. I am Kora the Maiden, the goddess of renewal and spring. I rule over Orcus, and soon enough I will rue over Plato's Cave as well."

"What the hell, Cora? I'm your twin, Cleo. I climbed this bloody mountain to find you!"

"Twin? I have no twin. You are not my sister. You are my antigrafo."

CHAPTER 51

There are moments in life when seconds last longer than years. That was one such moment.

Cleo stood still for the duration of a couple of heartbeats, feeling her entire life rearrange itself.

Long-forgotten memories surfacing. Stories she had told so many times they were polished by repetition into the truth were revealed as fiction. Identities and relationships revolved in her mind like pieces in a kaleidoscope and fell into a new pattern.

She had always been the strong one, the dominant one. True?

No. She had tried so hard because Cora had not needed to. Cleo had had to fight for every grade, every award, every gesture of acceptance. Cora had only had to smile, and accolades, sympathy, even love flowed to her.

Daphne was equally indifferent to her daughters. True?

No. When they were kids, Cora had been the favorite. Later on, Daphne seemed to be afraid for her. Still later, she became afraid of her. When Cora disappeared, Daphne had not been indifferent. She had been relieved. Did she know something that Cleo did not?

Before her disappearance, Cora had descended into addiction. True?

No. Before her disappearance, Cora had dropped out of the university and her behavior seemed erratic and weird, with long-winded texts and social media posts studded with mystical references. People, including Cleo, seized upon the easiest explanation: drugs. But what if she had discovered Orcus and her true nature, and tried to express herself without sounding insane?

Cleo lifted her eyes and looked into the cruelly beautiful face that was no longer hers.

"We were born together," she said.

"So what? Antigrafos can slough off their divine paradeigmas at any stage. I am the original. You are a copy. You don't matter."

The shrunken crone by her side made an inarticulate moaning noise, and Cora twisted her hand, bringing the pitiful creature down to her knees.

"Who is this?" Cleo asked, but deep inside, she knew.

Cora tittered.

"The goddess of harvests and agriculture. The last of the Olympians. The former Ruler of the Final Level."

"Demeter," Cleo whispered. "Your mother."

"Our mother, actually. You are right, we were born together. We were abducted together, and replanted in the womb of that stupid chav, Daphne. But it makes no difference. I am the original, the one and only. Kora the Maiden, the goddess of the underworld, of death and rebirth, of bones and flowers, dust and seeds. I am the one who poured pomegranate wine into the water of the shadow world, so it has forgotten its true nature and has fallen easy prey to the new gods of the Upheaval. I am the Ruler of the Final Level, and I am going to make sure that Plato's Cave is a true reflection of Orcus. The Nine Levels are but a draft of what the cities, the villages, and the wilds of our world are going to be. You are a hindrance, sister. You are superfluous. You must be gone."

Cleo could imagine how it all unfolded. When Demeter discovered what Artemis and Apollo had done, she flew into a rage and conspired with the chthonic deities of Orcus to overthrow the tired and sleepy Olympians. Did she actually plan to create the Nine Levels, turning the pit into the mountain? Who knew? Perhaps her plans had gone awry, as plans often do, but she kept her foothold on the Final Level, still searching for her daughter. And then she found her and brought her to the Final Level, where Cora repeated the act of parricidal rebellion that had inaugurated the reign of the

Olympians. Zeus dethroned Cronos and locked him up. What Cora had done to her mother was even more cruel.

"Enough!" Cora declared and waved her hand. A dusky band began to form on the stony plain behind her.

"I will grant you one last favor," Cora said. "Gods can only be killed by other gods. Antigrafos are mortal. I can kill you with a single wave of my hand, but I will let you choose the manner of your death. All the Rulers of Orcus have pledged their allegiance to me. You can choose whose domain you will inhabit forever as a doleful shade."

The band of darkness behind her solidified, became three-dimensional, and fell into a lineup of larger-than-life figures.

Nyx, swathed in the velvety folds of a black cloak, her raven eye regarding Cleo with a sideways stare.

Briareus, a chaos of writhing limbs and clustered heads, drooling, laughing, baring their teeth. A harpy perched on top of the biggest head.

Hekate, a giantess as broad as she was tall, naked, with pendulous breasts and a featureless moist membrane at the front of her crescent-crowned head. Three miniature faces on her heavy body stuck their tongues at Cleo. All three faces were Cleo's own.

Hypnos/Thanatos, a double body, two misshapen lardy torsos melting into each other, the four-eyed face staring at her with a barely disguised hunger. An Oneiroi demon was held on a leash by two out of the four hands.

A swarm of Furies, a funnel of angrily buzzing enormous bees, their flickering stingers shaped like rose-colored arrowheads: love transmuted into poisonous zeal.

Echidna's breathtakingly beautiful and mindless face suspended in the cradle of hairy crawling vines.

"Choose!" Cora commanded.

"You lie, sister," Cleo retorted. "You said all the Rulers of Orcus are your vassals now, but I only see six out of eight!"

Cora laughed a tinkling, silvery, mocking laugh.

"You are clever, antigrafo!" she retorted. "But do you really want to rely on the Mistress of Stone and the Child-Eater as your allies? I know they plotted to depose me, or rather my mother, as they mistakenly thought she was still the sovereign now that they have seen who is really in charge, do you think they will stick with their insane plan for a second? Either of them will be happy to Rule their

Level as my vassal and to have you as their slave. Right, Medusa? Right, Lamia?"

In the hammering flood of revelations, Cleo had all but forgotten about Medusa and Lamia by her side. But now she saw them step forward and join the menagerie surrounding Cora. Medusa was a pale penitent in a nun-like habit, but her head was a nest of coiling vipers. Lamia had reverted to her blind, voracious, zombie-like incarnation, her teeth glistening through her decaying cheeks.

"Choose!" Cora commanded again.

You are like the Dioscuri, the star twins, one mortal, one divine. But they always stood by each other, and now they are in the sky together. You have to stand by each other, girls. Always.

"I can choose any Level?" Cleo asked.

"Yes."

"Then I choose this one, the Ninth Level, the Final Level. I choose to stay with you, sister."

CHAPTER 62

ora's face was frozen in an expression of horrified disbelief that strangely reminded Cleo of Medusa. Behind her, the eight Rulers stirred uneasily. Demeter whimpered, her sunken eyes rapidly flicking around as if she was trying to understand what was going on.

"You can't!" Cora screamed.

"You said I could choose. I have chosen."

And before Cora could say anything else, Cleo walked toward Demeter and fell to her knees, bringing her face to the level of the erstwhile goddess' blank, wrinkled visage.

"Demeter," she called softly. She wanted to call the creature "mother" but could not bring herself to do so.

The rapid erratic eye movements did not stop, and there was not a vestige of recognition. Cora must have sucked all power out of her mother until there was nothing left but a grotesque empty shell. And if she could do it to a goddess, what would she do to humans when the shadow world fell into her hands? Cleo imagined a vampire deity presiding over Plato's Cave, reshaping it in the image of Orcus, each Level breeding innumerable reflections of itself, each one worse than the other.

Cleo gently touched Demeter's bony claw, and she let tears flow freely down her cheeks.

She cried for herself. She cried for her dead friends. She cried for the mother who had never loved her and for the grandmother who had.

Demeter lifted her withered hands and caressed Cleo's cheek. Something sparked at the tips of her fingers. A warm current flowed through Cleo, banishing the cold and despair of Tartarus; a simple warmth like a mother's embrace, a simple giving that asked nothing in return, a simple acceptance with no conditions and no strings attached.

Cora snarled, and the empty shrunken body of her mother toppled onto the ground and was still.

Cleo stood up, the heat of Mediterranean days throbbing in her blood, the sunshine of Mediterranean skies illuminating her mind, the blue of the Mediterranean waves glowing in her eyes.

Hē hēmetérā thálassa, Our Sea. The cradle of civilization, where humanity had invented stories woven through the millennia of history, always changing, never dying.

She cupped her hands, and they filled with liquid gold.

"Arachne!" she called.

A golden spider materialized between her palms.

She shook it to the ground and the spider exploded into growth so quickly that Cora, angry and confused, had no time to react.

In a moment, it was the same size as the creature who had first confronted Cleo in the hotel room in Ano Syros, almost causing her to jump out the window. The thorax like a polished bronze shield; the skittering chelicerae furred with sparkling hair, their joints the color of rosy gold; the abdomen seemingly filled with liquid metal. And as before, there was a human head perched on the front end, with a human face.

But the face was no longer a corpse's rotting mask. The patches of decay had disappeared, the greenish tinge of decomposition had been supplanted by the smooth olive skin, and the matted hair was now healthy and shiny, curling around the chiseled cheekbones.

It was a face Cleo knew and never hoped to see again.

"Hello, girls," Eleni said.

CHAPTER 63

"Eleni!" Cleo cried.

"Grandmother," Cora whispered.

"Neither, actually," Arachne said. "Eleni was my antigrafo, and I am sorry to say she is dead. When Koresh tried to bring her over to Orcus, his boat was waylaid by the Cyclops whom Demeter had set to guard the mountain of dead gods. No one comes in, no one goes out. She was very pissed, that one. Angry with the Olympians who had abandoned humanity to its own devices and had grown fat, lazy, and mindless. Angry with humanity who was ravaging Gaia. Angry with Apollo and Artemis for stealing her daughter. What she did not realize was that they had done her a service. Kora had been spending too much time in the eternal darkness of Hades, communing with chthonic deities and building up hatred and resentment against her indifferent husband and her mother, who she believed had sold her out. Being born again in the shadow world could be a real teaching experience. Unfortunately, it was not. At least, not for Kora herself. Her antigrafo, though…that's another matter."

Cora backed off, the red pomegranate flowers on her wreath curling up and blackening, as if singed by her emotions.

"You knew!" she whispered. "You knew all along who I was. And you let me…vegetate. Poor little Cora! Crazy lost Cora! An outcast, a misfit, no friends, no life. You gave me back to…her! That whore who called herself my mother! You would not let me stay in Greece!"

"First," Arachne said, "it was Eleni who sent you back to London, but I have to confess I approved the decision. You needed to learn to live between different worlds, navigate different realities, speak different languages, tell different stories. I was grooming you to take over from Demeter the Barren who was no longer fit to restore Gaia. Too bad you learned all the wrong lessons from your experience."

Cora's beautiful face twisted into something so ugly even Medusa and Lamia, cowering behind her, appeared attractive by contrast.

"I learned one lesson, Spider," she hissed. "If you want power, you have to take it!"

She grabbed the body of Demeter and squeezed it hard. The shrunken remnant of the last Olympian clung to her daughter's hand for a moment, and then shrunk even further into a dusty bundle of skin and bones, and was tossed away, drained, and discarded. Cora threw up her arms and started growing, towering into the inflamed sky like a pillar of darkness. And as Cora grew, she changed.

Her face remained the same, heartbreakingly familiar to Cleo, but the rest of her became gross and misshapen, ripping through the peplos that fell away like a molted snakeskin. Mangy fur sprouted along the limbs flexing in wrong ways, delicate fingers expanded into bony talons, rounded breasts were absorbed into the shaggy torso. Two smaller heads popped out on the hunched-up shoulders: mad-dog heads, with revolving white eyes and lolling red tongues. A revolting hybrid of a woman and a three-headed dog growled at Cleo, as tall as the Cyclops that had threatened her on her way out of Orcus. Persephone, the princess of the underworld, was blended with Cerberus, its guardian.

The Rulers behind her whispered uneasily and clumped together into smaller factions, some backing off, some trying to slink away unobtrusively. Clearly they were not happy with this latest development, and Cleo understood why.

The chthonic deities, suddenly recalled from the darkness of their long slumber and thrust into the bright light of the pit-turned-mountain, did not necessarily want to remake the human world into the shadow of their archaic realities. They were, after all, neither good nor evil – just different from the gods humanity worshipped after their departure. They were experimenting with new spaces humanity had created during their long slumber – cities, suburbia, and preserved wilderness – trying to find places for themselves. They were cruel, predatory, callous, but they were not malicious. And what they saw in the entity who had declared herself their Queen was curdled malice, envy, and resentment, such as they had never known before. But Cleo had.

She stepped toward the creature that lunged at her, its dog heads dripping rabid saliva, its talons outstretched. She had nothing in her hands. The Eye of Charon was gone, and so were the rest of her enchanted toys. But she had herself.

It may not protect you anymore but at least it will remind you of your courage. There are worse things to be reminded of.

Worse things such as her own blindness at not seeing what her twin was really like. Worse things such as abandoning her family to pursue a climb up the corporate ladder. Worse things such as never forgiving her mother. But without remembering and embracing these things, Cleo's courage was a shallow thing, unable to withstand the power of the Final Level. With them, though…

"I love you, sister," she said. "We shared the womb. We shared our stories. We shared our languages. What is mine is yours, and what is yours is mine. Your power is mine, and I take it back."

And she felt it flow into her like the warmth of the Mediterranean sun after the clammy English winter, like the sweet wine after a long journey, like the smell and taste of pomegranate. The power of Persephone, the goddess of flowers and spring. The power of Demeter, her mother, the goddess of harvest and plenty. And another power, which she suddenly discovered slumbering inside her, never used before but so irresistible it swept away the last vestiges of fear and regret. The power of Arachne, the Weaver of Words, the Spinner of Tales.

In her ascent of Orcus, Cleo had been a clever little mouse, skittering at the feet of gods, surviving by wit and subterfuge. She had had no power aside from the random odds and ends picked up from the forces she barely comprehended. But suddenly she was not a mouse anymore. She was not a refugee from Plato's Cave. She was a goddess.

She stepped forward and embraced the slavering monster, whose reeking breath stinged her face and whose talons raked her forearms. She did not even realize she was now the same size as the three-headed Cora. Either her paradeigma had shrunk or she had grown – it made no difference. She folded the monster in her arms and clung to her, disregarding the pain of its lacerations and bites, and the heat of the blood streaming down her arms and legs. She clung to her like Heracles had clung to Antaeus, the invincible giant who could only be defeated by being raised above the earth, his mother Gaia. And just like Heracles must have felt Antaeus' strength ebb as he was lifted in Heracles' arms, Cleo could feel the strength of the creature that used to be her sister ebb – and flow into herself.

It may have taken minutes or centuries, but when Cleo dropped to her knees, pumped up with power and yet as weak as a newborn, the thing in her arms was so small that she clutched it desperately, afraid to drop or lose it. The thing was mewling pitifully.

A pair of chelicerae removed it, gently but firmly, from her embrace.

"I know how to take care of babies," Arachne said, cradling the little girl.

CHAPTER 64

Cleo struggled to her feet.

She was afraid to look down at herself. She did not want to see her body reshaped into a classical statue, a monster, or a goddess. But when she did she saw that she was still wearing her tattered jeans and hoodie, and there seemed to be no extra limbs or heads protruding from her aching ribcage.

Arachne was rocking the crying baby, while the Rulers of Orcus seemed to have melted away, probably deciding to escape to their respective Levels before this new Upheaval had reshuffled their powers and domains. But not all. Cleo saw that a cloaked figure with the head of a raven was lurking at a distance, observing what was happening.

She turned to Arachne. Seeing Eleni's face on the body of a giant golden spider still gave her a pang of longing. She had to keep telling herself that her grandmother was dead. Arachne was the mold from which Eleni had been cast, not Eleni herself.

But was there a real difference? Was she herself Cora's reflection or her twin? Was she Cora?

She looked at the crying baby and remembered the photograph in their family album: Daphne in her hospital bed, two red-faced bundles by her side, and Eleni smiling proudly at her granddaughters. Jerrod Brown was not there. He must have known even then he was not the father of the twins.

"Will she remember?" she asked Arachne.

The spider shrugged – a very human gesture, grotesque on her arachnid body.

"Probably not until she is the same age as you are now. But a better question is what we are to do with her. Remember, she is a goddess, and a divinity can only be killed by another divinity. And with all due respect, you are not Persephone. You are only an antigrafo."

"Kill? I don't want to kill my sister! Don't you dare even say this!"

"So what are we going to do? Sending her back to Plato's Cave did not work out well last time."

"Which is why we are not going to do it again," Cleo said. She turned to the raven-headed figure.

"Nyx! Come here."

The goddess of the night, the Ruler of Ano Syros, approached cautiously, her birdlike hands nervously playing with the edge of her cloak.

"I will entrust my sister to you," Cleo said. "Take care of her. Give her to a good Greek family to raise as their own. And when she is of age, send her to climb the Nine Levels, ascending the pit-become-mountain. Tell her that her sister is waiting for her on the Final Level."

"Will do," Nyx said, bobbing her beak, and raising the baby to her chest. Cora stopped crying and stared, round-eyed, at the sleek, black-feathered visage looking down at her. Carrying her, Nyx passed through the doorway and disappeared.

Arachne tutted.

"Well, this would never occur to me, but you know what? It might work."

"It will work," Cleo said, sounding more certain than she felt. "She will see the Levels. She will learn her lessons. And when she reaches the Final Level, she will meet its Ruler."

"And who is that going to be? Again, you are an antigrafo, mortal. No matter your borrowed power, you cannot take the vacant throne of Demeter the Barren."

"I don't intend to," Cleo scoffed. "I have better things to do. But there are other divinities here."

"Like who? All the Olympians are dead, and I am needed as the Weaver of Stories, the link between Orcus and the human world. I cannot take over the Final Level and try to restore it to what it needs to be."

"But a child of a divinity is a divinity too, right?" Cleo asked.

"In most cases, yes."

"Well, then, there is a divine child here who can Rule the Final Level."

"Who is this?" Arachne asked, sounding skeptical.

Cleo pointed to the marble doorway, leading to the lower Levels. Brian stood there, in his faded rainbow unicorn t-shirt, with only two stripes left.

"A boy?"

"Why not? He is the son of Iris, the rainbow goddess, the goddess of peace, the bearer of good news. Mick told me she was only an antigrafo, but he lied in this as in everything else. She must have escaped in the shadow world and laid low to hide. Perhaps like Cora she had forgotten who she was for a time. And when Hendrick and Tomas, antigrafos of the double god of death and dreams, came after both of us, she must have rediscovered her divine power and spent it to hide her son in the last place anybody would look for him: the City of Glass."

Cleo's heart contracted painfully as she imagined the horror of Iris' split-second decision. A goddess willing to die in order to save her son!

She did not understand this decision, not really. She was not a mother, but she was a sister, a daughter, a friend. And she would do what it took to play her roles in all the stories, past and present and future, that were swirling around her at that moment, poised at the cusp of what Greeks called peripeteia, the reversal, when the plot turned on its pivot, disclosing the hidden truths and restoring lost connections.

"He has her power. He can do it."

"I can do it!" the boy said, a proud smile on his face. "I am grown up. I can take over. I am ready!"

"Well," Arachne said, "since there is nobody else left, why not?"

Brian clapped his hands, and the four blind kids emerged from the portal. Cleo started when she saw they were not quite blind anymore.

Embedded in their orbits were the blue-and-white porcelain talismans against the evil eye – mati.

"They'll help me," Brian said excitedly. "Right, mates?"

The children nodded, their porcelain eyes giving their faces a strange, doll-like quality.

Cleo smiled but for a moment, she felt uneasy, remembering what Brian had told her:

Everybody wants to reach the Final Level. There we will be made gods and rule over the Archipelago.

Epilogue

Cleo fished in her wallet for another ten-Euro note. Her credit cards had been canceled after she resigned and found out that the stock options she had been paid in lieu of bonuses were worth nothing.

Greece was not cheap, either. Even though the country had recovered from the last financial crisis, the new prosperity did not extend to hospitality workers, which was the best job Cleo could find in Ermoupoli. At least she had Greek citizenship, so the aftershocks of Brexit did not impair her right to vacuum carpets, make beds, and launder dirty sheets. The hotel where she was gainfully employed was not called the Villa Pharos, but it looked pretty much the same.

She placed her plate of tomatoes, cucumbers, and feta cheese on the rickety plastic table and relaxed in the sunlight pouring onto her face like a flood of rich honey. Her fellow workers, most of them Filipinos and Albanians, marveled at her capacity to bask in the sun without doing any damage to her skin or hair. But Cleo thrived in the Mediterranean climate – the same climate that had made olives and vineyards bloom at the dawn of human civilization.

She sipped her mineral water and studied the letter she had found this morning on her bedside table.

She had not seen Arachne in six months, since she came to on the beach in Syros, expelled from Orcus through the gate that the new Ruler of the Final Level had graciously opened for her. The transit had erased itself out of her mind, but she remembered Orcus, the Nine Levels, and her sister well enough.

She went back to London briefly, to hand in her resignation and to visit Daphne. She subconsciously hoped to resurrect her relationship with her mother. It did not work. Daphne was the same as she had always been: vain, self-centered, and rather silly. Cleo did not hate her, but neither could she force herself into loving the woman who had unknowingly given birth to the goddess of the underworld and her antigrafo.

She also looked up Mick and Iris. The results were spooky.

Mick was gone, or rather it was as if he had never existed. All Cleo's attempts to trace his back story were in vain, not that she fancied herself a private investigator or had money for the real thing. But she looked him up on social media, only to find no accounts. She checked with his employer who told her that he had never had an employee by that name. And after racking her brain, she realized that Mick had never spoken of his family and had not had any close friends apart from Cora and herself.

True death was final in Orcus, but it was as if Mick's death had erased his previous existence altogether.

This was strange.

Cleo thought of Brian and his mati-eyed friends ruling it over the mountain of dead gods. Had she done the right thing by installing a child on the Final Level? Children were amoral and often cruel. Children stepped on insects, teased each other mercilessly, and loved horror movies and dark fairy tales. The only reason children did not do much harm was that they were powerless in the adult world. And by the time they grew up, hopefully they had internalized morality's do's and don'ts.

But Brian had the power of a god. He was a god, and now, thanks to Cleo, he knew it. What would he do with this power?

What would Cora have done had she discovered her true nature when she was a child?

Cleo knew the answer, but she did not want to think of it. Instead, she tracked down Iris.

Yes, Iris Stableford was alive and well, but she was not the Iris Cleo had known.

The address was the same, and when the woman opened the door Cleo's heart skipped a beat. She looked like her friend – or at least, like the face Cleo had reconstructed from bits and pieces of broken memory, and some pictures she had found in her flat when she came back. Blond curls, hazel eyes like Brian's, a thousand-watt smile.

She was wearing a loose dress so drenched in clashing colors that it hurt Cleo's eyes to look at it.

"How can I help you?" the woman asked.

A brief conversation established that she did not know Cleo from Adam. And when Cleo inquired about her son, the woman frowned and practically slammed the door in her face. A little social-media snooping confirmed that this Iris was single and had no kids.

Another antigrafo? Why not? Cleo had never found out how many antigrafos a single deity could have. An infinite number, perhaps.

But if so, had there been two identical women with the same name living in London when Cleo was growing up? The goddess of the rainbow and her avatar? No, this seemed unlikely. And if somebody was messing with the shadow world, changing not only the present but the past, who could it be? The Ruler of the Final Level, perhaps?

She did not want to think about it either.

Cleo missed Arachne, but she knew the Spider could not enter the human world in her own guise. She had reconciled herself to not seeing her until she was Called again – if ever.

But she also remembered what Arachne had told her before they parted:

"Orcus is not the only mountain in the Archipelago," she had said. "Not even the most important one."

"I know," Cleo had said.

"The Nine are ruling – or ruining – Orcus on their own, but that is not to say that there is no communication between them and other…entities."

"What kind of communication?"

"Letters," Arachne had said. "Like the letter Mick left for you. It was not written by him. Or not entirely."

"I thought it was a lure to make me climb the mountain."

"It was more than that, and that was why I made you unable to read it. You got the eye of Charon and broke the spell, but not completely. There were things in that letter that I did not want you to see."

At the time, Cleo was annoyed at the Spider's presumption. She was not a child to be protected from bad words!

But now as she studied the letter, miraculously delivered into her tiny bedroom, she was thinking about the infinite Archipelago of myths where all the monsters, gods, and daimons that humanity had seen reflected on the walls of Plato's Cave lived, and breathed, and plotted to take over. Perhaps she was not meant to read their summons. Perhaps she was better off reconciling herself to living her entire life in the world of shadows.

And still, Cleo stared, as if the intensity of her gaze could pierce the golden glare of the spiders crawling across the sheet of paper.

ACKNOWLEDGEMENTS

As always, my profound thanks go to my husband Jim Martin, my sons Ariel and Eliran Gomel, and my writer friends, especially Kim Smuga-Otto, for keeping me on track with my writing. I am also grateful to Justine Alley Dowsett and the team at Mirror World Publishing for their support and helpful editorial comments. But most of all, I want to thank the wonderful people of Greece for their hospitality, warmth, unconquerable spirit, and pride in their heritage. This book was born from my trip to Greece in 2022, and I hope to see the ancient shores of hē hēmetérā thálassa, Our Sea, as the ancient Greeks called the Mediterranean, again soon.

ABOUT THE AUTHOR

Born in Ukraine and currently residing in California, **Elana Gomel** is an academic, an award-winning writer, and a professional nomad. She is well-known for her work on speculative fiction and narrative theory, represented by her academic books, which Beyond the Golden Rule, Bloodscripts, and The Palgrave Handbook of Global Fantasy. Twelve years ago she published her first fantasy novel and has never looked back. She is the author of more than a hundred short stories, two collections, several novellas, and seven novels. She writes dark fantasy, dark SF, fairy tales, and hard-to classify dreamlike stories, some of them connected to her roots in the former USSR. Her stories won several awards, and "Mine Seven" was featured in the Best of Horror 13 edited by Ellen Datlow. Her latest fiction publications are the dark fairy tale Nightwood (Silver Award in the Bookfest 2023 competition) and Girl of Light, an alternative history of the USSR with monsters. Many of her stories and novels have mythological and folkloric overtones, inspired by her travels and her academic research. Having lived in several countries including Israel, Italy, the UK, and Hong Kong, she now resides in the magical – and sinister – redwoods of the Santa Cruz Mountains with her husband.

To learn more about our authors and our current projects visit: www.mirrorworldpublishing.com, follow @MirrorWorldPub or like us at www.facebook.com/mirrorworldpublishing

Keep reading for a sneak peek at our upcoming new release:

LADY

by LCW Allingham

Chapter 1

My lips formed prayers, but they were poor tethers to hope as the pit seemed to open in my chest. Why should I not succumb? Alexander's shallow breath formed a cadence with Old Meg's soft weeping in the outer chamber, and the worried whispers of the household in the corridor. The sharp ache of my knees, ground into the cold stone floor, dulled with each hollow tug, the rest of my traitor body already numb, still, and surrendered.

The time for action was done, my failures complete. Now I could only force my body to stop and pray in the fading gray light. I should become like a stone saint, and earn my penance in finally achieving stillness.

For why though I shall go in the midst of shadow of death, I shall not dread evils, for thou art with me.

It was my fault that Alexander lay dying. My failures as a wife. So why should I not join him? He had given up, and so should I. We could, together, leave this world before our sins could damage our souls anymore.

My fingers twitched traitorously, sending a ripple of fresh ache through my heart and lighting a final desperate plea within me.

Please, my husband, do not let my failures be your end.

Please, my God, please let him awaken.

The clatter of Sir Simon's approach jolted me from the edge of the despair.

"How is the Baron FitzRoland?" His deep voice was hushed, but still too loud for our reverent misery.

"Much the same," I whispered, trying to hold onto the stillness, to the surrender.

"My lady." Sir Simon's voice dipped lower. "I fear our situation is dire. You know young Colbert Fellwater has made trouble the last week."

The last week while my body purged the last blood for my lost babe and my husband gave into his own despair, slipping into a fevered sleep, I had barely been aware of anything outside our chambers. I disrupted my stillness to give a mere lift of my chin.

"Baron Strumhale claims no responsibility for his son, nor for the damage he's done to the mines or the farms. Now Colbert is at the gate with a team of fifty men. I have come in hopes that Lord FitzRoland might be roused to turn him away before this scuffle turns into an attack."

The men and women clustered around the door gasped and I remembered that I was not alone in Alexander's rooms. The entire household prayed for Alexander's life. The entire household was now in peril of violent invasion.

My soul, which had been floating away, slammed back into my body with sudden, startling pain. The darkened chamber took on a sharp clarity in the flickering rushlight. Faces of people who Alexander and I were responsible for, who served us loyally, looked to me with terror.

My husband, Baron FitzRoland, was a mere pale phantom, shivering under pelts even as sweat beaded down his cheeks like tears. There was only me to rule.

I clutched to the spiraled post of Alexander's bed to heave myself to numb feet, my knees cracking in painful protest. As feeling flooded back through my body, I fought to keep from doubling over. It had not just been from emotional distress that I had been trying to flee. My body had not yet recovered from the stillbirth of my son.

"And why do you believe the baron's words will turn away Colbert Fellwater when our walls and garrison do not?" I asked Sir Simon.

Sir Simon kept his eyes on the blue carpet. Alexander's whole chamber was adorned in blue, with the exception of the sharply contrasting red tapestry of the FitzRoland griffon on the far wall. "Young Fellwater is reckless, still unknighted. Word must have escaped of Lord FitzRoland's ailing health or he would not dare. If the baron should appear on the wall, I believe the boy would balk."

The room erupted into despondent protests. Old Meg buried her weathered face in her hands and wept.

I lifted my hand for silence and the bellows dulled. "We are not well fortified here. The walls need repair. We lost many of our garrison to the flux. Crops are not yet sown and our supplies will not last through a siege, even if Colbert fails to break through our gate. Our allies are occupied in London, so we cannot expect a rescue."

"Yes, my lady." Sir Simon clenched his square jaw and still could not meet my eyes.

The fields would burn, the mines would be seized, and the people would lose all they had. Once Colbert penetrated the outer wall, the keep would fall and Alexander would be murdered.

I would be ransomed to my father. Possibly raped. But I would be better cared for than those with no one to pay for them. I had lived through such a thing before.

Something cold bloomed in my chest and spread to my limbs, pushing the ache away. I could die tonight. I could simply kneel back down on my warped knees and pray like a proper lady until I was cut down, but my inaction would condemn everyone else as well.

I rolled the stiffness out of my shoulders and flexed warmth back into my calves. I had to act. I had to move. I was suddenly awash with a strange, sterile gratitude.

I had to keep fighting.

I straightened my back. "I must rally the baron."

"My lady." Sir Simon tugged at the red trim on his surcoat. "In this state, the baron could not possibly—"

"He can, and you will escort him. Have our best men flanking him." My heart beat so hard I wasn't sure how loudly or softly I spoke.

"My lady—" Sir Simon's orange mustache fluttered nervously. I lifted my hand to cut him off.

"Do we have an alternative, Sir Simon?" I asked. "Could our garrison win against Colbert's men?"

He shook his head. "Lord FitzRoland would deter Colbert, in a challenge of single combat, but our men could not stand up to his."

"Then the baron must go to the gate," I said, ending the debate. My household retreated from the rooms. Old Meg shuffled past me, with a strange brightness in her milky eyes.

The knight took a deep breath, his thick chest swelling as he looked up at me. I was taller than Sir Simon. Taller than many of our soldiers. I was always so oddly out of place, yet I felt a sudden gratitude for my height as the knight deflated in my shadow.

"Yes, my lady. I will await the baron at the bailey gate."

When the door shut behind him, I sank to my husband's bed and took his damp hand.

"Oh, Alexander," I whispered. "Please awaken and save me from this folly."

My husband of two years took a rattling breath, but did not wake. A moment later there was a knock on the door. It was time to move.

I ushered in my cousin and lady maid, Aures. Her fair face white, and her lips tightly shut for a change.

"I need you to get Nicolas," I said. "I am in need of Alexander's squire."

"Rosalynde, what are you doing?" Aures whispered, twisting her skirts in her hands.

I lifted my hand. "I'm trying my best. Help me out of my kirtle before you go."

She pulled the laces from my overdress, then slipped from the chamber without another word.

A cool evening gust came through the open window and blew through Alexander's damp hair as I tugged the plain red dress off. The metallic stench of sickness and fear wafted through the room. This time of year, there should have been life, fragrance, joy, and music on the air, but it seemed Casstone's fortune had turned as sour as the stink in the chamber.

And now was I to seal that fate?

By the time Aures returned with Nicolas, I was dressed in Alexander's hose and quilted doublet.

"Rosalynde, you can't do this," Aures said. I suppose she felt she wouldn't be doing her job if she didn't protest.

Nicolas's sharp brown eyes assessed everything in a moment and his mouth quirked up. "You are almost the same height as him."

"I know," I said. Alexander had often jested that I could wear his armor.

Aures muttered in Welsh as Nicolas started with the chain mail, a chattering coat of weight, then the greaves on my ankles and poleyns on my knees. I should have wrapped my knees tight before he armed them, but it was too late now. Time was short. When Nicolas strapped on the breast and back plates, their heft nearly pressed me to the floor. If it came down to combat against Colbert, I was already defeated. The burden of the armor confined me, each motion a strain on soft muscles. I was not as strong as I had been a year ago.

"Make sure the visor covers my face." I kept my voice steady. "No one must suspect it is not Alexander on that wall."

Nicolas tied on the rerebraces and I winced as they dug into my skin. Alexander and I were close in size, but his steel plates did not conform to my shoulders.

Alexander favored a cumbersome longsword. Even when I had been strong it was too heavy for me to wield, so Nicolas armed me with Alexander's old broadsword. It would have to do.

"Keep your back straight and don't falter," Nicolas said as he pushed my visor down and draped the surcoat over me. It shone with Alexander's coat of arms, the red griffon, bright and bold.

"Speak in a gruff voice, and very little," Nicolas said, serious for a rare moment. "Leave the arduous speeches to Sir Simon. He is well equipped to make them."

"And for God's sake, be careful!" Aures cried. I was surprised she said no more to stop me. She must have known as well as I how little choice we had.

"I will." I regarded them through the slats of Alexander's visor. They looked far away from me. "If this fails, if Colbert's men get in the north gate, get Alexander and our people out, however you can. I am relying on you both."

Aures scratched her throat. "You look like a proper knight, Rosalynde," she said. "Don't fail."

"If it comes to combat, go for the neck and the head," Nicolas said.

"I am ready." That was a lie. It didn't matter. My friends needed to hear it, and I needed to forge ahead regardless of feelings.

I clattered to Alexander's side and leaned in. "I am going, my dear. Wish me good tidings. I hope to return with your barony still intact as well as my head."

A shallow breath was his only reply.

#

The metal rattled around me as I marched to the keep gate. Nicolas trailed behind me, as if he were my squire. Sir Simon waited at the north gate with our best men at arms. When he saw me, his shock and elation released a relieved breath from me. My pretense was convincing.

"Lord FitzRoland." Sir Simon gave a little bow and I raised my hand without thinking. The gesture gave me away. Sir Simon did not seem to notice.

I rumbled in my throat and said in a deep, rasping voice, "I would have this done with quickly, Sir Simon. Perhaps you will speak for me, to Colbert."

We marched forth from the castle into the bailey, each step a labor for my weakened body buried in metal. Two men at arms flanked me in case I faltered.

But I did not.

Casstone castle consisted of the keep, where Alexander and I lived with our household. Its walls were high and newly mortared, but the outer wall of the castle was not so fresh. Within the bailey were the productions of Casstone and the cottages of those who tended them. The butcher, the dairy, the kiln, the mills, and blacksmiths, as well as our store gardens and fields, our livestock, the gatehouse barracks, and the small inn. The bailey was the center of Casstone, where our people came and went through the gatehouse in the outer wall. A road ran from the keep to this gatehouse on the north end of the castle, where the walls crumbled in disrepair.

Around the castle was a nearly useless moat. It ran from the Grise Beck that streamed from the River Tees past the south end of the castle, dammed and widened at the keep gate. Because of the lack of recent conflict in Casstone, the channel around the castle had filled in and the trench outside the gatehouse was little more than a muddy dip.

People huddled along the road to the gatehouse, their worried faces flickering in rushlight. At the sight of Alexander's standard, their fearful faces lifted and they reached toward me.

I held a hand out to them, as Alexander would have done. I had to be Alexander. Rosalynde couldn't quell their fears. Rosalynde was merely the disappointing wife of their liege. Strange, too tall, and unable to birth a healthy heir.

I followed Sir Simon up the stairs of the gatehouse and found myself looking down at a team of horsemen in the market field just outside the gate. Colbert Fellwater, heir to the Barony of Strumhale, stood at their front on a white warhorse. Colbert had been a disappointment as a fighter when he was twelve, but that was three years ago, before he had been made a squire for a Neville knight. Had he improved or was he all bravado?

His smug expression melted when he saw me above him. My ruse as Alexander held, and a second burst of relief flooded my already tired body. I spoke to Sir Simon in the deepest, gruffest voice I could muster, and Sir Simon relayed my words to the boy below.

"Baron FitzRoland of Casstone asks you to retreat from his walls," Sir Simon declared.

"We've heard you've been quite unwell, Lord FitzRoland," Colbert called. "Since we all rely on the mines you currently control, we were concerned that you were unable to care for your land and people."

I spoke to Sir Simon and he relayed my message. "The Baron is quite well, although the rumors your heard aren't entirely unfounded. He's had a sore throat and has lost his voice. He does not believe, however, that is grounds for a squire to try to usurp the barony his family has held for over two hundred years. However, if you feel strongly about the matter, he will gladly face you in single combat."

There was a rumble of laughter among Colbert's men. The tightness in my chest loosened. Colbert sucked on his lower lip and sunk into his saddle. The knight beside Colbert whispered to him. If Lord Egbert Fellwater claimed to have no part in this attack, why was a knight with his wayward son?

"How can I even be sure that he really is the baron?" Colbert asked. "It could be anyone under that suit. If you're so confident, come on down and fight me."

My chest twisted tight again. So be it. I started down the wall to the gate. Nicolas and Sir Simon both put their hands on my shoulder.

"Don't let him goad you, my lord," Sir Simon cried.

"He must be taught a lesson, Sir Simon," I rasped. "Be ready to back me up should we come to blows."

They flanked me as I gave the command to open the gate. I prayed in whispered breaths as it rolled open enough for me to ride through. Alexander's Irish Connemara mare, Guinevere, was brought to me. She saw right through my disguise and snorted irritably.

"Please," I whispered. "If we play this out, I shall give you all my apples this summer."

Perhaps it was the pounding of my heart or the desperation in my voice but she allowed me to mount her, and it was through sheer will that I managed to haul my burdened frame onto her back without falling. The whole of me ached, my feeble muscles on fire.

Colbert's bravado faltered as I rode through the gate. I easily had five inches on him and in Alexander's gleaming armor, I looked every bit the champion.

"Do you wish to engage, Squire Fellwater?" Sir Simon asked, emphasizing the word 'squire'. If Sir Simon believed I was Alexander, then he knew I was not prepared for battle, yet he remained calm.

"Lord FitzRoland." Colbert's voice cracked. "I am pleased to see you well. I, uh, I merely wished to be sure your barony was well protected in these times of turmoil."

"Then you see," I uttered. "Go."

"I, uh…" Colbert looked at his knight, who raised a brow. If I was Alexander, at my full strength, Colbert would stand no chance. His challenge could result in his death and, because his father took no responsibility for the attack, his death would be considered righteous and without legal recourse. If he won, however…

"Yes. Certainly, we shall leave." Colbert's voice was quiet and tight. He had promised his men blood and glory, but he would not risk his neck.

He continued to watch me as they collected into ranks and started back down the road. I remained statue still, even as the burn in my shoulders and back became unbearable.

"I pray this misunderstanding will not damage the long-standing alliance between our baronies. King Edward needs all his lords in line behind him," Colbert mumbled as the last of his men began their ride up the Dere Road, back toward his father's lands in Ablekirk.

Sir Simon glowered at the young lord. "His Lordship prays we will not find you threatening our walls again, and that damages to the mines and farms will be compensated for."

Colbert cleared his throat. "Erm, good morrow, then."

He kicked his horse, leaving a cloud of dust as he sped to the front of the chastised march.

"His Lordship should return to bed," Sir Simon suggested at my side.

"When they are out of sight," I whispered, stilling the urge to lift my hand.

Walking back to the manor was exceedingly difficult, as I fought to conceal the shaking of my taxed body. My knees screamed with each step. Pregnancy had stolen all my previous strength. Had I been forced to fight…

Yet I forced my stance to remain straight as we marched back to the keep, raising the heavy steel on my trembling arms to wave assurance at the people who had crowded behind our walls. They cheered as we passed them.

Once in the manor, Nicolas whisked me back to Alexander's chambers, where Aures quickly shut the door against prying eyes. I collapsed next to Alexander, panting to catch the breath I had fought so hard to keep even. Alexander shivered in his bed, a sheen of greasy sweat coating his ashen face, as if he too was taxed to his limit.

"You are mad," Aures said, helping Nicolas pull the armor from my exhausted body. "What if you had been found out?"

"At least it would have bought you time to escape," I said, my voice still ragged from my attempt to sound like a man.

"And what will Lord Alexander say when he learns what you've done?" she asked. Now that I had succeeded, she felt free to scold me. "He could have you hung."

I ran my hands, now free of the gauntlet, down Alexander's cheek. "I pray for that ire, for it would mean that my husband had awoken and I am not alone the protector of Casstone."

This book is coming soon!

Follow our blog, newsletter, Facebook Page or
website for updates.

We are an independent publishing house based in Windsor, Ontario. We publish quality paperbacks and ebooks that feature other worlds, times and versions of reality. Our novels are for all ages and are creative, unique, imaginative and engaging.

We pride ourselves on our originality and 'outside the box' thinking, while taking a good look at the question, 'what if?' Our stories are never ordinary, the dialogue and action engaging, the characters believable, and there will always be some element of romance, adventure, science or magic. We are dedicated to bring our readers novels that will not only entertain them, but also teach them something about the world they live in by showing them one that mirrors it. We hope you'll consider picking up a novel from our collection today so you can see for yourself what we're all about.

You'll find a wide variety of our wonderful titles in our online bookstore and you can also purchase or review them through most major retailers worldwide.To learn more about our authors and our current projects visit: www.mirrorworldpublishing.com or follow @MirrorWorldPub or like us at www.facebook.com/mirrorworldpublishing

www.ingramcontent.com/pod-product-compliance
Lightning Source LLC
Chambersburg PA
CBHW030119010826
48973CB00002B/341